A Song of Thyme and Willow

CAROLE STRACHAN

Cinnamon Press
:: small miracles from distinctive voices ::

Published by Cinnamon Press
Meirion House
Tanygrisiau
Blaenau Ffestiniog
Gwynedd LL41 3SU
www.cinnamonpress.com
The right of Carole Strachan to be identified as author of this work has been asserted by her in accordance with the Copyright, Designs and Patent Act, 1988. © 2019 Carole Strachan
ISBN 978-1-78864-049-7
British Library Cataloguing in Publication Data. A CIP record for this book can be obtained from the British Library.
All rights reserved. No part of this publication may be reproduced, stored in a retrieval system, or transmitted in any form or by any means, electronic, mechanical, photocopying, recording or otherwise without the prior written permission of the publishers. This book may not be lent, hired out, resold or otherwise disposed of by way of trade in any form of binding or cover other than that in which it is published, without the prior consent of the publishers.
Designed and typeset in Garamond by Cinnamon Press. Cover design by Adam Craig © Adam Craig.
Cinnamon Press is represented by Inpress and by the Welsh Books Council in Wales.
Printed in Poland
The publisher gratefully acknowledges the support of the Welsh Books Council

Acknowledgements

Epigraph
Hilary Mantel on Grief
Reproduced courtesy of Guardian News & Media Ltd

Ariadne auf Naxos
Music by Richard Strauss, Libretto by Hugo von Hofmannsthal,
English translation by Alfred Kalisch
Reproduced with permission by Boosey & Hawkes Music Publishers Ltd.

A Grief Observed by CS Lewis
Reproduced by permission of Faber and Faber Ltd

Your former life still seems to exist, but you can't get back to it; there is a glimpse in dreams of those peacock lawns and fountains, but you're fenced out, and each morning you wake up to the loss over again.

Hilary Mantel

For my mother,

who told me stories and inspired my

life-long love of reading

A SONG OF THYME AND WILLOW

Prologue

The unknown benefactor had deposited the boxes outside the shop and disappeared. It was an unusual offering: a large collection of play scripts and a single song. An old ballad, warning young girls of the dangers of false love, handwritten in black ink on sheets of cream manuscript paper; on its cover, etched in fading pencil, a doe-eyed girl with a long plait, gazing over her shoulder as if yearning for something out of reach.

Steven Bennett was running late that morning and as he laboured up the hill from the car park, one of his shoelaces came undone. He stopped in the doorway of a charity shop to retie it and, as he bent down, he glimpsed his reflection in a dressing table mirror on display in the shop window. He winced at the sight of the inflamed scar on his jaw, the gash beginning to heal but still raw-looking and conspicuous. He pushed away the jagged images it triggered, trying to condemn them to the recesses of his mind; hoping to safeguard the shield of stoicism that had so far sustained him.

He was distracted by the smell of coffee and bacon wafting from the café on the corner. He contemplated stopping to collect a takeaway and, as he peered inside to see if there was a queue, an elderly woman, sitting alone at a table in the window, met his eye. He glanced at his watch and hesitated at the door, but turned instead to cross the road at the traffic lights. As he waited for the lights to change, he looked over to the opposite corner on which the shop stood, shielding his eyes against sharp shafts of sunshine. The double-fronted windows were covered with posters of all shapes and colours, and large signs below each window pronounced *Books—Old & New*. As he crossed the road, he could see that three brown boxes blocked the doorway, placed neatly side-by-side. He leant down to see what they contained but their lids were tightly sealed so that the contents were not visible. On the top of one box was a sheet of paper, torn from a small lined exercise book, on which someone had written: *If this were played upon a stage now, I could condemn it as an improbable fiction.*

He looked around to see if anyone was waiting for him, but the street was deserted save for a taxi parked across the road on double yellow lines just below the café, its driver absorbed in a newspaper he had spread across the steering wheel. Bemused but intrigued, Steven unlocked the door and heaved the heavy cartons inside.

The smartly-dressed woman drinking coffee in the café had watched all this from her seat in the window and wondered about the man's awkward gait and the grimace of pain as he bent down to lift the boxes. Half an hour earlier, she'd asked the taxi driver to slow down as the car made its way up the main street, so she could scan the frontages for a charity shop that looked likely to accept her strange gift.

It was the bookshop's name on the old-fashioned fascia that made her ask the driver to pull over.

Improbable Fiction

That would do perfectly.

She waited until the man had manoeuvred the boxes inside and closed the shop door behind him before she opened her handbag and took out a lipstick and powder compact. Having added another layer of both and eyed the results with a rueful shake of the head, she eased herself to her feet, relieved, if a little sad, that this final task—so long postponed—was at last discharged. Outside, she paused and looked over at the bookshop once more, imagining the boxes being unpacked, the contents examined. This was the last of him, given away to strangers for whom his name, after all this time, would mean nothing.

Seeing her come out of the café, the taxi driver scrambled out of his seat to open the rear door, ready to offer her his arm. With one last glance across the road, she walked slowly towards the waiting car to begin the long journey home to Italy.

The boxes felt gritty to the touch and gave off a faintly musty smell as if they'd been stored for a long time. He slit open the lid of the first box and saw what looked at first like several dozen hard-backed books in uniform colours of blue, red and black. Having opened a few, he realised these were not books in the usual sense, but play scripts that had been specially bound, their tall, slim spines bearing their titles in gold lettering. On the front page of every one he opened was the name Paul Eveson. The red covers contained the complete plays of Shakespeare, their pages dotted with faded pencil markings, few of which he could decipher. The plays bound with blue and black covers bore the same illegible notations in the margins; those in blue covers were contemporary classics—Beckett, Miller, Pinter —while the works with black covers contained older classics—Sheridan, Wilde, Shaw. The cover of one of the black-bound plays was coming away from its spine and the pages were worn and thin, suggesting the script had been well used. He opened it carefully and turned to the title page: *Crime and Punishment*—a play for radio based on the book by Fyodor Dostoyevsky. Underneath, someone had written in emphatic capitals: *Dostoyevsky's characters tell me a lot about myself. I can be innocent and guilty both. That, to me, is life.*

One of the boxes was smaller than the others and though there were more bound scripts on the top, underneath were bundles of others that had flimsy paper covers and were in a poor state of repair. Some were adaptations of novels by the likes of Arnold Bennett, Thomas Hardy and Charles Dickens, but most were by writers he'd not heard of. As he flicked through them, looking for names he might recognise, he caught a glimpse of a handwritten song sheet. It had been stapled into a large piece of cream card, which formed a simple cover, on both sides of which someone had sketched the outline of a young woman with her hair wound in a long plait. The artist had some skill and the woman was shown from a number of different angles, from the side and the back as well as with her face fully in view.

He inspected the manuscript with a mixture of interest and sadness. Just as the sight of his disfigured face had sparked unwelcome memories, the music stirred regret for a life that was gone.

The score was a duet arrangement for soprano and baritone of 'Let no man steal your thyme', the notes and lyrics as neat and clear as if they had been professionally typeset, the name Nigel Nixon and the words *Under the Greenwood Tree* written in perfect copperplate in the top right-hand corner.

He turned back to the front cover where below the title of the song was a single drawing of the girl looking wistfully over her shoulder. She might not have been a real woman, merely an idle fantasy conjured in a moment of boredom, but she seemed to hold his gaze with a pensive sweetness that caused his heart to catch.

Alongside the drawing, there was a date he could just make out as 1962, but the three words next to it were as illegible as the jottings in the play scripts. He peered closer and with the help of a magnifying glass, he at last deciphered them: Hope Street Theatre.

Alice

As the taxi made its way from the station towards Sandleheath, I peered through windows streaked with condensation, straining to make out familiar landmarks in a landscape swathed in mist, willing the driver to take his time, dreading my arrival at the empty house overlooking the graveyard. The roads were quiet, the streets almost deserted, and only the pubs and takeaways had enticed people from the warmth of their homes. At last, through the gloom, the lights of the Johnny Jim shed a watery welcome onto the wet pavement outside and I knew we were getting close. At the corner of Hope Street, I waited for the brightly lit frontage of the theatre to emerge from the shadows, a welcome beacon in this desert to which I'd returned, but the building was in darkness apart from a solitary light casting a faint pink glow from the back of the foyer.

I turned my head away and sighed, knowing the taxi would soon be at the top of the hill, near the church, and the turning to Vicarage Road.

'Number 1 were it, my duck?' the driver called over his shoulder.

'You can drop me by the church, thanks,' I called back. 'Save you turning off the main road.'

And giving me a little longer to ready myself for my first night in Imogen's house.

My house.

I had yet to get used to that idea.

'Right you are,' said the driver, slowing to a halt and reaching round to accept my ten pound note. 'Are you going to the service then?' he asked, nodding in the direction of the church.

'Service?' I asked, with little interest.

11

'There's a service on tonight for All Souls' Day. My missus is there with her sister. You'll have missed the start, mind,' he added, glancing at the clock on the dashboard.

'No, I'm not,' I said. 'I've been travelling for hours—I need to stretch my legs.'

I stood on the pavement, my one small bag at my side, and watched the taxi do a U-turn in order to head back to the station. The mist was thicker and the air cooler up here and I shuddered at the prospect of a chilly night alone in an uninviting house and, though it felt incongruous, I thought a few moments in the warmth of the church might bolster my spirits. I walked up the gravel path between the graves, the air echoing with the crunch of tiny stones beneath my boots, when a sustained, ethereal chord on the organ tolled across the churchyard, startling me, as if to reprimand me for disturbing the solemnity of the service. I hesitated before continuing towards the entrance, where I could see that one side of the heavy outer door had been left ajar. I stepped into the porch, from where I could just make out the opening bars of Fauré's 'Pie Jesu.' The porch opened into a vestibule and from there I could see into the church through wide double doors of almost floor-to-ceiling glass. The soloist was a young girl, who looked no more than seventeen, her voice a pure, clear soprano.

Twenty years ago in a different church, not far from here, that might have been me. I blinked back tears that came unbidden and lifted my left hand to my neck as if to massage my throat, flinching at the mental image I now carried with me of my vocal cords trapped in a vice-like clamp.

I gazed at the people gathered there, seeking consolation for the loss of a loved one, their heads bowed in sorrow and remembrance, and I felt an unexpected need to seek my own solace. I tip-toed into the back of the church, picking up an order of service from a pile on the end of an empty pew and sat down alone, relieved that my late arrival seemed to have gone unnoticed. The vicar was inviting the congregation to light candles from the Paschal candle, and to place them on a large table below the pulpit. Almost everyone stepped forward to take a small candle and, as the surface of the table began to disappear under a carpet of flickering lights, the choir stood quietly to sing a setting of words from the *Wisdom of Solomon*.

> *But the souls of the righteous are in the hand of God,*
> *and the pain of death shall not touch them.*
> *In the eyes of the foolish they seemed to perish:*
> *but they are in peace.*

Though I had no deceased loved ones to remember—I had barely known Imogen in recent years and could not claim that I mourned her—I stood with my head bowed and did not feel out of place amongst the ranks of sorrowers.

The music started slowly and quietly—at first almost inaudible—but as it reached the end, the organ accompaniment swelled to a crescendo of sound just as the vocal lines rose to a climax of joy and reassurance.

The words moved me and, though religious faith had long ago disappeared from my life, I felt a flicker of hope that I, too, might find peace at the end of my journey.

For now, the journey was a short one, round the corner to Vicarage Road. I stood outside the house at the end of a terrace of identical-looking cottages and forced myself to breathe deeply as I turned the key in the lock and let myself into what had been my godmother's house and was now mine. The front door opened onto a narrow passage which led to the kitchen at the back of the house but which also gave access, via a door on the right, to the front and middle rooms. I switched on the overhead light and opened the door into the room Imogen had called her sitting room.

From there, I moved through all the rooms, upstairs and down, switching on lights as I went, trying to banish the dark corners and to challenge my conviction that this was an old woman's house full of mismatched furniture and dusty antiques.

I took in little of my new surroundings apart from a general sense that it was a world away from the bijou flat I had left behind in London for a newly-qualified solicitor to rent for the next six months and enjoy its muted colour scheme and minimalist style. I'd left her most of my furniture but stripped the place of anything personal. Now I negotiated my way around rooms that seemed already cluttered and wondered how I would assimilate my belongings amongst Imogen's. After her death, everything had been left untouched for me to sort and decide what to keep. I dreaded this task, fearing it would be dreary and dispiriting, though I knew I should do it with care and choose some mementos of my godmother to keep.

My solicitous mother had been there to take receipt of my possessions from the removal firm a few days earlier and had made sure that the carefully labelled boxes were placed in the correct rooms. I was grateful for her support but couldn't share her optimism that I was making a wise move, one that would help me get my life back on course. She believed it would do me good to root myself again in the place of my childhood and, though part of me yearned for respite from the hot-house world that had been my life ever since I left school, I feared that I no longer belonged here and that I would feel like an exotic bird trapped in an alien habitat.

Though it was not yet ten o'clock, I felt weary, and went into the kitchen to find the box in which I'd packed a bottle of whiskey. I thought it might help me sleep and with bottle in hand, and not wanting to look for one of my own, I went in search of a suitable glass. I wandered back into the middle room—the parlour—where I'd noticed an unusual bamboo cabinet, on one shelf of which was displayed a small collection of glassware. I helped myself to a cut-glass tumbler in which the honey-coloured liquor looked surprisingly pleasing, and stood in the middle of the room with my eyes closed, savouring each sip.

I opened my eyes and saw my reflection in a large ornate mirror above a Victorian fireplace surrounded by blue and amber tiles. How worn out and defeated I looked.

I turned away from this wan image but found myself looking with interest at the mantelpiece beneath the mirror. An assortment of china ornaments and vintage *objets d'art* was bookended by two blue and white vases that had a curious Japanese appearance, while nestling among the curios were a couple of fine art postcards. The one that first drew my eye was a reproduction of a nineteenth century painting showing a young woman, dressed in white, captured in a moment of deep contemplation, leaning against a mantelpiece and gazing dreamily into a mirror, her face reflected there and silhouetted against a seascape which must have been hanging behind her. I turned the card over and saw that it was called 'The Little White Girl' by James McNeill Whistler. The credit said that the painting had been part of an exhibition at the Tate Gallery in 1977 exploring Whistler's influence in Britain.

The card bore no address or stamp so I assumed it must have been sent in an envelope, meaning there was more room for the hand-written message:

I come here whenever I can to make silent communion with this woman whose sad and careworn expression seems to reflect my own despair. She won't be here for much longer—the exhibition closes at the end of October—but I expect to have left London by then.

I like Swinburne's poem, which Whistler had pasted onto the frame—

Glad, but not flushed with gladness,

Since joys go by;
Sad, but not bent with sadness,
Since sorrows die;
Deep in the gleaming glass
She sees all past things pass,
And all sweet life that was lie down and lie.

I read the verse quietly out loud and when I turned the card over to study the painting once more, I could see that the words seemed to reinforce the picture's theme of reverie and regret.

The other card was half hidden by a small black and gold fan but caught my eye because of a flash of red. It was a publicity still from the film *Gone with the Wind* and showed Vivien Leigh as Scarlett O'Hara and Leslie Howard as Ashley Wilkes, faces close together in deep conversation, his expression kind and concerned, her limpid blue eyes liquid with tears, her lips aflame with scarlet lipstick.

I turned the card over and was sure that the slightly agitated handwriting was the same as that on the Whistler card.

I loved something I made up, something that's just as dead as Melly is. I made a pretty suit of clothes and fell in love with it. And when Ashley came riding along, so handsome, so different, I put that suit on him and made him wear it whether it fitted him or not. And I wouldn't see what he really was. I kept on loving the pretty clothes—and not him at all.

I had seen the film when I was a teenager and recalled my irritation that the feisty Scarlett could so inexplicably pine for such a spineless weakling. Now, I gasped at the acuity of these words, and shuddered as I realised how much they resonated with me—as they clearly had to the sender of the card. A woman, I felt sure, from the confessional style in which both messages were couched.

Underneath, in the same handwriting, but this time without quotation marks, there were two questions:

This is what I did; did you never do this? Can you not find a crumb of compassion for me?

Neither card was signed nor bore an address. Who was this woman, I wondered, and what was her story?

Alice

I woke early after a miserably disturbed night, though I couldn't claim it was sleepless since I'd been tormented by dreams that were surreal and unsettling. My mouth felt dry and I knew I'd drunk too much whiskey on an empty stomach and gone to bed exhausted but restive.

There were three bedrooms and a bathroom upstairs and, at my request, my mother had made up the bed in a room that was not Imogen's. It was more than I could face to sleep in the room where she had lingered for weeks before she died, in a nearby cottage hospital. The bedroom Mum had chosen for me was the largest and lightest of the three and looked out over the long narrow back garden. My white embroidered bedspread was welcomingly familiar, but my mother had achieved an unusual and stylish effect by using some of Imogen's cushions for decoration. I remembered they used to be on the sofa in the front room, where they made little impact amongst the jumble of dark furnishings but, here, the Golden Lily design of soft greens and creams and burnt oranges gave the bedroom a soothing warmth.

That had not been enough, however, to elicit a restful sleep. So incongruent and chaotic were my dreams that I woke to the sense that I'd spent the night in the company of a bizarre troupe of players, some real, some fictional, but brought together as if they inhabited the same lopsided world. For the most part, I remembered only snatches and fragments, brief encounters with a motley cast, who came and went, leaving me increasingly frazzled and upset.

One encounter seemed more lurid than the rest and was still a powerful memory when I was fully awake. I was sitting in a church with Ashley Wilkes complaining to me that the soprano on stage was producing nothing but rasps and gasps, and was delivering high notes that sounded like a sow squealing in labour. I had looked at the stage to see myself—one minute as Gretel with long socks crumpled round my ankles and a little girl's white dress that was too small; the next as Zerbinetta, dressed in rock-chick leathers and tall black boots, my mouth smeared carelessly with bright red lipstick.

There was no point in trying to sleep again so there was nothing for it but to get up and face the day—and the job of unpacking. I hitched up the hem of my long silk dressing gown and edged my way down the steep and uneven staircase. At the bottom was a door which opened into the parlour, which even in daylight was a dark room, the only natural light sneaking through a tiny window overlooking a small paved area. The mist of the previous night had dispersed and I felt my spirits lift as I saw soft wintry sunshine streaming through the French windows in the kitchen, revealing a space I felt I could happily spend time in. On one side of the windows was a pale oak table, with two chairs facing towards the garden and a settle, on the other side, covered with a long cushion upholstered in another colour-way of the William Morris Golden Lily design.

As I waited for the kettle to boil, I looked down the garden and took in the full extent of its neglect. Imogen had clearly abandoned it some while before she died and allowed nature to overwhelm what had once been carefully tended. This garden had been one of her greatest joys and I felt sad to see that it had become too much for her. I had never before been responsible for a garden, having lived only in flats since I left home, and this felt a challenging one on which to learn.

My mother had left some provisions for breakfast and I was enjoying the comforting smell of toasting bread when the phone in the parlour rang.

'Hello?' I said cautiously, though I suspected it would be my mother, eager to hear how my first night had been.

A similarly tentative female voice replied, 'Hello?'

Not my mother then.

I waited, unsure what to say to a stranger calling me in a house I had only just moved into.

'I'm sorry to bother you,' the woman said, 'but does Isabel Grey live there please?'

She sounded hesitant and nervous and, feeling groggy and not fully awake, I felt unsure what name she'd asked for. I assumed she was looking for Imogen, so feared I was about to be the bearer of bad news.

'No,' I mumbled. 'Imogen Grey lived here for a long time but I'm afraid she died some months ago and I live here now.' For no obvious reason I added, 'I'm Alice.'

The woman said nothing, though I heard her catch her breath and, before I could ask if she was alright, she'd apologised and hung up. I stared at the receiver before replacing it softly on its cradle. I was about to ring 1471, to retrieve her number so that I could call her back, when the phone rang again, this time an automated message urging me to claim some money that was owing to me.

'Damn,' I said, slamming the phone down in frustration. If only I'd been able to keep her talking, I might have discovered who she was and who she was looking for.

Steven

The job in the bookshop was only meant to be a stop-gap, an opportunity for Steven to help his ageing uncle, (who wanted to work shorter hours but was always short-staffed) and, at the same time, to rebuild his strength before he began the next chapter of his life, whatever and wherever that was to be. He'd always loved books, and was widely-read, but this was no ordinary bookshop. It was deceptively large, a labyrinth of tiny rooms and cubby-holes crammed with volumes, catering for readers looking for new titles across all genres, as well as those seduced by the diverse second-hand books interspersed among them, including a few antiquarian treasures. He was particularly proud of the large collection of second-hand sheet music which, when he'd first arrived, had been nothing more than a jumble of papers in a large trunk. He'd set about organising and categorising it and within a few weeks he'd created a whole new 'department'.

To his surprise, he enjoyed the job more than he'd imagined possible and ended up staying for six months, proving himself good with customers and even better with the books, able to recall titles across the whole range of the stock and to readily find even the most obscure request. His uncle hoped he might stay for good and take over the management of the shop but, unexpectedly, a new opening had arisen.

Steven had never envisaged returning home to the Potteries, and indeed the work that had come his way was short-term and might lead nowhere, but he'd leapt at the opportunity to work again in the arts, even if only tangentially.

The sense of loss was never far away, had not yet been fully absorbed into the tapestry of his life and he was keenly reminded of the rawness of his pain when, a few days before he left, a customer arrived looking for music for her son.

'He's only fifteen,' she said, 'but he's preparing for his Grade VIII exam on the bassoon.'

She shook her head and smiled, as if surprised she could have produced such a prodigal child.

'He's really keen,' she continued, 'wants to go to music college, and I wondered if you have any suitable pieces he might work on to improve his playing.'

It was an unusual request—most parents came looking for music for the piano or the recorder—but Steven was able to say that the shop did have a small selection for bassoon and he would look to see what might be appropriate. He asked the woman to wait while he went to a room at the back, glad to escape her gaze. People still occasionally stared at his scar but, more than that, he didn't want her to see how much her request had ruffled him.

He'd not stayed for a drink in the bar with the others after the concert, but had headed across the bridge to meet an old college friend at the Ship and Shovell, a pub they'd discovered when they were students. They were meeting there for old times' sake, their professional careers having taken them in different directions many years earlier, Steven plying his trade mainly in London, his friend almost entirely in Scotland. As young men, exchanging the Potteries for the capital, they'd enjoyed the pub's eclectic, cosmopolitan atmosphere and relished the bizarreness of its location underneath the platforms of Charing Cross station, its two buildings separated by Cravens Passage, linked only from below by a vast cellar.

It was a cold, murky night and there was a light covering of snow on the ground and the hint of more to come. Though it was only ten o'clock, there were few people around. The Embankment gardens loomed away to his right as he made his way northwards, the misty half-light making the Victorian pleasure grounds appear unnervingly eerie. Up ahead near the railings, he saw the briefly flickering flame of a match being held to a cigarette, its smoke catching in his throat as he got closer. Later, he recalled that instinct had warned him to quicken his step but at that same moment his mobile phone had buzzed into life. His gloved hand fumbled to find it in the depths of his coat pocket and he later rued the irony of that instant when he felt the first of a series of blows to his head while the good-natured melancholy of the *Rumpole* theme played on, the sonorous and stately bassoon oblivious to the ugly scene to which it was adding its surreal accompaniment.

It was the third punch that felled him, the kicks to his ribs and legs making him curl into a ball on his side, trying to shield his face from further attack, flinching as a hand reached roughly inside his jacket to extract his wallet.

He had no idea how long he lay there before the first passer-by stopped to help and summon assistance. He heard a man's voice giving directions to the emergency services and telling them he'd wait at the scene until they arrived. He was breathing fast and hard, his heart thudding in his chest, as he took in the enormity of what had happened. His mouth felt full of loosened teeth and his jaw was broken, he was sure of it. As blood dribbled down his face and down his throat, he started to cry.

It was then he heard her voice and felt her touch. A woman was leaning over him, stroking his matted hair with one hand, her other laid gently on the arm he had used to shield his body. He shifted his position in an attempt to ease the pain but the woman urged him to stay still, while the man leant down to say that help was coming. Steven closed his eyes, wishing that unconsciousness might claim him, and he was drifting in and out of awareness when he heard the woman say:

'He's a bassoon player. See, there's his case.'

At first he was flooded by an irrational wave of relief to know that his instrument had not been taken but, at the woman's next words, every bone and sinew in his body seemed to dissolve as if they'd been liquefied.

'Whatever they do, they must take care of his mouth. We must tell them that.'

At those words, he saw at once the wreckage of his life, knew that his playing days were over and foresaw a purposeless and impoverished future.

All the while they waited, the woman murmured words of reassurance, trying to soothe and calm him. He could just make out her face and guessed she was in her seventies and, though she was a curious sight, her large eyes and well-defined cheekbones suggested she might once have been beautiful.

His mind drifted back to the concert hall and became a blur of beautiful women, their faces and voices seeming to clamour for his attention. The diminutive soprano soloist had been vocally underpowered, pleading a heavy cold, and as she turned to bow to the orchestra at the end of her performance, he'd been struck by how haggard she looked, the vivacious charm for which she was known decidedly subdued. The Russian pianist was tall and statuesque, physically arresting in her low-cut glittery dress, but she'd been shockingly heavy-handed and much of the orchestral playing was similarly coarse, as if the musicians were subconsciously mimicking the vulgarity of the soloist. He willed his ears to shut out the cacophony of brass and timps and crashing glissandi that assaulted his shattered nerves. His head hurt and he pushed away the thought that his final concert had been such an uneven, dispiriting affair.

'What's your name, sweetheart?' he heard the woman ask quietly.

Through bloodied, broken teeth he somehow managed to splutter an answer.

'Steven,' he said. 'Steven Bennett.'

She was still leaning over him, stroking his forehead, when the paramedics arrived and took charge. She stood back while they examined him and turned him onto his back, asking him if he could tell them what had happened. As they lifted him gently onto a stretcher and prepared to take him to the waiting ambulance, Steven saw the woman clearly for the first time: the coarse grey hair rolled onto the back of her head like a straggly bird's nest, the pungent earthy smell that clung to her eccentric clothing, and the melodious timbre of her voice with its hint of a familiar accent. Strangely, he felt sure he had seen her before.

He tried to thank her but she had moved away to talk to one of the paramedics. And then she was gone, into the night from which she'd briefly emerged as a guarding angel.

As he flicked through the small section of bassoon music, he wondered yet again who she was and wished he could thank her for her kindness and concern, tell her that despite the best efforts of surgeons and dentists, his mouth was so altered by the attack that his playing days were over, but reassure her that he believed he would survive to do other things.

He was sad to be leaving the shop and he regretted abandoning his uncle, though the old man had been magnanimous and confessed he had never dared hope that Steven would stay a month, let alone six, so was resigned to him going and wished him well. As a parting gift, his uncle invited him to help himself to anything he liked from the shop, so on his last day, Steven browsed through the rooms for a keepsake that might link this life with the new one about to begin and, though he'd intended to pick out a book, he chose instead the simple song of thyme and willow that an unknown soprano and baritone had once sung at Hope Street Theatre.

Steven

He was early and, as he waited in the plant-filled atrium at the university's main entrance, he studied the stream of people arriving to begin their week and felt a sense of wry gratitude that his former lifestyle had prepared him for being the new boy facing his first day. For a busy musician, there were countless 'first days' at work, sometimes for a job that might run for weeks or months, or even years; sometimes for one that would be over by eleven o'clock that night. Though that thought bolstered his fortitude, he nevertheless had to brush aside fears that this new job might be a poor substitute for all the 'new' jobs that had gone before.

Tony Fletcher arrived on time and hurried over to seize his hand.

'Welcome!' he said. 'It's very good to see you again. I'm glad you didn't have second thoughts after that gruelling inquisition the Dean saw fit to inflict on you.'

Steven laughed, deciding not to confide that at one point he'd wanted to tell the supercilious academic where to stuff his job.

'And what exactly makes you think you might be suited for this position, Mr Bennett?' Tony mimicked, his voice assuming the punctilious and over-refined enunciation of Morningside. 'A trombone player weren't you? Oh my!'

Steven laughed, relieved to feel the butterflies settling, and confident that Tony would be a congenial colleague. He was the Archivist at Sir John James University, a former Polytechnic in the Potteries, and he and Steven had met and become friends at school, though Tony was two years older. They'd both played bassoon in the school orchestra—a first for the school to produce one let alone two bassoonists— and Steven had been a Library volunteer when Tony was Library Monitor. They'd kept in touch, as much through their mothers, who were also friends, as through direct contact with each other. Tony had been shocked to hear about Steven's injuries and keen to help him get back on his feet.

They made their way up to the fourth floor and down the long passageways that dissected the different departments of the extensive, well-lit library that occupied the whole of this floor and the one below. Tony chatted as they went.

'I remember at school you were an avid reader and one of the most diligent helpers in the library, so I think this job will suit you very well.'

Steven nodded, grateful for the reassurance.

They collected coffees from a drinks machine situated next to a bank of photocopiers and settled themselves in the office to talk. The archive was housed in a large space at one end of this floor and, while the storage area's lighting and heating were carefully controlled, its offices and reference area had large windows overlooking a public park flanked by houses built in the style of the arts and crafts movement.

Tony looked at Steven over tiny steel-rimmed glasses which he wore perched on the end of his nose.

'So, how are you then?' he asked. 'No more surgery needed I hope?'

'No, thank goodness,' Steven replied. 'They've done all they can. My jaw still aches at times from the last operation, but they tell me this will pass as everything settles down. My hip's healing nicely, too,' he said, 'so in time I should be able to walk without a limp—but I'm still a bit of a patched-up job.'

'Poor you.'

'I'll live,' he said, not wanting sympathy for fear it would hijack his hard-won equanimity, 'and I'm grateful for this chance. I could have stayed on at my uncle's bookshop, but to my surprise, I wanted to come home.'

Tony nodded, indicating this made sense to him.

'When I went off to college, I couldn't wait to get away,' Steven went on. 'Going to London seemed like such an adventure, but when this happened,' he said, stroking his jaw, 'I didn't seem to mind the prospect of coming back.' He paused. 'Mind, I'm not sure how I'll cope living with my Mum but, until I know how long I'll be staying, I'm loathe to sell my flat in London and buy something here.'

Tony laughed.

'Your Mum's fine—try living with mine. Kate and I moved in with her when our kitchen was being rebuilt and matricide was only narrowly avoided.'

This time they both laughed.

'So,' said Tony, drawing a buff folder from out of a drawer in his desk. 'I'll fill you in with the basics and then I'll show you around and we can talk in more detail about what we're dealing with.'

He took out a sheet of A3 paper but for the moment didn't refer to it or show it to Steven.

'Ever since it opened,' he said, 'Hope Street Theatre has been building an archive but hasn't had the space or the expertise to organise it properly. The entire collection has been stored across the road from the theatre in a little terraced house which was lent to them some years back when the owner went into a residential home. She died over a year ago and her executors want to sell the house, so the theatre has had to find a new home for a helluva lot of material—basically a small houseful.'

He took a last mouthful of coffee and got up to put the empty beaker into a recycling bin.

'They approached the university to ask if we could help and we jumped at the chance to take it, but even we don't have the resources in-house that it needs to get it into shape, so we applied to the John James Foundation for financial support. The grant they've offered will pay for my post to be covered so that I can be seconded to the project for at least a year—perhaps longer if need be—and will pay for administrative support for a year in the first instance—which is where you come in. We're also taking on two of the theatre's own volunteers—a couple of retired teachers who've done a pretty good job of at least gathering the right material and keeping it safe. Very little seems to have been chucked away—ever!—but it's all in a bit of a muddle to put it mildly and until we get down to it, we won't know what's missing or lost or simply misfiled.'

Steven nodded, having heard much of this when Tony first approached him.

'Looking further ahead,' Tony said, 'to when we can see the collection taking shape, the Artistic Director of Hope Street has suggested we might mount occasional exhibitions in the theatre foyer—to mark key milestones or anniversaries, that sort of thing.'

'I like that idea,' Steven said. 'I'd love to be involved in that.'

'Good man! Now one of the most important parts of the collection,' Tony went on, 'is the music—commission contracts and briefing notes, manuscripts, recordings, show tapes, et cetera. The Artistic Director once said that music was the blood stream of every show the theatre ever produced, and so every single play or documentary at Hope Street Theatre has contained music, much of it original and commissioned by the theatre. And, as well as the music produced for the shows, there are the occasional Sunday night concerts and the Hope Street Summer Festival.' He paused. 'So, this is where I'd like you to focus first, on the music, though inevitably that work will overlap with all the other work of sorting and cataloguing and deciding what to digitise.'

As he drove the short distance to his mother's house he was glad that the evening rush-hour traffic was heavy and slow, giving him time to gather himself before he reached home.

Behind a queue of cars stopped at slow-changing red lights, he tried to adjust to the reality of being back in his childhood home, of once again inhabiting the bedroom of his boyhood. As a young man going to college in the early nineteen nineties, his plan was to leave home and not return other than for vacations and obligatory filial visits. He had longed for his freedom, to make his way in a world beyond the confines of the Potteries.

He recognised that his return demanded an adjustment for his mother, too, and though she'd welcomed him back with the love and warmth that had nourished his childhood, it had been over two decades since he had last lived with her and in that time, she had built her own life, independent of him, and had forged an interesting career and a committed relationship. She and Frank didn't live together, but they'd been a couple for almost twenty years and Steven had come to think of him as the father he'd never had.

He had done little more on his first day than begin to familiarise himself with the vast scale of the archive's new holdings and study the painstaking plan for the collection which would provide the guide to the sorting and cataloguing work that lay ahead.

'It looks complicated,' Tony had said, opening out the large sheet of paper and placing it on the desk between them, 'but it's just a multi-layered flowchart.'

Steven nodded, letting out a long, low whistle of admiration as he absorbed the logic and detail of the plan.

'This is quite something,' he said. 'Must have taken you an age to produce this.'

Tony smiled.

'I have to confess that much of this is down to the theatre's Production Manager. He's been at Hope Street for over thirty years and he helped me begin to make sense of everything we've acquired. I use it as both a hierarchy of information and a route map,' he told Steven as they poured over a plan that comprised different-sized boxes linked by arrows which emanated from a central box with a thick black border containing the words *Hope Street Theatre Plays, Concerts and Festivals in date-order since 1958.*

Steven had made a photocopy of the plan and was studying it at the dining room table when his mother, Jenny, arrived home.

'Sorry I'm late,' she said, taking off her coat and coming to stand behind him. He turned round and smiled.

'No problem. I guessed you might be held up when I heard the dismal traffic news on the radio.'

She groaned and nodded.

'Have you eaten?' she asked.

'No,' he said. 'I thought I'd wait for you.'

Her eyes widened with surprised pleasure.

'I put the casserole in the oven on a very low light when I got in,' he went on, 'so it might be an idea to turn it up now, but it should be almost heated through.'

'Lovely,' she said. 'I'll do that and bring us both a glass of wine while I'm at it.'

He heard her busying herself in the kitchen and a few minutes later she came back holding two large glasses of red wine. She sat down opposite him and raised her glass.

'Here's to your new job!'

They clinked glasses and both took a large sip.

'Mm, that's better,' she said. 'Long day.'

She closed her eyes and drank again.

'How was it?' she asked at last. 'Have you survived?'

He laughed.

'Pretty well,' he said, feeling suddenly hungry and looking forward to a meal and the chance to tell someone about his day. Jenny knew the theatre well, having been a regular attender since she was a teenager, growing up at the other end of Hope Street, and was a volunteer usher there for several years after she left school.

'What's the particular significance of these boxes?' she asked, leaning forward and pointing at a number of boxes he'd marked with a yellow highlighter pen.

He turned the sheet around so that she could see it properly and got up to come and sit next to her.

'The material's come to us in a bit of a muddle,' he said, 'though there's been some attempt to file relevant stuff together. This chart shows how we plan to organise every different category of material—programmes, press cuttings, production photographs, correspondence and so on—and the boxes I've highlighted are going to be particularly relevant to me as I start work on the music.'

He pointed at each box in turn and read out its name.

'Production Files in Date Order; People List (actors, writers, directors, designers, composers in alphabetical order of surname); Card Index (who did what, where and when); Show Music (manuscripts); Show Music (rehearsal tapes); Production Tapes (sound effects and music); Show Tapes (sound recordings of first night performances); Concerts and Special Events (sound recordings).'

She reached for the reading glasses that hung on a red ribbon round her neck and perched them on the end of her nose before pulling the sheet towards her so that she could study it more closely.

'This is fascinating,' she murmured, moving her finger slowly over the plan, lingering in places as if recalling her own memories of the Theatre.

'I wish I'd made you go more often,' she said, shaking her head. 'Think how useful you'd be finding that now.'

He laughed.

'I probably went more often than most teenage boys. You dragged me there quite a few times, I seem to remember.'

Jenny laughed, too and, while she went through to the kitchen to serve up the meal, Steven cleared his papers off the table and reached into a drawer in the sideboard for table mats, napkins and cutlery, just as he had as a boy.

His mother arrived with two steaming plates which she put down hurriedly.

'Careful, they're hot,' she said, going back into the kitchen to fetch the bottle of wine.

'Good old fashioned stew and dumplings,' he said approvingly. 'Frank's a good cook—I'm impressed.'

'He's a treasure,' Jenny said. 'I'm very lucky.'

'Cheers Mum', Steven said, holding up his glass to chink against hers again. 'Thanks for having me.'

'It's lovely to have you here,' she said. 'I just hope I don't get on your nerves.'

He smiled, feeling guilty about what he'd said to Tony that morning, and coloured when, as if she had overheard their conversation, she added: 'I know it can't be easy coming back to live with your old mum.'

He shook his head.

'It's fine, Mum, don't worry.'

'Are you fine, love?' she said with emphasis. 'I know you don't like to talk about it, but I do worry…'

'I just feel I have to get on with things,' he said, between mouthfuls. 'No point in looking back. It's what I do next that matters.'

'I do worry about you, though,' she said, putting down her fork. 'I don't like the thought of you being unhappy or lonely, stuck out here in the sticks after life in London.'

Steven shook his head and took a gulp of wine.

'Bit heavy for a first evening, Mum,' he joshed.

'Sorry, love,' she said and fell silent, but he knew she fretted about his lack of wife or partner, of children.

'How's the book coming on?' he asked.

She brightened.

'Really well,' she said. 'It was worth driving all the way to Lichfield. Zoë loved the drawings I've done so far, but she had some interesting ideas about the illustrations she'd imagined for the ending. So, I've lots to get on with before we meet up again.'

Steven looked at his mother in admiration, thinking that since he left home she had stepped centre stage in her own life, no longer regarded as the plucky single mother, but as a successful artist. She was the illustrator of a popular series of children's books, the writer of which had recently had her fourth child just months ahead of their publisher's deadline.

'What about you?' she asked. 'Do you feel positive about the new job?'

'I do,' he replied. 'I think it'll be interesting and Tony seems to think it will suit me.'

'It's such a worth-while project—the theatre has done so much for this area, it's right that its records are preserved.'

'What are your first memories?' he asked, wondering if his mother might know anything about the singers of the song he had brought back from his uncle's shop.

'Well, it may not have been the first show I saw, but the first one I remember clearly, because we were doing it for O level English, was *Under the Greenwood Tree*. 1962 it would have been.'

He gasped and she looked at him in surprise.

'I found a song from that production when I was sorting through a load of second-hand plays that were donated to the bookshop. Uncle Bill let me keep it.'

He got up from the table to get his satchel bag in which he'd packed the manuscript, intending to show it to Tony. He handed it to Jenny, who pushed away her plate and wiped her hands on her napkin before taking it from him. She handled it with care, looking with interest at the sketches.

'Who did these—do you know?'

'It might be someone called Paul Eveson as his name was on all the play scripts that formed the bulk of the donation. I guess he was an actor, but I'm not sure.'

His mother was studying the words of the song.

'I remember this part of the production,' she said. 'The song isn't in the original book but I recall the way they staged it was very effective.'

She looked again at the drawings.

'Who's this?' she asked, looking at Steven.

'I'm afraid I've no idea.'

'She certainly wasn't the girl in the production,' she said, looking puzzled. 'She looked quite different: her hair wasn't as long as this girl's and she wore it in short curls and ringlets.'

Steven reached for his wine glass, feeling surprisingly disappointed. His mother, though, was still studying the girl closely.

'But I think I might have seen her in something else—those eyes are so distinctive. I'm pretty sure she played Gertie Gitana a few years later in a semi-documentary piece.'

Steven frowned, recognising the name but not recalling who she was.

'Gertie was born locally and became a big music hall star in the early twentieth century.'

'Ah, yes, of course,' he said. 'Do you remember this woman's name by any chance?'

He held his breath, expecting Jenny to shake her head, but to his surprise she said:

'If I'm right, this is Isabel Grey, another local girl who went on to be a singing star. An opera singer.'

Steven raised an eyebrow in anticipation but his mother was frowning as if perplexed.

'She was well-known for a while—I remember hearing she was singing regularly at Covent Garden and the London Coliseum—but then she seemed to disappear.'

Alice

Though I struggled to adjust to my changed circumstances, to accept that life was going to be different from now on, to my surprise, over the coming weeks, Imogen's house began to reveal unsuspected charms. She had clearly been an avid collector of Victoriana and, though her style was not instinctively mine, she had endowed every room, including the bathroom, with an enviable individuality, so that before long I began to appreciate that she had created a home full of character. I had feared the house would be dark and oppressive, but it had been recently painted in an acceptable shade of pale mushroom and I realised the problem lay with the lighting, which was cold and dim, and I felt sure it would be possible to achieve a warmer, cosier effect.

This reversal of my expectations meant that I tackled the previously dreaded tasks of sifting and reorganising with more enthusiasm than had seemed likely on that gloomy first night. I remained fascinated by the two cards on the mantelpiece and was struck that one—perhaps both —had been sent as long ago as 1977 and kept in view almost forty years later, albeit half-hidden among an array of other knick-knacks. With their enigmatic messages, the cards seemed to bestow upon Imogen an unexpected air of mystery and when I began sorting through her papers, I did so in the hope I might discover more secrets.

The bamboo cabinet in the parlour had a series of drawers below the shelves, while in another corner of the room there was a second piece of bamboo, this one an elaborate and unusually tall bureau, with drawers above and below the desktop. Having opened a drawer in each cabinet at random, I guessed that both units would be stuffed full of papers. Imogen's solicitor had given me all the legal and practical documents relating to the house, as Imogen had entrusted them to him when she first fell ill, so I wasn't expecting to find anything of that sort. At a quick glance, it looked as if Imogen's passion for collecting had extended to all kinds of ephemera.

'There could be a lifetime's paraphernalia here,' I groaned as I made a start on the drawers beneath the shelves of glassware.

The first drawer seemed to consist of playbills and programmes for plays and other events at Hope Street Theatre going back as far as the late 1950s, when the theatre was founded. Though I'd planned to simply bundle the different categories of papers together and decide later what I would do with them, I was soon absorbed in these records of plays and players, finding it hard to pass over them without opening and at least scanning their contents.

I was particularly side-tracked by programmes of shows I'd seen with my parents as a young child or later when I went on school trips. I smiled at the discovery of a flyer for *Mary Poppins*, the Christmas production in 1986, as my own love of singing began with an overwhelming desire to become Julie Andrews. Seeing *Mary Poppins* live on stage ignited a fervent belief in my seven-year old heart that I could one day be as big a star as Julie was. I would make my father sit and watch as I 'performed' scenes from the show, trilling my way through 'Feed the Birds' and 'A Spoonful of Sugar' as he pretended to listen while surreptitiously working on *The Times* crossword.

I sighed and forced myself to concentrate. At last, in order to feel I was being systematic, I started to sort and tidy the programmes and playbills into years, and that was when my eye was caught by a name on the front of a leaflet:

The Life of Gertie Gitana with Isabel Grey as Gertie.

'So, I didn't mishear the name,' I said out loud, remembering the bemusing phone call.

I turned the flyer over and read:

37

Music hall singer Gertie Gitana was born at Shirley Street, Longport, Stoke-on-Trent, on 27th December 1887. Her first appearance was at the age of four as a member of Tomlinson's Royal Gipsy Children and by 1900 she had made it to London. Gradually she became a firm favourite with music hall audiences all over the United Kingdom and in the 1914-18 war she was the Forces' sweetheart. She had a sweet, childlike voice that particularly suited her famous signature tune, 'Nellie Dean'. For many years the tune was so familiar that the Nellie Dean pub in London's Dean Street, Soho, boasted a gallery of photographs of the popular singer.

I looked for a date: 1965. The show had played for three weeks and I guessed it had been a dramatised documentary of Gertie's life.

'So Isabel Grey was an actress, or perhaps a singer,' I mused, wondering if she was related to Imogen and, if so, why I'd never heard of her.

I pressed on with renewed purpose, hoping to discover further appearances by Isabel Grey at Hope Street Theatre, but I found nothing in any of the drawers of this first cabinet.

The bureau presented a greater challenge because there were more drawers here, some very small, and there was also a row of pigeon holes into which Imogen had crammed anything she couldn't decide where else to 'file'. The contents of the bureau were more varied and in some ways less interesting. Notices of horticultural lectures, coach trips to famous gardens, antique fairs, recipes and the like had been kept for no apparent reason. Some of the recipes had been cut out of magazines and local newspapers and it was as I was bundling these together that I noticed that a recipe for carrot cake had been cut out incompletely and half the instructions were missing. I turned the cutting over and saw that it was from the *Daily*

Telegraph of September, 1974, and had been preserved not for the recipe but for the feature on the other side, which was a review of a performance of *Rosenkavalier* at the Royal Opera House. The name leapt out at me:

> *Isabel Grey dug deep into her character and, in her graceful, poised performance revealed the Marschallin's sophistication and courage, yet at the same time she touchingly conveyed the disillusionment she feels over her wasted life.*

There must have been a photograph accompanying the review because there was a gap within the centre of the text where an oblong section had been neatly cut out. Perhaps it would be somewhere else in the bureau, I thought (though it might take me an age to find it amongst all the flotsam that Imogen had hoarded). I reasoned that if you went to the trouble of cutting a photograph out of a newspaper, leaving the remainder of the article amongst a confusion of other papers, you might want to keep it safe, especially as newsprint creases and tears so easily. An envelope, I thought, and looked hopefully at the row of jam-packed pigeonholes, several of which seemed to contain letters and cards. At the same time, I realised that apart from a solitary photo in a silver frame of Imogen's parents on their wedding day, there were no other photographs on display anywhere in the house.

I was tired and decided to leave this particular search for another day and for now return to the job of sorting and tidying, resolving not to allow myself to be further distracted or deflected. It was in this desultory mood that I found it: in an envelope, as I'd surmised, but simply in another drawer amongst a jumble of church bulletins and gardening pamphlets.

The name Isabel was written in pencil on the front of the envelope and the same date in 1974 I'd seen on the review. It was a full length close-up of the Marschallin and though the black and white photo had faded, Isabel Grey's face was still clear enough to make out. I didn't know her, but she was a powerful likeness to an unknown woman once painted by Thomas Gainsborough in a portrait I had seen at a house in London a few months earlier.

Alice

We were making our way on foot to Bloomsbury for a party at the home of Matthew Markham, a major donor. In the past I had relished these first night receptions, had embraced the opportunity they offered to unwind and celebrate, to 'glitter and be gay' and gradually come down from the heady high of performance. But on that occasion in February, more than anything else, I wanted the night to be over, longed to get away from the gaggle of noisy singers in their boisterous high spirits.

I hung back, listening despondently as Damian and Marie recounted moments of hilarity from the performance, while I cringed at the prospect of the reviews, their likely criticism playing out in my head like a form of torture.

> *Damian Kent gave an uproarious virtuoso display as the gleeful, child-eating witch, and Marie Oliver was a convincingly gawky yet endearing Hansel. The major disappointment was the horrible vibrato and sour intonation which beset Alice Wade's erratic Gretel.*

My throat felt odd—not sore, just strangely tight—but as always, I pushed away the thought that something was wrong. The night air was cold and I tilted my head back to feel it cooling my blazing cheeks. The group at the front had stopped and were climbing the steps of a large house with a Queen Anne frontage, its wide double doors open to welcome us. Christian had walked ahead with the director, but turned and waited for us to catch up, before standing aside to usher us into a spacious and brightly-lit reception hall. Its pungent perfume was a mixture of furniture polish and the scent from extravagant displays of white lilies, while at the foot of an impressive cantilevered staircase, immaculately groomed waiters were on hand to take our coats and offer us champagne.

I took a glass and forced myself to go with the crowd, to mingle and smile, to say the right things, but always with half an eye on Christian. I could see him across the room deep in conversation with a glamorous, elegantly clad woman who'd been introduced as a member of the board. I turned away, feeling not for the first time like a latter-day, putative Mrs Hemingway, always wondering who would succeed me, though in truth I enjoyed the status of neither wife nor mistress.

I heard a gust of laughter from the other side of the room and saw Marie making a great show of refusing the food on offer by miming the scene in the opera where she was force-fed with cake to fatten her up for the witch's oven. I laughed too and, as she threw me one of her winks of encouragement, I gave silent thanks for her. Without her friendship and unfailing support, it would have been unbearable. The performance overall had gone well enough and the applause had sounded enthusiastic, but it had been folly to allow a hopeless infatuation to expose me to the risk of humiliation and failure.

I drifted around, smiling at the clusters of partying guests, catching snippets of conversation, completing sentences in my head with my own morose reflections.

'The interaction between the two of them was good.'

'Yes, they made a sparky pair.'

'My problem was that not enough of the text was audible, especially from Gretel.'

I frowned, but couldn't push away a disloyal grievance.

The orchestra, conducted by Christian Kennedy, was generally rather too loud for comfortable listening, tending too often to drown the singers. Humperdinck's music is wonderful, but the Wagnerian-size orchestra seemed to be relishing it too much to pay heed to the balance needed with the cast.

I needed to escape the jollity, to find silence and solitude, and I helped myself to more champagne before stealing away unnoticed. I wandered through a couple of well-proportioned rooms with panelled walls and high ceilings, grand fireplaces and dark portraits in heavy frames. In a corridor, well away from the reception rooms, I stopped in front of a large gilt-framed mirror and examined my flushed complexion and my tired-looking eyes, now revealingly dark-ringed without the layers of clever stage makeup. If nothing else, I knew I had looked every inch the pert and impish Gretel and that, with my wobbly pirouettes, my girlish smiles and self-righteous sulks, I could at least act the part and bring her to life.

Behind me, the sounds of the party grew fainter and an outbreak of cheering and clapping indicated that speeches were being made.

I turned away from the mirror and sighed. Christian had said almost nothing since the end of the show. It had fallen to me to bring him out of the wings and onto the stage to join the rest of the company for the curtain call. I had skipped towards him with all the zest I could contrive, longing for reassurance but dreading any sign of disappointment he might fleetingly betray. He had leant down to peck my cheek but his smiles were for all of us, his eyes not meeting mine. Having first acknowledged the orchestra, he manoeuvred himself between me and Marie to join the line of singers. I couldn't resist the urge to look up at him and, when he squeezed my hand and raised it to his lips, I seized on this as cause for pitiful and transitory rejoicing.

Through the half-open door of a room at the back of the house, I could see a jumble of music stands clustered together in a corner. There was no one around so I slipped through the narrow opening, leaving the door still ajar behind me.

I guessed this was the famous Music Room, large enough to accommodate a small audience for the recitals which were held here. It was a long, wide room with the same highly polished parquet floor which began in the hall and continued through all the reception rooms. In the middle of the echoing, empty space was a grand piano and, down one long wall, chairs were stacked one on top of the other, ready for the next event. The lights were dimmed and, with its walls painted a rich crimson pink, the room gave off a strangely calming glow. Here and there were framed prints it was too dark to see, but at the far end of the room was a large oil painting, hung above a beautiful marble fireplace. Though the painting was illuminated by two carefully positioned wall lights, from where I stood near the piano, I could only just make out the subject of the composition. Intrigued, I moved closer to see it more clearly.

It was a full-length portrait of a woman wearing a salmon-coloured silk dress and a transparent gauze shawl, trimmed with a gold fringe. Small dabs of white and gold paint applied to the shawl gave it a flickering, sparkling effect, and the artist had somehow created the illusion that the fabric of the dress shimmered and rustled. There was such immediacy about the woman that she seemed to actually breathe and move and I had to stop myself reaching up to test if she was real or merely a life-like vision conjured by miraculous use of colour and brushstrokes.

I took a step back to better take in the whole effect.

The woman was standing against a backdrop of dense foliage, with a distant view of green and gold fields beyond her. Her abundant blonde hair was swept up to reveal the graceful curve of her neck and shoulders, and she was smiling with an expression that suggested both spirit and tenderness.

'What are you up to?' asked a booming voice behind me.

I turned round with a jolt. Caught off guard and embarrassed at being found loitering alone in someone else's home, I tried to concoct a plausible answer but stopped mid-stammer. The man, who'd been peering round the door, made his way towards me and, judging by his unsteady, portly gait I guessed that he was slightly drunk. He seemed friendly, though.

'Ah,' he said, 'I see you've found the Marschallin.'

He too, was studying it closely now.

'The Marschallin?' I said, turning to look.

'It's said to be a Gainsborough,' he said after a while.

I looked at him in astonishment and he promptly offered me his hand.

'Hello,' he said. 'I'm Ted, friend of our host.'

I summoned a smile.

'Alice Wade. Pleased to meet you.'

'Ah! You were Hansel—excellent!'

'I'm afraid not,' I said, with discomfort. 'I was Gretel.'

The man's ruddy face seemed to cloud a little but he quickly recovered his *bonhomie*.

'My apologies, but you looked very alike on stage.'

Hansel and Gretel were perfectly matched visually—(Gretel for once looking convincingly like Hansel's kid sister)—but vocally it was a different matter. Marie Oliver was able to spin effortless lines of delicious warmth and subtlety whereas though Alice Wade looked good and moved well, the part seemed to sit too low in her voice for comfort, and overuse of an obtrusive vibrato meant some of her higher notes were not perfectly floated, and indeed sounded a bit flat.

'God,' I thought, with a shudder, 'I'm too good at this.'

'Haven't I seen you in something else?' the man was saying.

'Possibly,' I smiled, seeing he was trying to make amends. '*Ariadne auf Naxos* perhaps?'

45

He looked me up and down and then exclaimed.

'That's it! Zerbinetta! You were wonderful!'

'Thank you,' I said. 'It's one of my favourite roles.'

One of my most successful, too. In the past, at least.

Miss Wade has been a consistently dazzling Zerbinetta but one fears for her when she reprises the role here in a few months' time.

I felt my eyes fill up and quickly brushed the back of my hand against my cheek to hide the tell-tale tears. Understandably alarmed, the man was relieved to see a grey-haired woman heading towards us clutching two large glasses of red wine.

'Elsie—meet Miss Wade. Gretel. My sister, Elsie.'

The woman handed one of the glasses to her brother before shaking my hand. She looked at me kindly.

'I see you're admiring the Gainsborough lady. Beautiful isn't she?'

We stood in a line, as if at a gallery.

'Do you know who she is?' I asked her.

'I don't think anyone knows for sure,' she answered. 'Matthew bought it some years ago. He said she reminded him of a singer he once knew who looked just like that when she played the Marschallin in a production of *Rosenkavalier* at Covent Garden.'

She edged closer and whispered: 'If you ask me, I think he was a little bit in love with her.'

I looked back at the painting with renewed interest and asked: 'Who was the singer? Do you know?'

The woman shook her head.

'I'm afraid I don't remember her name—it was before we knew Matthew. I seem to think there was some mystery surrounding her but Matthew has never wanted to talk about it.'

Steven

'I've been thinking about her,' said Jenny.

'Who?' asked Steven, as they were having dinner a few weeks later.

'Isabel Grey.'

'Ah, her,' he replied.

'Her—and Gertie Gitana.'

'Oh?'

'Next year it will be sixty years since Gertie died—perhaps you could mount an exhibition in the foyer to mark it? 'The Longton Songbird' or 'The Tommies' favourite songbird', that sort of thing.'

Though this was sooner than they would have expected to mount anything substantial, Steven agreed it was an anniversary they should take advantage of as a way of showing off some of the archive's holdings.

'Good idea, Mum,' he said, impressed by her thinking and feeling it would be an interesting project to go alongside the painstaking work of sorting and cataloguing.

Jenny smiled and spooned herself another helping of cauliflower cheese.

'And,' she said, in a tone that signalled she had something significant to add, 'I've remembered that Isabel had an older sister, Imogen, who was the Librarian in Stoke for years. Quite a formidable old girl I seem to recall. I'm sure she still lives in the old family home in Sandleheath. Vicarage Road. You could write to ask if she has any memorabilia of her sister you could borrow to include in the exhibition.'

Yes, Steven thought, and Imogen might also be able to add to the little information he'd been able to find so far.

'Having been a librarian all her life,' his mother went on, 'she'll no doubt have kept family history stuff like that safe and tidy.'

A reasonable assumption, Steven thought, and resolved to check the address in Vicarage Road and write the next day.

'How's it all going anyway?' Jenny asked, pushing her plate to one side.

Steven paused to take a final mouthful, before sitting back in his chair, wine glass in hand.

'It's slow work,' he said, 'but it's rewarding seeing order emerge out of chaos.'

'Made any interesting finds?' Jenny asked.

'Well, funny you should ask that, because I found a small folder of press cuttings about Isabel Grey. They were amongst some of the Gertie Gitana material, which coincidentally I've just started going through—research on the songs, press coverage of the show in 1965 and so on— but someone had obviously followed Isabel's career for a while afterwards because there were reviews of her appearances at the Coliseum and the Royal Opera House during the 1970s. Sadly, after some glowing reviews of *Rosenkavalier* in 1974, and some concerts in 1975 and '76, there was nothing else.'

Jenny shrugged.

'I guess the person—a volunteer perhaps—who'd been filing the cuttings left or lost interest.'

'Yes,' said Steven. 'That's possibly what happened, but it also ties in with your sense that Isabel seemed to disappear.'

Jenny stood up to clear the table.

'Perhaps she's dead?'

'No,' Steven replied, piling the dirty plates together to take them through to the kitchen. 'I can't find any record of that.'

Alice

At the start of rehearsals, Christian had told the cast: '*Der Rosenkavalier* is not, as so many people seem to think, about a woman who's concerned about ageing. The Marschallin is only thirty-two, after all. The opera is actually about 'letting go' in as graceful a manner as possible.'

'Mm,' I had thought grimly. 'Must try that next time.'

The first time I met Christian was at my audition for *Rosenkavalier*. I'd arrived early and they were running late and I fell into conversation with Marie Oliver, the girl who was up for the role of Octavian. I knew of her but our paths had never crossed because she'd spent the last six years on contract at the Komische Oper in Berlin.

'So what brought you back?' I asked.

'My husband,' she replied. 'He'd been teaching at the British International School, but it wasn't his thing, and when he got offered a job at a comprehensive in Bristol, we decided this was the time to come back to the UK. So here I am—trying to remind people that I still exist!'

She chatted about the house they'd bought, the new friends they'd made through the school, and the thriving village in which they'd settled, and I found myself envying the normality of her life. I was newly single following the end of a volatile relationship with a fashion photographer that had somehow lasted almost eight years, and I was in that vulnerable state of longing to be loved again, needing to matter, to be important to someone. My life with Jake had been almost wholly a torment, in which from the start I had been what Auden described as 'the more loving one'. He was extremely attractive with a swagger and confidence that I was not the only woman to find hard to resist, and I came to realise that flirting and cheating were part of his DNA. My obsession with him was powerful and tenacious and I clung to it, despite the shame and anguish my fixation caused me, believing that love inescapably involves struggle and suffering. Long before he left, it was clear we had come to the end, but my heart and brain spoke different languages and I languished over him, refusing to accept that he didn't want me anymore—perhaps had never really wanted me.

There had been others before him, but none who'd stuck around for as long (though Jake's longevity owed as much to his inertia as anything more meaningful). Many of my earlier relationships had been short-lived and little more than flings, but I was rarely on my own for long, as I pursued my wearisome search for 'the right one'. Being in a relationship was an all-consuming need. Though I had learnt that love is hard when you love someone who doesn't love you back, I continued to believe that, with enough determination, I could awaken something within a man of which he himself was initially unaware. If you try hard enough, you'll get your man—well that's how it works in romantic fiction—and that's what I hoped would work for me.

Strangely, the confidence and certainty that carried me through challenging roles in different theatres in unfamiliar places all over the world seemed to desert me when I engaged in affairs of the heart. The same pattern of disillusionment and disappointment played out with sickening regularity: I would identify someone I liked and in an attempt to impress him and make him notice me I would lavish time and attention on him, over-investing in someone I barely knew. We would end up in bed sooner than I really wanted, because I assumed he would expect sex to be readily on offer. I went along with it, hoping it would lead to love. At first my efforts would appear to work but, after a brief period of bliss and enchantment, I would watch in dismay as he began to distance himself, any attraction he may have felt for me extinguished by my increasingly unattractive doggy devotion.

Now, alone and lonely, free-floating between obsessions, and searching desperately for a new berth, I was dangerously susceptible.

In some ways I lived a double life. At work I lived a life of pretence inhabiting characters whose devil-may-care philosophy might have served me better than did my own. With my clear, agile voice, my petite physique and my youthful energy, I was destined to play the coquette. So I made a career of playing girls who were young and frisky, coy but flirtatious, fickle and whimsical. These women were saucy and street-wise, mischievous and gossipy, and above all, light-hearted—never taking men or love or life too seriously and mocking all those who do.

The queue of singers was dwindling and I knew that soon I'd find myself before the casting panel, hoping to convince them I could be the innocent Sophie von Faninal.

'Have you worked with Christian Kennedy before?' I asked Marie, knowing that he, too, had spent periods in Berlin.

'No, I haven't,' she said. 'He came as a guest conductor to the Deutsche Oper when I was in Berlin, and in fact I heard him conduct *Rosenkavalier* there. I never met him but I did go to an insight event he took part in.' She paused as if thinking how best to describe him. 'He's a cool customer —he doesn't give much away.'

She gave a wry laugh.

'He said that the Marschallin was his favourite character in all opera, so you and I will have to work extra hard to impress him.'

'Oh?' I said, not really interested, as it wasn't a particularly original choice, the Marschallin being widely regarded as one of the most sympathetic female figures of the opera repertoire.

Marie paused.

'I remember him saying that if you didn't know that Hugo von Hofmannsthal had written this character, you'd

51

swear only a woman could have created such an intimate portrait of someone forcing herself to face the truth about the passing of time, about her fading youth and the fleetingness of love and happiness.'

I felt my interest quickening. She seemed to be describing an unusually sensitive man, interested in the psychological make-up of characters, and moved by their disappointments and sadness.

'Strauss did write some wonderful music for her,' I said with a sigh.

The Marschallin was a role to which I sensed I would never graduate, and though I liked Sophie well enough— *nouveau riche* and naïve though she is—she could only ever provide a pale and inadequate contrast to the complexity of the more interesting older woman.

'Does he live in Berlin?' I asked.

'No,' Marie replied. 'Hamburg—his partner's a pianist on the music staff of Hamburg Opera.' She hesitated. 'Though I'm not sure they're still together. I heard some talk…'

She stopped, because the door to the audition room had opened and a singer came out, followed by the pianist who'd come to collect me.

Marie squeezed my arm: 'Sock it to them girl—I fancy you as my Sophie!'

And so I breezed into the audition room determined to suggest I could embody Sophie's charm and vulnerability, and at the same time could sing the role with all the polish and precision it demanded.

The three members of the panel—Christian and two women—stood up to greet me and shake my hand. Christian's grasp was dry and firm, his manner seemingly shy and slightly reserved, but his pale blue eyes held my gaze for longer than I expected and when I told him what I proposed to sing, he smiled.

And I was charmed. That was all it took.

Isabel

The card had been left at the stage door, delivered in person. It was hand-made on fine ivory card, a sprig of thyme drawn in ink, the small oval leaves a deep green on a narrow, wiry stem. On the reverse of the card were the words:

> *To the fairest and tenderest maid of all. I'll be in to watch tonight—perhaps you'll be kind enough to receive me afterwards? P x*

Just the letter P and a single kiss, but she knew who it was from.

From time to time she'd seen his name in a theatre review or a television listing but she'd not seen him or heard from him since the autumn of 1962, yet even after all these years, she still dreamt of him and wondered if he remembered her. His reappearance after all this time was unexpected and startling, but she was pleased he would see her in a role that had won her so much acclaim and for which she had been dressed to perfection.

She propped the card against a vase containing half a dozen white lilies that Matthew had brought round to her dressing room—as he did for every performance she gave in London—and then moved it so that it was half-hidden amongst the clutter of other cards and lucky charms, feeling it was indiscreet to display it so conspicuously alongside Matthew's very obvious token of affection.

'Dear Matthew,' she sighed.

He was four years older and, in most people's eyes, was the perfect eligible bachelor: educated, wealthy and kind— and in search of a wife. She knew he loved her, and she loved him, too, but as a friend or brother, not as a lover or husband. Though she had told him this, as gently as she could, he remained a loyal friend and concealed as best he could his hope that in time she might change her mind.

Isabel knew, however, that she would never change her mind, that he was destined for a life of disappointment if he cleaved to her and forsook the chance of finding happiness elsewhere. For she knew she could not love him or anyone else while she continued to carry within her the flame of passion for a man she had met when she was an impressionable student.

She was a private, self-contained woman and few of her colleagues knew much about the life she lived away from the stage and many imagined her to be lonely. Matthew's interest in her was well-known and her rejection of him was thought incomprehensible and led some people to assume she was simply wedded to her career and had no time for a husband or family.

In fact, from her early teenage years, she had begun formulating theories of what the perfect lover and the ideal marriage would look like, but these ideas were gleaned from the heroes who populated the romantic novels she devoured. Her sister had no time for these literary delusions, scoffing that Jane Austen seemed little interested in her male characters beyond what financial security they could provide for her heroines, and dismissing the Brontës as incapable of writing male characters who were any more than overheated adolescent fantasies.

Isabel, however, had been happy to be seduced by the gallery of handsome toffs, dreamy romantics and sexy rogues who populated the classic novels she found on her mother's bookshelves. The brooding, misunderstood hero, tamed by the love of a good woman, remained an enduring archetype of how the course of true love should play out. Heathcliff, Mr Rochester, Maxim de Winter, Mr Darcy, and Rhett Butler were all potential templates for future non-fiction men in her life.

But there was one love story she found irresistible, two protagonists who spoke to her in a way no other literary creations did: Lucy Snowe and Paul Emanuel in Charlotte Brontë's *Villette*. She was sure that the isolation and disappointments of Charlotte Brontë's own life gave *Villette* its peculiar emotional tension, and she relished the way that out of a lonely woman's love of an unattainable man, Brontë had fashioned an intensely passionate love story.

Though less obviously likeable than other romantic heroines, Isabel loved Lucy Snowe all the more for this; she was a woman deemed plain and insignificant, little regarded by gentile society; but was a woman of fire beneath ice, a woman physically weak but mentally and morally strong, a woman of fierce nobility of soul, of ardent passions. She loves first one man, the handsome Dr John—who is out of her reach—and then another, 'magnificent-minded, grand-hearted' Monsieur Paul—who is better suited to her but still tantalisingly hard to pin down.

Isabel loved Monsieur Paul's learning and his cleverness, was excited by his fieriness, and admired his upright character and his decency. She liked the idea that such a man might appear cool, but once loved and in love, would show his ardour, and that still waters did indeed run deep.

But crucially for Isabel, because *Villette* conveyed so powerfully Charlotte Brontë's personal sense of despair and her lack of belief in the traditional 'happy ending', the novel reinforced Isabel's view that God predestined certain people for happiness and others for sorrow.

As is so often the case in any love story, timing was all, and up until the point when Paul Eveson appeared in her dressing room, suggesting dinner, Isabel had begun to lose hope of ever finding her very own Monsieur Paul.

Isabel

She sometimes marvelled that such a simple song could have played such a significant role in her destiny. It was an arrangement for soprano, baritone and piano of a traditional folksong, 'Let no man steal your thyme', and Nigel Nixon had written it for a stage adaptation of Thomas Hardy's novel *Under the Greenwood Tree*.

Nigel was the music teacher who'd inspired and encouraged Isabel at school and she had been his star pupil. He was also part-time Music Director at Hope Street Theatre and when Isabel was home for the vacation at the end of her first year at the Royal College of Music, she was invited to perform in the theatre's annual summer showing of extracts from plays in the forthcoming season. The actress who would play the heroine in the Hardy production was not joining the company until September, so Nigel thought it a good opportunity for Isabel to sing on the stage of her local theatre and show what she could do.

'Do you know the book?' he asked her while they waited for the other singer to arrive.

Isabel shook her head.

'Fancy Day is the comely new School Mistress in Mellstock, where the story is set, and young Dick Dewy falls for her at first sight,' he explained. 'Dick tries to insinuate himself into her affections, but Fancy's beauty has already gained her other suitors, including a rich farmer and the new vicar at the parish church.' Isabel laughed. 'Fancy and Dick sing this song at a party where the villagers persuade Fancy to show off her voice. She sings the first two verses alone, but Dick joins in quietly on the last line of verse two before daringly turning the rest of the song into a duet that's both innocent and suggestive.'

Isabel blushed.

'And who's playing Dick?'

'A fairly new member of the company called Paul Eveson,' Nigel replied, with a hint of tartness. 'He has a good voice, I'll give him that, but in all honesty, this is strange casting. To my mind, he's rather cerebral and too severe to capture this young man's innocence and naïvety. More Hamlet than Dick Dewey—not to mention that he looks at least ten years too old for the part.'

Isabel smiled. Nigel did not appear to like Paul Eveson very much but, like most men describing and dismissing another, he underestimated the effect that man might make on a member of the opposite sex, particularly one whose taste was idiosyncratic. When Paul arrived for this first rehearsal in Nigel's music room, he took Isabel's hand and said quietly: 'If Fancy's lips had been real cherries probably Dick's would have appeared deeply stained'.'

Taken by surprise by this gallant, albeit literary, greeting, Isabel was lost for words and stared at him, wide-eyed. He wore a shabby sports jacket and wasn't classically handsome —he wasn't tall or well built enough and his close-cropped hair and prominent nose gave him a somewhat ascetic appearance—but he exuded an intelligence and intensity that held her transfixed. His blue eyes looked sharp and penetrating and when he looked into hers, she felt an unfamiliar sense of danger that was strangely exciting.

She was still flushed and flustered when Nigel suggested they make a start, but Paul interrupted him.

'Won't you tell us something about the song before we sing it?' he suggested. 'About the symbolism it uses perhaps?' He looked over at Isabel. 'I like to understand what I'm being asked to speak or sing.'

Isabel could tell by Nigel's sceptical expression that he suspected Paul knew all he needed to know about the symbolism and was hoping to embarrass him—and perhaps her—by discussion of the imagery.

'Well,' said Nigel, lifting his music off the piano. 'The song probably dates back to the seventeenth century and there've been many variants of it since then.'

'Ah yes,' Paul said.

He started humming the tune and Isabel was struck by his perfect intonation and the warm, dark resonance of the sound.

'It uses obvious botanical symbolism,' Nigel went on, 'to warn young people of the dangers in taking false lovers.'

Isabel stood to one side of the piano, trying to avoid Paul's unsettling gaze and studying her copy as Nigel identified key words that appeared throughout the song.

'So,' he said. 'Thyme is virginity and, to an extent, time —T-I-M-E. Rue is regret; Red Rose is romantic love or wanton passion; Violet is modesty; and Willow in this context is forsaken love—so stands for sorrow, grief and despair.'

Paul looked on with an ironic smile, and made great play of taking off his reading glasses and fixing his attention on Isabel.

'I heard that thyme was also used as an aphrodisiac,' he said. 'Wearing a sprig of thyme in a woman's hair was reported to make her irresistible.'

Isabel blushed again and seeing this, Nigel turned the pages back to the beginning of the piece and with more than a little irritation in his voice said: 'At one time, it was also the custom for someone who'd been jilted to wear a willow garland.'

The song was straightforward so required little musical rehearsal. There were, however, to be stage rehearsals with the show's director and at the first of these the designer found Isabel a simple pale blue dress similar to the one Fancy would wear at the party scene and suggested that Isabel's long blonde hair be wound into a single plait. Barbara, the Wardrobe Mistress, led her away to the dressing rooms to get ready, Isabel following on her heels, admiring the woman's distinctive thick red hair cut in the sharp, geometric style made famous by Vidal Sassoon, and in her wake, feeling girly and provincial. As she sat in front of the dressing room mirror in a dress the colour of cornflowers, watching the transformation to her hair take shape, Isabel thought how large and blue her eyes appeared against her small, pale face, and hoped the overall effect would be suitably fetching.

She loved these days spent at the theatre, watching the actors rehearse and, when not required on stage, Paul sat with her. Though they spoke little, she felt an intimacy grow between them, despite the fact he was married—though this in no way deterred him from spending time with her over lunch or in the pub after work—and he took to scribbling notes and sketches for her which he left at her place in the ladies' dressing room. At the end of the dress rehearsal, the day before the performance, she found his copy of their duet on the floor near the table where they'd had lunch and saw to her delight that he had drawn her outline on the front and back covers.

The staging was simple—no set or props—and began with Isabel standing alone on the stage with audience on all sides of her, the lighting low and focussed on her head and shoulders. The first verse was unaccompanied, with the piano joining her quietly at the start of the second.

> *Come all you fair and tender maids*
> *That flourish in your prime.*
> *Beware, beware keep your garden fair.*
> *Let no man steal your thyme;*
> *Let no man steal your thyme.*
>
> *For when your thyme is past and gone,*
> *He'll care no more for you,*
> *And every place where your thyme was waste*

Will all spread o'er with rue,
Will all spread o'er with rue.

On the last line of the second verse, Paul could be heard—but not seen—singing with her in unison. As the third verse progressed in harmony, he stepped forward into the light and they stood facing each other for the remainder of the duet, both now bathed in a single warm spotlight.

For woman is a branchy tree,
And man's a clinging vine,
And from your branches carelessly
He'll take what he can find,
He'll take what he can find.

The gardener's son was standing by;
Three flowers he gave to me
The pink, the blue, and the violet, too,
And the red, red rosy tree,
The red, red, rosy tree.

But I forsook the red rose bush
and gained the willow tree,
So all the world might plainly see
How my love slighted me,
How my love slighted me.

Come all you fair and tender maids
That flourish in your prime.
Beware, beware keep your garden fair.
Let no man steal your thyme;
Let no man steal your thyme.

During the last verse as the lights gradually dimmed, Paul stepped forward. Unrehearsed, and with great delicacy, he pinned a sprig of thyme to Isabel's hair.

Isabel

Twelve years had passed since that simple song brought them briefly together. Though in that time Isabel's professional career had flourished, privately, she felt as if her life was on hold; that she was waiting for the fulfilment she believed would come only from union with a man whose love would release her from the isolation in which she lived out most of her life. She socialised only occasionally, but was a popular colleague, valued for her quiet professionalism and gentle kindnesses as much as for her gleaming tone and compelling stage presence. But she was reserved and appeared self-reliant and colleagues learnt she would give little away, her guard being securely in place at all times, her focus centred on her work and the roles she was learning or performing. It was to these characters she related; in their clothes she sprang to life as if real and fully-formed. Away from the stage and these exotic creatures, she felt flat and insignificant and longed to inhabit her own life as intensely as she did theirs.

Secretly, she longed for a composer to fashion an opera out of *Villette* so that she could bring Lucy Snowe to life in all her psychological complexity; could intrigue audiences with a heroine so physically plain and emotionally throttled, who is yet so sensuous, so intelligent and so keenly feeling. What a challenge, she thought, for a composer to translate to the stage a first-person narrative that withheld so much, and yet communicated such powerful emotion. Isabel knew she carried within her all Lucy's passion and disappointment, and that it was rigorous self-control that enabled her to hold herself together.

She confided this to no-one, fearing they would think her eccentric for relating so closely to a creation of fiction. She recognised this oddness about her personality, knew that she indulged in a life fuelled by fantasies, but once she had given way to these dreams, she could not banish them or even keep them at bay. They were ever-present. It saddened her that she wasn't more 'normal' and couldn't fathom how and when she'd become this way. She had never been short of male admirers, but she'd had few boyfriends and had never allowed any to get too close to her, or to become casually involved with anyone who didn't match her ideal.

She had been a cherished daughter, favoured by her mother over an older sister with whom Isabel's life had become an endless competition. Their mother was ambitious for them both and after the early death of their father—a dutiful, caring man but one who always remained just beyond a real connection—they were always in her gaze, subject to her scrutiny and judgement, her praise or disapproval. For her sister, Imogen, this led to jealousy and dejection that in time hardened into thinly-concealed anger.

And then there had been Ralph, whose infatuation with her was unlooked for and unwanted but led Imogen to view Isabel as a bitter love rival. The Royal College of Music had provided a fortuitous escape, where Isabel hoped she could strike out alone and find her own happiness. But it was back home in Sandleheath where she first encountered the man she came to believe was her Monsieur Paul.

That he was even *called* Paul was a beguiling coincidence.

The belief had sustained her through the early weeks of the first term until she'd returned home for a weekend, ostensibly to see her mother and sister but, in truth, to see a performance of *Under the Greenwood Tree* and hopefully meet up with Paul again. For a long time afterwards, she would redden at the image of herself hanging around in the foyer waiting for him to emerge from the dressing rooms, remembered wondering anxiously about the dark-haired woman in the glamorous fur coat who also waited;

shuddered at the excruciating experience of being introduced to her.

'Gina,' Paul had cried, in a voice more actor-ish than she remembered, 'this is Isabel who sang Fancy's part in the summer concert. Isabel, meet my wife, Gina.'

Though inwardly wincing, she forced herself to smile. The woman smiled back and, as they shook hands, Isabel tried to ignore her unmistakable sophistication, her well-cut clothes worn with casual grace, her face well-defined under skilfully applied make-up. With a pang of dismay, she thought how physically well-suited she and Paul seemed— both neat, compact and dark—and by comparison she felt colourless and gauche. She cursed herself for her foolishness in assuming he'd be glad to see her, in hoping he would sweep her off for a drink, and was instead mortified to look like a silly girl hankering over an urbane, older man.

As she walked home alone up Sandleheath Hill, the bubble of excited anticipation in which for weeks she'd lived so blissfully, dissolved into the chill October air.

But she had never stopped believing that one day they would meet again. She'd fantasised about how and when this might happen, hoped he would learn of her success and contact her at whichever theatre or concert hall she was performing, and that they might resume the intimacy that twelve years earlier had so tantalisingly begun. Strangely, she ignored one of the lessons that life in the theatre had taught her: that the immediate familiarity, the trust, the instant family, so often achieved among a company of singers embarking upon an intense period of rehearsals and performances—though wonderful—is not real. She had felt an instant connection to Paul, and it had never occurred to her that the person she'd fallen for was a man she barely knew. While she was careful to avoid the temptations of succumbing to her leading men, she'd allowed herself to nurture the intense feelings she'd developed for Paul during their brief interlude at Hope Street Theatre, had fed and watered her memories of that time so that all these years later they were still vivid, and his eventual return into her life seemed to be in the natural order of things.

And now, he was sitting on the other side of the footlights while she lay *en déshabillé* on a huge crumpled bed behind plush red and gold curtains that draped across the proscenium arch. It was the fourth performance in a run of eight of Richard Strauss's opera *Der Rosenkavalier*. At thirty-two years old, Isabel was the exact age that Strauss had specified his heroine should be and though she had feared she was not yet ready to play the part of the 'older' woman forced to renounce her teenage lover to the young girl with whom he's fallen helplessly in love, the role seemed to suit her well. The underlying melancholy in the opera, as the Marschallin muses on the temporal nature of life and love, resonated with her own growing suspicion that love was hard to find and happiness ephemeral.

The curtain would rise after an orchestral Prelude that was an unambiguous musical depiction of the Marschallin and Octavian making love. As she lay on her side, facing the woman who was playing the young man, waiting to begin, she felt an unfamiliar sense of abandon that was both liberating and frightening, and that night she impressed as much for her sensual playfulness as for the sadness and dignity she habitually brought to the role.

At the end, the ovation for all the singers was prolonged but to Isabel's delight, no-one else received the sustained roar of approval that greeted her when she stepped through the closed curtains to take her solo bow. Standing alone at the front of the stage, she remained in character for as long as she could, allowing the audience to stay with the woman they had grown to love across the course of the previous four hours, the spotlight catching her shimmering, salmon-coloured silk dress with its transparent gauze shawl, trimmed with a glittering gold fringe. At last she took one long graceful bow and, as she slowly raised her head, she blinked through the lights, hoping to pick him out somewhere in the stalls but, in the half-gloom, the faces remained a blur of smiles, many concealed by hands raised in vigorous applause. She relaxed and smiled but her anticipation of what was to come next was tinged with anxiety that he might rush away without seeing her.

She hurried back to her dressing room to change, trying to hide her agitation and excitement. Kevin greeted her with his usual 'Let's be having you then' and, just as she did before and during the show when he helped with her costume changes, she gave herself over to his skilful ministrations and listened and smiled as he worked and chatted. In the warm, brightly-lit room, the pungent scent of the lilies was over-powering and as Isabel glanced at the beautifully presented bouquet, she sighed, and thought again, 'Dear Matthew.'

Kevin followed the line of her eye and shook his head.

'Do you think you could you ask him to send roses instead?' he teased. 'After ten minutes in here with those lilies my aftershave just lies down and dies.'

Isabel laughed and patted him lightly on the cheek.

'Turn round so I can undo you,' he scolded, 'so to speak.'

She laughed again.

It was the same script, the same ritual every time, but no other dresser anywhere looked after her better than Kevin. He helped her slip out of the layers of clothes that made up the final extravagant costume in which she appeared at the end of the opera, carefully smoothing out and hanging up the top garments, checking for any signs of wear that might need attention, discreetly tidying the undergarments to one side, ready for the laundry.

When she'd shed all the layers, he turned away and busied himself to allow her to get dressed into her own clothes.

'So what was going on with you and little Miss Octavian tonight then?' he quipped.

'What do you mean?' she said, turning to look at him as he stacked her shoes in boxes in a corner.

'You seemed to be going at it with a fair amount of relish—not like you.'

She laughed and blushed, knowing he was right and that she had been more uninhibited than usual in the opening scene.

'That's just your dirty mind at work,' she teased, but there was no concealing the heightened colour in her cheeks or the gaiety of her riposte.

'Ah yes, that will be it,' Kevin said, with one eyebrow raised.

She was still laughing when there was a knock at the door and she felt her heart skip a beat when she heard a man's voice asking:

'Would Miss Grey receive an old friend—Paul Eveson?'

Kevin glanced at her and she nodded to indicate that the visitor was welcome.

She held her breath as Kevin stood aside to let Paul into the small room. At a glance she could see that though he looked all of the twelve years older than he had been the last time she saw him, he was still recognisably the same man. His beard was close-cropped as before but was now peppered with grey and he was still too slightly built to carry off his baggy Norfolk jacket, but there was no denying the quiet force of his personality, even before he'd said a word. And when he did speak, his voice was as deep and resonant as she'd remembered.

He stepped towards her and held her gently by the elbows.

'You took my breath away,' he said. 'You looked as if you'd stepped out of a painting by one of those Great Masters of the eighteenth century.'

She was pleased that the effect she'd created on stage had been so striking, but wished she was not now wearing an unassuming day dress in navy and white, with a thin vinyl belt with a metal chain, the overall effect of which was rather prim. She struggled to know what to say, conscious that not only was Paul a matter of inches away from her but Kevin was still there, studying them with a wary eye. Ever the professional, however, he quickly gathered up the washing and left them alone.

They walked up Bow Street towards an Italian restaurant off Long Acre, the air as chilly as it had been twelve years earlier when she'd watched him walk arm-in-arm with his wife towards the Johnny Jim before she made her lonely way home to Vicarage Road.

Now it was her arm he took, as if claiming her as his.

The restaurant was hot and busy, the air heavy with the smell of garlic and candle wax. They were shown to a table set slightly away from the others, in an alcove which gave them some privacy, albeit under the benign gaze of a statue of a naked woman. Paul helped her choose from a menu he knew well before toasting her—and them—with red wine. As she raised her glass, she looked around to soak up the scene: the red and white gingham tablecloths and matching red candles, the walls covered with posters of famous Italian tourist sites and the ceilings draped with fishing nets and, a little incongruously, the sound of Nat King Cole crooning quietly in the background.

When their prawn cocktail starters had been delivered, he leant across the table and took her hand.

'If Fancy's lips had been real cherries probably Dick's would have appeared deeply stained'.'

'*Under the Greenwood Tree*,' she gasped.

'A magical time,' he said, holding her gaze until she blushed and looked away.

'How much opera do you get to see?' she asked at last.

'Not much, I confess,' he said, refilling his glass, though she refused another. 'Ah yes,' he said. 'You must look after your precious vocal cords.'

She wondered if he was making fun of her and laughed uneasily.

'So what did you think of the performance tonight?' she asked, hoping to conceal the awkwardness she felt, and concentrating hard on a prawn that kept slipping off her spoon.

He swirled the wine around the large bulbous glass and considered the question.

'I enjoyed it—beautiful music, quite stunning at times.' He took a large swig of wine. 'Though it's exceedingly long. I think that's what stops me seeing more opera. I don't know how audiences do it!'

She gave a tight little smile, waiting for more.

'I suppose that was what you'd call a traditional production?' he asked. 'Grand sets and handsome period costumes, painted flats trying to evoke mid-18th century Viennese interiors: very plush but a little too obvious, for my taste.'

She felt deflated, hurt that he couldn't find anything more positive to say, and she fiddled with the stem of her glass to cover her disappointment. He reached over to take her hand, just as a waiter arrived to clear their plates.

'Seriously,' he said, when the man had gone, 'I loved the tension between superficial propriety and unmanageable sexual impulses. I thought the production conveyed that brilliantly.'

He looked at her intently, all the while stroking the top of her hand. She'd only drunk half a glass of wine but took a large gulp, wanting to relax but nervous about being alone with him in such an intimate situation.

'What made you come tonight?' she asked.

'A wild impulse to see you again,' he said in a mock-declamatory way. 'I saw the review in *The Stage* this morning saying you were *nonpareil*, and rang up on the off chance they might have the odd return and here I am.' He paused, as if for effect, but said more quietly. 'Here we are.'

Isabel realised to her shame that she didn't want to hear about anything or anyone that might spoil the idyllic scene that was playing out in her mind's eye, but was guided by her notion of what was polite when you were being treated to dinner by a man about whose current life you knew little.

'Are you working at the moment?' she asked.

'No,' he said, pausing as the waiter returned to reset the table in readiness for the main course. 'No,' he went on. 'Nothing much doing right now, I'm afraid.'

She looked surprised, having imagined him continually away on location making films and television, or immersed in rehearsals for the next play.

'I'm sure something will come along soon,' she said brightly. 'I can't believe you'd ever be out of work for long.'

He shrugged.

'It's no matter,' he said. 'In fact, I think I'm rather bored of acting.'

Isabel had barely absorbed this unexpected comment before she rushed on with her next question.

'And what about your wife—Gina wasn't it?' she asked, trying to feign only the most casual recollection of her.

He leant back in his chair as the waiter, with an ostentatious flourish, placed two ceramic dishes of lasagne in front of them and wished them *bon appetit*.

She watched him cut through the cheesy topping to reveal the layers of steaming meat and pasta underneath. While he waited for it to cool, he looked up:

'She's away for a while,' he said. 'With her family in Milan.'

Something about the answer and his tone of voice dissuaded her from asking more, but to her surprise he added.

'Tired of me, no doubt.'

Before she could stop herself, she exclaimed: 'Surely not! How could she be?'

He smiled and shook his head, before taking another slug of wine.

'She's a city girl—loves Milan. Loves London even more —but I don't care for it. I'd like to move to the country.'

He scooped up a forkful of lasagne and studied it closely.

'We don't seem to be able to resolve that particular conundrum.'

Her eyes widened. He seemed to be suggesting a marriage that was less than perfect.

'And what about you?' he asked. 'Do you miss the Potteries, or does London suit you?'

'Oh, I love London,' she said with feeling.

He raised an eyebrow, as if surprised.

'I was a bit overwhelmed at first by how big it is,' she said, 'but now I love its variety. There's so much going on, so much to see all around you, and even in the midst of all the buildings and traffic, there are so many parks and green spaces.'

He smiled, humouring her.

'I've always loved parks and gardens,' she went on. 'At home, we had the Linda Vista Gardens and I went there as often as I could, it was so tranquil and beautiful and I liked to get to know all the unusual trees and shrubs.'

'So you're something of a botanist are you?' he laughed.

'No, no,' she blushed. 'But I do love trees and I love being amongst them. I'm sure they have personalities just like we do, feelings even. I'm sure they feel pain if they lose a branch just as we would if we lost a limb.'

He was watching her intently and she felt suddenly foolish and self-conscious.

'So where do you go to enjoy your trees?' he asked.

'The usual places,' she said. 'Hyde Park, Green Park, St James's Park, but I like to find less well-known gardens, too, that not so many people know about.'

'And do you have a favourite specimen of tree?' he asked.

She thought for a moment before answering.

'Yes,' she said, at last. 'I do.'

He waited.

'I like willows best of all. They're so beautiful and expressive and they're loners—their seeds fly far away from other trees.'

He raised an eyebrow and laughed.

'Are you a loner?' he asked. 'I can't believe that! Surely you're fighting off suitors right, left and centre, just like Fancy Day? Leading them all a merry dance!'

Seeing her shake her head, he lowered his voice as if in mock horror.

'Married then?'

She shook her head again and for a moment they were both silent.

'You still have that same look about you,' he said at last, having studied her face for what felt to her like an age.

'What look?' she asked.

'That look you had when we sang together all those years ago.'

She waited, feeling the hot anticipation in her cheeks, as he lowered his head and closed his eyes as if trying to summon up the right words.

At last he looked up.

'As if you're still looking for the Christmas present with your name on it because all the parcels under the tree are for other people.'

She blinked and gulped.

'You're a dreamer,' he said. 'Not like Fancy Day at all.'

For once, she held his gaze.

He shook his head.

'Don't look at me like that.'

'Why not?' she asked.

'All that glisters is not gold',' he said quietly, sitting back in his chair.

She shook her head, as if to say she knew otherwise. For the rest of the evening he continued to flirt and flatter, while she dismissed his self-deprecation as misplaced humility. He intrigued her and she believed there was much more to know about him. She wondered if his life had been a disappointment and that he, as much as she, was looking for something or someone special.

He was good company—cultured and entertaining—and to her delight, he seemed charmed to be with her. In the background, Bing Crosby was singing 'Some Enchanted Evening' and, by the end of the evening, Isabel had no doubt that her long-delayed magical adventure had at last begun.

Alice

I sat at the kitchen table and looked out at the bedraggled garden, now almost bereft of colour, a forlorn sight beneath the bleached, white sky. A large envelope bearing a Bristol postmark brought a short note from Marie and a copy of the latest edition of *Music Matters* magazine.

> *I know this won't make pleasant reading,* she wrote, *but I thought you'd want to see it for yourself. Dear old Hilary, she's tried to be fair so don't feel too bad about her.*

I frowned. I was anxious about what the day ahead might bring, and was further discomfited by knowing that the extent of my problems would be public knowledge, even if only amongst a discrete readership.

> *I'm at home for a few weeks, thank goodness, and here all over Christmas. I guess you haven't felt much like calling or emailing, but I'm here whenever you want to be in touch. Come for Christmas or New Year if you like—it would be lovely to see you. Whatever you decide, I'd like to know how you are and what the docs have said.*
> *Much love, Marie xxxx*

I sighed. I knew I was neglecting—perhaps avoiding—my friends, even Marie. Even my mother. I had turned in on myself and lacked the will—or the confidence—to engage. I'd never lived my life on Facebook or Twitter so, to all extents and purposes, I had disappeared from view. I lived in near silence where once sound had been a constant companion. There was no piano in Imogen's house—though I recalled there had once been a battered black upright—and I couldn't bear to listen to music on the radio; my music centre and my large collection of CDs remained stashed away in a box in a corner of the small front bedroom. Even Radio 4 was a hazard to be negotiated with care, its arts shows avoided for fear of features on music and musicians.

In contrast to the hectic existence I'd known before— the repeating cycle of learning, travelling, acclimatising, rehearsing, performing, and trying to rest, before starting all over again—my life had shrunk to what seemed like nothingness in a few short weeks.

I braced myself and opened the magazine at a page that Marie had flagged with a pink sticker. It was the lead article and the headline in bold black type—*Lost Voices*—was an ominous indication of what was to come.

> *It worries me that young artists feel pressurised to do too much too soon. I see too many young singers taking on the wrong roles and damaging their voices. Just this week, we learnt that acclaimed Argentinian tenor Roberto Castellan has been told to take an indefinite break from singing in order to rest his voice and try to resolve the problems that have led to a series of high-profile cancellations and withdrawals, including a concert last month when he was due to sing at the White House.*

There was a small black and white photo of the singer, his handsome head with its shock of curly hair tipped back, his eyes dancing, his whole face alight.

I shook my head and grimaced.

> *Castellan has consulted vocal specialists and been told there's nothing physically wrong, but for some reason his voice has simply stopped working. Alistair Mackenzie, a throat specialist at London's Royal Free Hospital, says that Castellan's problems are probably caused by a combination of factors. He was undoubtedly putting a lot of strain on his voice by travelling constantly, all over the world, going from job to job without a break. Castellan himself admits that the roles*

he was singing were not only challenging but extremely varied
—for one part he would be singing very high in his range and
the next he'd be singing very low. On top of that, he developed
the constant anxiety that some notes did not sound right and
might disappear altogether. The stress, the fatigue, the gruelling
rehearsals, the countless performances in the public eye must
have taken great toll.'

'Might Dr Mackenzie say the same to me?' I wondered. It
was much what all the other specialists had told me and it
depressed me to think that the man I regarded as my last
chance might have nothing new to add, no wonder cure to
offer.

Castellan's 'crash' has drawn attention to a problem that can
afflict singers at any stage in their careers. In four decades of
writing about opera and opera performers, I have too often seen
the heartbreak of singers whose stars have blazed brightly but
all too briefly, their performing lives cut short by crises that
were often a mixture of physical and psychological.

The news that English soprano Alice Wade was to step in
at short notice to make her role debut as Gretel in a revival of
Humperdinck's opera at Covent Garden caused many
observers to express concern about a voice that already seemed
under pressure. Looking at her crowded schedule for the next
couple of years, one has to ask why she would do this. The
singer she replaced withdrew for unspecified reasons but
rumour has it that she felt the role sat uneasily in her voice and
she preferred to risk short-term management displeasure rather
than long-term damage to her reputation and perhaps her
career. If only Miss Wade had been as wise, for she was
unable to produce the clean, even soprano needed to capture
Gretel's youthful freshness.

After a meteoric rise, she's enjoyed a glittering career, but
has increasingly gained a reputation for sounding below par.
Her performances this summer at the Met as the coquettish

Valencienne in The Merry Widow *provoked particular disquiet. Critics said she seemed lost and ill at ease; that though she was at home in the dialogue and the dancing, her voice sounded tentative and tremulous. We're used to hearing her dash off her dazzling, coloratura pyrotechnics with smiling ease and aplomb in her signature role of Zerbinetta, but even this is apparently beyond her at present, with the Covent Garden management advising her to withdraw from the recent production after what insiders described as a fraught dress rehearsal.*

We don't want to lose this sparkling talent from our opera houses, but right now, it's Alice Wade who has most to lose.

Hilary Forbes, Editor

It was shocking to read about myself in this way and I shied away from the thought that what I was calling a 'break' might become permanent, that there might be no going back and I might one day have to stop describing myself as a singer.

Later that morning, I walked down Sandleheath Hill to catch the bus to the station. As I waited outside the fruit and veg shop, with its array of Christmas trees crowding the pavement, I looked over at the theatre on the other side of the road. Perhaps it was envy or simply sadness that made my heart shrivel as I saw the splashy displays advertising the current run of *Singing in the Rain*.

'Room at the back for a little one, my duck,' said the driver as he took my fare.

I made my way down the aisle to an empty seat next to a window, my shy awkwardness met by kindly smiles and cheery greetings from other passengers. I sat on the crowded bus, listening to the reassuring din of animated gossip, surrounded by people who seemed completely at home and accepting of their lot. I'd grown used to a life of rootlessness, where all urban spaces, all hotel rooms and airport departure lounges looked the same, where people were generally harassed and distracted, running to catch up with themselves and worn out by the stresses of lives lived too fast. I'd long ago stopped talking to people on trains and in queues, fearing they would back off, thinking me strange and overly-familiar. But here everywhere I went, I met people who were unfailingly friendly. Here, people were curious and concerned, had time for each other, for me; but feeling so out of sorts with myself and my life, I was finding it hard to accept this easy sociability as normal.

It had started to rain heavily and I rubbed the steamed-up windows with the back of my glove so I could peer out at the familiar landscape—the weathered purple sandstone of the large Victorian villas and the tiled roofs of the red brick terraced houses, some of which still had Brexit posters propped in their windows.

I sighed, feeling out of place and alone, and sorry I'd rejected my mother's offer to come with me to London. I'd barely seen her since I moved into Vicarage Road but we'd arranged to meet for coffee near the station before I caught the train. I had thought she would suggest the North Staffs Hotel and though it was not as grand now as it had once been, I assumed Mum would take us there for old time's sake. But she wanted to meet at a new Italian café that was run by the daughter and son-in-law of an old school friend of hers.

I pushed open the door to Viazzani's and looked around. The mid-morning rush was in full flow and I was met by a cacophony of chattering customers and cappuccino machines in full chorus. I was early and Mum was not yet there, but as I hesitated in the doorway the bearded man behind the counter winked at me and called out:

'Coming in then my lovely, out of the wet?' in an accent that was a peculiar hybrid of Italian and Welsh.

I smiled and looked for a table from where I could see the door and look out for Mum.

'What can I get you then, love?' he asked.

I hesitated. I needed some caffeine so decided to order, hoping that Mum wouldn't mind that I hadn't waited for her.

'I'll have a double espresso please.'

'Have a seat, love. We'll bring it over in a minute.'

I took the only empty table I could see amidst the clutter of shopping bags and buggies. A few people looked up, obviously wondering who the newcomer was. As I took off my red duffle coat, I struggled to disentangle one of the toggles from the strap of my shoulder bag and tried to look unconcerned when two young men at the next table, wearing replica Stoke City shirts, stared at me with undisguised curiosity. I hoped Mum would arrive soon and make me feel less conspicuous.

A girl appeared with my coffee but, before putting it down, she gave the table a vigorous wipe, giving me time to take in her impressively sassy appearance. Despite the inclement weather, she was dressed as if for a surfing bar on a beach somewhere hot and sunny. A daring deployment of black Lycra showed off a glowing, tanned physique, while around her wrists and neck were layers of gold bracelets and necklaces. To complete the look, she had a crop of spiky blonde hair set off by earrings from each of which dangled a black skull and crossbones.

'There you are duck,' she said. '£2.50. Pay us when you go.'

I watched as she made her way back towards the counter, picking up empty crockery with practised ease as she went, stopping to coo over babies and toddlers. She seemed to inhabit a world that glowed in technicolour, whereas even in my bright red coat, I seemed by comparison to fade into monochrome.

I was pleased to see Mum waving at me through the window. She made her way over to my table and we hugged, just as the bearded man came over to take her order.

'Shirley', he said, 'how are you, my lovely? Cappuccino is it?'

I looked at them in surprise. Given the warmth of the welcome, my mother must be a regular and yet the café was nowhere near where she lived.

'Nico,' she smiled, sitting down and taking off her coat. 'This is my daughter Alice.'

'Alice!' he cried. 'We hear so much about you.' He shook my hand with enthusiasm. 'How you doing?'

I managed to splutter, 'Pleased to meet you,' before he hurried away to make the coffee.

I laughed and my Mum laughed, too.

'It's good to see you smile, darling. How are you?'

'Oh you know,' I said, 'a bit up and down.'

She frowned and patted my hand.

'What time's your appointment? I wish you'd have let me come with you.'

'It's OK, Mum,' I said, lying. 'I'll be fine. My appointment's not till four o'clock.'

'Will you meet up with anyone afterwards?' she asked. 'It might do you good to have some company, might cheer you up.'

I shook my head.

'No, I'll come straight back. It's likely to be quite draining. I doubt I'd be good company.'

Nico reappeared with Mum's coffee and a plate of almond biscuits.

'Coffee's on the house,' he said. 'Enjoy!'

Several of the tables emptied at the same time and the noise level dropped significantly so that the café took on an altogether calmer ambience.

'How does Nico know you so well?' I asked as my mum dipped a biscuit into her coffee. 'Do you know his wife? Is

79

that her in the black Lycra?' I nodded in the direction of the counter.

'No!' she said in a whisper. 'She works here part-time. Vicky doesn't seem to be around right now.'

'But how do you know Vicky?' I persisted.

'Well, it's her family I know really, not her so much.'

There was something unusually vague—evasive even—about her answer, but I was too preoccupied to pursue it. I reached into my bag to find the music magazine and handed it to her, open at the leader article.

She looked at me inquiringly.

'Read it,' I said glumly.

She took a case out of her handbag and put on a pair of bright green reading glasses. 'Nice colour,' I thought. 'Very stylish.'

As she read, I noticed her face twitching from time to time and wondered what she was thinking, feeling suddenly protective of her and sorry to be the cause of so much worry. She was still an attractive woman, her face lined but flatteringly made-up, her hair cut short in a soft natural style that seemed to emphasise her pale blue eyes. She'd been on her own for a long time, but she took care of herself and was interested in looking good. I admired her for that.

She closed the magazine and handed it back to me with a sigh.

'You're not the only one, then,' she said sadly.

'No,' I said. 'It happens.'

'Is it the same Dr Mackenzie you're seeing this afternoon?'

I nodded.

'Well,' she said, trying to look more cheerful, 'if he finds nothing wrong, there's always the hope that with rest your voice will recover.'

If so, I thought, only time would tell and what would I do in the meantime?

Isabel

Isabel floated through the remaining performances, buoyed by its critical success and her burgeoning relationship with Paul. The bitter-sweet scene at the end of the opera was a world away from the love-struck bubble in which she now existed and she had to dig deep to summon the necessary sense of resignation and despair that had been her silent companions for so long. While the Marschallin had to face the outcome of the masquerades that had gone before and set her young lover free, Isabel revelled in the gratification of feelings she had harboured for over a decade.

She told no-one about her new-found happiness, partly because she was by nature private and discreet, but largely because it troubled her that her lover was married and that they were deceiving his absent wife. She also felt a nagging sense of disappointment that their affair progressed at Paul's chosen pace, not hers. She would have liked an old-fashioned courtship where they took time to get to know each other so they could savour and linger over each new stage of intimacy. Paul, on the other hand, having made affecting displays of chivalry at the outset, before long could not contain his ardour. She allowed herself to give way to him, but was saddened by a sense that in pressing ahead so quickly, something precious and important had been lost that they would never regain.

Paul had time to spare, with little work and currently no wife to limit his freedom; and though Isabel had music to learn for future engagements, she allowed Paul to take priority, to disrupt the normal discipline and routine of her life, to transport her to an unfamiliar place where love set the rules. On days when she had no performance, she and Paul spent time together, visiting the museums and galleries he loved, walking and sometimes picnicking in her favourite parks, enjoying long dinners in cosy restaurants or romantic trysts at her flat.

Paul said little about Gina, though Isabel learnt to spot the signals when it was clear they'd been in touch. If Gina had phoned or written, he was noticeably tetchy and agitated, and even though he said little about this contact, at those times Isabel sensed the woman's presence intruding upon their idyll and felt a mixture of resentment and guilt casting a shadow over their liaison. He avoided discussion about the future, with or without Gina, with or without Isabel. He seemed able to enjoy the present with no thought of where it was leading, whereas, as the weeks turned into months, Isabel became increasingly consumed and constricted: consumed by her infatuation with Paul and her hopes for a future with him; constricted by her desperate struggle to conceal that passion from the people around her. At times this conflict threatened to tear her into two equally powerful parts, the one part loving and yearning, the other sternly self-controlling. To those who knew her away from the stage or the concert platform, she was a quiet, undemonstrative woman. Inside her head, however, she was vulnerable and passionate, and it was an iron-will that was holding those feelings in check and preventing the two conflicting parts from splintering apart.

Autumn succumbed to winter and winter dragged by until the first green shoots of regrowth signalled the promise of spring, and still Paul remained unforthcoming about his intentions. It was wrong that nothing was said about anything and on some level she knew this. But when they were together, she felt complete.

She had no close women friends in whom she might have confided. Women who might have counselled: 'Don't waste another moment with this man! He'll never leave his wife.' She alone knew how ardent he could be, how special he made her feel, how essential. And yet, she recognised that he remained somehow distant, that even during lovemaking he seemed sometimes disconnected from her, but she didn't allow these unsettling contradictions to undermine her belief that they were meant to be together, whatever the obstacles. As she had done for so long, she fed and watered her hopes and dreams and made her own fantasy of the moment in *Villette*, when Paul at last beseeches: 'Lucy, take my love. One day share my life. Be my dearest, first on earth.'

In the absence of any such declaration and certainty, the shadow of disappointment and loss seemed always to be lurking near the surface, even during happy times. Women friends might have said: 'Real love should make you happy and contented, not miserable and anxious,' or asked: 'Does he love you as you love him?' She longed for some indication of commitment that might have sustained her, but though Paul's desire for her remained undimmed, it was increasingly matched by periods of disconcerting distraction.

She had engagements which frequently took her away, as her career continued to blossom and her diary filled with work for almost three years ahead. She was much in demand for roles that had already brought her success, but promoters increasingly wanted her to venture into new territory and new roles. She was careful to ensure she didn't take on too much new work while she was busy repeating her existing repertoire, but some offers were too enticing to resist, chief amongst them, an invitation to sing the title role in *Ariadne auf Naxos* in two years' time. Her agent advised caution, fearing the offer had come too soon, that her voice was not yet full enough, and concerned that the production was to be sung in English when he felt she should learn the role in the original German. Though Isabel knew the role would require her to be emotionally and physically robust, she also believed it was one she was born to play, an operatic heroine to whom she could relate like no other, one of those rare women who surrenders to one lover only.

Then, in April, just as she was leaving for a concert tour of Germany, Paul told her that his wife was returning to London.

Alice

As the weeks before Christmas dragged by, I slowly made my mark on Imogen's house so that, though it did not feel entirely like mine, it was no longer simply hers. I reorganised the middle room so that it functioned as a cosy sitting room, with two new comfy chairs on either side of the mantelpiece, the hearth below which was still usable for coal fires. Mum and I shopped together for new lighting, and I was grateful for the unexpected skill with which she helped me tackle the gloom that encased some of the rooms. More than that, I was touched by her endless store of love and kindness, and though I'd become rather reclusive, I was nevertheless glad to know she was close by.

I had tidied all the materials relating to Hope Street Theatre into a box, which I kept in the small front bedroom and to which I added whenever I found anything I thought might be of interest to someone at the theatre. Most of what I found, however—the copious flyers, church notices and random cuttings—I threw away, enjoying a sense of tidying and decluttering that helped persuade me I could make the house my home.

I continued to work my way through the muddle of Imogen's cupboards and drawers, always on the lookout for anything about Isabel, but I'd found nothing to add to my early finds. Anticipation of further discoveries sustained me through what was frequently tedious work—envelopes tucked in the back of drawers promising much until opened to reveal ever more recipes for puddings and cakes.

The next find was in such an unlikely and unexpected place, I began to imagine Imogen as an absent-minded squirrel who stowed stuff away with little logic as to where and why. One day, as I was making a birthday cake for my mum, I reached into a kitchen drawer for a large wooden spoon and found a small brown envelope lodged at the back, almost invisible against the brown wood. Inside the envelope I found a clutch of reviews about a production at Covent Garden in 1977 of another opera by Richard Strauss, *Ariadne auf Naxos*, in which Isabel had played Ariadne. I put aside the mixing bowl and spread the cuttings on the kitchen table in front of me. Even at a quick glance I could see that the tone of these reviews was very different to the glowing appraisals of *Rosenkavalier*. As I read, I found myself shaking my head in dismay, so unanimously unfavourable was the collective critical verdict.

> *One glaring cause of this show's dysfunction is its miscast star... As the tantrum-prone Prima Donna in the Prologue, Isabel Grey was unable to capture the tempestuous, temperamental diva required to dominate the proceedings in the first half with a wonderful air of indignation, and to tear up the stage with formidable hauteur. She was also in worryingly poor voice and was only intermittently up to the task of the demanding titular role.*

'Pretty damning,' I thought.

> *The voice had little of its famed sheen or glow and in the short time since we last heard her in this house, it's alarming how much of the power has diminished. Indeed for much of the evening, her voice had little presence or richness and her tone sometimes disappeared into the lush orchestral textures.*

I frowned, recognising the signs of a voice under pressure, a singer possibly experiencing extreme levels of anxiety.

> *The production served her badly, weighing her down with a hideously stiff auburn wig and fussy costumes which made her look lumpy in all the wrong places. Even allowing for that, however, she looked weary, her discomfort and fatigue all too apparent, physically and vocally.*

I sighed, knowing how hard it could be to overcome unhelpful designs or a muddle-headed production. In my own recent debacle in the same opera, the production included a bizarre range of styles, from eighteenth century elegance to nineteen eighties grunge.

Memory—or was it vocal problems?—seemed an issue for Miss Grey: the audience soon became aware that whole chunks of words were missing and once or twice she stopped singing completely, causing her fellow singers to wait in vain for their cues.

'Poor woman,' I thought, my stomach fluttering in sympathy at the very public collapse being described.

No announcement had been made to say Miss Grey was unwell and she made it through to the end of the performance, but on this showing, something is surely gravely wrong and you have to question the management's judgement in allowing her to go on.

'At least I was spared such public shaming,' I mused, though at the time, the management's decision—while an unexpected relief—was a shock and a humiliation.

A star has fallen from the heavens.

This seemed the saddest judgement of all.

I knew that reviews like these were all it took for the knives to come out and for a singer's confidence to crumble. Did Isabel recover from this disastrous debut, or was she so devastated and ashamed that she slunk away without finishing the run?

'I don't suppose she ever wanted to sing Ariadne again,' I thought, feeling certain that even if my voice recovered enough for me to resume my career, I would never again attempt to scale the heights of the fiendishly florid coloratura that Strauss wrote for Zerbinetta, even though she had once been my ever-reliable calling card.

I refolded the clippings and put them back in the envelope, deciding I would add them to the Gertie Gitana playbill and the *Rosenkavalier* cutting and photograph which I was keeping in a large white envelope in the bureau.

I stood up and looked out of the window. In the gloom of the December day, the garden looked more ragged and abandoned than ever. I shivered and went through to the parlour. Despite the new lighting, this morning the room had an eerie chill that made my spirits sag. As I opened the lid of the bureau to slip the small brown envelope into the larger white one, the whole house seemed steeped in melancholy; sadness permeating the rooms as if they were haunted by Isabel Grey.

Isabel

A radio adaptation of *Crime and Punishment* marked the beginning of the end of Paul's life as a performer. Though he was an avid student of theatre, he had become increasingly disinterested in life as an actor, more inclined to study the great texts than itching to perform them. Isabel worried that his career was stalling, that he was wasting his talents, and was pleased when, soon after her run in *Rosenkavalier* ended in October 1974, he accepted a job with Radio 4 in Birmingham.

Not previously having known the novel, he researched it with a rigour that was academic and forensic.

'I love the way the book grapples with such profound political, social, and religious issues,' he said, one night when they were having dinner at her flat. 'I'm fascinated by how it delves into the tortured psychology of characters whose destinies were shaped by those issues. They seem to live their whole lives confronting despair and mortality, and wrestling with…' He hesitated, before pursing his lips as if to force the words out, 'the anxiety of choice.'

As Isabel busied herself at the stove, he leant against the sink with the book in one hand and the radio script in the other, describing the mental anguish and moral dilemmas of the character he was playing, Rodion Raskolnikov, an impoverished young man who formulated a plan to kill an unscrupulous pawnbroker for her cash.

'He's the most challenging character I've ever played,' he said.

Isabel spooned out servings of chilli and rice, struck by his animated manner, and pleased to see him so enthusiastic about his work. She took off her apron and moved through to the dining area of the large living room, plates of food in each hand.

'The book attempts to defend his actions,' he said, pulling out a chair for her at the small, round table. 'It argues that with the pawnbroker's money he can perform good deeds to counterbalance the crime, while at the same time ridding the world of a parasite.'

He sat down and poured two glasses of wine, while Isabel lit a pair of candles on the sideboard and another pair on the table before turning off the bright overhead lighting. He waited for her to sit down and then began to eat while continuing to talk.

'He also commits the murder,' he said between mouthfuls, 'to test his theory that some people are naturally capable of such actions, and even have the right to perform them, that murder by such *Übermensch* is permissible in pursuit of a higher purpose.'

Isabel listened and shook her head.

'Dostoyevsky has such an obsession with evil,' she said. 'I don't like him. I prefer Tolstoy, he conveys so much love of life. He transports me to another world—I can see myself ice-skating in Moscow or dancing in elegant ballrooms in St Petersburg—and there's always that poignant longing for what might have been.'

He smiled at her over his glass.

'You're such a romantic,' he said.

'I am,' she agreed, 'but Dostoyevsky makes me feel uncomfortable and anxious—all that over-the-top desperation, that sense that tragedy is just around the corner.'

She shuddered.

He laughed.

'So speaks the opera diva,' he joshed. 'What about *Tosca, Rigoletto, Forza del Destino....?*'

She pulled a face and mimed the word: 'Touché!'

'So, tell me,' he said, 'who's your favourite character in Tolstoy?'

She stared into the large yellow church candles flickering between them in the middle of the table, considering the question and wondering if her answer would betray her as frivolous and shallow.

'It has to be Prince Andrei in *War and Peace*,' she admitted at last.

Paul snorted.

'But he's so arrogant, so convinced of his own superiority, so unlikable!' he cried.

'No, no,' she protested. 'You have to see beyond the façade to the passionate heart beneath. He has this fateful belief that glory on the battlefield will give his life meaning.'

He held her gaze and shook his head.

'You're seduced by the dash and the gallantry.'

Perhaps so, she thought, but said nothing.

'I prefer Pierre,' he said. 'I can relate to him—the way he fumbles from party boy and reluctant soldier towards a meaningful life he can live well, on his own terms, true to his political convictions.'

Isabel raised an eyebrow in surprise, Pierre having struck her as a buffoon, given to endless philosophising.

'I enjoyed the opera,' he said.

'You saw the Prokofiev?'

'I did,' he said. 'I went to the London premiere.'

'So did I!' she said and blushed, recalling that Matthew had taken her and soon after had declared his feelings for her.

'Well, well,' he said. 'What a coincidence.'

'Yes,' she murmured, relieved they hadn't bumped into each other on that occasion.

She was quiet for a moment.

'What made you go?' she asked. 'It's very long—I know you're not keen on long operas.'

'No, indeed,' he grimaced, 'but a friend was working on the costumes and she got me a free ticket.'

Who was this friend, Isabel wondered with alarm, but before she could ask, he got up with an air of insouciance to help himself to more rice from the kitchen.

'What did you think of it?' she asked when he sat down again.

He pulled a face that conveyed mixed feelings.

'Well it's obviously a wonderful spectacle,' he said, 'but it doesn't measure up to the novel.' He paused. 'It seemed to me to lack emotional depth—and god, it was long.'

She laughed.

'It had its moments, though,' she said. 'I was in tears when Natasha and Andrei danced that last waltz, just before he died.'

She sighed and they both laughed. She enjoyed their discussions about books and art and philosophy, particularly when these conversations overlapped with their work and seemed to bring them closer together.

The radio adaptation was a success but, once back in London and again 'resting', Paul dismissed Isabel's concerns about his lack of work, grateful for such lulls when he could legitimately devote his time to his growing interest in philosophy, psychology and ethics. To her surprise, she learnt that, as a student in the 1950s, he'd begun a degree in Philosophy and Theology before switching to English and Drama. With its focus on the 'big questions' of life, *Crime and Punishment* had ignited in him a fascination with the extremes of behaviour of which people are capable and the ethical dilemmas human beings have faced throughout the ages.

She was impressed by his intellect and erudition; it gave her a sense that she was sharing her life with someone more substantial than herself, someone with whom she would learn and grow as they went through life together. At moments of misgiving and doubt, however, she recognised what a small portion of his life she did in fact share and knew there was no guarantee that this would ever change.

Isabel

'I've not been a good husband,' he said quietly. 'She's ill and she needs me.'

Isabel knew that, unlike Gina, she had no claim on his loyalty or commitment, yet the words froze her heart. Paul bowed his head and his next words were almost inaudible.

'She's my wife. I have a responsibility to her.'

They were sitting on a bench in the gardens near Russell Square, Isabel having suggested they spend her lunch break there together. The gardens were busy and the sounds of shocked laughter from around the raucous Punch and Judy show pierced the usual tranquility of the green oasis in the heart of Bloomsbury.

Isabel looked over to the red and white striped booth and the clusters of spell-bound children sitting cross-legged on the grass in front of it, flanked by parents and other adults who stopped to watch as they idled through the park, on their way north to Euston, or south towards Covent Garden.

'That's the way to do it!' cackled Mr Punch as he thwacked the unsuspecting Judy round the head.

Isabel looked down at her lap at the half-eaten sandwiches and felt a wave of nausea sweep through her. She wrapped up the remnants in the crinkly grease-proof paper and placed the unwanted package carefully on the bench beside her, all appetite banished. She closed her eyes and frowned, hoping that if she stayed still and concentrated hard, the queasiness would pass.

'It was over two years ago. Why didn't you tell me about the baby?' she asked at last, wishing the question didn't sound so accusing but unable to hide her dismay at his concealment. 'You said she went back to Milan because she was tired of you.'

Paul sighed.

'I know,' he said. 'I was less than candid about that.'

She looked up at him, trying to make sense of it.

'She wanted a baby,' he said. 'I didn't. She wanted to live in London. I didn't. We were at odds with each other. She wanted a break from me so she went back to stay with her family.'

His packet of sandwiches sat unopened on the bench beside him and, with his mug of tea in one hand, he sucked greedily on a cigarette, a new habit she disliked but tolerated because he said it helped him focus on his work.

She waited for him to continue.

'Not long after she arrived in Milan, she discovered she was pregnant.'

He paused.

'She lost it at five months. I wasn't there and it was traumatic for her.'

Isabel swiveled slightly to her right so that she could see his face, but he looked away, and she guessed he found it easier to open up when freed from the intensity of her scrutiny. She adjusted her position and waited for more.

'She came back to London soon after that.'

He blew out a last circle of smoke, before scrunching the butt under his foot into the gravel beneath the bench.

'Said she wanted to make a go of it, even if it meant not having children.'

Isabel took a sharp intake of breath and shuddered, feeling the nausea return and threaten to overwhelm her.

'How old was she when she lost the baby?' she asked at last.

The question seemed to surprise him.

'Thirty-seven,' he said. 'Why do you ask?'

Isabel shook her head, embarrassed.

'I thought she was older than that,' she mumbled, recalling the sophisticated woman she had met at the theatre over fifteen years earlier, shocked to learn that she was little older than herself.

'She's not been well for a while,' he went on. 'A series of seemingly unrelated symptoms, inconclusive tests, different doctors, more tests.' He turned to look at Isabel. 'Now it seems it's serious.'

Paul had rarely talked much about Gina and Isabel preferred to know as little as possible, hoping that the less his wife occupied her thoughts or her time with Paul, the less real she might seem. But much as Isabel had tried to deny the reality of her, Paul had now made it clear that he would stand by her, that she would face the gruelling treatment and unpredictable prognosis with her husband at her side.

Birds chirruped in the trees above their bench and children shrieked in delight at the outrageous antics of Mr Punch. Isabel shielded her eyes and watched as she had done long ago on summer Sundays in Linda Vista Gardens. This was the same anarchic Mr Punch she remembered from her childhood, with his relentless baton, his trying baby, and his hapless wife.

She sighed and closed her eyes, and though the bright sunlight penetrated her eyelids, all she could see in her mind's eye was a darkness so intense it seemed almost solid.

He walked her back to the rehearsal room, promising to meet her at the end of the afternoon, take her home and cook her supper. Throughout their relationship it had been his way to occasionally make flamboyant gestures of affection, often after periods of appearing distant and evasive. He would turn up at her door with extravagant bouquets of flowers or take her shopping for expensive clothes, and these tokens had become more frequent after his wife came back to London, as he somehow divided his time between the two women. Isabel realised that this could not have been easy and determined to be understanding and accommodating, not wanting him to think her a nag, preferring to make allowances for his absences, to reassure herself that he was simply fulfilling obligations from which it would have been wrong to extricate himself.

Now, however, Isabel resented Gina for the time and attention she would need and expect from Paul, and the more so, as she was worried about her own health and was struggling with a role that even though they were in only the first week of rehearsals, left her physically and emotionally drained at the end of every session.

She had never asked him to choose between them, perhaps because she feared which way he would choose. The decision was his alone. Only rarely did she admit to herself the shame she felt from being the one without the power, of being the one who waited and hoped that patience would at last be rewarded. Her love for him was steadfast but she feared the pain of rejection and abandonment, unable to imagine how she could survive and carry on if her hopes turned out to have been illusions.

He left her at the door and she watched as he made his way towards the hubbub of Leicester Square. He didn't look round, and though she knew he would come back for her in just a few hours' time, she knew in the end, she would lose him.

The windowless rehearsal room in the basement of a large, unused church, though high-ceilinged, was unpleasantly stuffy and as the afternoon wore on, Isabel felt increasingly uncomfortable. Her short-sleeved cotton dress should have been perfect for the unusually warm spring weather, but she could feel perspiration pricking her armpits, and her unsettled stomach felt constricted, despite the loose-fitting drop waist. She sat at the side of the rehearsal area, next to the production table, watching her colleagues, glad she would not be required to sing until the next short scene had been blocked. On the table next to her was a sheaf of papers that Grant, the Australian director, had been studying during the lunch break, printers' proofs of the show's programme book. He stood up and swung round the table move onto the acting area, and in his haste, his hip dislodged the pile of papers, sending them fluttering to the floor at her feet. He stopped and turned, but Isabel raised her hand to indicate that she would pick them up, happy to have something to distract her.

She gathered the sheets together on her lap, shuffling them quietly to form a neat pile, before checking they were in the right order. The page on top included a brief summary of the story and as she read it, she gave a smile of approval, thinking it a neat précis of a plot that could seem problematically complex.

> *Richard Strauss's opera* Ariadne auf Naxos *is a curious cross between a sitcom and a Greek tragedy. It is set in the home of a very rich man who has hired the services of two very different groups to provide some after-dinner entertainment.*
>
> *On the one hand there is a rather precious composer and a group of opera singers; on the other, a team of burlesque dancers. Each group despises the other and they start bickering about who should perform first.*
>
> *That problem is both solved and worsened when they are informed that because of time pressure, the rich man has decided that they must somehow combine their efforts and perform together.*
>
> *The first act of Strauss's opera tells of the below-stairs squabbling between the two companies; the second act is their joint performance, telling the tale of Ariadne's abandonment by Theseus on an island, deserted except for a burlesque troupe that happens to be there...*

She glanced up, and seeing that the singers involved in the next scene were still being talked through their moves, she read on. After the synopsis there was an article about the genesis of the opera.

The figure of Ariadne, abandoned by the man she loves (Theseus) and longing for death on the island of Naxos, had haunted von Hofmannsthal's imagination since he was a youth, just as it had haunted Monteverdi and Haydn. By contrasting her with the flirtatious Zerbinetta, he could explore the natures of two types of women: Ariadne eternally faithful to one man and yielding herself to another (Bacchus) only because she at first believes him to be Hermes, the messenger of death, sent to lead her to Hades; Zerbinetta happily off with the old and on with the new.

The piece also quoted from letters between Strauss and his librettist. In July, 1911, von Hofmannsthal had written:

'It's about one of the most straightforward and stupendous problems in life: fidelity; whether to hold fast to that which is lost, to cling to it even unto death—or to live, to live on, to get over it, to transform oneself, to sacrifice the integrity of the soul and yet in this transmutation to preserve one's essence, to remain a human being and not to sink to the level of the beast which is without recollection.'

She sighed and put the papers back on the table, her thoughts veering from Ariadne's despair to her own seemingly inevitable, and perhaps imminent, desertion by Paul. As if from a distance, she heard Grant coaxing the members of the comedy troupe through the scene, guiding them into position, occasionally asking the choreographer to demonstrate a dance step.

She looked around the rehearsal room—its acting area marked up with gaffer tape, the untidy clutter of chairs and props and rehearsal costumes—as if seeing it all with new eyes, the break for lunch seeming to mark a before and after. During the morning session, she had sung of Ariadne's inconsolable despair, endeavouring to find a way into the character's heart.

How beauteous once were Theseus–Ariadne,
And went their ways in light and life rejoicing
Why knew I aught of them? Let me forget them—
One question must I answer. It is shame
Still thus to be distraught
Then let me rouse me. Yes, whither has she vanished,
The maid that once was I?
I know now—Let me not forget, ye gods,
Nay, not the name –The name is with its fellow
Grown intertwined so closely: For one thing
With a second mingles soon...

Now that scene seemed to foreshadow the desolation that lay ahead for her.

The sound of the piano launching into the scene being rehearsed brought her back to the present with a jolt. Isabel watched as the charming American baritone who was singing Harlequin peered into the area on the stage that would represent the cave into which Ariadne had retreated. He was trying to cheer her up, urging her to give life another chance, to be open to its surprises and joys. He strummed on a mandolin as if serenading her, trying to cajole her out of her misery with his caressing tones and his clumsy boyish charms.

Love and hate and every pleasure,
Hope deferred and every pain
Human heart can bear in measure
Once and many a time again.

He was an attractive man, with large, brown eyes and a wide mouth and she knew that anyone but Ariadne would have been enchanted by his good-hearted efforts to console her.

But, bereft of sense to languish
Painless, joyless, numb and cold,
Who can bear such cruel anguish
Worse than death a hundredfold?
Rest thee from such gloom and sorrow,
Wake, if but to fiercer pain –
Live, for joy may come tomorrow
Live, and wake to love again.

But Ariadne would not awake, would not be swayed.
She was the one who couldn't forget.

Isabel

That night, Paul cooked an elaborate meal of beef, olives and duchesse potatoes and, as he removed the string that held the thin slices of topside together, Isabel was touched by the trouble he'd taken. He said no more about Gina and showed only half-hearted interest in how her rehearsals were going, but talked instead about *The Self in Crisis*, the book he was writing and which he described as an exploration of the crises in faith which afflict modern man and the challenges that attend his journey to a life of spiritual values.

'I've always related most closely to characters who struggle and vacillate between good and evil,' he said. 'Whose fates are unpredictable, however virtuous they are.'

She looked at him across the table and realised how much of their conversation was intellectual and abstract; how little intimate communication there was between them. How he showed less and less interest in her work; in her.

She looked down at her plate and wondered if he would notice how little she had eaten and she cut the meat into morsels so small she might manage to swallow them.

'The anxiety of choice,' she thought to herself, had become an increasing preoccupation of his, no doubt brought into focus and heightened by his wife's ill-health and his faltering efforts to do the right thing by her, to rid himself of the guilt of being a faithless husband.

Isabel had prepared for the role of Ariadne for almost two years. She began learning the music as soon as the role was offered her and, in the months leading up to rehearsals, she had regular sessions with her vocal coach and with the conductor so that, by day one, the words and music were learnt and locked in her memory. At the same time, she'd immersed herself in the character, quickly developing an understanding and empathy for a woman who was defined by her love for a man who had deserted her. Isabel saw the fiery, flighty Zerbinetta as her antithesis, a foil to Ariadne's fidelity unto death. While Zerbinetta was in her element drifting from the arms of one man into those of another, Ariadne could be wife or mistress of one man only, be just one man's widow, and forsaken by one man only.

To her dismay, it seemed the hard work had been in vain. She found the rehearsals an ordeal and, in truth, she now knew why her agent had worried that the role had come too soon: it was too heavy for her and required a voice with a more metallic ring and enough heft and volume to cut through the rich orchestral textures. Her problems meeting the demands of the music led her at times to over-compensate, to try too hard, so that her pitch wobbled and her tone hardened, and all the while her vocal stamina was fading.

She tried to steady her growing anxiety by telling herself that the unusually warm weather and the airless room meant that the rehearsals were exhausting for everyone. But while the rest of the company escaped to enjoy cooling drinks at pavement bars around Leicester Square, she decided that, away from the rigours of rehearsals, she needed as much rest and solitude as possible. She even persuaded herself that Paul's preoccupations were a blessing, since she could retreat to her flat alone at the end of each day to recharge her flagging energy with no sense that she was neglecting him.

Though she envied the others their light-hearted camaraderie and the ease with which they seemed able to reconnect with their own selves as soon as rehearsals ended, she felt too pre-occupied and self-conscious to join in the playful teasing and good-natured banter with which they liked to relax and dissect the events of the day. Her dwindling confidence made her feel painfully awkward around colleagues so buoyant and assured and, though the

102

rest of the cast were kind and forbearing, she was too embarrassed to seek out a confidant or ask for help. She avoided conversations with her agent and vocal coach, trying to convince herself that if she could hold her nerve, it would come right in the end, but she was painfully aware of the frustrations and concerns of the conductor and director, though neither confronted her with them and preferred instead to flatter and encourage.

She continued to feel unwell and her appetite came and went. She ate like an invalid, choosing only simple foods she felt her system could tolerate. In the evenings, she adopted a comforting routine of curling up on her sofa with a plate of cheese and biscuits or egg sandwiches. She began re-reading her old friend *Villette*, hoping to absorb some of Lucy Snowe's ferocity and resolve. She lost herself in the colourful descriptions of public events—a night at the theatre; a birthday party; a picnic in a park on a public holiday—but was more at home with the long passages during which Lucy was alone, when the narrative followed her whirling thoughts, her repressed but palpable emotions, and described the way her mind reeled under pressures both imaginary and actual.

Having longed to sing the role of Ariadne, she felt oppressed by the woman's obsessional, all-encompassing grief and sought refuge in the story of Lucy Snowe and Monsieur Paul. She seemed to have forgotten the despair its muted, melancholy ending always aroused in her. Briefly, wonderfully, Paul's return to Villette seems inevitable, but although Charlotte Brontë denies her readers the finality of death, there is a storm at sea, one that will wreak havoc on the ship carrying Paul back from the West Indies. The promise of destruction overtakes the certainty of a lover's reunion. 'He is coming,' Lucy tells us, but it is never written that he came.

Isabel, however, clung to what hope she could find in the teasing last paragraph and adopted that as her truth:

Trouble no quiet, kind heart; leave sunny imaginations hope.
Let it be theirs to conceive the delight of joy born again fresh
out of great terror, the rapture of rescue from peril, the
wondrous reprieve from dread, the fruition of return. Let them
picture union and a happy succeeding life.

Whereas the clues in the novel pointed to tragedy and heartbreak, so thoroughly weighed down and disenchanted was Isabel with Ariadne, she failed to recognise that by contrast, the opera's final message was redemptive: choose love and life over misery and death.

She shared little with Paul about her struggles with the role and remained silent about her inner turmoil. His visits anyway became increasingly infrequent and he took to leaving early, claiming pressing demands at home. He rarely stayed the night; sometimes hurrying away after engaging in lovemaking so hasty and perfunctory that Isabel was left feeling more lonely than ever and unable to sleep.

One Tuesday evening, about half way through her rehearsals, she reminded him about the Verdi Requiem at the Royal Festival Hall in which she was singing that coming Saturday night.

He frowned and she realised he'd forgotten.

'You said you would come,' she said. 'I've got you a ticket.'

'I'm sorry, darling,' he said, taking her gently by the shoulders. 'I thought it was next week.'

'But you can still come, can't you?' she said, hearing a note of wheedling in her voice but unable to conceal her disappointment.

He shook his head.

'I'm afraid something's come up. I'm really sorry.'

She resisted the urge to ask what but looked sceptical, and immediately felt guilty. He was probably tied up with Gina and didn't want to admit it for fear of upsetting her.

'It's OK,' she said. 'There'll be other times.'

But she'd wanted him there and felt he'd let her down.

The afternoon rehearsal for the Verdi did not go well. Her usual sweetness and steadiness of tone had seemingly deserted her and she'd resorted to attacking some of the fearsomely high notes from below, some of which emerged as vibrato-less squeals.

In the break after the rehearsal she decided a walk in the fresh air along the river might do her good. The walkway beyond the Festival Hall and the National Theatre was busy with day-trippers and tourists. She walked on until the crowds thinned and stopped to take in the scene, squinting in the rays of bright sunlight that bounced off the water. She reached into her bag for her sunglasses and sat down on a bench to enjoy a moment of peace and solitude before heading back to the Hall to change. Two boys ran along the path behind her chasing seagulls which were wheeling and screeching over something enticing they'd spotted on the path ahead. She closed her eyes and breathed deeply and slowly, trying to visualise herself standing tall and erect on the stage of the concert hall, hoping to hear her voice soaring effortlessly above the choir and orchestra.

She opened her eyes and shivered. The sun was warm but the breeze had a chilly bite and she decided to go back to her dressing room to do some vocal exercises. She looked round, momentarily startled by the sounds of cries and laughter coming from a pleasure boat which was making its way towards Festival Pier. She followed its steady progress and saw it pull in to the jetty, her attention caught by the familiar outline of a man sitting on a bench at the back of the boat.

It was Paul, wearing his shabby Norfolk jacket, with one arm around the shoulder of a woman with bright auburn hair cut into a striking, jaw-length bob.

Alice

I wondered about Christmases past in this house that had been Imogen's solitary home for over half her lifetime. I imagined visitors falling away as she got older, shuddered at an image of her alone and perhaps lonely, knowing to my shame and regret that in her last years I had been a negligent goddaughter. I was not relishing the prospect of my first Christmas in Vicarage Road, but not wanting to inflict my low spirits on Marie and her husband, I'd declined her invitation. I knew my mum wanted me to spend Christmas Day with her, and I was happy to do that, but felt the need to spend the rest of the time quietly on my own.

I disliked many of the trappings of Christmas but decided a tree, prettily decorated, might inject some festive cheer into the house, and in particular to the front room, a room that remained sombre, despite the introduction of stylish floor lights. The room had been 'kept for best' and used by Imogen only on special occasions but, overcrowded with furniture that was dark and heavy, it had the appearance of an uncomfortable doctor's waiting room. Two ugly upright chairs with splayed wing arms were taken away by a charity that assisted people newly-released from prison and the space created enabled me to re-organise the remaining furniture—a low-backed sofa and two matching arm chairs—and position the tree in front of the window so that the room would look more inviting.

The sofa was against a wall and it half concealed a piece of furniture I had not till now inspected. It was an oak bookcase, raised on a plinth base and with an intricate carved detail along the top edge. It had glazed doors, with a lock and key, and inside there were four shelves, packed tight with hard-backed books, some still bearing their original dust covers.

I knelt down, turned the key and opened the doors. The books were arranged in alphabetical order of author, and contained a collection of literary classics—from Austen, Bennett, and Brontë through to Thackeray, Tolstoy and Trollope. I pulled out a few books at random and flicked through the first few pages of each. A few, newer publications, bore Imogen's name but most had the name 'Evadne Grey' written in confident black ink inside the cover. I was ashamed how few of these titles I had read, my own tastes running more to thrillers and crime novels, and at a cursory glance I counted only some childhood favourites—*The Secret Garden, Little Women,* and *Anne of Green Gables*—among my literary experience. The latter was one of the shabbiest books in the collection and the colour of the cover reminded me of my own once-loved copy, now presumably consigned to my mother's attic or long since gone to a charity shop. This copy, too, was a russet-coloured hard back, though its spine was worn and faded and, as I picked it off the shelf, I saw that many of the pages were loose. I opened it carefully but the frontispiece fell out and fluttered to the floor. It was a colour illustration of Anne standing over Gilbert Blythe and about to bring her slate down on his head because he had called her 'Carrots'.

You mean hateful boy, she exclaimed passionately.

I smiled. As a girl on the brink of adolescence, I'd been enchanted by Gilbert. So intelligent, caring and strangely, not dull, but utterly dreamy in a way I had never encountered in real life.

I put the book back in its place and was about to close the doors, when I spotted another book I'd read several times, admittedly out of duty because the school curriculum had demanded it, but which I had loved nevertheless: *North and South* by Elizabeth Gaskell. I opened it at the beginning and flicked through the chapters, reminding myself of the characters and their struggles, until I reached the last page. I read it in full, wallowing in the exquisitely tender ending, each line so rich with trembling passion and love at last requited. I sighed, remembering the relief I had felt on reading it for the first time, when all the tensions and misunderstandings between Margaret Hale and John Thornton melted into heartfelt apologies and a long, silent embrace.

I bent down to return the book to its place on the shelf, between another Gaskell novel and several by Thomas Hardy, and as I pushed it back into position, I spotted an envelope lodged against a lovely leather-bound edition of *Under the Greenwood Tree*, its deep red spine bearing a tiny gilt outline of a girl leaning against a tree.

I reached for the envelope and, as I straightened up, I studied the handwriting on the front and knew at once that it was unmistakably the same as that on the two postcards propped on the mantelpiece in the parlour. The envelope was addressed to Imogen and, beneath the smudged and indistinct postmark, I could see a lilac-coloured stamp for nine-pence, commemorating the Queen's Silver Jubilee 1952-1977. I perched on the edge of the sofa and eased out the contents of the envelope, a single sheet of good quality writing paper. I looked over my shoulder in bemusement at the shelf where I'd found it, not tucked inside one of the books, but simply half-concealed amongst them.

I turned the paper over and looked for the name of the writer, hoping she would reveal herself and confirm the source of those intriguing postcards. The letter was written in dark blue ink, the handwriting sometimes drifting unevenly down the unlined page, but the signature was clear.

Isabel.

Isabel

Isabel watched the boat sway gently on its berth as a handful of passengers disembarked and made their way onto the walkway. A sudden gust of wind whistled across the river, blowing long strands of hair across her face and causing her to shiver in her light-weight cotton cardigan. At the same time she saw to her dismay that Paul was hugging the woman closer to him, as if trying to keep her warm. He was taking no notice of the activity on the pier but when a dog on the jetty barked excitedly at another dog perched on the front of the boat, he turned to look and as his eyes scanned the riverbank, he saw her. She felt the muscles of her face give way, and any hope of maintaining a mask of composure crumpled. Paul looked momentarily alarmed, but as the boat jerked away from the pier, he shrugged as if to say sorry. Sensing some change in his demeanour, Paul's companion looked back to where Isabel stood watching them. The woman stared at Isabel in surprise before turning away and huddling closer to Paul. As the breeze disturbed her gleaming, helmet-like bob, Isabel remembered who she was.

She was Barbara, the Wardrobe Mistress from Hope Street Theatre, who had ironed the blue dress Isabel wore as Fancy Day and pleated her hair into a becoming plait.

She felt suddenly overcome with nausea and hurried back to the Hall, afraid she might not make it in time before her churning stomach overwhelmed her. She hurried through the artists' entrance, barely able to acknowledge the greeting of the Stage Doorman, before moving more cautiously along the corridor that led to her dressing room. The nearest ladies' toilets were thankfully deserted and once inside, she was violently sick. She had eaten little that day so the retching was painful. As the bile burnt the back of her throat, she knew she would be in a pitiable state to tackle the rigorous demands of the Requiem, but realised that if she cried off now, the management would almost certainly have to cancel the concert.

She supported herself against the washbasin and looked at her reflection in the mirror. Her face was drained of colour and strands of hair clung to her neck. Hot tears poured down her face and, as her nose started to run, she sniffed hard which caused her to cough and then retch some more. She took a handful of coarse paper towels from a pile on the counter and dabbed at her streaked and puffy face, before blowing her nose.

She would have to go on.

She turned round carefully, fearing the nausea had not completely subsided, and made her way across the corridor to the privacy of her dressing room. Next door she could hear the mezzo soprano warming up. Further away, the sound of ribald laughter, quickly stifled, signalled the tenor and bass soloists sharing a risqué joke.

She struggled to make sense of what she had seen and imagined Paul and Barbara enjoying a carefree boat trip along the Thames, unconcerned about her confusion and distress and oblivious to the foreboding with which she now approached the impending performance.

As she stood waiting in the wings with the conductor and the other soloists, she could hear the discordant strains of the orchestra tuning and the hubbub of chatter and rustling as the audience settled itself. She adjusted the neckline of her dress, worried it was too low-cut, and was conscious that her breathing was shallow and uneven, her throat inflamed and sore. The Stage Manager reminded them that the performance would be preceded by a minute's silence, during which the lights would stay up. The door onto the stage opened and Isabel led the quartet of soloists onto the front of the platform. A hush fell over the audience. Even the musicians seemed muted, the massed choirs sitting silently as if in prayer, the players bowing their heads in solemn concentration on their instruments.

After a short pause, the conductor made his entrance and the choristers and musicians rose to their feet. When he reached the podium, he signalled to the audience to also stand. Isabel glanced up at him, thinking how young he looked, what big shoes he had to fill in stepping in after the sudden death of the orchestra's Music Director. She looked away and bowed her head, knowing the occasion demanded she retain her composure, but afraid that under pressure, the thinness of tone that seemed to now beset the top of her range would be cruelly exposed by the work's more high-lying passages. After a minute of silence, she heard the conductor let out a deep breath and saw him raise his head. The lights in the hall dimmed and he waited patiently with his arms at his side until the mandatory outbreak of coughing had stopped. After checking that the soloists were ready, he lifted his baton to begin.

In an elegant black dress and with her blonde hair swept back off her face to leave her neck and shoulders bare, Isabel looked beautiful, but she was painfully nervous, and was fighting back emotions that threatened to spill over the heads of the expectant concert-goers in the front of the stalls below.

In the rehearsal room on the following Monday morning, the Company Manager, concerned by Isabel's haggard appearance and general air of despond, arranged for her to be released early so she could see her GP before the end of his afternoon surgery. She had spent much of the previous day in bed, sleeping fitfully between bouts of sickness and, as she waited her turn in the surgery's cramped reception area, she began for the first time to ask herself what might be wrong. She was rarely ill, so this anxiety about her health was a new and unfamiliar experience. A man sitting behind her got up when his name was called and left his newspaper amongst a pile of dog-eared magazines on a low table in front of her. With little interest, she saw that it was the afternoon edition of the *Evening Standard*, but after a few minutes of staring at the front page without really seeing it, she realised it might carry a review of Saturday's concert. She leant over to pick it up, opening the pages just wide enough to scan their contents. At last she found it and a cursory glance confirmed her fears.

> *What should have been an immaculate line-up of soloists did not really gel as a quartet. Isabel Grey achieved moments of shimmering beauty, but far from floating ethereally in a pristine pianissimo, her pleading for mercy in the final* Libera Me *had an unintended ring of truth.*

She read no more and returned the paper to the table, just as a brusque voice over the Tannoy summoned her to a consulting room on the first floor.

Isabel

Dear Imogen,
You will no doubt wonder why I am writing to you after such a long
silence between us. The truth is I'm in trouble and despite our
estrangement, I have no-one else but you to turn to; nowhere else but
home I can escape the shame I fear will soon befall me. I admit this is
a calamity I have brought on myself, but I beg you to take pity on me
and consign our differences to the past.

All my troubles seem to have come together and I feel overwhelmed
and afraid. I'm rehearsing for a production of Ariadne auf Naxos
which opens in just over three weeks' time, but the role is beyond me
and I half expect to be sacked, though the management seem inclined
to think it will come right on the night. I doubt that. No music has
ever seemed so taxing, so unforgiving of any vocal or emotional frailty,
and while I struggle at work, my personal life is a mess. I've been in a
relationship with an actor—Paul Eveson—I first met at Hope Street
Theatre. We met again after many years of no contact and fell in love.
Or I thought we did. You see, he's married and says he must remain
so as his wife has cancer and her treatment is debilitating and when
she's through it, she wants to complete her recuperation at home in
Italy. I concealed from him that I, too, have been feeling unwell but
now I discover I'm to have his baby in October—news at which he
does not rejoice. So I expect to be on my own with our child. It would
be hard combining motherhood with a career like mine, but that career
seems likely to hit the rocks of Naxos and sink without trace.

Even if I get through the run of performances, I fear I will not
feel strong enough to work for much longer before the baby comes. I
have some savings from Mother's will, but London is expensive and
will soon soak them up. I have so far told no-one but Paul about the
baby, but before long, my pregnancy will be as hard to conceal as is my
sense of hopelessness.

I have loved this man for so long, but I fear he will leave and not
come back. I have striven hard to be self-sufficient, to make my own
way in the world, but right now I feel quite alone and when I look into

the future, I am fearful for myself and my child. I have been re-reading Villette—do you remember how much I loved it?—and Lucy's utter loneliness and inner, hidden torment seem to match my own. Sometimes I think I will go mad like Lucy does when she's left alone in the holidays at the deserted school; when the silence and the rows of empty beds multiply in her mind and drive her out in to the streets, needing and at the same time, afraid of company.

Can I come home Imogen? I need time to work out what I will do and where I will live once the baby arrives. You and I have no other family and I need your support. Is it not time we made up?
Please write soon.
Isabel

Alice

I pictured Isabel sitting where I was now, a woman in crisis, hoping to find comfort and companionship from the sister from whom she was estranged. I laid her letter to one side and shuddered, feeling the shadow of her unquiet soul. Despite the years that separated us, we seemed somehow connected, not just by the shame that the same opera had caused us, but because the pursuit of love and happiness had brought us both disappointment and regret.

I was struck by her reference to *Villette*, a book I'd not read, and was intrigued by how strongly she related to the heroine. I stood up and slipped behind the sofa to check if there was a copy among the collection of Brontë novels I'd seen on the top shelf of the bookcase. *Agnes Grey, The Tenant of Wildfell Hall, Jane Eyre, The Professor, Shirley*, and *Wuthering Heights* were all there, but not *Villette*.

I moved across to the window and pushed the curtains to one side. Apart from the muffled hum of traffic on the main road, there was nothing to disturb the silence of the house. I shivered and hugged my arms around my body, hoping to warm myself. I decided to busy myself by decorating the Christmas tree and made my way to the kitchen, where the young man from the grocery store had left the tree when he delivered it that morning. It was a handsome Douglas fir with soft, dark green needles and had been sold in a sturdy black bucket around which someone at the shop had wrapped bright red crepe paper dotted with large silver stars. A pretty touch, I thought, and smiled, already cheered by the thought of the task ahead.

I lifted the bucket and breathed in the tree's lovely citrus fragrance before carefully easing it through the house to the front sitting room, skirting round any obstacles that might catch the branches and cause the needles to tumble. From the kitchen I collected two large carrier bags of trimmings

I'd bought when I ordered the tree. I'd thrown away the tangle of fairy lights, the threadbare tinsel and chipped baubles with which Jake and I had decked our last Christmas tree, and treated myself to some silky cream ribbon and a collection of beautiful glass decorations, each one slightly different, made by a local designer. I'd chosen an array of colours, some plain, some multi-coloured, some decorated with stars and stripes or frosted snowflakes, all of them bright and pleasing to the touch.

I positioned the tree in front of the window and leant down to choose the first piece. As a child I would litter the branches with anything I could get my hands on, but I recalled the care with which my mother dressed her tree, and with time to spare, I could try to achieve something not dissimilar to the stylish effect that seemed to come so easily to her.

I knelt on the floor and began adding the decorations from the base upwards. As the tree began to take shape under my unschooled hands, I lost myself in my task, and tentatively, I opened a window into my heart and allowed myself to look inside, to face memories and fears which for months I'd pushed away.

I knew I was no longer the bubbly, outgoing girl I had been, growing up in these six towns, before escaping to London and a career that took me to far-off places. I grieved for my disappearing self and yearned for my former life. Every day, I realised how many things I missed about being a singer, not least the license to be backstage in a theatre, a thrill I had never grown tired of. When not on stage, I spent little time in my dressing room, preferring to listen in the wings to the audience's reactions, to soak up the energy of the other singers, watching their routines and rituals, admiring the industry and skill of the stage management crew, loving the sense that I was part of a team that was bringing a story to life through music and drama.

An existence I once took for granted, now seemed unattainable, part of a golden age when my voice worked without me giving it another thought. It was hard to know when the problems began, because at first—and for some time afterwards—I ignored and denied them and instead made excuses or shifted the blame.

I had a cold and was feeling under the weather.
I was jet-lagged and dehydrated.
I'd been up all night with a stomach virus.
We'd not had enough rehearsal.

I recalled that around the time that Jake and I split up in the autumn of 2012, I had a cold that wouldn't shift. No sooner did I begin to feel it had cleared up than I was laid low again with a cough or catarrh or a sore throat. I became accustomed to feeling below par and simply carrying on, not reducing my travelling or cancelling engagements, so that by Christmas that year, I was run down and miserable and went home to my mum's to be cosseted. The break appeared to revive me and by the time I auditioned for *Rosenkavalier* a few months later, I seemed fully recovered— still sad that Jake had turned out not to be 'the one' but physically well again and able to tackle the role of Sophie with no sign of difficulty or strain.

But since my appointment with Dr Mackenzie, I realised I had underestimated how my voice might react to the emotional pain and personal self-doubt with which I was increasingly beset.

'Unlike an orchestral player,' he said, 'a singer's instrument can't be packed away when they're done performing—real care has to be taken to keep it in peak performance and that demands emotional well-being as well as physical health.'

I had seen all the obvious voice specialists in London and Dr Mackenzie was in many ways a last resort. He was much younger and less experienced than the others, but he was making a name for himself not only for his clinical expertise but for his holistic and empathic approach to patients and in particular, his astute understanding of singers. I was nervous about my consultation with him and didn't know what to expect as he was clearly not entirely conventional in his approach, and at the point I went to him, I didn't feel ready to confront anything other than my physical symptoms.

I smiled as I recalled the inauspicious start to my visit. I was seeing Dr Mackenzie privately at a new clinic he was establishing in west London and the walk from the tube had taken longer than it should because at one point, I turned right when I should have turned left. When I arrived in a cul-de-sac of small mews houses crawling with an American film crew, I realised I was lost. With the aid of animated directions from a trio of Polish electricians, I retraced my steps and was soon turning through wrought iron gates onto a short driveway of crunchy grey gravel.

It was a large Victorian house and looked like the traditional notion of a ramshackle country rectory. The area around the drive was laid to lawn, edged with raggedy flower beds, while the house was shielded from the peaceful avenue on which it stood by three enormous weeping willows.

Despite the cold weather, the front door was open, and an elderly man in white overalls came out carrying a toolbox and some folded dust sheets. He nodded and headed down the side of the house, leaving me standing on the doorstep. There was no sound of any activity in the hall, so after a few moments, I rang the brass doorbell which chimed in the distance like a church bell. Through the stained glass of the inner door, I saw the figure of a woman walking across the hall to let me in.

'Yes?' said the woman, giving no indication that I was expected.

'I've an appointment at four o'clock with Dr Mackenzie,' I said, trying hard not to be intimidated.

'You'd best come in,' the woman said, 'though he's not here.'

I did my best to hide my dismay and surprise.

'He said to come in and wait,' she said tersely.

At least I hadn't been forgotten.

The woman stood back to allow me to step into the hall.

'No telling how long he'll be. His wife's just had a baby,' she said, marching towards a room on the left. 'You can wait in here.'

'Mrs Danvers, eat your heart out,' I thought.

As I watched her disappear through a door at the far end of the hallway, I heard the inner door open behind me and a man in a loose-fitting mac that was too big for him burst into the hall. I judged that he was in his forties but he had the face of a slightly gawky fifteen-year old, and a smile and a manner that told me he was kindly.

He offered me his hand.

'I'm so sorry I've kept you waiting,' he said, glancing behind me to the door at the back of the hall. 'I had hoped to be back in time to greet you myself.'

I smiled, realising he was aware of the shortcomings of the receptionist.

'Come through,' he said, opening a door on the right.

I guessed this was where the elderly man had been working, because although the walls were lined from floor to ceiling with bookshelves, they were empty and the carpet in one corner was covered with boxes of books and other personal possessions. It was a handsome room, overlooking the drive and, when it was finished, and everything was unpacked and in its place, it would be impressive. I breathed in drying paint, new wood, fresh varnish—and a faint hint of antiseptic. Apart from the unpacked boxes of books, the rest of the room was set up and equipped as a consulting room.

'Do sit down,' he said, ushering me to a chair at the side of the large desk behind which he was now sitting. 'We're not quite up and running yet and Mrs Snoddy agreed to stay on until our two new receptionists start next week.'

'Ah,' I said, draping my duffle coat over the back of the chair.

'Yes,' he laughed, 'we inherited her from the GP practice that moved out last month to a purpose-built surgery. Your referral said you were anxious to have an appointment before Christmas, so I hope you don't mind a little un-readiness on our part.'

He took off his glasses and began to wipe away a smear on one of the lens.

'Have you read my notes?' I asked, aware there was a file on the desk in front of him that he hadn't opened.

'I have,' he said, not seeming to take offence. 'Do you want to tell me in your own words what's been happening?'

I sighed.

'I know,' he said kindly. 'You've been through it many times before with countless other doctors, whose notes are here, but I'd like to hear it from you please, and I don't only want to know about your voice and when it first started misbehaving, but about you—about your general health and your life away from work.'

I shook my head and sighed again, but knew I owed it to him and to myself to fully co-operate if this consultation was to be of any use at all. He said nothing, just sat leaning forward on the desk, looking at me and waiting. To my surprise I heard myself telling him my story, trying to make it sound coherent, wanting to hear it out loud as if that would help me make sense of it, too. At first, I felt awkward as I laid it hesitatingly before him—the repeated colds and sore throats, the endless travelling, the grueling schedule, Gretel, Valencienne, Zerbinetta, my growing sense of shame, Jake, all the men before him, Christian, my father, the belief I was not good enough, the fruitless search for the one.

At last I stopped, aware I had told him far more than I'd told any of the other specialists or even some of my closest friends.

I held my breath before letting it out slowly and sitting back in my chair.

Dr Mackenzie nodded gravely.

'I think the concept of 'the one' is one of the most destructive beliefs we can have.'

His words took me by surprise, but I searched in vain for a reply. He stood up.

'Can I take a look please?'

He pressed a buzzer and spoke into it: 'Nurse, will you come in, please?'

The examination of my throat was uncomfortable but thorough and, as the doctor and his friendly Scottish nurse hovered over me, I felt strangely at ease and reassured.

'Good girl,' he said encouragingly from time to time. 'Stay nice and relaxed for me, we're almost done.'

When he'd seen all he needed to, he led me back to the desk and as he made notes in the file, the nurse tidied away the medical paraphernalia.

'OK?' Dr Mackenzie asked when we were alone again.

'I'm not sure yet,' I said. 'I'm afraid of what you might be about to tell me.'

He nodded and smiled.

'I hope I can offer some reassurance,' he said, and I felt my stomach flutter with anticipation. 'I agree with my colleagues that there's nothing sinister going on.'

I let out a long sigh.

'But what *is* going on?' I asked.

'I think you might have some of the answers to that,' he said. 'Don't you?'

I frowned and shook my head.

He moved his chair away from the desk so that he was sitting closer to me.

'You can't get through life without something happening to you that is more than you can stand,' he said quietly, 'and you've endured your fair share of travails.' He paused and patted my hand. 'I think you've not always recognised their impact on you.'

I looked at him in surprise.

'Your father, your difficulties with relationships, your fear of childlessness, your vocal problems, the humiliation of your last experience at Covent Garden.'

I nodded.

'Is that enough to be going on with?' he asked.

I managed a rueful laugh.

'There are many reasons why someone might lose their voice, both physical and emotional,' he went on. 'Common physical ones are associated with extremely hard work— overload, too many singing engagements, and fatigue developing in the musculature which then can no longer hold the weight of the voice so that you tire early. You start off singing fine and then the voice fatigues and you can't sustain the role, let alone the workload.'

I nodded to show I understood.

'I've become an expert on the workings of the voice box.'

He smiled.

'The voice box is very sensitive to stress,' he said. 'If a person becomes distressed it's possible for them to lose their voice down to a whisper or lose their ability to sing efficiently or even at all. And singing's a scary business at the best of times, isn't it?'

I nodded.

'Every time you go out on stage you're expected to give a fantastic performance. It's terrifying for a singer if all of a sudden they're not sure what's going to come out when they open their mouth to sing, and that uncertainty can tighten you up and take away your ability to do it.'

He spoke slowly and quietly with a natural unassuming assurance and I listened intently.

'And at the same time you're supposed to be a magical combination of able-to-bare-your-soul one minute, and thick-skinned-and-armoured-against-criticism the next. Yes?'

We both laughed.

'It's a conundrum,' he continued, 'because in truth, this vulnerability is precisely what we ask of you as a performer. Resilience is of course a virtue to be prized but, on stage, the business of a singer is the ability to project emotion— and to do that, you have to be prepared to open up your inner life, explore your liability to hurt, expose your frailty.' He paused. 'After all, a singer has to penetrate the heart, not just please the ears.'

I was impressed by the subtlety of his insights, but what he said next shook and saddened me.

'I'm afraid that too many careers fail because however strong the voice, the person who possesses it isn't strong enough in other ways.'

The words seemed to hang in the air between us and I looked down at my lap, my attention momentarily distracted by my badly-bitten un-manicured nails, with tiny traces of red nail varnish showing around the cuticles. There was a light knock on the door and I looked up to see the nurse holding a tray of tea and biscuits.

'Thanks Nurse,' the doctor said as she made a space on the edge of the table on which to settle the tray.

As the door closed behind her, Dr Mackenzie said: 'Let's have a cup of tea. You look like you need it.'

I was glad of the respite, but keen to continue. Having handed me a cup, the doctor heaped two spoons of sugar into his own and sat back in his chair.

'I'm sure you feel a great sense of shame about losing your voice,' he said.

'I do,' I replied. 'It's what I am, who I am.'

I bit my lip.

'My voice started sounding different, as if it wasn't my voice,' I said, 'and I didn't like it.' I paused. 'I don't think anyone liked it.'

He nodded and smiled.

'We have a face that people recognise us with, and in the same way, they recognise our voice, so if you alter that voice, people don't recognise you—and after a while you don't recognise yourself.'

I winced at the truth of his words.

'Losing the very thing that you want most or that you believe is what defines you is one of the greatest forms of suffering.'

At that, I thought I would cry, but he put his cup on one side and leant towards me.

'Look,' he said, 'there's no doubt that it's hard to come back from a voice problem, and you need a really good state of mind, but it's not impossible and I think understanding what went wrong can be helpful.'

I waited for him to go on.

'You already know some of this,' he said, before holding up his left hand and counting off on his fingers.

'One: singing the 'wrong' roles juxtaposed can be a problem—like Gretel and Valencienne and Zerbinetta for instance. They make different demands on different parts of your range and it can be hard to adjust quickly from one to the other.

'Two: Gretel gives you far more to contend with musically than other roles you've sung, where I'm guessing you were able to use the force of your personality and be your sparky self.

'Three: I think you may have done too much too fast too soon and that caught up with you and became a problem.

'Four: You—or your agent—may have found the offers from the big houses hard to resist.

'Five: You never allowed your body time to recover from illness or the rigours of travel—you were driving yourself into the ground.'

'Wow,' I said. 'That's quite a list.'

'But do you agree with it?'

'I do,' I said.

'And six,' he said, 'you've lived on an emotional level that was constantly incredibly highly charged. That's got to be very stressful and draining.'

I nodded vigorously. The list was an accurate one.

I reached over to put my cup and saucer on the tray.

'What do you recommend?' I asked. I trusted this doctor, confident that even on one meeting, he had begun to understand me.

'Continue to take time out. Settle into your new home. Develop other interests. Don't turn your back on your friends. Be kind to yourself. And try not to worry about your voice for a while—give yourself a break from constantly angsting about it.'

I flushed, knowing how obsessively I still continued to steam my vocal chords. I pulled a face.

'I know,' he laughed, 'that's easier said than done, but you need to let it go for now—and worrying about it and blaming yourself won't help.'

That made sense.

'I'm not suggesting surgery—there's no need for that—and I don't want to prescribe any medication,' he said, 'but it may be that some sort of counselling or psychotherapy is worth considering. It might help you to understand why there are these recurring patterns in your life and decide how you'd like things to be different.'

He looked at me kindly.

'Have a think about that and come back after Christmas and we'll see how you are then.'

'OK,' I said and stood up.

He helped me into my coat.

'Despite all the emotional upsets you've experienced,' he said, 'you've led a successful and independent life. You're stronger than you think.'

I looked at him closely and nodded. I could tell that he believed this. The challenge was for me to believe it, too.

He led the way to the door but paused with his hand on the door knob.

'Your heartache because neither Jake nor Christian turned out to be the one...' He hesitated. 'Perhaps there's another way of looking at it.' He paused again. 'Try to see that the pain doesn't come from losing your soul mate but from the disappointment that neither of these men turned out to be your soul mate. It's sad but it's not catastrophic. You can move on to find someone you will be happy with, but you must be open to it.'

Alice

My relationship with Christian was played out in the company of three very different women, beginning with Sophie—all heady delight during *Rosenkavalier* (its high point)—through the slow deadening of the affair during *Hansel and Gretel,* until I was rehearsing *Ariadne* and he walked away for good, without needing or wanting to talk, and seemingly without regret.

After my audition for *Rosenkavalier,* I didn't see him again until we began rehearsals in Cardiff eighteen months later. Jake reappeared a couple of times but, though we dallied with each other, and even had some fun along the way, we both knew there would be no point in allowing ourselves to slip back into the old routine.

And by then I'd set my sights on someone else.

I was rarely free-floating for long; in that uncomfortable condition, I needed to re-establish my equilibrium by latching onto someone new around whom I could weave a new story. That short encounter with Christian in the unlikely setting of an audition room was enough.

Most of Christian's work was in Germany with the orchestra of which he was chief conductor, but he made occasional visits to the UK. I made it to just one of his performances in London, a concert of Beethoven at Cadogan Hall. I bought a seat in the gallery overlooking the orchestra from which vantage point, I would also have a perfect view of Christian.

His expressive gestures and balletic movement seemed to communicate powerfully to the players, his smiles of delight suggesting he was urging them on every inch of the way. Afterwards, I longed to hurry backstage to offer congratulations, but feared an encounter out of the blue might prove disappointing, that he might not remember me, and that I would take away a memory tainted with awkwardness. I preferred instead to wait for our assignment in Cardiff, far off though that still was.

Until then, I followed Christian's career from a distance, devouring features in music magazines and coverage of his performances in the press. I scoured his reviews for insights into what he was like as a musician and, from that, it was a short step to imagine what he was like as a man.

> *The orchestra plays its heart out for Christian Kennedy and it's clear he has established a wonderful rapport with the players*
>
> *That the performance gives enormous pleasure is due to the radiant conducting of Christian Kennedy—full of grace, merriment and charm*
>
> *Christian Kennedy is making a name for his superb operatic interpretations. This was a performance of tremendous sincerity and integrity that avoided overt histrionics in favour of a reflective exploration of the work's deeper resonances. Kennedy's reading juxtaposed sensuous detail with spine-tingling excitement.*

On rare occasions, when reviews were less favourable, I would speculate about what might have been going on in his life away from the pit or concert platform to account for such lapses.

> *It takes a really searching, insightful conductor to make sense of Mahler's Seventh Symphony and Kennedy seemed out of his depth.*
>
> *Frustratingly, the singers were frequently drowned by an overloud orchestra, swept along on a tsunami of decibels under the brusque baton of Christian Kennedy.*
>
> *Overall, too few details were made to count and the performance was disappointingly lifeless and lacklustre.*

I would allow my imagination free rein, surmising that he was tired or stressed, that he was unhappy and could not prevent his sadness communicating itself to the musicians. During the long months before I met him again, I was never without a story about him. I conjured up a whole life's narrative for us, one I could replay to my heart's content, and in this way keep loneliness at bay.

Before I even knew him, the infatuation filled the entire spaces of my life and possessed me, even with no external reinforcement. I existed in a state of limbo as I waited for 'it' to happen, ignoring any creeping sense that my obsession was draining life of its reality and obliterating new experiences that might have brought me happiness.

I turned up in Cardiff for rehearsals for *Rosenkavalier* a few days before Christian arrived and discovered that the Company Manager had found us flats in the same large Victorian villa overlooking the sea in Penarth. Growing up in the land-locked Potteries, I had loved my childhood holidays in Llandudno and Anglesey and, as my work enabled me to travel, I seized any opportunity to stay near the coast, however briefly, so I'd asked the Company Manager to bear that in mind when finding somewhere for me to live.

My studio was on the top floor under the eaves and overlooked the back garden, whereas Christian was to have a large, airy apartment on the first floor, spacious enough to accommodate a baby grand and with uninterrupted views over the channel to Somerset. Throughout those first few days when I walked back and fore to the station to take the train into the city, I would look up at the large bay windows on the first floor, waiting impatiently for him to take up residence, imagining myself inviting him to share the occasional dinner in my flat, hoping he would return my hospitality.

I was delighted that Marie had been cast as Octavian. I looked forward to working with her and sensed our friendship might grow into a bond that was strong and important enough to survive our nomadic lifestyles.

Marie's flat was on the other side of Penarth within sight of Cardiff, and after the first day of music calls we walked from Cardiff Bay across the barrage towards the new marina where she was staying in an apartment overlooking pontoons crowded with yachts and sailing boats. It was late August and the route was busy with families and cyclists enjoying the picturesque walkway in the early evening sunshine. We passed the Norwegian Church with its white painted clapboard and stubby spire and headed around the water towards the grand Custom House building on the edge of the marina. Once there we stopped and looked back towards Cardiff Bay.

'Do you notice how the most striking and interesting architecture here is the oldest?' Marie said, shaking her head at the tacky new development of Mermaid Quay.

I followed her gaze and nodded, before turning round to face the Custom House, a Victorian dock building, now a restaurant, with a handsome façade and an elegant clock tower.

'That's quite something,' I said.

'Rather different to this concrete jungle,' Marie grimaced, leading me towards the blocks of flats and town houses which straddled the waterfront. Her apartment was on the second floor of a building about half way along, and though the exterior and the stairways were stark and functional, the flat was neatly proportioned and had a cool, stylish interior with plain white walls, pale wood flooring, and a flourishing array of dark green potted plants.

'Hey, this is nice,' I said, moving to look out of French windows that opened onto a small balcony.

'It is,' Marie said. 'Much better than you might expect from the outside.'

'Tidy, too,' I said. 'I'm impressed!'

'Oh yes,' Marie laughed. 'I'm not keen on clutter and mess.'

She opened the fridge door and took out a bottle of white wine.

'What's your place like?' she asked, as she opened several cupboards before finding one containing glassware.

'Probably too cluttered for you, though it's very nice,' I said. 'It's slightly shabby, but it's comfortable and the owners have given it a distinctive character. The wife was a singer and the husband a foreign affairs journalist and the place is crammed full of books and CDs and all sorts of interesting bits and pieces they collected on their travels.'

'So where are they now?' Marie asked, handing me a glass.

'They're retired and spend half the year in Buenos Aires where their daughter lives. When they're away, they let the company use the flat for visiting artists.'

Marie had piled the contents of her fridge onto the kitchen table and we washed and chopped the ingredients for a salad, getting into a relaxed and companionable rhythm.

'So how are things with you?' Marie asked, scooping out the inside of an avocado with a large spoon and beginning to slice it.

I blushed, because though there was nothing to tell, I was excited at the prospect of Christian's arrival and the weeks ahead when we'd be working together.

'Oh fine,' I said, nibbling at some cucumber and glad that she'd turned away to reach into a carrier bag. I learned soon enough, though, that Marie didn't miss much and as she placed an olive ciabatta onto a small bread board, she looked at me closely and her eyes narrowed.

'Glad to hear it,' she smiled, 'but I can see there's more to tell.'

I laughed and stepped to one side as she opened a drawer to take out some cutlery.

'Do you think it's warm enough to eat on the balcony?' I asked, having noticed a white plastic table and a couple of chairs.

'Let's give it a go,' Marie said, unlocking the double doors and sliding them open. Immediately, the flat came alive with the sounds of the marina—laughter and loud voices from nearby boats, footsteps clattering down pontoons, masts clanking together as the breeze caught them.

Some of the pontoons were busy with people preparing to head out to sea. Immediately below us a small powerboat called *Pirate Party* was berthed between a larger cruiser on one side and a travel-worn sailing boat on the other. Bulging Tesco bags and crates of lager were blocking the narrow pathway as three young men loaded overnight bags into the cabin.

I laughed.

'Pirate party indeed!'

We squeezed the food and wine onto the table and settled down to enjoy the simple supper. We clinked our glasses together and smiled.

'This is the life,' I said. 'Doesn't feel like work, being here.'

I took a sip of wine and closed my eyes.

'Makes me fancy a trip out into the channel,' I sighed.

'When I arrived yesterday afternoon,' Marie said, 'I had a good look around and there's a stretch of water out in the channel that's jam packed with small boats moored on buoys. It's very pretty but lots of the boats look neglected and abandoned as if they never go anywhere.' She dipped a chunk of bread into a dish of hummus. 'I thought they looked rather sad.'

I visualised those forsaken moorings and the image cast a fleeting, melancholy shadow.

'Will you go home at weekends?' I asked.

'Probably,' Marie replied. 'Though I think Peter would like it here so I'll suggest he comes down at some point before term starts.'

I wondered what Christian would do at weekends and hoped that with home being in Germany, he would stay in Penarth.

'How about you?' Marie asked.

'I'll stay here,' I said. 'I fancy a few weeks by the sea, away from London.'

'No-one to go back to?' she asked, over her glass.

I shook my head.

'Afraid not,' I said. 'I'm on my lonesome right now.' I took a large gulp of wine. 'I'll be on the shelf if I'm not careful.'

Marie laughed.

'I haven't heard that expression in ages.'

She looked at me closely.

'I take it, you don't want to be on the shelf, so what's the problem?'

I shrugged.

'I seem to attract the wrong men.'

'What do you mean?' she asked.

I thought for a moment.

'Oh, you know. Men who seem like a good thing and then go cool and start messing me about, so I feel under-appreciated and resentful until they walk away, leaving me feeling even worse.'

'But surely,' Marie said, topping up our glasses, 'you're not actually attracting the wrong men. You're just dating the wrong men and there's a big difference.'

I frowned and opened my mouth to protest but before I could speak, she'd continued.

'Ask yourself this: when you notice warning signs early on with a man you're dating, why do you choose to ignore them? Is it because you don't want to be alone? Or are you worried you won't find someone else? Or you don't think you deserve any better?'

'Mm...' I said ruefully. 'Probably all of the above.'

'Oh Alice,' she cried. 'You do deserve better. Of course you do!'

'But where are all these better options then?' I asked her defiantly. 'I seem to have an unfailing talent for choosing the guy who other women can see has a red mark emblazoned on his forehead and a large sign hanging round his neck saying TROUBLE in capital letters!'

Marie laughed.

'I get it—I really do,' she said, when I shook my head to suggest she didn't understand. 'I know that fancying someone isn't always a choice, you can't stop yourself, but believe me, pursuing a lost cause is definitely a choice. We can always choose to move on and begin the process of getting our sanity back.'

If only it was that easy, I thought. If only.

At the end of the first day of rehearsals with Christian and the director, I was at a loose end, uncertain how to spend the evening and too restless to stay cooped up in my flat. I dumped my music bag on the low table in the sitting room and went straight out again. The rehearsals had been intense and I sensed that Christian would be a demanding conductor, something that made me question whether I would measure up to his expectations. I made my way down to the esplanade, glad to be out in the fresh air, taking deep breaths and straining for the familiar smell of sea and seaweed.

I walked around the headland and up onto the cliff. An old cottage, that looked out of place alongside the imposing villas around it, had been converted into a restaurant. A piece of grey slate alongside the front door was engraved with the words 'Trattoria Pierre'. It was closed so I peered through the windows to see square tables set out on a flagstone floor and, beyond them, an attractive terrace open to the sky under a leafy trellis and with a view of the sea. There was no sign to say when it would open, but I could hear sounds coming from what I took to be the kitchen.

I looked at my watch: it was not yet seven o'clock so I walked back to the esplanade, past black wrought iron benches on the seafront on which people sat looking out to sea while eating ice cream or candy-floss. On the sand, a few feet below me, a young boy was doing back-flips and attracting admiring looks from passers-by. The boy prepared to repeat his party trick, first glancing behind him to see if his father was watching. I felt sad to see that the man was absorbed on his mobile phone and taking only cursory notice of his son and I gave the boy an encouraging nod as he launched into his acrobatics. I continued to clap as he scurried back to his dad. He gave me a cheeky smile and held his chest to mime exhaustion after his efforts. I laughed, but jumped when a voice behind me said:

'I asked him to teach me how to do that but he said I was too old. The cheek of it!'

'Christian,' I cried in surprise. 'I didn't see you.'

'Sorry to startle you. I was walking aimlessly along the front back to my flat when I spotted you watching the boy, so I thought I'd come and say hello.'

To my horror, I blushed bright red, convinced he could read my thoughts and see all the graphic fantasies I entertained about him.

'We made a good start today. You did very well,' he said, seemingly unconcerned by my awkward behaviour but, when he smiled, I felt a plucking sensation in my stomach and turned away to cover my embarrassment, trying to look riveted by a gaggle of girls at the water's edge intent on pushing each other—fully clothed—into the sea. At last I turned back to him.

135

'Thanks,' I said. 'I enjoyed it.'

'Good,' he replied. 'I look forward to tomorrow.'

And with that he turned away and headed off to his flat.

'Damn!' I cursed after he was out of earshot, frustrated that despite all my endless rehearsing of potential encounters between us, I'd been so socially inept that I couldn't even make small talk, let alone have a coherent conversation. My shoulders sagged and I felt completely out of sorts with myself. I walked slowly up the hill, not wanting to catch up with him but, once back at the flat, I knew it could not contain my restlessness. On any other evening, I would have called Marie but her sister was visiting, so I would have to make do with my own company. I went into the bathroom intending to spruce myself up but did no more than repair my lipstick. Back in the sitting room, I picked up the thriller I'd almost finished, stuffed it into my bag and headed out the door.

The wind was getting up as I walked around the headland towards the restaurant, the front door of which was now open. A waiter stopped in the doorway and smiled.

'Table, Madame?'

I hesitated but I was hungry and there were good smells emanating from inside.

'Yes, please,' I said.

Only four tables were occupied and the young man led me to one in the window overlooking the terrace. He handed me a menu and I chose quickly—spaghetti carbonara and a large glass of Merlot. At first I felt conspicuous sitting there alone with no one to talk to and was glad I'd brought a book for company. The wine arrived almost immediately and I drank with enthusiasm, relishing its full-bodied flavour and enjoying the feeling of warmth and well being that seemed to seep through my veins. I took out my book and opened it at the bookmark, but looked up as a couple made their way past me to a nearby table.

I looked around. At all the occupied tables there were couples. Couples making plans, taking stock, trading grievances. Just being.

I sighed and went back to my book and was soon engrossed, stopping only to estimate if I might finish it before the meal arrived and would find myself with nothing to distract or conceal me while I ate.

I shrugged and looked down, just as I heard Christian ask:

'May I join you?'

Much later—and not that she needed telling this—I admitted to Marie that I should have recognised Christian was trouble right from the start. As she'd told me when we first met, he had a partner in Hamburg, but he'd been married before that to a singer who was herself already married when they first got together.

'She left me,' he told me that first night in Trattoria Pierre, 'not long before I went to Hamburg to conduct *Rosenkavalier.*'

He paused.

'There hadn't been any arguments, and I had no idea why she wanted to divorce me. The whole thing came as a complete surprise.'

I brushed aside a thought that came unbidden, wondering if any divorce ever really came as a complete surprise and, if it did, that was probably your answer as to why someone was divorcing you.

'That was where I met Monica,' he was saying as I banished such unfair cynicism to the back of my mind. 'She was the *répétiteur* for the show so we spent a lot of time together.'

He laughed.

'Separation, lust and work is a dangerous mix.'

I blushed, knowing immediately what he meant.

'It seems there's plenty of sexual energy around the loss of a relationship,' he went on. 'I should have known better,' he laughed again, 'because if that sexual energy starts ricocheting around at work, it's probably wise to avoid rushing into a new relationship.'

I felt a tingle of excitement and a twinge of unease, not at all sure I wanted to hear this, when to my surprise, he looked suddenly sheepish and said: 'I guess I was on the rebound.'

I nodded and felt my heart swell, interpreting this as an important moment of connection between us.

Over the following weeks we had dinner together occasionally, sometimes with other members of the company, other times alone in his flat or mine. One Sunday morning we took the boat over to Flat Holm Island and watched as the air filled with swirling gulls getting ready to depart for sunnier climes. The Warden told us that Herring Gulls stake out their territories on the cliffs and wait patiently for their life mate to return so they can reconnect in preparation for breeding come the spring.

Christian told me that Monica was five years older than him and was struggling to accept the fact they seemed unable to have children. His constant travelling was putting a further strain on their relationship, but he said that despite the separations and the challenges, they were committed to making it work.

Throughout the rehearsal period we were professional and discreet, though Marie, of course, guessed something was brewing and was not slow to urge caution. I listened to her warnings, but was sure that Christian and I were set on a course from which I would not turn back, and that an affair was inevitable once we were on tour.

I was buoyed and inspired by this sense of anticipation, and the production—and the role—proved a great success for me. Vocally I was in good shape, able to float effortlessly through Sophie's high lines and blending exquisitely with Marie in our scenes together. Christian seemed charmed by me, both personally and professionally, while he, too, won acclaim for the rich and idiomatic reading he had drawn from the orchestra.

At the first night party, he made it clear he hoped we would spend the night together and, after that, with two performances a week for eight weeks at eight different theatres, our relationship became an open secret. Christian had other engagements between our performances but when we were both free, we spent the time together, either at my flat in London or on snatched breaks away in romantic hotels. Our idyll was interrupted by Monica's unexpected decision to fly to London for the first of the performances at the final venue of the tour. Though I glimpsed her and Christian together at the stage door after the show, I slipped away without meeting her. I was too uncomfortable to join the other singers for a drink, realising they would all know why I was there with them and not with Christian.

Monica's visit cast a shadow over the final performance, as, for the first time, relations between Christian and I felt awkward and strained. She had made a big effort to see the show and spend time with Christian, and I had to face the fact that she had every right to be there and it was I who was the cuckoo.

Though we stayed late at the end of tour party and he spent the night at my flat, something had shifted in his demeanour towards me. The next morning, before he left to fly back to Germany, he said nothing about seeing me again and was vague when I asked about his immediate plans and the possibility we might arrange to meet up again soon when our schedules coincided. He merely said he'd call or text me.

When he'd gone, after a worryingly casual goodbye, I felt racked with shame, knowing I'd been foolish to let myself think that this liaison was special. I tried to tell myself that it wasn't worth this anguish and uncertainty, but another voice told me I couldn't give up on it.

I moped about the flat feeling let down and depressed and was grateful when Marie rang to suggest meeting for coffee. She was at Paddington waiting for a train to Bristol and expected to be stranded there for at least another two hours due to signal failure near Ealing Broadway. She'd found a table in a quiet corner of the foyer lounge at the Paddington Hilton and a cafetière of coffee and a jug of hot milk were delivered almost as soon as I arrived.

'Thanks for coming,' she said, as she paid the waiter. 'I'm so frustrated by this. I missed the train I was booked on—which left before the signals failed—because of endless delays on the dreaded Circle line!'

I smiled wanly and she leant forward and studied me closely.

'Hey,' she said. 'What's up with you? What's happened?'

I told her about my unsatisfactory parting from Christian and how I had virtually begged him to agree to see me again.

'I feel so humiliated,' I whispered.

'Oh Alice, I'm sorry,' she said, squeezing my hand.

'I know,' I said. 'You told me so.'

She shrugged her shoulders and sat back in her chair, saying nothing for a while.

'But Alice, you must have known he'd be going back to Monica when the run ended.'

I hung my head. In truth I'd not allowed myself to think about it.

'Perhaps you have to accept that it was a pleasant interlude, but now it's over and he's going back to his real life.'

I looked at her aghast.

'Are you saying that it was simply the equivalent of a holiday romance?'

She raised her eyebrows and said: 'Maybe it was. I can see that you thought it was more than that, but face it, he's in a relationship and you told me he said right at the outset that he and Monica are trying to make it work.'

I nodded glumly and looked away.

She leant forward and forced me to look at her.

'Listen, it seems to me that in situations like this, there's a crucial moment when you can choose whether to over-invest in a losing proposition, or take the short-term pain and move forward, and find someone who is available and who actually reciprocates your feelings.'

I nodded but said nothing. Christian had filled my imagination and my fantasies for so long, I couldn't survive without the hope and the pleasure they brought me. I simply couldn't make the choice she was advocating. I was not ready to renounce him.

A few weeks later, at the beginning of December, by which time I'd had only superficial contact with Christian, my agent rang with an offer of work that seemed to vindicate my constancy: a production of *Hansel and Gretel* had lost its Gretel and needed a replacement. The management wondered if I would step in. I knew this was a production in which Marie was booked to sing Hansel so I was immediately interested. The next piece of information made my heart race: the production had also lost its conductor (the husband of the original Gretel), and Christian Kennedy had agreed to take over. My stomach fluttered: I was a surprising choice to step into a role I had never sung before at such short notice so I felt sure he must have suggested me for Gretel; that he wanted us to work together again as much as I did.

I accepted the engagement without hesitation, but in allowing infatuation to govern my decision, I underestimated how taxing I would find Gretel and how difficult it would be to master what I quickly understood was a very testing role. I was booked to do a series of concerts at the end of the year, in six European capitals, so my opportunity for sustained learning time was limited but, almost immediately after the tour of *Rosenkavalier* was over, I developed a cold I couldn't shake off and which left even my speaking voice sounding weak and rasping. This had become a recurring pattern: I would succumb to all sorts of viruses at the end of a long engagement, especially during the autumn and winter months. My body might be telling me that I needed to hunker down in my flat or go home to my mum for Christmas, but this year I was working throughout the festive period, with the last of the concerts a New Year's Day Johann Strauss gala in Vienna.

Fortunately, I was a quick learner, so the notes were not a problem, but my vocal coach was concerned that I would find the extended vocal range much harder to master and was unhappy that I'd agreed to sing Gretel at a time when she felt I was already over-extended and would be juxtaposing a role that was almost certainly too low for me alongside singing high-lying roles like Valencienne and Zerbinetta which I was scheduled to sing over the coming months.

But I was determined to do it and so I brushed aside her concerns, and worked hard to learn and memorise a very challenging part so that I would be well-prepared when rehearsals started in the middle of January.

But when rehearsals began, I was still unwell. I'd been forced to cancel the penultimate concert in Budapest and even a few days later in Vienna, I could hear I was vocally out of shape, my performance lacking finesse and control in music that I had hitherto been able to sing with ease.

I arrived back in London in no condition to start work on a new production but I was determined to be there because Christian would be. I was also anxious not to reveal any signs of frailty or flakiness, so I put on my game face and turned up on day one armed with a box of throat pastilles and as much lighthearted cheeriness as I could muster.

I'd not seen Christian since *Rosenkavalier* finished because, despite all my attempted maneuverings, our schedules had not allowed it. He was friendly and seemed happy to see me but, from the start, he was careful to be circumspect at all times and not display in public anything that would have hinted at our earlier relationship. I was therefore confused about where we were in that relationship, having hoped we would pick up where we'd left off and that this period of working together again would consolidate and cement our previous intimacy. We did spend time together, both within a group and alone, but I could rarely relax enough to enjoy those times as I could sense that his previous enthusiasm had been replaced by a manner that was lukewarm and non-committal.

Patient and kind though she was, Marie was not afraid to speak her mind about what she regarded as a misguided fixation. Whereas I tried to read deep meanings into Christian's every action, she was quick to point out that what was probably happening was simply his attempt to maintain a professional relationship.

'You're confusing the intensity of agony with the intensity of real love,' she said during one of our many conversations on the subject. 'You'll know when you've found the real thing, because it will flow in both directions.'

We were good colleagues, though, and as if we had known each other all our lives, we developed such a close sibling dynamic that audiences would see that Hansel and Gretel got along well and looked out for each other. Throughout rehearsals, she was unfailingly supportive and good-humoured, though she must have been aware of my vocal shortcomings. To my horror, I could not control a tendency to sing with a vibrato that was sometimes so wide that I lost pitch, so that in some of our duets the balance and blend of our voices sounded as if we were singing against rather than with one another.

While we were rehearsing with piano in a large studio, Christian allowed the director to take the lead so that the focus was on the staging. Thankfully, I felt confident about developing my characterisation of Gretel, but it was when we started rehearsing with the orchestra that the extent of my difficulties was revealed. Whereas the rest of the cast seemed able to cut through an orchestral score so dense and richly embroidered that it could obscure the voices on stage, I had to sing at full throttle to be heard above an accompaniment that often seemed impenetrable. I hated to hear how my tone hardened under pressure and how much the glow had faded. Worse of all, no part of my voice sounded right for the music: I could find neither the caramel lustre required in its lower range nor the pure sugary magic demanded at the top.

It was now that Christian's earlier restraint disappeared. He seemed impatient with my vocal difficulties, on one occasion dismissing them as a symptom of incipient prima donna tendencies, an accusation I knew was unfair, whatever the limitations of my performance.

The reviews were much as I had feared they would be. Throughout the agonising run of performances, I became increasingly desperate to cling on to Christian, but had to endure an undisguised cooling on his part that was obvious to our colleagues, making my fears about my vocal decline all the harder to deal with.

Alice

It was time to inspect my handiwork.

'Not bad,' I thought, as I reached into one of the bags to find the topper I'd bought. I'd rejected a traditional angel or a star and had chosen instead a white iridescent peacock with long glittering tail feathers. I stood on tiptoe to clip it to the top of the tree and then stepped back and smiled. I was pleased with the effect.

While I'd been absorbed in the work, I'd allowed my thoughts to flow freely, without censoring or banishing them, but I was stiff and tired now and wondered what to do next. I rubbed my lower back before bending down to gather up a stray ribbon and tidy away the carrier bags. I rolled my shoulders backwards and forwards, and then moved to the side of the tree to pull back the curtain. There were lights in the church and, on an impulse, I decided to wander over for no better reason than to have a change of scene.

The church was quiet but there was activity at the far end as two elderly women knelt down to pick out blooms from huge boxes of cut flowers that covered the floor between the choir stalls. I sat at the back, from where I could see that all the pew ends were decorated with purple and ivory bows, the centres of which contained a small heart made of white crystals.

The church was being readied for a wedding.

The lighting was dim, as only some of the lights were on, but wintry sunlight struggled through the stained glass windows and here and there I could see motes of dust dancing in the air. I watched as one of the women went out through a door into the vestry and thought how uneven and ungainly her gait was, until I noticed the caliper she was wearing on her left leg. The other woman was absorbed in her task of arranging a combination of purple and cream flowers in a stand beneath the pulpit.

The organ was on the left of the choir stalls, its high, narrow seat only inches away from where the back row of singers would sit. I closed my eyes and tried to imagine Imogen and Isabel coming here to worship, first as children and later as young women. I wondered if Imogen had become one of those aging volunteers who helped the vicar prepare the church for occasions that marked life's rites of passage: weddings, christenings, funerals.

Imogen's funeral in March had been a muted affair, but perhaps that was as much a reflection of my own low mood as anything else. She died during my run of performances of *Hansel and Gretel* and I'd not seen her during her final weeks at the cottage hospital in Leek, and for that I felt great remorse.

Mum and I went to the funeral together, grateful that it had been organised by one of Imogen's former colleagues from the library. I recalled how self-conscious I'd felt about joining in the singing of the hymns. The congregation tried valiantly but could manage a rendition that was at best thin and warbling. I knew I could add substance to this meagre sound, but was afraid my voice sounded thick and curdled and I could hardly bear to hear it ring out through the resonant acoustic.

At the end of the service, the vicar said that in her last days and weeks, Imogen did not shy away from discussion of her funeral and the final hymn—'Dear Lord and Father of Mankind', sung to the tune of 'Repton' by Hubert Parry —was one she had particularly requested. My mother nudged me as if to urge me to do better than I had in the earlier hymns and so I tried. The Quaker words, passing through repentance to trust to stillness and silence were very beautiful and by the final verse I was close to tears.

Dear Lord and Father of mankind,
Forgive our foolish ways,
Reclothe us in our rightful mind,
In purer lives Thy service find,
In deeper reverence, praise.

In simple trust like theirs who heard,
Beside the Syrian sea,
The gracious calling of the Lord,
Let us, like them, without a word,
Rise up and follow Thee.

Drop Thy still dews of quietness,
Till all our strivings cease;
Take from our souls the strain and stress,
And let our ordered lives confess
The beauty of Thy peace.

Breathe through the heats of our desire
thy coolness and thy balm;
let sense be dumb, let flesh retire;
speak through the earthquake, wind, and fire,
O still, small voice of calm;
O still, small voice of calm.

I sighed and decided to leave. The door to the vestry opened and the elderly woman limped back into the church, having covered her light grey dress with a gaily patterned overall. She peered at me for a moment, then walked slowly down the aisle towards me.

'Are you alright, my duck?' she asked quietly. 'You look very pale. Can I help you at all?'

'That's very kind,' I said. 'I'm fine.'

The woman was studying me intently and I blinked under her observant gaze but her grey eyes looked kind.

'You're new around here, aren't you?' she asked. 'I'm Betty.'

'I'm Alice,' I replied. 'I grew up nearby, but I've just moved to Vicarage Road into what was my godmother's house.'

The woman looked interested.

'Who was your godmother?' she asked. 'If she worshipped here, I might have known her.'

'Imogen Grey,' I replied. The woman murmured and nodded in silent assent, and I wondered if she might also have known Evadne and Isabel. Before I could ask her, however, the other flower-arranger looked round and coughed.

'Ah well, my duck,' Betty said. 'I'd better get on.' She nodded in the direction of the other woman and said under her breath, 'I don't want Eileen there getting her knickers in a twist.'

I smiled and watched as she turned and hobbled up the aisle away from me. I stood up and made my way quietly out of the church. The light had faded while I'd been inside and I thought how pretty and welcoming my tree would look. I took a few steps down the gravel path before I stopped and turned back, deciding to make my way to the side of the church where Imogen was buried. Her grave was on the side of the graveyard that overlooked Vicarage Road. The headstone was new and plain, with no inscription other than Imogen's name and the dates of her life span, while next to it were the weathered headstones of her parents, Arthur and Evadne. I was thinking how peaceful it was when the harsh cackle of chattering crows made me spin round to look over towards the cypress trees that marked the furthest perimeter of the churchyard, where there were fewer grave stones and the grass was thick and overgrown. As I was turning to take a final look at Imogen's grave, I stopped, my eye caught by something white glimmering faintly in the gloom. Half-expecting to find a straggle of stray sweet wrappers caught in the clumpy, long grass, I walked over to have a look. I was wrong and instead I found little sprinklings of snowdrops, encouraged by the mild winter to bloom early and, as I bent down to cradle one of the tiny, white drooping bell shaped flowers in my hand, I smiled, thinking that perhaps their beckoning was a reminder that the hope and warmth of spring were not far away.

Isabel

Rhona Winters was five months pregnant and her rapidly changing appearance was the subject of much discussion. She glowed with good health but was beginning to widen round the hips and develop a pronounced bump. When Isabel arrived at rehearsals the day after she'd been to the doctor, the designer and director were rethinking the tight-fitting and revealing basque they'd intended her to wear as Zerbinetta.

Isabel slipped quietly into the room, and after acknowledging everyone with a friendly wave, tried to make herself as inconspicuous as possible, happy to allow Rhona to be the focus of attention.

'No-one could ever accuse me of being svelte,' she wailed, holding her wide hips and looking down at her swelling tummy, 'even before this little mishap.'

Isabel smiled feebly, knowing this was no mishap and that after fifteen years of marriage, Rhona and her husband were delighted at the prospect of becoming parents. The pregnancy had been confirmed only weeks before rehearsals started, Rhona having not considered that her symptoms were anything more than an aberration caused by tiredness and jet lag. From the first day of rehearsals, when she'd announced her good news, the mother-to-be had exuded a sense of contentment and well-being that Isabel envied more than ever that morning.

She tensed as Yvonne, the Company Manager, headed towards her, knowing she needed to deflect concerns about her health.

She was not ill, simply pregnant, but this was not something she could talk about, let alone revel in.

'How are you?' Yvonne asked kindly.

Isabel tried to hold the other woman's gaze and appear unconcerned.

'A little better,' she lied.

'Good,' Yvonne said brightly, looking genuinely pleased. 'What did the doctor say?'

'He thinks I might have some sort of sickness virus that's knocking me out.'

Yvonne nodded sympathetically.

'Viruses can be so hard to shift, you must look after yourself, but I'm glad it's nothing to worry about.'

She squeezed Isabel's arm and moved away to join the discussions about how Rhona's expanding girth could best be concealed. The designer was gathering up his drawings and preparing to leave, and Rhona was shaking her head at him in mock despair, with just the slightest swing of her hips.

'I'm doomed to look like a baby whale whatever you come up with,' she drawled in her nasal American accent.

While everyone laughed at this, Isabel blanched, knowing that despite the fact she was currently eating so little, she too, might soon start showing tell-tale signs it would be hard to disguise or dismiss. It had not occurred to her that she might be pregnant, Paul having taken pains to prevent such a 'mishap'. She had spent the previous night in shock and was still trying to process the potential impacts on her life. She had no hope that Paul would be glad at the news—he'd been clear that he did not want children—and coming now when he was concerned about his wife's health, the timing could not have been worse.

And then of course there was Barbara.

But perhaps there had always been Barbara.

She'd not heard from Paul and though she wanted to confront him about what appeared to be his duplicity, she resolved to wait for him to contact her, knowing the longer he stayed away, the more precarious his commitment would be revealed to be.

Only she and Rhona were called for the first part of the morning and she tried to steel herself for the alarmingly

151

prescient scene they were about to enact. Grant was standing in the middle of the room holding his score and Isabel forced herself to focus.

'So, let's recap where we've got to,' he said to them and proceeded to list the events that had gone before. 'Ariadne's been abandoned by Theseus, she lies motionless, attended by Naiad, Echo and Dryad. She wakes and expresses inconsolable sorrow at her heartbreak.' He was pacing around the acting area absorbed in the story. 'Meanwhile, Zerbinetta and Harlequin are commenting from the side, and Harlequin even tries to pep Ariadne up with a little song, but to no avail. The comedians have one last try to lift Ariadne's spirits, but Zerbinetta sees their efforts are pointless and sends her troupe away. And this is where we are now.' He stopped and looked around. 'Zerbinetta faces Ariadne directly, to share some feminine solidarity with her, and implores her to find an inner strength despite the inconstancy of men.'

Isabel had little to do other than listen and react to the lengthy discourse contrasting true love with cheerful promiscuity, but for Rhona, the aria was one of the most fiendishly difficult in the soprano repertoire In its sheer length, the variety of moods it reflected and its coloratura pyrotechnics, the aria required prodigious technical resources of agility and range to bring it off. But as she dashed off its incredible cascades with smiling ease, the long scene seemed to hold no terrors for her. Isabel sat, as instructed by Grant, like a frozen marble effigy, subdued and sorrowful, but was all too aware of the aplomb with which Rhona confirmed herself as the free and easy star of the troupe, offering not only a voice that was full of colour, light and shade, but a personality of natural warmth and winning charm.

Will you not deign to hear me—
Fair and proud and moving not,
As if you were an effigy on your own monument.
You would have none to share your sorrow's secret
But yonder rocks and tumbling waves of ocean?

At times Isabel was directed to turn away or cover her face
or make as if she would leave, but whatever she was doing,
she found herself compelled to listen.

Most noble lady, lend an ear:
Not thou alone, all women,
Yes, all women, all, have suffer'd it.
Deserted and abandoned, desolate!
But of such desert isles there is a multitude
Ev'n in the haunts of men. I, I, myself
Know them full well: in many have I dwelt:
And yet I did not learn to load all men with curses.
Faithless are they,
Past all believing, without measure.
A few hours of a night,
A feverish day,
The sigh of a breeze,
A languishing glance—
And lo! They are changed.
But are we, are we immune
Against these pitiless enchantments, these changes.
That pass all understanding?
Full oft when I think that for ever unshaken
My constancy every attack will repel
Strange promptings assail me, that in me awaken
A longing for liberty long lost, a yearning—
The moment I think I'm true to one lover,
And soon 'tis a new flame in secrecy burning,
That holds my heart fast in its conquering spell.

Isabel sighed. Her feelings for Paul could not be dismissed as an every-day love affair, where an old lover can be readily exchanged for a new one. Isabel turned her back on Rhona and hung her head. When at the end she stood up and looked at Zerbinetta in non-comprehension, Rhona sang:

> *Yes, it seems the lady and I do not understand each other's language.*

Silently, Isabel nodded and smiled.

At the end of the morning rehearsal, Rhona came over and took her arm.

'Are you OK, honey?' she asked quietly. 'Reckon you could do with more than a lonely old rock for a friend.'

The day was still warm as they made their way down a secluded side street half way between London Bridge and the Tower of London. They'd finished earlier than scheduled and Rhona was taking Isabel to visit a hidden garden that had only recently been restored and opened to the public. She hooked her arm in Isabel's and steered them through the tall wrought iron gates.

They walked up the wide path and into the garden that had been created from the ruins of a bombed-out church. It was overgrown with trees and ivy, and wall-climbing flowers grew amongst the ruined arches, but enough of the original walls survived to suggest what the church would have looked like in its heyday, and the garden had been cleverly created with an exotic mix of plants and trees.

'How did you discover this?' Isabel gasped, gazing up at the enormous steeple standing high above them on four sturdy buttresses.

'I can't take credit for that,' Rhona laughed. 'Henry brought me here. He's been researching the church and said it was an astonishing place.'

Isabel had never met Rhona's husband but knew he was an eminent church historian and imagined they might be something of an odd couple.

Rhona nudged her.

'I know what you're thinking,' she said.

Isabel couldn't stop herself blushing.

'But you're right.' Rhona laughed again. 'Me and Henry —I'm Marilyn to his Arthur Miller.' She paused and shook her head. 'Except we seem to have a marriage that works.'

Isabel smiled.

Rhona was guiding them towards a bench near the original doorway to the church, from where they could see the old gravestones and take in the strange but wonderful mix of ruin and garden. Before she sat down, Isabel wandered a short distance away to peer through a window and was surprised to see palm-like trees growing on the inside.

'How did you meet?' she asked.

'At college,' Rhona said simply as Isabel sat down next to her. 'I was studying music in Chicago and he came for a year on a Junior Fellowship to study American ecclesiastical architecture.'

'Is he American?'

'Well, he's a mongrel like me—American mother and English father. But unlike me, he's lived mainly here so he talks like the Cambridge don he is, whereas I still sound like a good-time girl from the Midwest.'

Isabel laughed.

'How did you get together?' she asked, glad to deflect the conversation away from herself for a while before the inevitable cross-examination she knew would come.

'He came to one of my concerts,' Rhona replied, 'and we got talking at the bar afterwards.' She laughed. 'We didn't get off to the most auspicious start.'

'Oh?' Isabel asked.

'Oh no,' Rhona said with emphasis, shaking her head. 'He asked me out for dinner a few nights later and we arranged that he'd collect me from my hall of residence, but I'd gone down with the most godawful stomach bug, and when he turned up at my door, I could barely get out of bed to let him in.'

'Poor you!'

'Holy shit. Imagine this picture of loveliness: faded, baggy pyjamas, greasy hair, grey and pallid complexion. Mm—lovely!'

Isabel laughed.

'And y'know what?' Rhona went on. 'He came in, took off his jacket, put me back to bed and made me tea and dry toast.' She stopped and watched as a white butterfly settled on the bench next to her. 'He was just so kind,' she said quietly, 'and he sat on a chair by the side of the bed and he looked at me as if I was the most beautiful creature he'd ever set eyes on.'

She looked over at Isabel.

'And y'know, he still looks at me that way.'

Isabel held her gaze and then looked away, unable to suppress a sigh. Rhona took her hand and held it in hers.

'So, tell me,' she said. 'Spill!'

There was something about Rhona that was irresistibly open-hearted and so Isabel told her the story—about Paul, how they had met, their covert relationship, his wife, her illness, the possible other 'other' woman.

Of the baby, she said nothing.

When she'd finished, Rhona let out a long, low whistle and let go of her hand.

'Does he love you?' she asked at last.

Isabel shook her head.

'I don't know any more. I thought he did.' She paused. 'I was sure he did. I was sure that we had waited so long to be together that it was meant to work out for us.'

'You thought he was the one?' Rhona said.

'I did,' Isabel replied. 'Right from the start.'

'Honey, that's dangerous,' Rhona replied. 'The concept of someone being 'the one' assumes that when you meet someone, they're already 'the one'.'

Isabel frowned and asked: 'So, didn't you think Henry was 'the one' as soon as you met him?'

'Hell, no!' Rhona exclaimed in surprise. 'To be honest, I was worried he might be a bit geeky.' She laughed. 'He had this quiet, earnest way about him and looked like he was wearing his dad's clothes and he didn't seem interested in the stuff that all the other guys I knew were in to.'

'So what happened to change that?' Isabel asked.

Rhona thought for a moment.

'I got to know him I suppose and learned to see him for the man he really is.' She laughed. 'He's so patient, so unflappable, you wouldn't believe it. And I liked how he treated me,' she said. 'How thoughtful and caring he was. We both work hard but he always makes time for me, to be interested in me.'

Isabel fell silent, struck by how straightforward Rhona made it sound, how unlike her own experience.

Rhona shifted her position and turned to look at Isabel. Her expression was kind but perplexed.

'Are you in love with a fantasy?' she asked at last.

Isabel frowned, not sure what she meant.

'What is it about this man, this Monsieur Paul?'

'As soon as I saw Paul,' Isabel replied, 'I thought of Monsieur Emanuel in *Villette*. Paul had exactly the same fiery blue eyes and close-cropped black hair and shabby coat that Charlotte Brontë describes in the book.'

Rhona looked at her long and hard, as if struggling to understand.

'He just seemed so *different*. So unlike anyone else I'd ever met before.'

'But you were nineteen, yeah? First year in college?' Rhona replied.

157

Isabel nodded and Rhona shook her head.

'The way you tell it,' Rhona said, 'it's like you saw someone whose look you liked, who for some reason made you think of a character in a novel with whom you were in love, and you filled in all the blanks, and when you felt that first, powerful rush of attraction, you projected every good quality you desired onto him, even though you had absolutely no basis for doing so.'

Isabel winced and shook her head but Rhona was not finished.

'It sounds like you fell in love real deep, real quickly, so you feel and believe as if you really 'know' this man, but if he's mainly a concoction of your own imagination—well, yours and Charlotte Brontë's—then it's not surprising you felt an instant connection.' She paused. 'But the truth is, you may not love the real him at all, because you don't know him. You made him what you wanted him to be.'

Isabel felt her eyes filling with tears and bit her lip.

'Honey, I don't mean to be unkind,' Rhona said, placing her hand lightly on top of Isabel's, 'but I can see you're obsessed with this man and from what I'm hearing, he's not worth it.'

Isabel opened her mouth, intending to say: 'Worth it or not, I can't give him up.'

But Rhona held up her hand as if to stop her.

'Any man worth taking seriously as a potential mate will cherish you, and believe me, it's simple: if he cherishes you, he shows it.'

Isabel opened her mouth to defend Paul, to cite examples of how he cherished her, but feared Rhona would see them as mere empty gestures and signs of his guilty conscience. Instead, she watched in silence as an elderly man sat down on a nearby bench. He was wearing a brown pinstripe suit and carrying a briefcase, out of which he took a large silver hip flask from which he proceeded to drink, his head tipped back, his eyes closed.

She lowered her voice.

'You're saying I projected my ideas of love onto someone I barely knew?'

Rhona nodded.

'So does it follow that what we had was never a shared experience? That we were two people who had entirely different experiences? And one of them mistakenly thought that his experience was the same as hers?'

'Maybe,' Rhona replied gently.

Isabel shifted her position and fell silent, watching through eyes prickling with tears as the man in the pin-striped suit unloosened his tie and took off his shoes. He caught her staring at him and she turned away to look at Rhona.

'Don't be too hard on yourself,' Rhona said, squeezing her arm. 'People in love can lose even the most basic critical faculties and become capable of monumental self-deception.' She laughed bitterly. 'We've all done it.'

Not getting any response, Rhona asked: 'So you've not heard from him since Saturday?'

Isabel shook her head and bit her lip.

'You caught him out so perhaps he's lying low for a while—or else he's gone lukewarm on you,' Rhona said. 'And here's the problem: what if 'the one' doesn't want you? Then what happens? Are you going to stay single for eternity because 'the one' doesn't want you?'

Isabel hung her head, fighting back a sense of rising dread.

'I know right now you can't imagine ever loving someone else,' Rhona said, 'but you have to give up this obsession. Take back your life! Get a new man—now there's a thought.' She nudged Isabel and winked. 'Even Ariadne succumbs to Bacchus in the end.'

She paused and pulled a face.

'That said, I guess you may not have the option of falling into the arms of the God of Wine or sleeping in a Greek cave that turns into an erotic bower.'

She laughed out loud and Isabel couldn't help laughing with her but, almost as quickly, her laughter turned to tears.

'No one will want me now,' she said quietly, wiping her eyes on the back of her hand and turning to Rhona. 'I'm pregnant and Paul has made it clear he's never wanted children.'

Rhona blinked and gasped.

'Oh honey, I'm so sorry. I wouldn't have gone on like that if I'd known.'

Isabel was crying unashamedly now, Rhona's earlier words having hit home. She knew she'd ignored all the obvious problems and obstacles that came with Paul and now, they were coming back to taunt her.

Alice

Christmas cards arrived, forwarded from my London address and, though I was pleased to hear from friends, every card provoked a sharp pang of guilt, because the cards I'd intended to send had stayed firmly in their wrappers. I couldn't face the interminable task of inscribing a news bulletin that would make depressing reading, and I baulked at taking the cowardly route of writing simply 'love Alice'.

A couple of cards arrived for Imogen, but as neither sender had included an address, I couldn't write and convey the news of her death. As I was throwing the cards away, I remembered my mother telling me that when she was readying the house for my arrival, she had tidied away a pile of post that had come for Imogen. I'd forgotten this and the letters lay untouched in the drawer of a small table near the front door. All but one of the envelopes contained circulars from charities Imogen had supported. The other was addressed by hand and bore the franking mark of one of the local universities. I expected it to be an invitation to a lecture or other event, so was surprised that it was a personal letter from someone called Steven Bennett, who described himself as an Administrative Assistant in the Hope Street Theatre Archive. I thought it likely to relate to Imogen's career as a librarian, so I read it with little interest —until I came to the words 'your sister Isabel' and re-read it more carefully.

September 30th

Dear Ms Grey,
I'm writing to ask for your help. You may have heard that Sir John James University is now housing the archive of Hope Street Theatre and as part of our work, we plan to showcase some of the holdings in

exhibitions we'll mount in the foyer of the theatre. We've decided that the first of these will be a celebration of Gertie Gitana who died almost sixty years ago, and who the theatre celebrated in 1965 in a play starring your sister Isabel. We've found some material to put in the exhibition, but wonder if you have any memorabilia of your sister that you'd be prepared to lend us please? We would, of course, look after it and let you have it back afterwards.

I'd be happy to come and see you to discuss this further and to collect anything you think might be of interest to us. I'd love to hear more about your sister. My mother remembers her as Gertie and I have a song sheet with a drawing on the front, which I think may be of Isabel. I'd be delighted to let you see it.

You can contact me at the university—my details are at the foot of this letter. I look forward to hearing from you.

Yours sincerely,

Steven Bennett

So, I thought with surprise, someone else is interested in Isabel. I added his letter to the large white envelope in the bureau and resolved to contact him in the New Year.

Isabel

Her ghost-like reflection in the mirror suggested a silent Victorian woman living on the border of dreams and reality. There was something ethereal about her, as if she was not really there, but was passing through life without touching it, not allowing the harshness of reality to taint the whiteness of her lovely muslin dress.

It was early and the gallery was quiet. Isabel stepped back to view 'The Little White Girl' from a greater distance, from where she could imagine her slowly and elegantly walking across the room, before standing by the fireplace, her hand barely touching the mantel, while the other held a Japanese fan. The reflected image seemed so sad and dejected, and Isabel wondered if there was a link with the wedding ring so prominently displayed on her left hand.

Isabel had been a regular visitor to the exhibition ever since it opened, drawn back time and again to stand in front of this pensive girl and share her wistful reverie. That morning, the young woman's careworn expression seemed to match Isabel's mood more perfectly than ever. Her back ached and she looked round for somewhere to sit. The room steward got up from the bench from where he'd been watching her and made way for her to sit down. She nodded her thanks and eased herself onto the low, hard bench. She was glad of this time to be alone, before she summoned the energy to return to her flat.

The first time she'd come here, in July, she and Paul had come together, with Isabel studying the paintings in silence while Paul quoted extracts from the catalogue he thought would be of interest to her. The painting had caught her eye as soon as they entered the room where it was displayed —the patterned fan, the red pot, the blue and white vase on the mantelpiece, and the spray of pink azaleas providing brilliant splashes of colour against the background of black, white and cream. Isabel had gone straight towards the girl, while Paul read her the relevant entry in the catalogue. The model was Whistler's mistress and Isabel wondered if Paul had ever valued her as much as Whistler had apparently prized his muse. She doubted it.

She was still struggling with nausea and suggested they go somewhere for a cup of tea. Paul made as if to demur but something in her manner seemed to persuade him to agree and they made their way slowly towards Pimlico tube station, stopping on the way at a café with tables set outside on the pavement. Though the air was warm and dusty, the interior was even hotter, so they chose a table under an awning which gave welcome shade.

While they waited for their drinks to be delivered, Paul continued to flick through the catalogue. Isabel watched and waited. She knew he was discomfited by the awkwardness between them, an unease that had been growing since she learnt of his wife's illness and understood he would be putting her first.

He was a coward—she saw that now. After that chance sighting on the South Bank, he had stayed away from her for over two weeks. Eventually, he'd appeared at her door one Sunday afternoon wearing a sheepish expression and bearing flowers in one hand and a box of brightly coloured macaroons in the other, the appearance of which had made her feel queasy. While she sipped peppermint tea, he made excuses for his duplicity.

He had known Barbara for a long time and had a casual relationship with her. Barbara expected nothing from him. They simply enjoyed good times together now and then.

He hadn't wanted to hurt Isabel. Really, it was nothing to be upset about.

These things happen…

Isabel didn't seem to want him that way anymore…

He did try to warn her from the start.

It need not make a difference…

But it did make a difference. They continued to see each other, but these meetings became more infrequent. He said nothing about her changing shape, though admittedly the bump in her belly was small and neat and could be concealed by the long, loose sundresses she wore that summer. Similarly, he seemed unmoved by her troubles at work and when catastrophe struck he had nothing to offer —neither solace nor understanding.

Rhona was perplexed by Isabel's reluctance to tell Paul about her pregnancy. Now, after their first outing together for some time, she resolved at last to tell him, even though she'd begun to accept that he was drifting away from her.

He closed the catalogue when a young boy placed two cups of tea on the table between them. His expression was pricked with anxiety, as if he knew she was about to tell him something he wouldn't want to hear. She, on the other hand, was calm. She couldn't stop herself loving him, but she'd adjusted her expectations, knowing he would choose a sick wife over a pregnant mistress, even if at first he dressed up his intentions in noble fashion. In fact, when she told him the news, he made no attempt to disguise his dismay and fell silent, at a loss to know what to say or do.

She thought of Lucy Snowe and the famously ambiguous ending of her story; recalled the passion and despair of the penultimate chapter when Lucy tells Monsieur Paul:

> *It kills me to be forgotten, Monsieur. All these weary days I have not heard from you one word, and I was crushed with the possibility, growing to certainty, that you would depart without saying farewell!*

Paul had gone without a word of farewell, and she had come back to see 'The Little White Girl' for one last time. By the time she got home, Paul would be on his way to Italy, leaving Isabel to face an uncertain future alone.

Alice

My mother had disposed of Imogen's clothes, but her bedroom still had the distinctive smell I associated with her. She had dressed smartly but her clothes always smelt of mothballs. The bed had been stripped so the room looked bare and unloved, but I felt sure the drawers of the two bedside cabinets would be full of the same sort of clutter I'd found downstairs. I stood by the window and looked round the room. It was not unattractive and, in the pale afternoon sunlight, the view over the graveyard was peaceful and strangely pleasing, though I shuddered as I realised that Imogen's grave was amongst those I could see beyond the high grey wall.

I moved over to the cabinet nearest the window and sat on the edge of the bed. There was little in any of the three drawers here—a pair of scissors, a couple of greying handkerchiefs, a few pencils and a glass paperweight in the shape of a rose—so I imagined Imogen had slept on the other side of the double bed and hoped I might find more in the cabinet there.

I sat on the other side and leant down to open the top drawer. It was stiff and seemed to be stuck so I tried the second and third drawers which slid open easily. Again there was little of interest—a small, unused notebook, some more pencils and a dried up lipstick which smelt old and stale. I tried the top drawer again but it was shut fast and wouldn't budge. I wondered if something was wedged at the back so opened the second drawer again and reached in to see if I could feel anything. I got down on my knees and peered in to see what looked like a pamphlet stuck between the first and second drawers. I eased it out carefully and put it on the bed while I checked that the top drawer would now open. It did and, as I'd hoped, it contained more than the others. There was a small torch, a hand mirror in a pretty decorative case, a silver pill box, a stainless steel comb, a small sewing kit and a cream envelope, addressed to Imogen. I knew at once that the handwriting was Isabel's.

My breathing quickened and my hands were unsteady as I took a single sheet of paper out of the envelope. I sat on the bed to read it and, as I shifted my position to get comfortable, the pamphlet fell to the floor, dislodging a small piece of card that must have been inside it. I leant down to pick it up and saw that it was a theatre ticket for a seat in the balcony at the London Coliseum for a performance in October 1972 of *The Magic Flute* by Sadler's Wells Opera. What I'd thought was a pamphlet was the programme for that production and when I looked at the cast list on the first page, I saw that Isabel had sung Pamina. I assumed that Imogen had gone to see her sister on stage—either before their estrangement or despite it. I flicked through the pages until I came to the cast biographies. The small black and white photograph that accompanied Isabel's showed a woman with loose shoulder-length blonde hair and large, hopeful eyes that seemed tinged with trepidation.

I turned back to the letter. It was shorter than the one I'd read a few days earlier and the handwriting was more uneven and at times hard to decipher.

Flat 5, 9 Parkfield Gardens
London W11

10ᵗʰ October 1977

Dear Imogen,
Did you receive the cards and the letter I sent recently? My baby has come early and I'm desperate to get away from London and from everyone here who knows me. I plan to come home to you in a few days' time—on the afternoon of the 14ᵗʰ October all being well. I will

travel as lightly as I can so I'd appreciate it if you could buy or borrow a cradle for the baby please. I won't impose on you for any longer than I need to. I simply need time to gather myself and think about what I'll do and where I'll live.
Your sister,
Isabel

Did she come, and if so, did Imogen set aside whatever differences had caused them to fall out?

Isabel

She struggled down the platform heaving her suitcase in one hand and cradling the baby in her left arm. The wind and rain tore at her hair and clothing with such ferocity that she stumbled and almost fell. A man who disembarked from the same carriage looked at her with curiosity but neither he nor anyone else offered to help. Her fellow travellers—most of whom were less encumbered than her —made their way quickly across the bridge and down the steps towards the exit and, when she arrived there, she found the taxi rank deserted. The lights from the station gave the glistening forecourt a ghostly pallor and she felt her spirits falter. It was a wild night to be out with a new-born baby who seemed to be sickening, and there was no guarantee of a warm welcome when they reached their destination. She huddled against the outer wall of the station building, the overhang of the roof giving some protection against the elements, and rocked the baby gently from side to side. The child slept, wrapped up in blankets like a tiny mummy, but her breathing was uneven and crackly and her face was flushed.

Two cars stopped at the traffic lights at the end of the road ahead, waiting for the green light, and with relief she saw that the second car bore a yellow sign on top displaying the word TAXI. The first car pulled in to collect two men waiting to her left, and slid away before the passengers had even shut the doors. As the taxi slowed to a halt she heard through the driver's open window the distinctive voice of Bing Crosby singing 'Pennies from Heaven'. The driver sprang out to help her, taking the suitcase and opening the back door for her. Once safely inside, she was glad of the warmth and comfort of the car, relieved that the wait had been short and that she would soon be home.

'He's died today—had you heard, duck?' the driver called over his shoulder, before leaning forward to turn the sound down a little.

At first Isabel was confused, unsure what he meant, but when the man spoke again she understood.

'He was one of my mother's favourites. She's right upset, she is.'

'He had a beautiful voice,' Isabel said in reply, recalling how his light, velvety baritone had serenaded her and Paul while they basked in the glow of that first date.

'Where to, my duck?' the driver asked.

'Sandleheath please,' she replied. 'Vicarage Road, by the church.'

The driver pulled away, humming along to the tune, until the song came to an end and he gave his own rendition of the first line.

'I like that,' he said, peering through the rain-streaked windscreen. 'No matter how much it rains, it will all turn out OK in the end.'

Isabel laughed and momentarily allowed herself to hope that all would be well. She looked down at the baby, whose laboured breathing had turned into rasps. As Isabel stroked her burning cheek, the child's eyelids flickered and she began to whimper, un-consoled by Isabel's whispered endearments, urging her to hush.

The driver was looking at her in his mirror.

'Babbie OK?' he asked.

'She's tired,' Isabel replied. 'I need to get her to bed.'

Would Imogen have remembered to buy a cot, she wondered, suddenly anxious about what they'd be met with.

'Soon be there,' the driver said reassuringly, and sure enough, in the distance she could just make out the shape of the church.

His taxi radio spluttered into life and he leant down to pick up the mouth-piece.

'Just dropping off in Sandleheath.'

A man's voice crackled through the handset but the driver seemed to understand the instruction.

'OK,' he said. 'Ten minutes it should take me.'

He turned into Vicarage Road and pulled up at the first house on the right. Isabel peered through the window and saw the faint glow of a light through the narrow pane of coloured glass in the front door. She leaned forward to pay the driver, who pulled up the hood of his anorak and hurried out to lift her suitcase out of the boot before helping Isabel and the baby out of the back seat. The rain seemed heavier than ever and she hugged the baby close while she knocked tentatively on the metal ring on the front door, not wanting to alarm the child who was whining steadily now, her face distorted and distressed.

'Take care, duck,' the driver called as he got back into the car.

She watched as he did a nifty three-point turn in the narrow roadway and sped away to his next fare.

She waited a while longer, thinking perhaps she hadn't knocked hard enough. She tried again more forcefully, the welcoming hallway light a steady beacon and surely a sign that Imogen would soon appear. But she heard no doors opening inside nor footsteps approaching. The baby was crying now and she felt panic rise within her. She had written to say that she would come on this day, Friday, the 14th October, but she was later than she'd said she'd be. Perhaps her letter had gone astray and Imogen was unaware of her plans. But with a growing sense of dread, Isabel knew that she had written before and had no reply.

She was desperate now. Either Imogen was not at home or she was deliberately ignoring her. She pushed against the letter box and leant down to look inside, hoping to sense whether the house was deserted or simply still and watching. She called her sister's name, feebly at first and then with more urgency, but her cries made the baby howl with more anguish and she knew she had to find somewhere dry to take shelter and wait. The house next door was in darkness and the one beyond that was up for sale and appeared to be empty.

Through eyes that were wet and stinging with rain, she peered up at the church. She thought she saw a light somewhere within but then as quickly feared it was a trick of the moonlight. She picked up her suitcase and hurried as fast she could round to the main road and up the long path that led to the entrance. When she opened the door into the porch, the building was deathly quiet and seemed to be deserted. Though the church itself was locked, she was content to rest in the porch for a while and decide what to do. It wasn't warm, but it was dry. She huddled uncomfortably on the hard wooden bench, increasingly worried by the child's agitated breathing. She shivered and held the baby close to her, to feel her warmth and breathe in her clean, sweet smell.

From the other side of the locked door, she heard music —the faint, sonorous harmonies of the church organ—and closed her eyes to listen. She dozed fitfully until the air resounded to the triumphant swell of Mendelssohn's 'Wedding March'. She shook herself awake, confused and disoriented.

A wedding?

No, it was still dark night outside.

She sat up to listen more closely.

The organist played on, but at last the church once more fell silent. She felt hope ebbing away. Help had been close by and now had gone. The door into the porch had been blown slightly ajar by a gust of wind, but she was too tired to stand and push it shut and her attention was taken with the baby who was once more crying piteously. She kissed her forehead and tried to soothe her. Back and forth she rocked her, crooning *Rock a Bye Baby* gently above the child's head.

The baby would not be comforted and her cries rose to an ear-splitting wail. At this, the door of the porch opened to reveal a man in a dark overcoat and a white dog collar. She looked up into his face, expecting to recognise the stern visage of the vicar of her childhood, but this man's appearance took her by surprise. He was young and he looked kindly. She held his gaze, pleading wordlessly for help, and he sat down beside her and took her hand, and for now she knew she was safe.

Alice

I was more relaxed than I'd felt for a long while. Christmas lunch and a couple of glasses of Rioja combined with the hypnotic effect of the glimmering fairy lights, and the warmth and sweet smell of the log fire, meant I had let down my guard and Mum and I were talking openly for the first time since I moved to Sandleheath.

'You were lonely,' she said, 'and looking for someone to take away the loneliness.'

I nodded and wondered if she had ever done that in the thirty years since my father left.

'But he wasn't really available, was he?'

'No,' I conceded, 'but I persuaded myself that he might be.' I paused. 'In the end, he just walked away without explanation, without saying anything, really.'

Mum shrugged and put down her glass.

'I suppose, once it was over as far as he was concerned, he didn't need to talk because he had nothing to talk about.'

'That may be true,' I said, 'but I was prepared to talk until the cows came home to persuade him he could be happier with me than he was with Monica.'

'But all the time and effort in the world will never change someone's mind about loving you and wanting to be with you once it's been made up.'

She looked suddenly downcast.

'Mum, what's the matter?' I asked, concerned.

'I want you to be happy. That's all.'

'I know you do.'

I caught her eye and smiled.

'Let's have another glass of wine.'

She laughed and we raised our glasses in a mock toast.

'This is good,' I said. 'It's working wonders.'

Mum was fiddling with the stem of her glass.

'Would you consider trying on-line dating?' she asked at last.

I pulled a face.

'My internet profile would have to say: can give off a whiff of desperation!'

We both laughed.

'I don't want you to give up on happiness,' she said at last.

She hesitated before speaking again.

'I'm worried you may feel you've lost the only person in the world you can feel like this about. That you can't imagine ever loving anyone else.'

I didn't contradict her.

'But if you allow this belief to take hold,' she went on, 'not only will it add to your heartache, it will make it more difficult for anyone else to come into your life, because you'll feel and behave as if you've already lost 'the one' and so no-one else will mean anything to you.'

I thought of Ariadne, transformed by the arrival of Bacchus into a radiantly happy woman, ecstatic in the arms of a new lover who she at first mistakenly welcomed as the Messenger of Death. I smiled at this image and my mother smiled back, pleased to think that her words had helped.

And in a strange way, they had.

'Let's have some pudding,' I said, jumping up and going through to the kitchen. Mum followed and watched as I put the Christmas pudding into the microwave and took some ice cream out of the freezer.

'Shall we have some dessert wine to go with it?' she asked. 'I've got a lovely sweet Greek red that will be perfect.'

'Let's go for it,' I said. 'It's Christmas.'

And over pudding and sweet wine, I asked her about Isabel.

I told her all I knew, but Mum's bemused expression told me that none of it meant anything to her.

'I never heard Imogen talk about anyone called Isabel,' she said, when I'd finished. 'You'd think that someone would have mentioned her at the funeral.'

'That's what I thought.'

I dipped my spoon into the softening ice cream and licked at it absentmindedly.

'Why did you and dad choose her as my godmother?' I asked, realising I didn't know what the connection had been between my parents and Imogen.

'She was your father's choice,' Mum said. 'He did a holiday placement at the library where Imogen worked and they got to know each other. When he and I first met, just after he'd qualified as a Librarian, he told me how encouraging she'd been throughout his placement and his studies in Sheffield. She seems to have been supportive at a time when his own parents were distracted and disinterested.'

'Did he say what she was like when he first met her?' I asked.

'He said she was extremely good at her job and had a real love of learning and knowledge.'

I had never thought of Imogen as a woman with a career she enjoyed and was good at, perhaps because when I was setting out on my professional life, she was about to retire.

'It seems strange Dad didn't come to her funeral.'

Mum looked uncomfortable and said nothing.

'Do you know why he didn't come?' I persisted.

'I do,' she said quietly. 'I was relieved you didn't ask at the time because I knew how difficult things were for you then.'

I waited.

'His daughter, Flora, was getting married the same day.'

I felt myself stiffen and stood up to return the ice cream carton to the freezer. Seeing this, Mum said: 'Let's clear away and sit somewhere more comfortable to have coffee.'

'Would Dad have known Isabel?' I asked, closing the freezer door with a thud.

'Why don't you ask him?' she replied. 'Have you been in touch with him since you moved back?'

I leant down to load the dishwasher while she made the coffee.

'I sent him a card,' I said, 'with my new address and an edited version of what's been going on.'

'Did you hear from him?' Mum asked cautiously.

'A Christmas card and a note. I didn't read it that carefully.'

'Oh, Alice,' she said and touched my cheek. 'He's still your father and I'm sure he's never stopped loving you.'

I shrugged and pulled away and we spoke no more about it.

We whiled away the afternoon watching a black and white film starring Bette Davies.

'They don't make them like that anymore,' Mum said later as we drank tea and ate mince pies.

'They don't,' I agreed. 'I'm going to spend the rest of the festive period doing more of the same: eating mince pies and watching cheesy films. I have a pile of them ready: *Shrek, Toy Story, The Muppet Christmas Carol*. Bliss!'

Mum laughed.

'How about you?' I asked. 'Do you have any plans?'

She put down her cup and I sensed she had something to tell me.

'I'm going to spend tomorrow with my friend, Derek,' she said. 'He's Vicky's father.'

It took me a moment to work out who Vicky was and when I did, I recalled how evasive Mum had seemed when I'd asked her how she knew Vicky and Nico.

'Tell me more,' I said, watching her blush.

She described how she'd known Derek at school but not met him again until six months earlier when she'd gone to a concert in which he was singing.

'After his wife died a couple of years ago,' she said, 'he joined a choir. It's the same one my friend Joan sings in and I met Derek at a post-concert party she dragged me off to.'

'Oh Mum, I'm so pleased for you,' I cried.

'He'd love to meet you,' she said, 'and you'd be very welcome to join us tomorrow, but I realise you might not feel up to that.'

I didn't.

'I'd love to meet him, Mum, but another time. What's he like?'

'I always liked him at school,' she said, 'though all my friends thought he was dull because even then you could see he was a really loyal, dependable sort of chap. Teenage girls then and now tend to dismiss those qualities in favour of more glamorous ones.'

'Guilty as charged!' I laughed.

'He's still loyal and dependable—and he's very kind. He works hard, too—he runs his own landscape maintenance business.'

She chattered away and I saw how happy she was.

'By the way,' she said suddenly. 'I meant to ask you this weeks ago: did you find the box of music I left at the bottom of the wardrobe in Imogen's bedroom?'

'I didn't look in there,' I said in surprise. 'What is it?'

'Just some battered old scores, I think. They were loose on the top shelf of the wardrobe so I found a box to put them in. Probably nothing of much interest, but you might want to go through them and decide if they're worth keeping.'

'I will,' I said, but I was still absorbing the news about her and Derek.

I had never stopped to think that she, too, knew what it was like to be rejected, and now, here she was, after half a lifetime alone, opening her heart and moving on. I knew I shouldn't define moving on as simply finding a new partner, and that maybe she had moved on long ago, but clearly Derek had come along when the time was right for her to allow him into her life.

And I wondered what it would take for me to move on, to start living a real life, free from fantasies and obsessions.

Alice

I'd not felt lonely during my self-imposed solitude. I'd made a conscious decision to indulge myself, so I ate when and what I wanted, (cheese on toast was a particular favourite), and on New Year's Eve I was not feeling any desperate need to be anywhere rather than on my own. I decided I would wish myself a happy new year, and go to bed as early as I liked, but during the afternoon, after days of being cocooned by the fire watching Christmas television, I itched to be outside in the fresh air.

I looked through the front room window and was surprised to see that in the time it had taken me to put on my coat and walking shoes, the wispy mist which had clung to everything for days had thickened into a dense and cloying fog, while the pavement was covered with a light dusting of snow which looked as if it was settling. The main road was unusually quiet and everywhere seemed smothered in the deep silence that usually only descended in the early hours of the morning when the traffic briefly abated.

I zipped up the front of my padded coat and collected a torch from a drawer in the hall table, but when I opened the front door, I winced as a gust of icy air made my eyes sting. As I struggled to ease on my tight leather gloves, I looked up to the graveyard that loomed above me on the high bank at the front of the house. I started when I saw someone looking down at me from behind the wall that encircled the edge of the churchyard. I blinked, thinking I'd been misled by the thickening fog and a trick of the rapidly fading light, but no, I was sure there was someone—an elderly woman I thought—standing amongst the grave stones. I coughed, hoping the watcher would realise she'd been seen and would move away. But still the figure stood and watched me. Unsettled and alarmed, I decided to create a blaze of light, as if that might chase away anyone sinister lurking in the shadows of the graves, but in fiddling with the switch, I almost dropped the torch. While I juggled it clumsily back into my clutching hand, the beam momentarily swooped over the woman, the light catching her face and making it look ghostly and ageless. I peered through the snow that had begun to fall more steadily and, all of a sudden, the air seemed laden with a sadness that radiated from this stranger.

At that moment a tall man appeared behind her and, with his hand on her shoulder made as if to steer her away, but he, too, looked down at me, long enough for me to get a view of him. His skin was dark and his hair was tight and crinkly and I speculated that the flash of white I noticed at his neck might be a dog collar. As I watched them, they turned and walked away out of sight, leaving me unsure if they'd been real or imagined.

If I'd been braver, I might have gone after them, waited at the bottom of the path, so that I would meet them as they made their way out of the church yard and could ask them why they'd been watching me. That's what a plucky fictional heroine would have done, I thought, but the encounter had perturbed me and taken away my appetite for a solitary walk in the fast-falling darkness.

All my efforts to keep loneliness at bay were undone by this wordless encounter. I switched off the torch and went back inside. As I took off my boots and hung up my coat, I wondered what these visitors wanted in the graveyard of Holy Trinity on this bleak midwinter's day.

Isabel

Her absence is like the sky, spread over everything. I have no photograph of her that's any good. I cannot even see her face distinctly in my imagination.

Isabel sat at the window and stared out at a landscape that looked as frozen as she felt inside. The trees of the convent garden were bare, the lawns hard and white with frost and the heavens a resolutely dull grey as if the natural world was grieving with her, its November bleakness mirroring her own mood of despair.

She looked down at the words she'd just read and pushed the book away. She had no photograph of Lucy, but her baby's face appeared indelible, so sharply etched was it upon her mind's eye.

It was one of the younger nursing sisters, a novice, who had pressed the book upon her, in the hope it might one day offer comfort.

'C S Lewis wrote it,' she explained, 'as a memorial to his love for his dead wife.'

Sister Angelica traced her fingers across the book's title, *A Grief Observed*, before taking Isabel's hands in hers.

'This is one man's perspective of grief,' she'd said, 'but though each grief is different, all griefs bear similarities.'

Isabel was grateful for the kindness of the nuns, but despite their care and concern, she felt cut off from everything around her, encased in sorrow and stranded in a solitary, debilitating state in which she travelled endlessly from shock to denial to yearning and back again, with guilt and hopelessness being ever present foes.

She believed she had somehow predestined Lucy's death by surrendering to such foreboding when she discovered she was pregnant. Now she cursed her self-centred preoccupation with Paul and with her vocal troubles, and feared that her unborn child had sensed she was unwanted. Though she had loved Lucy with a burning intensity through every day of her too-short life, she presumed that even her quickly aroused maternal devotion had not been enough to banish the baby's subconscious belief that she was an unwanted burden.

The child's grasp on life had seemed secure, so bonny and well had she looked despite her difficult, premature birth and the anxiety displayed by the medical staff when they whisked her away before Isabel had even set eyes on her. When the emergency was over and a nurse placed Lucy in her arms for the first time, Isabel had been enchanted with her daughter, gazing into her dark blue eyes and stroking her peachy skin and silky hair. Though the labour had been long and debilitating, Isabel took to motherhood more readily and instinctively than she had thought possible, feeding and changing and bathing her baby as skilfully as the nurses.

At the end, though, she felt she had failed her: a long journey in harsh weather, with no guarantee of safe haven at the other end now seemed a foolhardy undertaking.

Isabel stayed for four weeks at the Convent of the Good Shepherd, a few miles from Sandleheath, and on the day she left, Father Kyle drove her first to Holy Trinity Church and then to the station to catch the train back to London. He took her case and helped her down the platform. When the train approached, he put his hands on her shoulders and briefly held her close.

'Thank you,' she said. 'I'll never forget your kindness.'

He nodded.

'Remember,' he said, 'Stella Maris. If you ever need me, that's where I go next.'

She smiled. He was so young and striking, with his spiky black hair and lively dark eyes. He and the sisters of the Good Shepherd had saved her.

But saved her for what?

Steven and Alice

It was the final week of the Christmas show and the theatre was busy with families eager to collect their tickets and find their seats before the performance started. Steven recognised Alice immediately, though she looked smaller than he remembered. Her streaked blonde hair was slightly longer than the feathery crop that had once made her so distinctive, and her face looked pale and pinched, much as she had looked when he'd last seen her two years earlier.

The crowd dispersed, so that at last they were visible to each other, and Steven waved and went over to greet her.

'Hello,' he said, trying not to sound as self-conscious as he felt. 'Thanks for coming.'

'No problem,' she replied. 'I'm intrigued. Keen to know more.'

They'd spoken on the phone a few days earlier and shared some of the information they each had, and Steven had sensed that Alice was as curious as he about Isabel and what had become of her.

'I've arranged for us to use the Artistic Director's office,' he said. 'He's not here tonight.'

He led her up the stairs and across the bar to a door in the far corner that led into the offices. Here, the walls of a large, open plan space were covered in framed posters of past and future productions. A young woman, peering at a computer screen, looked up briefly as they headed into an office that opened off the main area.

It was a large room, with a desk and filing cabinets at one end and two comfy chairs at the other. Alice took off her coat and sat down.

'How are you?' Steven asked, sitting next to her and taking a folder out of his satchel. 'I was surprised to hear you'd moved back to Sandleheath.'

Alice looked puzzled, and he realised that though he knew who she was, she had no idea that their paths had crossed before.

'You were one of the soloists in what turned out to be my last concert as a professional bassoonist,' he explained.

She looked surprised, but interested, too.

'When was that?' she asked.

'Southbank Centre, November 2014,' he answered, trying to sound as blasé as possible, but not quite managing to disguise the despondency he still felt whenever he recalled the events of that night and was forced to confront his altered circumstances.

'I'm so sorry!' Alice exclaimed. 'I didn't recognise your name, but I remember hearing about what happened to you.'

She shook her head.

'I'm so sorry.'

He was quick to bat away her sympathy and recover his hard-won self-control, but at the same time, he guessed why she, too, had come home. He was about to say something, when she nodded as if to stop him.

'Yes, I've come home to pick up the pieces, too,' she said quietly.

It was his turn to apologise.

'It was crass of me to ask,' he said. 'I heard about *Ariadne*—I had friends in the band...'

Her head drooped and he saw her wince. She looked so small and forlorn, he couldn't stop himself from leaning forward to touch her arm, before pulling away, fearing she would dislike such familiarity from a stranger.

Instead, she looked up, and her startlingly blue eyes held his with a look of unexpected gratitude, before she turned away and reached into her bag.

'I'm not sure I can be of much help with your exhibition,' she said, taking out a large white envelope, 'but I'm happy to share what little I know.'

On the low table in front of them, she laid out the Gertie Gitana playbill, the *Rosenkavalier* cutting and photograph, the reviews of *Ariadne,* and the programme for *The Magic Flute.*

'There are some personal postcards and letters Isabel wrote to Imogen, but otherwise, this is all I've found so far.'

'I'm afraid I have only a little more,' he said, opening his folder. He handed Alice two plastic wallets, one containing a mixture of press cuttings from a variety of concerts and operas, and another which held material relating to the Gertie Gitana show. Finally, he handed her the song sheet.

'This is the song I told you about,' he said. 'The one written for *Under the Greenwood Tree.'*

Alice put down the plastic folders and took the manuscript from him, turning the pages carefully and studying the music closely.

'It looks a lovely arrangement,' she said at last, beginning to look at the drawings on the covers. 'Who did these sketches, do you know?'

'I'm guessing it was Paul Eveson, whose copy this was and who presumably sang the baritone part.'

'Was he in the Gertie Gitana show as well?' Alice asked.

'No,' Steven replied. 'He left the company the year before.'

As she continued to study the drawings, he was able to observe her closely without feeling rude. There was a touching frailty about her, though at the same time, he got the sense of a strong spirit, only temporarily diminished.

'She looks very young in these sketches,' Alice said at last.

Steven nodded.

'We don't know how old she was then. Have you been able to find out when she was born?'

Alice shook her head.

'I didn't even know she existed until a few weeks ago. The first inkling I had was when I got a phone call from a woman asking for Isabel Grey.'

'Who do you think that was?' Steven asked.

Alice shook her head.

'I've really no idea.'

'She might still be alive,' Steven said. 'I've found no record of her death.'.

Alice's eyes widened. She picked up the folder of press cuttings and skimmed through them. There were reviews of *The Magic Flute* and *Rosenkavalier* and she picked out one that included a photo of Isabel as the Marschallin and held it up for him to see.

'I saw a portrait of a woman who looked just like Isabel does in this costume,' she said. 'The portrait's owned by a man who once loved a singer who resembled the woman in his painting.'

'An interesting coincidence,' said Steven. 'Perhaps worth pursuing?'

'Possibly, yes,' Alice said.

She put the cutting back into its folder and turned to the other, in which there were clippings about the Gertie Gitana show and some black and white production photographs. They showed Isabel transformed by a series of dark wigs, her hair long and loose with a centre parting in some and short and sleek in others, when she was meant to be older. As Alice flicked through them, Steven went over to a shelf near the desk and lifted down a large, old-fashioned cassette player.

'Do you have recordings of Isabel singing?' she asked.

Steven nodded.

'We have a recording of the Gertie show,' he said, 'but sadly, the tape of the concert at which Isabel sang 'Let no man steal your thyme' is missing.' He paused. 'It may have been misfiled and may still turn up somewhere. I'll keep looking.'

He took a cassette out of its case and pushed it into the player.

'The recording quality's not great but I thought you might like to hear her sing 'Nellie Dean'.'

He pressed the play button before coming back to sit next to her, just as a pure, sweet voice filled the room.

There's an old mill by the stream, Nellie Dean
Where we used to sit and dream, Nellie Dean
And the waters as they flow,
Seem to murmur sweet and low
You are my heart's desire; I love you, Nellie Dean.

At the old mill stream I'm dreaming, Nellie Dean
Dreaming of your bright eyes gleaming, Nellie Dean
As they used to fondly glow
When we sat there long ago
Listening to the waters flow, Nellie Dean.

I can hear the robins singing, Nellie Dean
Sweetest recollections ringing, Nellie Dean
For they seem to sing of you
With your tender eyes of blue
For I know they miss you too, Nellie Dean.

I recall the day we parted Nellie Dean
How you trembled broken hearted, Nellie Dean
And you pinned a rose of red
On my coat of blue and said
That's a soldier boy you'd wed, Nellie Dean.

All the world seems sad and lonely, Nellie Dean
For I love you and you only, Nellie Dean
And I wonder if on high
You still love me, if you sigh
For the happy days gone by, Nellie Dean.

There's an old mill by the stream, Nellie Dean
Where we used to sit and dream, Nellie Dean
And the waters as they flow,
Seem to murmur sweet and low
You are my heart's desire, I love you Nellie Dean.

'What a touching performance,' Alice said quietly. 'So unaffected and charming. The phrasing and the breath control were perfect, and she made it sound so effortless.'

Steven nodded.

'I agree,' he said. 'It's ironic—and rather sad—that neither Gertie nor Isabel are remembered now, though they called Gertie 'the Idol of the People', but nowadays, when she's remembered at all, it's usually just for that song.'

Alice smiled and raised an eyebrow.

'Fame surely is a fickle thing when the singer's forgotten but not the song.' She paused and pulled a face. 'I think someone famous said that—I don't know who.'

There was an awkward silence until Steven surprised himself by asking if she'd eaten.

'I've come straight from work,' he said, 'and I'm famished. There's a half decent Indian up the road just beyond the Johnny Jim if you're interested.'

Alice was tidying her papers away and when he saw her hesitate, he felt his face redden, but just as he was about to say it was no problem, he'd grab some fish and chips on the way home, she looked up.

'Why not?' she said, with a smile.

'So, you say this place is half-decent?' I asked, as we made our way out of the theatre.

'Well,' Steven said cautiously, 'in culinary terms, Sandleheath's not London by a long way, but if you like Indian, then you're in for a pleasant surprise.'

It was starting to rain and we reached the restaurant just as the heavens opened. We scurried inside, shaking

189

ourselves down and laughing as we took off our wet coats. We hovered in the entrance until an elderly waiter wearing a black sherwani shuffled over to take them from us before showing us to a table at the far end of the restaurant. Other waiters moved slowly and gracefully about their business while the buzz of taped sitar music reverberated gently in the background. The air was warm and laden with the powerful aromas of spicy food.

We ordered two bottles of lager, which were delivered almost immediately, along with a plate of poppadoms and a tray of dips and chutneys.

'How hungry are you?' Steven asked, glancing at the menu. 'Could you manage the meal for two? The chef chooses what you get, so it can vary.'

'Sounds great,' I said. 'Let's go for it!'

He closed the menu and pushed it to one side.

'Cheers.'

I held up my glass to his, thinking I was probably more fun when I'd had a drink

'So how are you adjusting to life back home?' I asked, after the elderly waiter had taken our order.

He told me about his job at the university following the six months in the Cotswolds with his uncle; about living once more in his childhood home, but how different that felt as an adult.

'My mum has her own life now,' he said, 'and most of the people I knew at school have moved away, so I sometimes feel a bit isolated.'

As he spoke, he was intent on smoothing out the pleats into which a red paper napkin had been fanned, which meant I could study him properly. He was dressed in blue jeans and an open-necked white shirt with a grey sports jacket that was a tad too small for him. He had floppy brown hair and kind, brown eyes and, with his slightly ruddy complexion and reassuringly solid physique, he looked attractively boyish, though I guessed he was older than me. He looked up and saw me staring at him, and as if it was now an automatic reflex, began stroking self-consciously at his jaw.

'Not very pretty is it?' he said, taking a large gulp of lager.

I realised he thought I'd been staring at his scars, whereas though I had noticed them when we'd been talking at the theatre, I was more interested in trying to work out what I made of him.

'I didn't mean to embarrass you,' I said.

'Don't worry,' he laughed. 'I used to wish I looked less boring, but there are drawbacks in having an interesting facial disfigurement.'

'You're not disfigured,' I cried, and then stopped short, realising that might be how he saw himself.

'The doctors say the scars will fade in time and look less angry,' he said, 'so that's some consolation.'

'What happened?' I asked.

He told me about the walk he was taking over the river from the South Bank and the sudden, brutal attack.

'It couldn't have been worse really,' he said. 'The epicentre of the injury to my mouth was exactly where you need everything to be right for playing the bassoon.' He laughed. 'If I'd broken both arms and both legs, it would have been better.' He paused. 'I'd still be playing.'

I shook my head at the horror of it.

'I remember rolling over and thinking: 'This is going to change my life."

He munched on some poppadoms.

'Eating and drinking and talking were difficult for a long while, so I'm grateful I can lead a normal life again—with the only lasting damage to my embouchure.' He paused. 'The means with which I made music.'

At that, we fell silent and, as I raised my glass to take a sip of lager, I caught his eye and knew we were both thinking about our ambushed careers.

'I need some idea of what I'm going to do long-term when this job finishes,' he said.

'Such as?' I asked, thinking the same might apply to me.

'Not sure yet,' he said with a shrug. 'When you've done something for so long, it's hard to think that anything can ever replace the experience of making music with other people.'

'I know,' I said. 'This last year, when I developed my vocal problems, I understood how important music is to me, how singing enables me to express myself.' I blinked back tears. 'I feel the loss of it almost viscerally, as if I've lost part of myself, some essential organ without which I'm not really here.'

He was looking at me intently, but kindly, and I felt myself relax.

'But you've not given up on your voice, have you?' he asked with concern.

I told him about my visit to Dr Mackenzie.

'I'm due to see him again in a few weeks' time,' I said, 'to review how things are.'

'Good,' he said hopefully.

'Maybe,' I said with a shrug.

'When did it all come to a head?' he asked. 'Can you talk about it?'

'I simply couldn't do it any more—any of it. Zerbinetta has this long and florid aria that includes a comic catalogue of her former lovers, all delivered with the most shameless and salacious trills and flourishes, and I was all over the place. Even allowing for the fact that I had to deal with a lot of strenuous stage business, I was underpowered and the tone was thin at the top. I heard myself resorting to the most excruciating swoops and scoops—God, it was awful.'

I shuddered.

'Mind, Strauss got it wrong, too. He made the mistake of continuing this 'show-stopping' aria for ages after it's actually stopped the show—a fatal miscalculation.' I laughed grimly. 'I sympathised with Ariadne, who'd had enough long before the end and made a dignified retreat into her cave.'

Steven tried without success to suppress a laugh and I laughed, too.

'The thing is, I'm finding this limbo land hard to deal with. I'm not singing and have no prospect of doing so, but I'm not ready to stop calling myself a singer.'

He nodded and I could see he understood.

'Perhaps for me,' he said, 'the situation was easier to come to terms with because the impact of the damage was incontrovertible. There was no uncertainty. It was just a matter of how long it would take me to accept it.'

He wiped his hands on the napkin and looked at me sadly.

'Some day,' he said, 'I hope I may find music consolatory, but ever since the attack, I've found it almost too painful to listen to anything that reminds me of my former life.'

I nodded.

'I might have tried to teach,' he went on, 'but I can't demonstrate sounds or techniques and I wouldn't want to be that sort of teacher.'

He laughed ruefully.

'I'm not sure what I'm good at any more.'

He thought for a moment.

'I'm pretty good at crosswords,' he said, 'but I don't see a career there.'

We both laughed and took a swig of lager.

I wondered what he would do when the job at the archive was over, and I had an image of him growing older and more stolid, living modestly with his mother in a quiet backstreet like my own. I found myself pondering why he was still single. For all he'd been through, there was something steady and decent about him, which many women would find attractive.

He sighed and rubbed his tummy.

'Sorry for the long wait, but the food is cooked to order so it can take a while.'

'Don't worry,' I said, though I had nearly finished my lager and could feel its effects going to my head and to my cheeks, which were hot and no doubt flushed.

'So tell me about your godmother,' he said. 'I'm intrigued that neither you nor your mother knew she had a sister.'

While I was telling him about Imogen, I thought I should do as Mum had suggested and ask my dad if he'd known Isabel. I knew Mum would be pleased if I made an effort to repair the rift between us, though the prospect of that seemed too enormous and difficult to contemplate and I pushed the notion away.

'Given the breach between them,' I heard Steven saying, 'I wonder why Imogen went to see *The Magic Flute*?'

'I wondered that, too,' I said, forcing myself to snap back into the present. 'Imogen didn't much like opera. She once complained to me that the plots were melodramatic and impenetrable and the acting amateurishly hammy.'

'Ouch,' Steven winced.

'I guess that *Flute* might have been one she liked,' I volunteered. 'She once asked me if I had ever sung Pamina.'

'And have you?' Steven asked. 'I'd have thought you were more of a Papagena than a Pamina, if you don't mind me saying.'

'I don't,' I said, helping myself to a poppadum, 'and thereby hangs a tale.'

'Go on then,' he urged, piling mango chutney onto his plate.

'I've sung Papagena many times,' I said, taking a sip of lager. 'I sang Pamina once at college, and decided it was not my role.' I paused. 'I could sing all the notes, but it really wasn't right for me—I just don't have the silky, creamy sound it needs—so it shows what desperation can do to opera managements when they've tried everyone they can think of to step in at a moment's notice and no-one half decent—to use your expression—is available.'

Steven wiped his mouth with his napkin and rubbed his hands in glee.

'I can tell this is going to be one of those theatre stories I love,' he laughed 'Go on—I'm all ears.'

I laughed, too.

'It's one of those stories I dine out on—talking of which, where is our food?'

I was about to continue when a convoy of waiters bearing trays arrived at the table, so I waited until the feast was laid out before us: an array of chicken and fish main dishes, vegetable side dishes, and bhajis, rice and nan breads.

'This looks great,' I enthused as Steven passed me a serving spoon and encouraged me to help myself.

As he, too, filled his plate with a little of everything, I carried on.

'I had a Saturday off at home in London when my agent rang—about two o'clock I think it was—to say that English Touring Opera had a problem and wanted me to bail them out.'

A waiter came over to ask if we had everything we needed and I took the opportunity to order two more lagers.

'They were in Poole,' I went on, 'and had a performance of *The Magic Flute* that evening, but the Pamina had cancelled with a sore throat the night before and during the morning, the cover—who was in the Chorus—went down with a stomach bug.'

'Oh dear,' Steven said.

'They'd tried everybody they could think of without success and apparently thought of me because I knew the opera inside out and because someone on the management had heard me sing Pamina at College and thought, at a pinch, I could do it.'

'Well, that's a vote of confidence then,' Steven said encouragingly.

'And apparently I was about the same size and shape as the girl who'd cancelled.'

'It all helps.'

'Yes, up to a point. The fly in the ointment—apart from the fact I'd only sung the role once years before—was that they were singing it in a new English translation which they'd commissioned and I only knew the one that most companies were using at the time.'

'Ah.'

I took another slurp of lager.

'So, I found my score, packed a bag, got myself to Waterloo and then on a train to Poole—spent the entire journey trying to remind myself of the music and the words (the wrong words, of course)—and arrived to have a walk around the set at about six o'clock.'

'Nerve-wracking.'

'Too right! I was introduced to the rest of the cast, taken to my dressing room and thrown into my costume and wig —which just about fitted me, so that was one less thing to worry about.'

I smiled as I pictured the scene.

'I remember the staff producer taking me on stage to walk me through some of the main moves and asking myself, 'Why am I doing this? I must be mad!"

'So, how did it go?' Steven asked.

'Everyone was so kind and solicitous and grateful. We were ready to start, about half an hour late, I suppose, and the Company Manager went out front to explain to the audience what had happened and he was brilliant. He really laid it on, how I'd saved the day with a mercy dash from the other side of London, but how I'd be singing the translation I knew, not theirs—no mention of the fact I'd only sung the role once, ten years earlier—and he got the audience so completely on my side, I honestly think that if people had brought flowers with them, they'd have thrown them the minute I made my first entrance. It was fantastic, the warm applause I got, before I'd even sung a note.'

I paused again for a spoonful of curry and a mouthful of lager. I could feel myself warming to my story and caught a glimpse of the old me and was pleased to see that Steven was waiting impatiently for me to go on.

'The thing about *Flute*,' I said, 'is that there's a lot of spoken dialogue. Have you seen it? Or played in it?' I asked him.

'I saw it in Edinburgh once,' he replied. 'A friend of mine from college was playing the birdman, Papageno.'

'Ah, Papageno was my hero that night!' I said. 'He was lovely: a beautiful voice and a wicked twinkle in his eye. He really took me under his wing—no pun intended—but we had a moment during our first scene together when the translations were so far apart it was surreal, as if we were having completely different conversations from different operas! He looked so goggle-eyed with alarm, wondering what I was going to say next, that I nearly had a serious attack of the giggles.'

'I imagine that at moments like that hysteria could easily set in,' Steven said.

I nodded.

'We had to sing a duet about Papageno wanting a girlfriend and wanting one there and then and he was so sweet, I was tempted to say, 'Forget this Prince Tamino, I'll be your girlfriend, happy ending, let's all go home and save me a lot of stress."

We both laughed heartily at that.

We were making inroads into the mounds of food but were slowing down and beginning to pick at what was left. At a polite distance, waiters hovered, with less to do as other diners paid their bills and left.

'Do you like opera?' I asked at one point.

'I do,' he said. 'Very much. I never saw you on stage, but I saw you singing operatic arias in a concert at the Bridgewater Hall in Manchester a few years ago,' he said.

He paused.

'It was lovely.'

I smiled, grateful for his appreciation.

'I can even remember some of the things you sang.'

'Really?' I asked, surprised.

'Yes, Micaela's big number from *Carmen* when she gives José a message from his mother. I felt myself saying under my breath, 'You great fool, José, stop messing around with that brazen hussy Carmen and go home with this girl immediately."

I laughed and then stopped when I saw how serious and awkward he looked. The words hung in the air between us and I felt myself blushing, so unexpected was this compliment from this slightly diffident man. Neither of us spoke for what seemed an age until he tried to diffuse the moment by saying:

'I expect most of the men in the audience felt the same.'

He took a long gulp of lager and looked down at his plate.

'Thank you, that's very flattering,' I said. 'I've never sung Micaela on stage—another role that's not for me,' I said. 'She has such a sweet, gentle nature, she's so obviously decent.' I paused and laughed. 'I never got to play that sort!'

We were down to the dregs of the meal and the elderly waiter hobbled over to clear the table.

'Sometimes, I wonder if I'll ever be able to do any of it again—cope with the nerves, the travel....'

Steven nodded again and let me continue.

'I think it's a form of madness, the way singers turn in on themselves and obsess about their voices. Musicians seem much more robust in that way.'

'Oh, we all have our neuroses, don't you worry,' he said, twitching and grimacing and going cross-eyed.

I laughed and at that moment, the elderly waiter delivered the bill, which we'd already agreed to split. We paid in cash and got up to go.

Outside, the rain had stopped but the wind was bracing and stepping out of an atmosphere that had grown oppressively stuffy, I felt suddenly woozy.

'Where do you live?' I asked.

'Not far from Linda Vista Gardens,' he said. 'I'll leave my car near the theatre and walk. It will do me good.'

We headed up the hill together.

'And how do you get on with your mum?'

'Oh, fine—really well in fact,' he said, 'but I know I won't want to live there indefinitely.'

'And no girlfriend?' I asked, the lager having emboldened me.

'No, I'm a latter day Papageno. My mum would love me to find my own little Papagena—or Pamina. She's not fussy.'

I laughed.

'There was someone,' he said more seriously, 'until just before I had my accident.' He shrugged. 'But she decided she preferred her boss to me.' He paused for effect. 'As he was a multi-millionaire, I tried not to take it too personally.'

I laughed and, still feeling slightly tipsy, I stumbled against him.

'Sorry,' I said. 'Can't take the drink. I'm out of practice.'

I stopped and steadied myself. The air was chilly, the sky clear and full of stars. I shivered and to my surprise, Steven took my hands in his to rub and warm them, as I remembered my father doing when I was a little girl.

'You're cold,' he said.

I shivered again and nodded and, as I began to feel the warmth of his hands slowly warming mine, I looked up at him.

'I'd like to find out what happened to Isabel,' I said. 'Will you help me?'

Isabel

Who said that death is rarely the end of any story; that the dead are silent and yet they speak to us? Isabel wished that Lucy could speak to her, could say that she did not blame her mother for her death; that the other world to which she had gone was a good place. But though Isabel dreamt about her night after long night, Lucy remained resolutely silent. In dreams, Lucy appeared just tantalisingly beyond her grasp, so that by day, Isabel clung to those dreams so that she might summon images of her baby's gentle, trusting gaze, her tiny, perfect fingers, her silky hair.

She returned to London before the nuns of the Good Shepherd believed she was emotionally robust enough to live independently again. Sister Angelica, who had cared for her most closely, saw a woman who was poleaxed by grief and questioned whether, without help or faith, Isabel had the means to process that grief and eventually move on. Isabel, though, was desperate to leave the Potteries—a place she associated now with rejection and loss—and hastened back to a city big enough to swallow her up and enable her to disappear.

She gave a month's notice on her flat in Westbourne Park, worried that the high rent would consume too much of her precious savings, anxious to survive, if she could, on the modest interest she received from astute investments made long ago by her fastidious father. She moved before the month was up to Shepherd's Bush, where no-one knew her, to a small bedsit in a rambling house which she chose because her room, in an attic at the back, looked out on a scruffy garden redeemed by a weeping willow, which with its long, hanging branches seemed to droop with a wintry sadness that matched her own.

The tree stood at the edge of a small pond overgrown with weeds and clogged with flotsam carried by the wind from the busy roads nearby. This did not mar the pleasure it gave her. She loved it not only for its grace and beauty, but for its association with love forsaken and melancholy, with grief and death. She believed it was the willow that stimulated her feverish dreams, and hoped that its magical powers might awaken her feminine energies and enable her to commune with Lucy.

There were other lessons of the willow, however, of which she was either unaware or chose to ignore; that willow can be used to bring the blessings of the moon and healing into one's life, and that the willow shows us how to bend without breaking, to let go of pain and suffering and take a path towards hope and safety.

She spent Christmas alone, seeing no-one and leaving most of her clothes and possessions in the boxes in which she'd packed them for the move a few weeks earlier. She knew that several friends were looking for her—Matthew, Kevin and Rhona, as well as her agent and vocal coach— but she had left most of their letters unopened in the hallway of the flat in Parkfield Gardens, and for a long time, she avoided places where she might have encountered any of them and gradually lost touch with everyone she'd known during her working life. Before long, her vocal coach went to work abroad and her agent retired to Devon, and with them, two key links with the musical profession were severed.

She missed making music and felt her sole means of expression had been extinguished, consigning her soul to a locked room for which there was no key.

She found ways to pass her time, so that though she was solitary, she was not isolated from the world. She took to roaming the furthest extremities of the underground for days at a time and sought out new parks and gardens to explore on the edges of the city. Sometimes she would sit in on local court cases. On other days she could be found examining scores in the music library at the Barbican, or attending matins or evensong at churches she discovered in the suburbs of west London.

As time passed and she was sure she had been forgotten by those on whom she had turned her back, she ventured into London to hear Sunday services at St Paul's Cathedral or Westminster Abbey, and sometimes—when she was feeling bold or reckless—to attend concerts. She had lost weight and her naturally blonde hair had become streaked with grey, so she hoped she looked different enough to avoid being recognised. Nevertheless, she stayed away from the South Bank and Covent Garden and yet, despite its proximity to the Coliseum, she went occasionally to St Martin's in the Field. On the second anniversary of Lucy's death, she went there to hear a performance of Duruflé's Requiem. It was a work she loved for its vision of serenity in the presence of death, but she'd underestimated the impact the two soloists would have on her fragile spirit: the soprano, an emblem of innocence, the baritone, a symbol of anguish. In the early hours of the next morning, a bemused tourist on his way back to his hotel in Russell Square, found her weeping inconsolably outside the British Museum.

That experience shook her so profoundly that for some time afterwards she left the flat only to shop for essentials and to change the library books on which she depended for distraction. Her eventual re-entry into the outside world was challenging, so much so, she feared she'd developed agoraphobia, but the pull of nature and green spaces drew her back into the open and she was soon once again roaming the streets and parks and public gardens.

In the summer, she began going to cricket matches, something she had done with her father as a child, trips to Old Trafford and Edgbaston being precious opportunities to spend time alone with him. Now she would sit unobtrusively amongst the spectators, keeping half an eye on the action, while doing crosswords and listening to the hum of conversation around her. She enjoyed watching the groundsmen tending to the wicket and the outfield and wished she had some piece of soil to tend. One day, she overhead two men in the crowd chatting about the produce they were harvesting at their allotments at St Dunstan's in Acton. She had visited the church of the same name, with its towering octagonal spire and magnificent organ and had noticed the sign to the allotments nearby. The words of the enthusiastic gardeners, extolling their marrows and runner beans, stirred hankerings for a new pastime.

Next day, she enquired at the council if there were any vacant plots at St Dunstan's and was told there was one available immediately, for which there were no other takers due to its neglected condition. Undeterred, she took it on, hoping the task of reclaiming the ground from weeds and nettles might help restore her to some vestige of living. Impressed by her determination and capacity for hard work, several of the other allotment holders—nearly all of whom were elderly men—let her use their water supply and borrow rakes and spades, and helped her install a shed to store her own tools and supplies. They were touched by her unassuming charm and air of faded gentility and they admired her perseverance, because they knew it would take time for the soil to recover and support new growth.

Her little plot of land gave her purpose and pleasure that sustained and nourished her even before it gave forth crops of fruit and vegetables. When the harvests came, they enabled her to live on a simple diet of home-made soups and salads and fruit puddings, and to make jams and chutneys which she shared with her fellow gardeners.

She enjoyed the long days of summer, liked the solitude of working at St Dunstan's at first light, or late into the evening, and during those times alone she would sometimes imagine Lucy playing alongside her and would talk to her and tell her stories. Some of the older gardeners would bring their grandchildren at weekends and show them how to weed or plant seeds and Isabel would imagine Lucy at the different stages of childhood, that unlike these young visitors, she would never reach: first words, first steps, first day at school, first boyfriend.

She would not describe herself as lonely, since she was never without Lucy. And yet she was always without her and grief held her in its tenacious grip, so that for all the poise she displayed, she was in truth a soul adrift, increasingly unmoored from everything except her grief. She had tried to read the book Sister Angelica had given her, hoping to find words of comfort, even hope, but the very first lines defeated her: *No one ever told me that grief felt so like fear. I am not afraid, but the sensation is like being afraid.* She *was* afraid. Her world had shrunk and with nowhere to go, she could not avoid her anguish.

Paul was never far from her thoughts. They'd had no contact since he left London for Italy in the late summer of 1977, and she had no way of knowing if he was abroad or if he and his wife had come back to Britain. Though he'd left her, as she knew he would, she still clung to her love for him and carried it deep inside her, not wanting to surrender it in case he might one day return, perhaps newly widowed, to seek her out. She pushed away the thought that even if he did, she would be hard to find, so completely had she relinquished her former life and identity.

She missed Rhona more than anyone else and more than she'd expected, given they'd been close for just a matter of weeks but, in that short time, the spirited American had proved a stalwart friend and it was to her only that Isabel wrote after she moved to Shepherd's Bush, though she gave no address or any hint of her whereabouts. Isabel would have liked to see her former colleague, but did not dare expose herself to the pain of reconnecting with someone whose life and career could only serve as a bitter contrast.

One evening in early November, at the end of a day when rain had prevented her working on the allotment, she made her way to Trafalgar Square, hoping to find something to distract her. The galleries were closed and the church of St Martin's was in darkness, and without thinking where she was going, she wandered round the corner towards the Coliseum, at the doors of which she allowed herself to be carried by a throng of people into the crowded foyer. Inside, under the glittering light of the chandeliers, she felt dazed and disoriented, so strange was it to find herself back at the scene of her greatest humiliation. She turned to leave but could see no way through the mass of people arriving for a night at the opera, queuing to collect their tickets and to buy programmes that bore an image of a young woman kneeling in front of a mill wheel.

Jenufa.

A woman wearing a shabby fur coat and red leather gloves pushed past her roughly and stopped to apologise. Isabel brushed away the woman's concern, anxious to find a way out, but just as she saw a path through the now thinning crowd and turned to head towards the doors, the woman caught her arm and thrust something at her.

'Do you need a ticket?' she asked. 'I have a spare. My husband's stuck in Edinburgh.' She raised an eyebrow and sighed. 'The airport's fog-bound apparently.'

Isabel hesitated, not knowing what to do.

'Take it,' the woman said. 'Shame to waste it.'

By now, Isabel was flustered and desperate to get away, but the woman had decided the ticket was to be used.

'Come on,' she said, taking Isabel by the arm. 'Let's go in.'

Isabel felt as if a force far stronger than her was in charge and allowed herself to be led through wide double doors towards a seat in the middle of the stalls. She was relieved that once seated, the woman showed no desire to talk and buried herself in her programme, explaining: 'I like to read the whole synopsis before the show starts so I know what the heck's going on.'

Isabel nodded but said nothing, afraid to look around the packed auditorium, and willing the lights to dim so she could sit in the darkness invisible to anyone who might recognise her. That was the main source of her unease, but the other was the growing dismay she felt at the prospect of sitting through *Jenufa*. She cursed her bad luck that the theatre was not showing an undemanding comic opera but instead a story of betrayal and infanticide she feared would be more harrowing than she could bear. She felt her chest tighten and her breathing become shallow, but was relieved that the woman beside her, having seemed intent on having a companion, took little notice of her other than to cast her the occasional sideways glance.

The curtain rose at last to reveal a stage dominated by a huge mill wheel. As everyday village life went on around it, Jenufa appeared, waiting anxiously to hear if the man she loved had been conscripted, singing of her need to marry him quickly so she could avoid the shame of becoming an unmarried mother in a society that made women pay for such mistakes. Though Isabel dreaded the terrible climax, for the next two and a half hours, she was drawn ineluctably into the emotional undercurrents of the claustrophobic world being depicted on stage. Every character seemed well drawn, every disastrous decision explicable, every relationship as complicated as those in real life. She felt as if she was watching a slice of her own troubled history play out before her. The central relationship between Jenufa and her stepmother, the Kostelnicka, gave the opera its raw power. The older woman, feared and respected by the villagers, was portrayed as fiercely tender, tormented, and authoritative, her decision to kill the child for Jenufa's benefit as moving as it was misguided and terrible. Jenufa's shock at discovering that the tiny corpse—still identifiable as her child—had been locked in deep ice over the winter, seemed so real that Isabel thought her heart would burst.

When the curtain fell at the end of the opera, the audience held its breath before the first applause and cheers broke a heavy silence. Isabel turned to her neighbour and saw that her cheeks were gleaming with tears she was shedding silently but unashamedly, with no attempt to wipe them away or shield her face. Their eyes met in the dark and Isabel recognised someone who had also met pain and loss. She squeezed the woman's arm and whispered a hurried thank you. 'I have to go,' she said. 'Goodbye.'

The people to her left were standing and cheering as the curtain rose to allow the cast to take their bows. Isabel seized the opportunity to clamber past them and make her escape ahead of the rush for the exits she knew would soon follow. She fled through the foyer out into the damp, mild air of the street, stopping in a doorway on the other side of the road, hoping to steady the painful thumping of her heart. She tipped her head back and looked up at the sky, across which she could see clouds sent scudding by a warm, blustery wind. She turned to go, when a woman's voice called her name with a mix of uncertainty and urgency. She looked round and took a step back in surprise as a red-haired woman hurried across the road to join her.

'Oh Isabel,' she gasped. 'I thought it was you when I watched you sit down a few rows in front of me.'

Isabel said nothing and the woman's face creased with concern.

'You do recognise me?' she said carefully.

Isabel nodded, disconcerted to have bumped into Barbara on a night that had already shredded her emotions.

'You haven't heard, have you?' Barbara said.

'Heard what?' asked Isabel, fear rising in her throat and causing her voice to catch.

Barbara closed her eyes briefly, before placing her hand lightly on Isabel's arm.

'It's Paul,' she said quietly. 'He's dead.'

Isabel never knew how she managed to get home that night. Disbelief and desolation overwhelmed her and as soon as she let herself into the flat, she ran to the bathroom and was violently sick. She sat slumped on the floor with her back against the bath until she felt it safe to get up. The flat felt stuffy and she lit a candle and placed it on the sill of the sash window which she opened a few inches. She felt the warm air rush in, as if the wind shared her agitation. She turned off the overhead light and stood looking down at the willow tree, its boughs straining and its leaves whistling in the wind. Exhausted and heart-sick, she sat down on her bed and let out a long, low moan.

Her copy of *Villette* was close at hand, kept in a drawer in a small table beside the bed. She opened the drawer and stared down at the book. She knew all too well that it ended with a storm raging at sea, Lucy's description of it laden with prophecy, as the certainty of a lovers' reunion was supplanted by the threat of disaster. But Paul Eveson had not drowned in a storm at sea. He had died on dry land, in his own home, in a village somewhere in the Cotswolds, drowned in his bath, cut down by a stroke.

Isabel pushed the drawer shut and tried to stand up, but her legs were shaking and as they gave way beneath her, she slumped back onto the bed. Without the energy to undress, she crawled under the bedclothes, turning on her side so she could see the candle flickering like a beacon in the darkness. A watery moon was struggling to reveal itself through the swirling, rain-filled mist and as the wind rattled the ill-fitting sash frame, she thought of the scene in the opera when a gust of wind blew open a window, and gripped by remorse, the Kostelnicka saw 'the face of Death' looking in at her.

Isabel shuddered and turned over onto her other side, at last falling into an unquiet sleep, while the candle burnt quickly and unevenly in the fretful draught.

Alice

We agreed to meet again a couple of weeks later at the Gertie Gitana exhibition.

'Keep looking for anything that might help us,' Steven had urged.

I'd at last finished sorting through the drawers and cubby holes in the parlour and could think of no other obvious places in which to look, when I remembered the scores my mother had mentioned. The box at the bottom of the wardrobe in Imogen's room was only half full, so I emptied its contents onto the bedroom floor with little hope of finding anything of interest.

There were a dozen or so scores, some in good condition, others dog-eared and fragile with their paper covers coming away from the spines. I inspected each one in turn: *The Creation, Elijah*, the Monteverdi Vespers, Requiems by Mozart, Verdi and Faure, Bach's B minor Mass, the *St John* and *St Matthew Passions*, books of motets by Bruckner and Byrd, *Judas Maccabaeus, Jephtha* and *Messiah*.

'Did Imogen have a Bible?' Steven had asked. 'People sometimes keep family papers in their old Bible.'

I'd found no Bible in the house and nor was there one here, but one of the two hard-backed books in the box was a hymnal with Imogen's name inscribed on the inside front cover, followed by the year 1957.

'A hymn book she'd had since she was a young girl,' I thought, handling it carefully.

The cover, though faded to a pale indeterminate rusty colour, was still reasonably robust and only the corners were shabby and beginning to fray, suggesting the hymnal had been well looked after. I hesitated, but judging it would not fall apart, I held it upside down by the spine and shook it gently, and was rewarded by a flutter of papers settling on the floor on which I was kneeling: a handful of small, square, black and white photographs and the order of service for a funeral at Lincoln Cathedral.

Ralph Liddell, 3 November, 1938–17 June, 2015
Organist and Director of Music
Lincoln Cathedral, 1965-2005

I didn't recognise the name, so I set the card aside and looked first at the photographs.

A young woman alone, sitting on a high bank, her hands on her knees, smiling nervously at the camera, an inscription on the back confirming it was Imogen.

Two young women sitting together on the same bank, Imogen in much the same position as before but this time with Isabel sitting alongside her, laughing at the camera as she held her hair off her face to reveal eyes as large and expressive as those sketched on the covers of the song sheet.

A young man in a smart suit, leaning against a car, one leg crossed over the ankle of the other, arms folded.

The same young man with a smiling Imogen, posing proudly for the camera, her arm linked in his.

And this time, the young man standing between the two sisters, Isabel, head down, turned away from the camera, Imogen looking up at the man with an expression of uncertainty on her face.

A note on the back of the photo of the man on his own said this was Ralph. His hair flopped untidily on his forehead, and something about his smile suggested he was pleased with himself—or perhaps with his car, which was a gleaming Morris Minor with its soft roof rolled back to reveal pale leather seats.

I laid the five photographs side by side on the carpet before me and peered at the smooth, bright-eyed faces, frozen in time; imagined them growing lined and worn as old age eroded the bloom and optimism of youth. Until death froze them for ever.

But was Isabel dead? According to Steven, there was no record of this.

I sighed and turned to the only other hard-backed book in the collection. It was a vocal score of the Brahms Requiem, its black cover in pristine condition, the signature in stylish copperplate on the title page that of Ralph Liddell. Who was he I wondered, looking down again at the photographs. I turned to the opening movement and ran my fingers over the staves, recalling the first time I ever heard this work. For my thirteenth birthday, Imogen had taken me to a concert at the Victoria Hall to hear the work performed by an orchestra, choir and soloists from Munich. It was that performance more than any other I recall during my teenage years that fuelled dreams of a career in music other than *The Sound of Music* and *Mary Poppins*. Everything about that performance had seemed perfect: the plush, sumptuously warm glow of the orchestral sound, the rich and radiant tone of the choir, the urgent baritone yearning to know the measure of his days; the statuesque soprano whose voice mesmerised me with a quality of tenderness that was not only moving but strangely consoling.

As I turned the pages of the score until I came to the fifth movement, I could still see her in my mind's eye, still remember how throughout the first four movements she'd sat and waited for her moment, occasionally glancing sideways at her baritone companion and up at the conductor, as if looking for reassurance. At the end of the fourth movement, as the chorus sat down with a gentle rustle, she rose to her feet. During the long orchestral introduction she stood tall and still, the earlier hint of insecurity replaced by an inner calm that seemed to shine through her, until the moment when at last her voice soared over the swelling accompaniment.

Pain and death; sorrow and separation; consolation and hope. With its focus on comforting the living, I still love this Requiem above all others, and even as a callow teenager, I was astonished that music could suggest so much hope and solace, while acknowledging the awfulness of death.

I flicked absent-mindedly through the pages, casting my mind back almost twenty-five years to that concert, recalling the rapt look on Imogen's face when we stood at the end to applaud. I was still wondering about Ralph Liddell and his relationship to the sisters, when something caught my eye. I stopped and turned back the pages until I found it, a pale blue envelope tucked between the pages of the fourth movement. It was addressed to Isabel Grey at Flat 6, 57 Parkfield Gardens, London W11, and to my surprise, the plain, precise handwriting was Imogen's, but the address had been crossed through with a thick black marker pen and, in the same pen, someone had written in uneven capital letters: *Not known at this address. Return to sender.* I turned the envelope over and saw that Imogen had written the Vicarage Road address on the flap, as if she feared the London address would no longer reach Isabel and this was a necessary precaution.

I heard my breathing quicken as I eased the letter out of the envelope. When I unfolded the sheets and prepared to read it, the first thing I noticed was the date, 30 June, 2015. I glanced back at the order of service of Ralph Liddell's funeral: Monday, 29 June, 2015, at Lincoln Cathedral.

Something had prompted Imogen to write to her sister the day after Ralph's funeral.

Imogen

Imogen let the envelope slide off her lap onto the bench beside her. From a shady corner, out of the heat of the late morning sun, she surveyed the waste of her garden, neglected throughout the spring as her health and strength began to desert her, and now an unsightly confusion of tangled undergrowth and overblown blooms.

She picked up the envelope and studied it, recalling the effort it had cost her to compose its contents, and the unexpected remorse and contrition that had seemed to propel her across the street to stuff it into the red post box set within the wall that bordered the graveyard opposite the house. Afterwards, she had sat watching at her bedroom window, waiting for the post van to make its midday collection, anxious to know that the letter was on its way to London, allowing her to feel that she had at last made atonement, even if the recipient might deem it too late.

But here it was, a little crumpled but unread, brought back by the post office because the addressee was no longer at the address. Imogen could not blame Isabel for not telling her where she could now be reached. No doubt she preferred not to be found by a sister who had turned her back on her when she most needed her understanding and compassion.

Imogen grimaced, recognising that neither quality had been much in evidence between siblings who, from an early age, had been competitors, not allies. Made so, she believed, by a mother who compared them constantly and who with unkind consistency found her older daughter wanting in all the characteristics on which she placed such store: looks, disposition, charm, talent. She had sent them both to Sunday school where they were taught that comparisons with others rarely promote goodness; that God told Jacob and his wives to find their worth in Him, but instead, the two sisters fell into a feud of jealousy and resentment. But Evadne Grey had openly favoured Isabel, her second child, the one whose birth had been straightforward, who was kind and sweet-tempered, who sang like a bird almost before she could talk.

Imogen could not accuse Isabel of pride or arrogance— she had to admit that Isabel was too good-natured for that —but endless unfavourable comparisons with her younger sister had created a rival not a friend.

And then of course there was Ralph, whose commitment to Imogen would surely mollify her mother's ill-concealed disappointment in her and with whom Imogen could find a place of significance. Ralph was Imogen's 'discovery'—she had met him at church during a time when Isabel stopped going—and she hoped to keep him to herself but, to her dismay, on his first encounter with Isabel, Ralph seemed as taken with her as Imogen had once thought he was with her. Imogen became the one who cared the most and longed the hardest, while Ralph trailed after Isabel like a devoted dog, undemanding and patient, impervious to her polite disinterest.

No sooner had Ralph become persuaded of Isabel's superior charms than she left him behind to begin her training at the Royal College of Music. Like a moth whose wings had been scorched by settling too long on a naked lightbulb, he'd seemed wounded by the experience, his confidence undermined. Imogen recognised this and saw a chance to rekindle their former attachment. Tentatively, they resumed their earlier closeness and, though on her occasional trips home from London Isabel avoided him, Imogen recognised that Ralph was different, subdued and restless, dissatisfied with his lot, and with her, too, she feared. He was stagnating in Sandleheath, he said, and before long, he left the Potteries for a job in the north east.

And now he was dead.

The journey to Lincoln had seemed never-ending: two tedious changes and several hours on noisy trains with no air conditioning, followed by a long wait at the station for a taxi to deliver her to Ralph's final resting place. The sunlight dazzled her eyes as she peered at the other mourners making their way towards the cathedral entrance. No one greeted her or consoled her. She felt old and insignificant, a forgotten relic of Ralph's past. In her heavy wool suit and smart shoes just a shade too narrow, she was overdressed and uncomfortable. Tired, hot, and slightly nauseous, she summoned the strength to endure this necessary ritual.

An usher handed her the order of service and she took a seat on the end of a pew so that she could observe the family as they processed up the central aisle. The great church resounded with the lachrymose swell of the organ and she looked up, hoping to catch sight of the organist tucked away in the organ loft. Was he young and lonely, separated from family and friends as Ralph had been so fatefully fifty-five years earlier?

She fumbled in her oversized handbag for a handkerchief and her eye was caught by a token of comfort she'd brought with her. Alone in her pew, and unnoticed, she took out a battered brown envelope addressed to her, Miss Imogen Grey, at number 1 Vicarage Road, Sandleheath. Now torn on three of its four sides and with a square cut out where the stamp had been, (requisitioned by a cousin for his embryonic collection), it contained a large, beautifully preserved postcard. An ornate, embossed border framed a garish pink rose with bright green foliage and the words, *With Love, dear Sweetheart, on your Birthday*. She turned the card over and gazed at the inscription: *With Best Wishes to Imogen xxxxxxxxxxxxxxx* (15 kisses), from *Ralph xxxxxxx* (7 kisses). Twenty-two kisses—she knew he had simply filled up the space available—but how she had rejoiced in them as a sign of his love for her and how those inky little crosses had warmed and cheered her during his absence.

The cathedral was beginning to fill up and she looked around and studied her surroundings. As a young woman, a lifetime ago, she had assumed she would often visit this celebrated example of medieval architecture; now, at the end of her life, she was seeing it for the first time, and an invisible stranger was playing laments for a man she had loved and who now lay in a purple-draped coffin just a few yards away. She turned to the order of service with its stark front cover:

> *Ralph Liddell, 3 November, 1938–17 June, 2015*
> *Organist and Director of Music*
> *Lincoln Cathedral, 1965-2005*

A man's voice summoning the congregation to stand signalled the arrival of the family. Imogen steeled herself and turned to face Ralph's widow and her children and grandchildren. Thoughts of Margaret Ellison had vexed her for years until at last she had lost the energy to harbour such envy for a woman she didn't know. Even curiosity in time had faded. Nothing had prepared her for this sweet-faced woman in a wheel chair, bent and disfigured by arthritis, mild and acquiescent in the care of a teenaged grandson.

The family's slow procession through the church was accompanied by the choir of lay clerks and boy trebles singing music that Ralph had loved more than any other, the fourth movement of the Brahms Requiem, its flowing tempo, he'd always said, creating a sense of deep repose and peace.

How lovely are thy dwellings fair O lord of Hosts,
My soul ever longeth and fainteth for the blest courts of the
Lord

my heart and flesh do cry to the living God,
Blest are they that in Thy house are dwelling,
they ever praise Thee oh Lord

The man who gave the address had clearly known Ralph well and she found herself drawn into the story he was telling of Ralph's life. Though much of it was a mystery to her, some of it she knew well. She had been part of those humble beginnings in Sandleheath. Their fathers had been schoolmasters and the two families had worshipped in the same church. The speaker recounted how Ralph had come to the Cathedral as Assistant Organist in 1963 and recalled how full of purpose he was and yet how lonely. He said nothing of the girlfriend he had left behind in Sandleheath who was also lonely, but prepared to wait until they could afford to be together. Instead, he spoke of Margaret Ellison, daughter of the Dean and the woman who was the love of Ralph's life, the friend and wife who had faithfully supported him through almost fifty years of marriage. Ralph's life, he said, had been a mix of devotion to music and to family.

Her attention wandered and she recalled how he had told her their relationship was over. What shocked her—but at the same time seemed strangely impressive—was the fact there had been no pretence at any wrestling with conscience. He had been kind and gentle but straightforward. Yes, he was genuinely sorry to hurt and disappoint her, he had loved and would always love her as a friend, but this woman was his destiny, he was sure of it, and marry her he must.

Yet again, she had come off second best and must endure the indignity of rejection. Recalling this now, she realised she had never overcome that sense of not being good enough. She had never forgotten Ralph or the promise of happiness he had once represented, and until today she had sometimes thought that if Isabel had not unwittingly disrupted and tainted their romantic journey or if Ralph had not gone away without her, they might have achieved the happy union that had once seemed possible.

In the pulpit the speaker was drawing to a close, inviting the congregation to stand to sing the next hymn, *Dear Lord and Father of mankind, Forgive our foolish ways; Re-clothe us in our rightful mind, In purer lives thy service find.* As choir and congregation raised their voices to the sweet, simple tune, the words of the hymn, with their powerful sincerity, seemed to pierce her heart and vanquish the grudges and grievances that for so long had fuelled her estrangement from Isabel. As the music reverberated around the vaulted pillars, Imogen realised she had wasted her life in holding onto a resentment and a fantasy.

Alice

Steven and I met at the theatre soon after the exhibition went up. A panel at one end was devoted to photographs and materials from the theatre's own production about Gertie Gitana, but the rest focussed exclusively on the real Gertie. The theatre archive contained a large number of her photographs and posters, and Tony and Steven had put them together with captions which described her life and long career. Steven talked me through the display, but allowed me to read and absorb it at my own pace.

> *While Nellie Dean seems a song that should rightly be sung by a man, in Gertie's rendition a young girl recalls idyllic trysts, and the endearments whispered by the boy she loves. A report in the Sentinel of Isabel Grey's performance said: 'Resplendent in a cornflower blue dress identical to one that Gertie herself once wore, Isabel Grey entranced the audience with her warm personality and a singing style that perfectly captured the sweet, childlike voice for which Gertie was famous and which perfectly suited her signature tune, Nellie Dean.'*

'Even in wigs that didn't really suit her,' I said, 'she looks lovely.'

'She was lovely.'

A man's voice over my shoulder made me jump and I turned round to see who had spoken those words with such feeling. A wiry, cheery looking man wearing a tweed flat cap and a matching muffler was edging himself forward to take a closer look at the display.

'She was my cousin,' he said.

I felt my eyes widen—in surprise at the unexpected connection and alarm at the use of the past tense.

'Really?' I said. 'I didn't know her but her sister, Imogen, was a friend of my father's and became my godmother.'

'Ah yes,' he said. 'Imogen.'

He paused.

'She used to help me choose books from the library when I was a little lad.'

I held out my hand.

'I'm Alice,' I said, 'and this is Steven. He's put the exhibition together.'

'Les Morrison. Pleased to meet you,' he said.

I looked at Steven and he gave an imperceptible nod of encouragement.

'Mr Morrison...'

'Les,' he corrected.

'Les,' I smiled. 'I'd love to know more about Isabel. Would you have time for a cup of tea and a chat?'

'I've all the time in the world, my duck,' he said. 'Or at least until the missus stops by to pick me up on her way back from the hairdresser.'

Steven led us to a table in a corner of the foyer where there was a small café and went to the counter to order. I watched Les take off his cap and muffler and lay them neatly on the table, and guessed he was in his mid- or late-sixties. He saw me studying him and smiled.

'I was ten years younger than Imogen,' he explained, 'and only nine or so when Isabel went off to London.'

'My father knew Imogen through the library,' I said. 'He worked with her for a while, but I've only just discovered she had a younger sister.'

Les looked surprised.

'I'm interested in her,' I said, 'because I'm living in what was their family home.' I hesitated. 'And I'm a singer, too, like Isabel.'

At that point, Steven came back carrying a tray laden with mugs of tea and slices of carrot cake, which he set out on the table, before returning the tray to a pile near the counter.

Les took a sip of tea and tore a corner off his cake.

'I heard Imogen died,' he said, as Steven sat down to join us.

'You weren't at her funeral, were you?' I said, sure I'd never seen him before.

'Sadly not,' he said. 'I've been living in Glasgow these last thirty five years or so. Once we both retired last year, the wife and I decided to move back to the Potteries.' He took a mouthful of cake. 'Moved into a little place in Sackville Street last September.'

'And what about Isabel?' I asked cautiously. 'Do you know where she is now?'

He shook his head, and I was struck by how perplexed he looked.

'What happened to her?' I asked gently. 'Do you have any idea?'

'Something happened, that's for sure,' he said. 'One minute she's a singer in London; next minutes she's gone.'

I nodded, hoping to encourage him.

'I'd not long left home and moved away,' he went on, 'but that Christmas, when I came home for the holidays, I heard my mam and dad talking about her when they thought I couldn't hear them.'

He shook his head again.

'I asked my mam,' he said, 'but she'd never say, and she and my dad are long gone, so there's no asking them now.'

I sighed and said nothing, but Steven, who'd been listening closely, asked:

'Can you think of anyone, Les, who might remember Isabel and know what became of her?'

Les put down his mug and frowned, but after a long silence, his face brightened.

'There is someone you might ask,' he said, looking at us both. 'I remember hearing Mam whispering something to Dad about the organist at Holy Trinity Church.'

'Can you remember his name, Les?' I whispered, crossing my fingers under the table.

He shook his head sadly.

'I can't,' he said. 'And anyway, I heard he died last year.'

He frowned again and began thrumming his finger tips on the table, as if trying to summon something else from the depths of his memory.

Go on, I urged him silently, not wanting to break his concentration. After what seemed an age, he slapped his palm on the table and beamed.

'I can remember his wife's name, though,' he said. 'Same as my missus.'

He paused, as if for effect.

'Betty.'

The next morning, I walked over to the church, to find out when Betty would next be in. I was studying the noticeboard in the porch for clues as to when the flowers might normally be changed, when the door opened and a woman came out who I recognised as Eileen, the other flower arranger. She looked at me suspiciously as if she thought I was up to no good and I felt momentarily thrown. She narrowed her eyes and tightened the belt on her coat before starting to walk away from me.

'Excuse me!' I called after her.

She turned.

'I'm looking for Betty. Do you know when she'll next be here, please?'

The woman stopped briefly before setting off again.

'She's there now, waiting for the florist,' she called over her shoulder. 'He should have been here over an hour ago.'

'Thank you,' I called after her.

I pushed at the heavy door and made my way into the church. It was empty save for a woman sitting in a pew at the front, who turned round as she heard the door close behind me. She stood up, expecting to see the florist, and I could see her take a moment to register who I was. I walked towards her and she smiled in recognition.

'Alice, isn't it?' she said.

'Hello, Betty,' I nodded. 'Happy New Year!'

'And to you, my dear. What brings you here?'

'I was hoping you might be able to give me some information,' I said.

She raised an eyebrow in surprise.

'Well, I will if I can,' she said, clearly intrigued. 'Come and sit down.'

She hurriedly moved the paperback she'd been reading and as I sat down next to her, I smiled to see it was an American crime novel with a lurid cover.

'Elmore Leonard,' I said. 'He's one of my favourites.'

She smiled conspiratorially.

'I never feel it's quite right to bring him into church, though.' She paused. 'But he keeps me company.'

I nodded, remembering that she had lost her husband.

'I wanted to ask you about my godmother's sister, Isabel,' I said.

Her eyes widened in surprise but I felt emboldened to go on.

'I didn't know of her existence until I moved into Imogen's house and she seems to have disappeared, so I'm trying to find out what happened to her.'

Betty looked puzzled and shook her head.

'And you think I can help you?' she asked.

'Possibly,' I said, cautiously, realising I might be about to reveal information about Isabel that Imogen had kept quiet.

'The last news I have of her is that she intended to come back to stay with Imogen in Vicarage Road in October 1977, but there's no sign that she came or any indication of what happened to her after that.'

'October 1977, you say?' she asked carefully.

'Yes, that's right. 14th October to be precise. I met a cousin of Imogen and Isabel's last night and, though he has no idea what happened to Isabel, he heard his parents whispering about the organist here perhaps knowing something. Your late husband, I think?'

She nodded.

'My John,' she said. 'He was the organist then.'

'Do you remember anything about that time that might be relevant?' I asked.' Something he might have told you?'

She was plucking at the hem of her long cardigan and I could tell that she was lost in thought.

'My youngest son was born in October 1977,' she said at last, 'so I was away from church for a while and relied on John for news.'

'Did you know Isabel had a baby around that time?' I asked.

She gasped and put her hands to her mouth.

'So it was her then,' she said. 'John swore for certain that it was.'

'What do you mean?' I asked, my voice disappearing to a whisper.

'He came home one night quite shaken up. I remember it because our baby was only a week old and I was not long out of hospital, and it was the first night I'd been in the house alone with the two other children and the baby. He'd been to the church to practice for a wedding the next day. The bride and groom were going to exit to Mendelssohn's 'Wedding March' but the bride wanted to walk in to 'The Arrival of the Queen of Sheba' and he found it a tricky piece to play well.'

I smiled.

'There are a lot of notes!'

'He said that after he'd finished practising, he spent a little while tidying up in the song room, before leaving through the vestry door, the way he'd let himself into the church. He locked up and walked around the side of the church, when ahead of him he saw the young vicar, Reverend Kyle, come out of the porch at the main entrance with a woman, who he led down the path.'

Betty closed her eyes and shook her head, and I held my breath.

'John said the woman was holding something in her arms—a small bundle. He thought it might be a baby but he couldn't be sure. But he was sure that the woman was Isabel Grey.'

I gasped.

'So, she did come, after all.'

'It seems so, dearie,' Betty said sadly. 'At the time I was sure John was mistaken. I certainly knew nothing about a baby. Imogen hadn't spoken of her sister for a long while, and never did again as far as I'm aware, so if it was Isabel, where she went after that, who knows.'

'What happened to the vicar?' I asked.

Her face lit up.

'He was very special,' she said. 'He was handsome, too, though it feels wrong to say that in church!'

I laughed.

'I'm sure God won't mind.'

She nudged me playfully and chuckled.

'His family came from British Guiana and settled in the Potteries. Benjamin was only here temporarily, standing in for the regular vicar who was ill.' She sighed. 'By the time I started coming to church again, he'd left and gone to London to be Chaplain to an order of nuns. Our Lady, Star of the Sea. Stella Maris.'

As I walked home, my head was racing. Yet more unanswered questions, but if I could find the Reverend Kyle, he might be able to provide some answers; might know where Isabel and her child went.

A child, I realised, who would now be the same age as me.

Alice

Matthew Markham showed me into a sitting room on the first floor where a small table was set with tea and biscuits. We sat down on either side of the fire and as he handed me my tea I looked round and thought how homely the room was in contrast to the formal public rooms I'd seen when I came a year ago.

Matthew saw my expression and smiled.

'I entertain downstairs and live up here,' he said, 'so this is where I can let my hair down and make myself comfortable.'

'It's lovely,' I said, admiring the understated elegance that had faded without becoming shabby. 'It's a beautiful house.'

'It is,' he agreed, 'though it's far too big for me. I'm lucky to have an excellent housekeeper to keep the place running. If she left, I think I'd sell up and escape to a cottage in the country!'

'Would you like to do that?' I asked.

He pulled a face.

'I'm not sure I'd adapt very well after so long living in the centre of London—and I'd miss the opera and the ballet, which are right on my doorstep here.'

I nodded, knowing how difficult I was finding the change I'd made.

He was watching me closely and, though at first I made a play of choosing a biscuit, I looked up and met his gaze. He was a strikingly handsome man, despite his advanced years, and I imagined he would have been regarded as highly eligible when he was in his prime.

'So,' he said at last, 'tell me about you. I was sorry to hear about your troubles. I've always been a huge fan.'

I summarised the story of my life over the last year, but when I got to the reason for my visit, I hesitated, unsure how to broach it, for fear I was mistaken about the link between the woman in the painting and Isabel.

He saw my discomfort and came to my help.

'In your letter, you said you were trying to trace a family member who had been a successful singer. That was it, wasn't it?'

I nodded.

'When I came here for the first night party last year,' I said, 'I couldn't help admiring the Gainsborough portrait in the Music Room.'

'Ah yes,' he said quietly.

'Your friends, Ted and Elsie, said she reminded you of a singer you had once known....'

I stopped, struck by a sudden change in his demeanour which made him look old and dejected. Though I disliked the thought of causing him distress, I guessed I was on the right track.

'While I was sorting through stuff my godmother left behind,' I said, 'I found press cuttings about a sister I didn't know she had. A soprano called Isabel Grey, who sang the Marschallin at Covent Garden wearing a costume identical to the dress worn by your Gainsborough lady.' I paused. 'The resemblance was unmistakable.'

He put down his cup and I saw that his hands were shaking.

'I've come to ask if you knew Isabel Grey and if you know what happened to her?'

He was leaning on one arm of the chair, his head turned away from me, with his hands pressed together as if in prayer, resting under his chin. When he looked up, his pale eyes were clouded with regret.

'I'm sorry,' I said. 'I can see the question upsets you.'

He shook his head and placed his folded hands in his lap.

'It's not the question, as such, that upsets me,' he said. 'It's the fact that I don't have an answer. Yes, I knew Isabel a very long time ago, but I have no idea where she is or what became of her. The last time I saw her she was on stage in *Ariadne auf Naxos* and that was almost forty years ago.'

He stopped and seemed to be trying to compose himself. When he spoke again, his voice was husky, the words swallowed.

'She simply disappeared.'

'What do you mean?' I whispered.

'You say you found press cuttings about her,' he said, pouring me another cup of tea. 'Did you read any reviews of the first night of *Ariadne*?'

'I did,' I said. 'The ones I saw were pretty grim.'

'Indeed,' he replied. 'The role was beyond her; something had happened to her voice.' He paused. 'To her.'

'I guessed that,' I said, recalling what she'd said in her letters to Imogen.

He shook his head.

'I saw very little of her at that time, I'm afraid. She was always very private, but I believe she was involved with someone. I never asked who he was. When I went to her dressing room on the first night, I could tell she was dreading the performance, but more than that, she seemed lost and unhappy.'

I wondered whether I should tell him about Paul Eveson, and decided that if I wanted him to be candid with me, I had to tell him what I knew.

'She told her sister that she'd been in a relationship with an actor called Paul Eveson.' I hesitated. 'She had his baby, but he was married and he moved to Italy with his wife.'

Matthew's pained expression told me he had not known of this.

'So, the last time you saw her was the first night? When was that?' I asked.

'The first night was at the end of June 1977, but I went to another performance later in the run, to see if she'd steadied herself and got on top of the role.'

'And had she?' I asked.

He shook his head.

'No. By now, it was July and she'd sung four or five performances since the first night and the reports I'd heard suggested she was somehow getting through the show, but no more than that. It can't have helped that the Bacchus and the Zerbinetta were tremendous—Isabel would, I'm sure, have felt inadequate by comparison. I went to the penultimate performance.' He closed his eyes. 'What happened was shocking.'

I waited for him to go on, hardly daring to breathe.

'Even in the Prologue—when Ariadne has relatively little to do, compared with the Composer and Zerbinetta—you could tell she was struggling. I feared for her in the second part, and presumably, she felt the same and decided she wasn't going to put herself through the ordeal, because she didn't reappear.'

I gasped.

'The interval was much longer than usual and I suspected something was amiss. It was forty-five minutes before they got the audience back into the theatre and made an announcement from the stage that Isabel was indisposed and someone else would be singing the part.'

He stood up and went to stand at the window.

'I didn't stay for the rest of the performance. I was too concerned about her, and I went round to see if I could do anything to help. I guessed something was badly wrong, but when I got to the stage-door, I bumped into the Company Manager. She told me that Isabel had disappeared—left the theatre without telling anybody.'

I gasped again.

'Poor woman.'

Matthew sat down again and I could see that the colour had drained from his face.

'And to think she was pregnant as well,' he said. 'I had no idea.'

'Pregnant and afraid,' I replied.

'I looked for her, of course,' he said, 'but I never found her. I don't believe anyone did. I asked around about her. I wrote to her and tried to reach her by telephone. I even called several times at her home in Parkfield Gardens, but she was never there. A few months' later, just before Christmas, I went again and this time, another tenant told me she'd moved out, but had not left a forwarding address.'

We were both silent. I was thinking about Imogen's letter to her sister, sent to an address Isabel had left almost four decades earlier.

'I know she went back to Sandleheath in October 1977, hoping her sister would take her and the baby for a while,' I said. 'But I don't know where she went after that. It's possible that a young clergyman may have helped her. I'm trying to track him down to see if he knows anything that might help us find her.'

Matthew looked dubious.

'Do you think she wants to be found after all this time?' he asked.

'I don't know,' I said, 'but I'm living in a house that, if she is still alive, would rightfully be hers. I feel I should try to find her,' I said. 'It seems only right that I do that.'

He nodded and leant forward towards me.

'And will you tell me if you do?' he asked.

I reached out and took his hands in mine.

'I will. I promise.'

He stood up and smiled.

'Would you like to see the Gainsborough lady again before you go?' he asked.

'I'd love to,' I said, and followed him down the wide, winding staircase and along the passage to the Music

Room. The door was ajar but as Matthew pushed it open, he stopped.

'You could ask Kevin what he knows or remembers,' he said.

'Kevin?' I asked, my hopes lifting.

'Yes, Kevin Stevens. He was Isabel's favourite dresser and he worked with her whenever he was available. Singers love him: he looks after them. He's still working, here and there. Last thing I heard he was doing *Les Mis* on Shaftesbury Avenue.'

'Thanks,' I said. 'I will,' and I made a mental note of the name.

The Music Room was in darkness and when Matthew switched on the lights, I could see the painting more clearly than on my first viewing, when the lighting had been dimmed. We walked towards the painting in silence and stood side by side to study it and, once again, I marvelled at its captivating sense of freshness.

'I remember when Isabel made her first appearance in that dress,' Matthew said. 'The audience gasped. It was so beautiful; it took your breath away. For me, it was as if the woman in this painting had been brought to life. It was remarkable.'

'So you'd seen the painting before you saw Isabel in *Rosenkavalier*?' I asked.

'Oh, yes.'

'And had Isabel seen it, too?'

'She had.'

Matthew walked towards the stack of chairs against the wall and I realised he wanted to sit down.

'Let me,' I said, and I lifted two folding chairs and set them down where we'd been standing.

'Thank you, my dear. My old legs ache more than ever these days.'

He eased himself onto a chair and I sat down beside him, hoping he'd continue with the story of the painting.

'I'd got to know the designer of *Rosenkavalier*—he advised me on colour schemes and furnishings for the bedrooms—and on one of the occasions he came here, he told me about an extraordinary stately home in the New Forest at which he'd been working on a television adaptation of a Wilkie Collins novel. He said the owners were as poor as church mice, the roof was leaking and the whole place was falling into disrepair, but he said the wealth on the walls was staggering. This is where he found the Gainsborough. He took some photographs and told me he planned to use it as the inspiration for one of the Marschallin's costumes.'

'So, when did you buy it?' I asked.

'Oh, many years later—long after Isabel disappeared,' he said. 'Sadly, she never saw it here.'

'So she saw it in its original setting then?'

'That's right. Before she started rehearsals, I suggested we drove down to the New Forest to see it. At that time, the house was open to the public for a few days each summer—a desperate attempt to raise some cash—so we spent a weekend down there and went to see it together.'

He sighed.

'It was one of the happiest times of my life.'

He saw me raise an eyebrow in surprise and shook his head.

'I admit it, Alice, I loved Isabel and I pursued her, but to no avail. She was never interested in me as anything other than a friend and, God bless her, she never led me on or gave me false hope.'

He frowned.

'I always had the feeling she was waiting for someone.'

We fell silent again until he continued the story.

'But we had a wonderful time down there. She really loved the Forest, its pretty villages and sleepy way of life. After we'd been to see the house, we drove a short distance away and settled ourselves on a patch of grass by the edge of one of the lakes in Beaulieu. We had a picnic and were there for hours, watching families mingle with the ponies and small children paddling in the shallows.'

'It sounds idyllic,' I said.

'It was, but it seems a lifetime away now.'

He sighed and closed his eyes and I guessed he was remembering that sunlit day.

'I remember her saying that as a child she'd loved Captain Marryat's book *Children of the New Forest* and being there, in the countryside he had used as the backdrop, gave her a real sense of connection.'

He paused.

'She loved the painting, too, and was excited at the prospect of being transformed to look like the woman Gainsborough had captured so strikingly.'

'Who was the woman, do you know?' I asked.

Matthew shook his head.

'There's some dispute amongst art historians as to who she was, but the family said she was Lady Mary Anne Bly, who was married off by her parents against her will and later disappeared.'

'Oh, no!' I said. 'That's too horribly prescient for words.'

'I know,' Matthew said sadly, 'but we didn't know that at the time, of course.'

'How did you come to buy the painting?' I asked.

'In the early 1980s the owners were on their uppers and started selling off their assets. This, and five or six other paintings, were sold at Sotheby's.'

'Ah, I see,' I said.

'Two disappeared women for the price of one,' he said bleakly. 'But somehow, having this likeness of them here means they've not completely vanished.'

'Nor been forgotten, I can tell,' I said, touching his arm lightly.

'No, indeed.'

He stood up.

'My parents would have loved this portrait but they were both gone before I bought it.' He laughed. 'It sounds like something out of a Henry James novel, but my buttoned-up English father married a stunning American heiress called Odile and it's her wealth that made all of this— including the painting—possible.'

I stood up and followed him to the door, where he stopped to let me through ahead of him, but before he turned the lights off, he looked back at the painting.

'Unlike the couples in many of Henry James's stories, however, theirs was a true love match.'

He switched off the lights.

'Not all of us are so fortunate.'

'Disappeared—left the theatre without telling anybody.'

I replayed Matthew's words in my head, wanting to know what drove Isabel to do this at the point when she'd got through almost the full run of performances—difficult though they must have been—and the end was in sight. Something, I was sure, must have happened that day to tip her over the edge.

I looked out of the train window and sighed. Given my own troubled year on stage, I could appreciate that someone in Isabel's predicament might make such a decision in a moment of desperation or madness.

And that would be hard to come back from.

It was dark now and there was nothing to see of the towns and countryside through which we were passing, but still I stared through the window, and in the darkness on the other side of the glass, I saw my own misadventures playing out before me.

After *Hansel and Gretel*, my next engagement was Valencienne, the coquettish wife of an officious, elderly ambassador—a role that had previously suited me well—in *The Merry Widow* at the Met. I loved New York but was in no mood for its bustle and its constant clamour. My lowered spirits craved tranquillity and privacy, but in my serviceable but soulless apartment there was no respite from neighbours within and without the building, whose incontinent lives seemed to leak into my solitude.

And thus sleeplessness and exhaustion were added to my list of woes.

I had never before sung in such an enormous theatre, and critics who said I seemed lost and ill at ease, that my voice sounded tentative and tremulous, were right. My experience with Gretel had left me bruised and afraid and my confidence was being steadily chipped away as if by a stonemason who was not yet finished with me. Even if I had been at my best, my voice was simply not big enough to carry across the cavernous expanses of that auditorium and at times I feared I was barely audible. I looked at my reflection in the train window and saw a performance that should have been vivacious and flirtatious but was instead hopelessly innocuous, and I wondered where I had gone.

I was not helped by the production, which would have looked old-fashioned in 1950, let alone 2016. An opera that should exude charm and fizz was more depressing than irrepressible and, in a show with a waltz in practically every scene, most of the cast couldn't dance a step—so I at least redeemed myself there. I recalled one critic saying that he prayed for symptoms of appendicitis—anything to get him out of the theatre and away from such a misfiring and un-merry performance.

It was a long season—nine performances spread over four weeks—and I was lonely. I took solitary walks in Central Park, wandered aimlessly through galleries and museums, and drank coffee in friendly bookshops, but I was out of sorts and could enjoy little of what the city had to offer. I heard hardly anything from Christian. My efforts to keep in touch felt brittle and forced and his tardy, lack-lustre responses to texts and emails served to further diminish my self-esteem.

I looked forward to going home, to being back in familiar surroundings, especially my own flat, but I was also returning to a production of *Ariadne auf Naxos* and I feared danger was lying in wait for me in a role that is nothing if not a celebration of coloratura. I feared my performance would be more of a disappointment than a celebration and that my voice and my spirit were no longer able to convey extrovert young women living and loving with blithe abandon.

The rehearsal period for *Ariadne* was the most gruelling I'd ever experienced, but at least I didn't have to humiliate myself daily in front of Christian as I had in *Hansel and Gretel*. I was still hankering after him, but by now he had almost completely disappeared from my life, his determined silence only serving to make me want him more. Rehearsals were punishing, not only because of my excruciating inability to negotiate without mishap the stratospheric demands of music I could once have sung in my sleep, but because I quickly realised the production was set to be a flop.

One consolation was that Marie was in London, rehearsing for a production of *The Marriage of Figaro* and, though our free times rarely overlapped, it was a boon to have her staying with me for a couple of weeks. One evening, when neither of us were called the next morning, we talked until late and, fuelled by more wine than was good for me, I held forth about everything in my life about which I was dissatisfied.

'I tell you Marie, this production is one of those 'someone should have said no' occasions.'

She laughed.

'For a start,' I said, counting off my grievances one by one on my fingers, 'the long final duet should not seem long; the comic interludes should be, well, comic; Bacchus should look and sound like a Greek God not a Friesian bull.' I paused. 'And 'Großmächtige Prinzessin'—all ten terrifying minutes of it—should hold no terrors for Zerbinetta, whose coloratura throughout should be sparklingly accurate and perfectly delivered.'

I folded my fingers away and sighed, but before Marie could get a word in, I babbled on.

'And can you believe it,' I said. 'How ironic is this? Ariadne and Bacchus—both of whom are married—are carrying on a shamelessly untroubled affair, while Zerbinetta—me—is going around with a face like a smacked arse. Temperamentally speaking, I should be playing Ariadne. I'm the one who can't forget.'

I laughed bitterly and was about to take another swig of wine when Marie leant across the sofa and took the glass from my hand. Putting it to one side, she said quietly: 'Enough, Alice.'

I wasn't drunk, but her unexpected intervention served to sober and quieten me.

'Sorry,' I said, running my hand through my hair until it stood up in crazy-looking clumps.

'It's okay,' she said, stroking my hand and smoothing my hair. 'I can see how unhappy you are.'

I nodded and fought back the tears.

'But don't you see how destructive this is?' she said. 'You can't go on clinging to someone who's made it clear he doesn't want you.'

I remember thinking how harsh that sounded, and tried to wriggle free of her, but she'd not finished.

'Don't you see a pattern?' she quizzed me.

I frowned, not knowing what she was getting at.

'You've told me about some of your other failed relationships, and it seems to me you're only drawn to men you think are glamorous—trendy fashion photographers, city high-flyers, starry conductors—because Christian wasn't the first of those was he? How likely are any of these men to be dependable life partners? Eh?'

I opened my mouth to protest but she held up a finger to stop me.

'And don't tell me dependable is boring. You could do with some stability in your life.'

I looked at her glumly and nodded. I knew she was right.

'And you're worth so much more than these men give you,' she said, shaking me by the shoulders. More gently, she said: 'When you love someone who doesn't seem to care for you, it can be easy to agonise over why they don't love you the way you do them. The fact is, you could be the prettiest, wittiest, brightest person in the world, and they would probably still not like you the way you like them. Trying to get something from someone who doesn't have it to give is like King Canute commanding the waves to stop flowing towards the shore. If they don't love you, it's not because you've done anything wrong or because you're not pretty, witty or bright enough, or because you're unlovable. You're simply not the one for them, and therefore they're not the one for you.'

This was quite a speech, and I was crying now. I'd never heard her talk like that before, but despite an edge of frustration in her voice, she was looking at me with such concern, that I let her take me in her arms and rock me until I stopped crying. When I was calmer, she held me away from her and said:

'This anguish and confusion must be going straight to your voice. You have to get help before you do real damage.'

'You're right,' I said miserably. 'I never know what's going to come out of my mouth or what it's going to sound like.'

'That must be so scary,' Marie said, squeezing my arms.

'It is,' I said. 'I'm terrified of this music and I'm sure everyone knows that. My coach has been sitting in on rehearsals and giving me notes, but I don't seem to be able to put into practice anything she suggests. My voice won't do what it should any more…'

Marie stood up to put the kettle on.

'Singing is so much about the mind,' she said. 'The minute your confidence goes, everything else starts to fall apart, too.'

The train was late and, by the time the taxi dropped me outside the Johnny Jim, Steven was already there, sitting in a corner, a pint of beer half drunk and his head in a newspaper. He looked up and smiled as I headed towards him.

'Good timing,' he said. 'You've just missed the UKIP candidate and his henchmen dishing out leaflets for the bi-election.' He pointed at piles of fliers they'd left on the tables. 'Fortunately, it was a flying visit.'

He made room for me to sit next to him on the scruffy red banquette.

'So, how was your day?' he asked, folding away his newspaper and putting it on the table in front of us.

'Good,' I said, 'though don't get too excited. I'm not sure that what I learnt takes us any further forward.'

'Oh,' he said, sounding disappointed. 'Let me get you a drink and you can tell me about it.'

'Large Sauvignon Blanc, please,' I said, taking off my coat and settling back in my seat. I picked up the newspaper and looked at what Steven had been engrossed in.

'Impressive,' I laughed, as he returned, holding my wine and another half for himself. '*The Times* cryptic is the pinnacle isn't it?'

He smiled modestly and sat down.

'*Times, Guardian, Telegraph*—they're all about the same in terms of difficulty.'

'I couldn't even get started on any of them,' I said, putting the paper back on the table.

'I reckon you've got to have the right sort of devious mind to get on with cryptic crosswords,' he said. 'Perhaps you're too straightforward!'

'I don't know about that,' I said, pulling a face and reaching for my wine.

'So tell me about it. What was he like?'

'He was delightful,' I said. 'He did know Isabel, as we hoped, and she was the singer who reminded him of the woman in the Gainsborough painting, but the last time he saw her was forty years ago, on stage. She disappeared in the interval of a performance of *Ariadne* in July 1977 and he's no idea what happened to her.'

Steven groaned.

'He said he'd seen less and less of her once she was involved with Paul Eveson. He had no idea she was pregnant, for instance. He went looking for her, but she moved house and didn't leave a forwarding address.'

I sipped my wine.

'I think he would have been a loyal friend to her through anything and everything, but she didn't turn to him.'

'Pity,' Steven said.

'What's even sadder is that he still loves her. He made no secret of that.'

We were both silent, perhaps both thinking what it would be like to spend a life-time alone, yearning for someone who has long gone, but you've no idea where.

'He did suggest someone else who might help,' I said. 'A dresser who worked regularly with Isabel.'

'Do you know how to contact him?' Steven asked.

'Yes, he does some work at the Queens Theatre on Shaftesbury Avenue. I left a note at the stage door for him before I left London this afternoon.'

'Well done,' Steven said, moving on to his fresh half.

'So tell me about how you are?' I asked. 'How's work for starters? Are you making order out of chaos?'

He laughed.

'Progress anyway. I'm enjoying it—and I'm keeping an eye out for material about Paul and Isabel. I'd love to find a tape of that concert. I'm sure they would have recorded it because right from the beginning, when the theatre first opened, there was a policy that everything was to be recorded.'

'Perhaps it was filed away with stuff relating to one of the shows featured in the concert?' I suggested.

'Yes, I wondered that, but it's not with *Under the Greenwood Tree*. I looked there.'

'Worth a look in the other shows then,' I volunteered.

He didn't appear to be listening, but at last he said: 'I do have some news—rather perplexing, I'm afraid.'

'Oh?' I said.

'Well, I discovered that the Stella Maris order in London was disbanded several years ago when the last surviving nuns went to live at the Mother House in Lichfield. The convent was pulled down and the site was redeveloped. I eventually tracked down Benjamin Kyle to a parish in west London and spoke to him on the phone yesterday. He was very friendly but he didn't have much time to talk. I caught him just as he and his family were leaving for Heathrow to catch a flight to Guyana for a family reunion. He'll be away for a month but said he'd be happy to talk again when he's back.' He paused. 'I think my enquiry intrigued him.'

He took a swig of beer and I waited for him to go on.

'But here's a surprise—and I think he was telling me the truth—he said he doesn't know anyone called Isabel Grey. The name meant nothing to him.'

Steven and Alice

'I've always liked this pub,' Kevin said, as three plates of pie and chips were delivered to the table. 'I came here sometimes with Isabel and whenever I come in now, I half wonder if she might be here, even after all these years.'

Kevin had suggested meeting at The Nellie Dean of Soho on Dean Street for a late lunch, and when Steven and Alice arrived, he was already there, recognisable by the yellow cravat he'd told Alice he'd be wearing. He looked youthful for a man in his late sixties, still trim and well-turned out, with touches of flamboyance in his colourful clothes and the sharp styling of his thick white hair.

'Mind you,' he said, tucking a white paper serviette into the collar of his shirt, 'it's been tarted up since those days. It was much more basic then, but it's always attracted a good crowd.'

Steven looked around and took in the other drinkers, most of whom seemed to be regulars who were on first name terms with the staff.

'So, you're still working then, Kevin?' Alice asked, blowing on a forkful of steaming hot pie.

'I do a bit. Normally three or four shows a week. Musicals mainly, sometimes ballet,' he replied, studying the colour of his beer before taking a sip.

'No opera?' she asked.

He shook his head.

'I lost the taste for it after that *Ariadne*,' he said sadly. 'I did a few shows at Covent Garden later that year, but...'

'You knew Isabel well?' Steven asked.

'As well as she'd allow,' Kevin replied. 'She didn't prattle on or gossip like some, but I guess I knew her better than most people did.'

'And did you meet Paul Eveson?' Alice asked hopefully.

'Oh yes,' Kevin sniffed, cutting into his pie with more vigour than was necessary. 'I could see she was smitten from the first time he turned up in her dressing room after *Rosenkavalier.*'

'And was he smitten, too?' Steven asked.

Kevin pursed his lips.

'Even if he was, I knew he was not to be trusted.'

'What do you mean?' said Alice.

'I knew about Barbara, that's what.'

He sniffed again and shook his head.

'I never knew how much she mattered to him, but he'd been seeing her on and off for donkeys' years. Isabel found out—during the rehearsals for *Ariadne*. Barbara told me that Isabel saw her and Paul together.'

'Who was Barbara?' Alice asked.

'She and Paul met back in the 1960s, in the Potteries, at your local theatre,' Kevin replied. 'Barbara came to London sometime later when I was just starting out, and I got to know her because she worked in costume. She was freelance, like me, so our paths crossed in all sorts of places.'

'Do you think Paul cared about Isabel?' Alice asked.

Kevin peered into his glass, as if the answer was to be found within its cloudy depths.

'In a way, I believe he did, but he was so self-absorbed, so feckless—else why did he lead Isabel on like that if he had no intention of leaving his wife?' He laughed sarcastically. 'His wife had money—she was from a wealthy family in Milan—so it meant he didn't have to work if he didn't feel like it.'

'Can I show you a couple of photographs?' Steven asked, reaching into his satchel.

He pulled out a brown envelope from which he took three black and white photographs. He wiped the table with his napkin and laid the pictures out on the envelope.

Alice had seen the photos on the journey down to London and watched Kevin closely to observe his reaction to them. He picked up each photo in turn, studying the image carefully before turning it over to read the caption on the back: Sebastian in *The Tempest*, Mr Casaubon in *Middlemarch;* Thomas Cromwell in *A Man for all Seasons*.

'That's him,' he said dryly.

'You didn't like him?' Steven said, putting the envelope and its contents back into his bag.

'I didn't like the thought of him messing her about and breaking her heart.'

'And did he?' Alice asked.

'I reckon so,' Kevin said, pushing his plate away before offering it to a passing bar tender. He'd eaten less than half of it, Steven observed. Talk of Isabel had perhaps dulled his appetite.

'She was in a bad way by the time we got to final production rehearsals for *Ariadne*. It didn't help that the costumes had been badly designed and didn't suit her and needed endless adjustments.'

He paused and gazed into his beer.

'That was when I guessed she was pregnant. It wasn't just the badly fitting costumes. She was changing shape.'

He took a long swig of beer.

'So what happened on the night she disappeared?' Alice asked.

Kevin shuddered.

'She'd told Paul she was pregnant—the day before—and he'd made it clear he couldn't help her, so she was shaken up by that and was obviously feeling unwell, and in that state, the role was too much for her.'

'But she got through most of the performances, Matthew said.'

'Just about, but it cost her, so by that night she had nothing left. It was quite an effort to get her out for the Prologue—she was all for cancelling—and I kick myself for not realising how distressed she was. If I'd known, I'd never have let her go out there...'

His head drooped with regret and Alice reached over and placed her hand on his.

'She tricked me,' he said at last with a half-smile. 'Came off stage and sent me on a fool's errand to find her some Lucozade. When I got back to the dressing room, she'd gone. Folded up her costume, got dressed, gone downstairs, and somehow, slipped away without anyone noticing.'

He pursed his lips.

'That was the last time I saw her.'

'But you looked for her?' Alice said quietly.

He nodded.

'I called, I wrote, I turned up at her flat at all hours, hoping to catch her there, but it was as if she'd vanished. I was even there at nine o'clock the morning after that last *Ariadne,* and she wasn't there. And then we heard she'd moved and not told anyone where, and that was when I realised she really wanted to disappear.'

'Did anyone contact the police?' Steven asked after a long silence.

'Matthew Markham was about to, I believe, but then Rhona Winters, the girl playing Zerbinetta, had a letter from Isabel, saying she'd decided to drop out for a bit and would be in touch when she was feeling better.'

'Did Rhona ever hear from her after that?' Alice asked.

Kevin shook his head sadly.

'None of us did.'

He drank the dregs of his beer.

'London's a big enough place to lose yourself in, I reckon, but I still look out for her, just in case. Sometimes I think I see her, but then I realise I'm looking at someone who looks like Isabel forty years ago.'

He sighed.

'Barbara saw her once, many years back, not long after Paul died.'

Steven looked at Alice in surprise.

'You didn't know he was dead?' Kevin asked.

They both shook their heads.

'Barbara saw Isabel at a performance at the Coliseum and looked for her afterwards to make sure she knew. Apparently, Isabel was dumbstruck and simply turned and fled—got into a taxi—before Barbara could stop her.'

'When was that?' Alice asked.

Kevin pulled a face.

'1980? '81? Round about then.'

'Was Paul living in London when he died?' Alice asked.

'Somewhere in the Cotswolds, I gather,' Kevin said. 'Barbara told me that Paul's wife was treated successfully for cancer and, after she recovered, they moved to somewhere near Burford.'

Steven and Alice leant back in their seats as the barman came to clear the plates and glasses.

'Not long after that,' Kevin went on, 'I saw a woman with short, shaggy hair that looked as if it had been hacked off with kitchen scissors and something about her reminded me of Isabel. Something about her eyes.'

His own eyes clouded with sadness.

'Another time, many years later, I saw a woman sitting on a bench in the gardens near Russell Square, long grey hair wound on the back of her head like a bird's nest. That might have been her, but this woman looked wild, ragged, not like my Isabel at all.'

He paused.

'And her eyes... They stayed with me, so full of melancholy. Bleakness, even.'

He fiddled with the rings on his right hand.

'I was a coward. I walked on. I couldn't bear the thought it might have been her.'

He looked at his watch and shrugged.

'I'd better be going,' he said. 'That laundry won't sort itself.'

He stood up.

'You'll let me know, if you find her?'

'Of course,' Alice said, standing up to give him a hug.

'Don't forget your paper,' Steven said, reaching over to retrieve a copy of *The Daily Mail* that was folded to a page containing a half-completed crossword. 'You do crosswords?' he asked, handing the paper to Kevin.

'Only the easy ones,' he said, laughing.

He looked at the unfinished crossword.

'Isabel used to help me sometimes. We'd do them in the dressing room during rehearsals. She could always get the clues about books or music or art—oh, and anagrams. She was good at those.'

Steven walked to the door with Kevin and shook his hand as they parted, and while Alice went to the ladies, he watched the man walk towards Shaftesbury Avenue, irked by a sense that among everything Kevin had told them, there might be something of consequence that he couldn't yet grasp.

Steven and Alice

Alice was gazing out of the train window and Steven was making notes in a large writing pad.

'I'm trying to piece together what we already knew, with what Kevin told us,' he said, 'to see if we're any further on.'

'And are we?' Alice asked.

'I'm not sure, but here are some random thoughts. First off, I've often wondered who left the boxes of plays and music outside my uncle's bookshop—could it have been Paul's wife? If it was her, she'd held on to them for a long time after Paul's death.'

'Perhaps she'd decided to have a clear out,' Alice suggested.

Steven nodded and continued.

'Why didn't Benjamin Kyle recognise Isabel's name? Was he lying or had he just forgotten it? Or was it because John the organist was mistaken and it wasn't Isabel he saw? Or, was it Isabel, but she gave the vicar a false name?'

Alice frowned.

'Who knows?' she sighed.

'But this is what's bothering me,' Steven said. 'The woman Kevin described sitting in the Russell Square gardens could have been the woman who helped me the night I was mugged.'

Alice gasped.

'I couldn't see her very well. It was dark and I wasn't really with it, but Kevin's description of her hair fits with what I remember of the woman who waited until the ambulance came. Even then I thought I might have seen her before, but I couldn't for the life of me think where...'

He broke off as Alice reached hurriedly into her bag to retrieve her mobile phone.

'I can't remember for sure,' he heard her say, as if with surprise, after a long pause while she'd listened to the caller, 'but I don't think so.' There was another long silence before she said: 'I will, thanks.'

He watched her frown briefly before scrolling through the contacts in her phone, until she found the one she wanted. 'Sorry,' she said, as she waited for the phone to be answered. 'This won't take long.'

'No problem,' Steven said, turning back to his pad which he was covering with scribbles and crossings out.

'Hello,' she said at last. 'I'd like to make an appointment for some blood tests please.'

Steven raised his head slightly but carried on with his doodles, a couple of which he had circled with thick black marker pen.

GAIL SEBREY

GISELE RABY

GAYLE BIRES

'Everything OK?' he asked, as Alice put away her phone.

'I'm not sure,' she said. 'A few days ago, I made an appointment to see the consultant again and that was his receptionist. She said he'd been reviewing my notes and couldn't find a record of a thyroid function test, so suggested I have it checked before I see him.'

A few days later, I walked home from the surgery on Hope Street, past the theatre on the corner, and stopped to look at the poster boxes on either side of the front door. They'd been changed since I was last there and were now advertising *Educating Rita* and *The Tempest*. I thought of Paul playing Sebastian here over fifty years ago, of Barbara looking after his costumes and sharing his bed, of his Italian wife out of mind in London, of Isabel dreaming of him and waiting for him to step back into her life.

I walked on up the hill, past the church towards the turning into Vicarage Road. The day was warmer than any that had gone before and there was a sense that spring might not be far away. Even in my untended garden, there were daffodils with large golden cups pushing upwards to herald the new season in a burst of cheerful colour. As I turned the corner, I noticed that a magnolia tree on the edge of the graveyard was showing the first signs of tiny star-shaped flowers and I thought what pleasure the tree would give me as it blossomed over the coming months. As I stopped on my door step to rummage for my key, I looked back at the tree and, as I turned round I saw a woman staring down at me from behind the high wall. The sight startled me, so reminiscent was it of the woman I'd seen in the same place on New Year's Eve. The woman didn't move, but I thought I saw her smile and lift her arm as if to beckon me. I narrowed my eyes, hoping to see her more clearly. Though I was sure I didn't know her, I waved back and began walking towards the front of the church. As I got to the corner, I saw that the woman had moved away from the wall and was waiting for me at the top of the gravel path. As I got closer, she held out her hand.

'I'm sorry I startled you,' she said. 'I saw you go out and I've been waiting for you to come back.'

I took the hand she offered me.

'Are you Alice?' she asked, looking at me with large, blue eyes that conveyed a mix of anxiety and hope.

'I am,' I said, in surprise. 'Do I know you?'

'No,' she smiled, 'but I rang your number a few months ago.' She nodded towards my house. 'I was enquiring about Isabel Grey.'

I looked at her aghast.

'I remember,' I said, my heart thumping and my voice sounding strangely hoarse. Something about her unnerved me. I cleared my throat and asked: 'How do you know Isabel?'

'I don't,' she said sadly. 'I'm looking for her.'

I held my breath as she seemed to summon the courage to say more.

'I think she's my mother.'

Alice and Sophie

Kevin's words were ringing in my ears: 'Sometimes I think I see her, but then I realise I'm looking at someone who looks like Isabel forty years ago.'

I realised why I'd been momentarily unnerved by this woman. Not only had I seen her likeness in old photographs but, with her eloquent eyes and gentle bearing, it was not hard to believe she might be Isabel's daughter.

I invited her for coffee and, as we walked down the church path together, she told me her name was Sophie Fleming and that she lived in Brockenhurst. I opened the front door and, as I ushered her inside, I guessed she would be wondering if this was somewhere her mother had once lived. I took her through to the kitchen into which bright, warm sunshine was streaming, making the room airless and stuffy. I saw her blow out her cheeks as if she was overheating so, after a few moments struggling with the stubborn old lock, I pushed open the double doors.

'May I?' she asked, indicating the garden.

'Of course,' I replied, 'but please forgive the state it's in.' I laughed. 'I promised myself I would tackle it once the good weather arrived...'

She smiled and raised her hand as if to dismiss my embarrassment. I followed her outside to test the temperature and after hesitating briefly, I went back inside, picked up a dish cloth and lifted the long cushion off the settle. I carried it down to a wrought iron bench to which I gave a quick wipe before dragging it out of its shady corner, so we could sit in the warmth of the sun.

'Do you take milk and sugar?' I asked.

'Milk, but no sugar, thanks,' she said.

While I busied myself making coffee, I watched her. She had short, thick blonde hair and fair colouring and looked striking in a loose-fitting, lemon raincoat. She was standing deep in thought beside the hedge that grew between my garden and that of my neighbour. Further along the hedge, a blackbird was perched with its back to her, chirruping loudly at something in the next garden until he spun round and saw her. He fell silent for a moment, before skipping along the hedge until he was alongside her, at which point he gave a raucous screech and flew off into the sanctuary of a tall tree several gardens away. She reared back in surprise and laughed, and was still laughing when she turned to look at me over her shoulder, but her face quickly became serious again and I had the uncanny sensation I was being visited by a ghost or a doppelgänger. The pose and the expression were unmistakable.

I stood in the doorway carrying two mugs, and she moved over to the bench and eased herself onto the cushion. As she did so, I realised she was pregnant. I handed her a mug and sat down beside her, unable to take my eyes off her.

'I'm sorry to spring myself on you like this,' she said. 'Call it a whim, perhaps, but when I went to bed last night, I knew I had to come, even if just to walk around the neighbourhood and see the house from the outside. When I saw the church was so close by, I went in to look for graves of the Grey family.'

'Did you find them?' I asked. 'There are three of them together.'

'Yes, I did,' she said. 'Imogen, Evadne and Arthur. I looked all over the graveyard before I found them. It's very beautiful. Have you ever explored it?'

'Not really,' I confessed. 'Imogen is the only person I know who's buried there.'

'On the far side of the church,' she said, 'there's a magnificent oak tree that fills that corner of the cemetery. Its branches have a tremendously broad span and a number of very young children are buried near it.' She closed her eyes. 'It's very tranquil there, nothing but birdsong to

254

disturb the peace. Some of the graves are decorated with a single rosebud. Very poignant.'

She sipped her coffee and looked around, taking in the scene, gazing up at the back of the house.

'It's such a strange coincidence that you should come now,' I said, shaking my head at the sheer unlikeliness of it.

'Oh?' she said.

'Yes, because I've been looking for Isabel, too.'

'Really?' she said, her eyes widening.

I nodded.

'I'd never heard her name until that day you rang. Imogen, my godmother, never mentioned her. It was only when I started sifting through the stuff Imogen had accumulated, that I realised the woman you asked about was her sister.'

'Ah!'

'Isabel and Imogen lived here as young girls, right up until Isabel went to music college in London. Eventually, I discovered there was some estrangement between them.'

'Why are you interested in her?' Sophie asked, frowning.

'I'm drawn to her story,' I said simply.

'Her story?' Sophie said.

'Yes,' I said. 'There's a mystery about her that intrigues me.' I hesitated. 'She seems to have disappeared in 1977...'

'The year I was born,' she interrupted.

'That's right,' I said.

As we sat in the sunshine drinking our coffee, I explained why I'd come back to live in Sandleheath and told her all I knew about Isabel, trying to convey it as coherently as I could because I suspected that much of it—if not all—would be news to her.

When I'd finished, she looked at me closely.

'I can see why her story would resonate with you,' she said quietly. 'Thank you for sharing that.'

'What about you?' I asked. 'What's your story and how much do you know about Isabel?'

I took her empty mug from her and put it with mine on the scruffy grass alongside the bench and looked at her expectantly. She clasped her hands in her lap in the protective way I'd seen other pregnant women do and told me her history in the clear and matter-of-fact way a teacher might.

'I was born in a cottage hospital in the New Forest in 1977. My parents were Wendy and William Hobday. Mum was a primary school teacher and dad was vicar of St Michael and All Angels Church in Lyndhurst. I was an only child—my mum had a hard time throughout her pregnancy and during the delivery and didn't want to go through that again. My childhood was happy enough, I suppose, though Dad could be rather strict and old-fashioned—he was quite a lot older than Mum—and Mum was prone to depression, but I wasn't aware of anything untoward in their lives until the day of Mum's funeral, three years ago.'

I shifted my position on the bench so that I could see her more easily. She moved, too, as if trying to get comfortable.

'Are you okay sitting out here,' I asked, 'or would you prefer to go inside?'

'No, no,' she assured me. 'It's lovely here, thank you.'

I waited for her to go on.

'After the funeral, we went across the road to the Crown Hotel for afternoon tea. It's an old coaching inn where we'd invariably gone to celebrate family milestones—birthdays, my exam successes—and until that day, it was a place with happy memories.'

She smiled.

'I can still remember how the place used to smell: a pungent combination of spilt beer and stale cigarette smoke. As a kid, I thought it was such a 'grown-up' smell.'

I smiled.

'It's no smoking now, of course,' she went on, 'but at that time, I still smoked a little. It was a bad habit I picked up at university. So, at one point during the afternoon I went out into a courtyard at the back of the hotel for a cigarette. There were other people around and I wanted some quiet time on my own so I snuck into one of the old stable buildings where chairs and trestle tables were stacked. I'd finished the cigarette and was about to go back to join the gathering, when I heard two women talking close by, and recognised one voice as that of my Aunt Dorothy and the other as a friend of Mum's called Pat.'

She stopped and I saw she was struggling to maintain her composure.

'Would you like a glass of water?' I asked, getting up.

She nodded in reply and I scooped up the mugs and went into the kitchen where I ran a tap until the water became clear and cold. By the time I got back to her, she seemed calmer, but she took a long gulp of water before continuing.

'They were having a good old gossip,' she said, wiping her mouth with the back of her hand. 'I could tell that immediately, from the furtive, whispered way in which they were both talking. Normally, I would have gone to join them, but some instinct told me to stay put.'

She took a sip of water.

'At first, I couldn't make sense of what they were talking about, and perhaps I didn't want to believe what I was hearing, but what I learnt then—and later when I confronted my Aunt about it—was that when my mother left hospital after my birth, she told my dad she suspected that the baby she'd come home with was not her baby.'

I gasped.

'Why did she think that?'

Sophie took a deep breath.

'It seems there were a number of reasons. She told Dorothy that after she gave birth, the baby was immediately taken away to be checked over and bathed—she wasn't even allowed to hold her first—but the child wasn't brought back wearing the clothes Mum had bought for her. The other thing that made her suspicious was that the child she was given was small and weighed less than six pounds, whereas by the end of her pregnancy, the midwife and her GP had predicted she would have a large baby. Despite her insistence to hospital staff, none of the nurses would admit to having swapped the baby clothes by mistake and her concerns were dismissed. My father attributed her concerns to what he called Mum's heightened hormonal state and anyway, he didn't want to put the hospital's reputation in a bad light so wasn't prepared to go back and challenge the staff. Mum shared her doubts with her sister, and Dorothy went back to the hospital pretending to be an academic researching birth rates in rural areas, and learnt that on the day I was born, two baby girls were born, five minutes apart. Dorothy found out that the hospital had been short-staffed that day and both births had been difficult for the mothers, so the small medical team was overstretched. Dorothy asked Mum if she could remember anything about the other mother and Mum told her she was called Isabel Grey and was a singer who originally came from the Potteries.'

'Didn't Isabel give the hospital an address?' I asked.

'She did,' Sophie replied, 'but it turned out to be a rented cottage in Brockenhurst which she'd left without giving a forwarding address.'

'Did your Mum tell your father this?'

'She did, but he said that the baby was theirs now, and that it was God's will.'

I couldn't stop myself letting out a snort of derision.

'I know,' Sophie said sadly. 'He wouldn't budge and that was that. Dorothy said Mum always loved me, but never shook off the belief that she'd been given the wrong baby.'

'You have to wonder,' I said, 'about the competence of a hospital that even when only two women give birth on a particular day, still manage to get something so wrong.'

'That's true,' Sophie said. 'I overhead Dorothy and Pat saying there was the possibility that one of the nurses might have been drunk…'

'What a terrible suspicion for your mother to live with,' I said, looking at her.

'I know,' she said sadly. 'She never hinted at any of this to me, but it might explain the depression she suffered as she grew older.'

She started to cry quietly.

'Poor Mum.'

I put my arm around her shoulder and pulled her close to me.

'And now, you're pregnant and want to know about your birth mother, is that it?' I suggested.

She nodded and took a paper tissue out of the pocket of her raincoat, wincing as she readjusted her position.

'I'm almost five months gone and I've already got a bad back,' she said, blowing her nose and laughing.

'Does your father know you're looking for Isabel?' I asked.

Her eyes filled again and she held the crumpled tissue to her face.

'When I found out I was pregnant,' she said, 'I asked him about Mum's suspicions but he wouldn't talk about it. In fact, he became quite agitated so I left it, but in the last couple of months, old age has caught up with him and he knows he's failing fast. I think that's why he's given me his blessing to look for Isabel. Last week I found her listed at this address on the 1961 census. I went to see Dad the day before yesterday, and as I left he said: 'Don't leave it too late."

I showed her the postcards and the envelope in which I'd saved the other bits and pieces. While I made sandwiches and coffee for lunch, she sat at the kitchen table and examined the cuttings and the other mementos of Isabel's life. I watched as she handled each item in turn before putting it carefully back in the envelope. Finally, she studied the postcards, seeming to re-read the messages time and again.

'She sounds pretty disillusioned, doesn't she?' she said, sadly.

'She does,' I agreed.

She stood up and went through to the parlour to return the cards to the mantelpiece. After a few minutes, when she hadn't come back, I followed her and found her with her head leaning against the mantle.

She turned to face me and said: 'I keep wondering what happened to the baby who went home with Isabel.'

Lunch seemed to revive her, so I suggested a walk to Linda Vista Gardens, about fifteen minutes away. Though some of the heat had gone out of the sun, the sky was still the brilliant blue it had been since early morning.

'This is one of the bonuses of living here,' I said, as we approached the weather-worn stone pillars that marked the entrance. 'I remember coming as a child once or twice, but now I come whenever I want fresh air and exercise. I find it very calming.'

'Perhaps Isabel and Imogen came here when they were children?' she pondered.

'Very likely,' I said. 'It's extremely popular, especially in the summer. It was the private garden of a large villa built in the late nineteenth century, but it's been open to the public since just after the Second World War. There's a sculpture in the centre of the garden that shows key events in the history of the area. The house was pulled down a long time ago and the council look after the garden now.'

'It's very well preserved,' said Sophie, as we stopped to take in the intricate layout of the formal part of the garden.

'I wish I knew more about it,' I said. 'I gather there are some unusual trees in the parkland that were planted when the house was built in the 1880s.'

Sophie let out a long breath and smiled.

'I like it here.'

'Do you have to get home tonight?' I asked tentatively.

She looked at me with interest.

'I'd like you to meet Steven. I could call him and ask him for supper—and there's a bed made up in the small front bedroom and I can lend you whatever you need.'

'I'd like that,' she said. 'Let me call my husband.'

'While you do that,' I replied, 'I'll ring Steven.'

She walked a short distance away and I saw her talking but couldn't hear what she was saying. Steven answered almost immediately.

'I was just about to call you,' he said.

'Oh?' I asked.

'Yes,' he said. 'I've found something I'd like to show you.'

'Can you come round for dinner tonight then? There's someone you should meet.'

'Really?' he asked, sounding curious.

I told him about Sophie.

'Wow,' he said softly. 'Then she really should see this.'

Sophie came towards me smiling.

'That's fine,' she said. 'Tim's on call tonight anyway.'

'He's a doctor?' I asked, as we carried on walking towards the sculpture we could see ahead of us.

'A vet.'

'How long have you been married?'

'Eighteen months. We met at Mum's funeral.'

'Really?' I asked in surprise.

'Apparently, weddings and funerals are surprisingly good occasions on which to meet a potential partner,' she said as if citing a well-known fact.

'Oh yeah?' I said dubiously.

She nodded, as if to say: 'Believe it.'

'Tim had looked after Mum's Welsh terrier, Bryn, for years and they got on really well. I'd heard her talk about him but hadn't met him before the funeral. He made a point of coming to ask how I was doing and shared some of his memories of Mum. She always said how kind and patient he was and I sensed that immediately. In fact, it was because I was taken aback by how much I instantly liked him that I went outside to be on my own for a while.' She paused. 'By the time I went in again, I was struggling to hide how upset I was and he saw this. He didn't say anything, just brought me a cup of tea and a piece of cake and sat quietly with me.'

'And?' I asked.

'We went for a walk a few days' later and we've been together ever since.'

'Had either of you been married before?'

'No,' she replied. 'We were both fine being single. We had good lives, nice homes, jobs we enjoyed...'

'What do you do?'

'I'm a Music Therapist. When Mum died, I was working at a hospital in Reading and living in Goring, but when Tim and I got together, I moved back to the New Forest and I'm self-employed now.'

'So you made big changes in your life all at once?'

'I did, though I wanted to be closer to Dad anyway. And I like to believe that we meet people for a reason. That they're meant to be in our lives to give us new experiences and change us.'

The timing of Sophie's visit was fortuitous for another reason: the night before, my mum had called in to bring me a shepherd's pie she'd made. (She worried I wasn't eating properly and I probably wasn't). It was more than big enough to feed three of us and all I had to do, thankfully, was put the dish into the oven for long enough to warm it through and make a green salad to go with it. In fact, Sophie made the salad, including an oil and vinegar dressing, and she was setting the table when Steven arrived. It was the first time he'd been to the house and I led him through to the kitchen, and stood aside to watch as Sophie turned round to greet him.

He gasped and was clearly astonished when he saw her, and even when he recovered himself, could only splutter hello.

'Hello,' she smiled, offering him her hand.

'You need a drink,' I said laughing and poured him a glass of red wine.

'Cheers,' he said, sitting down on the settle and dumping his satchel next to him. 'Sorry I'm late. I called home to pick up the song sheet.'

'Ah, yes,' I said. 'I hoped you'd remember that.'

Sophie and I sat opposite him and she looked from one to the other of us for an explanation. I let Steven tell the story and watched her reaction as he reached into his bag and handed her the cream-coloured manuscript. She handled it carefully, gazing at the sketches on the covers before turning the pages slowly to take in the words and music. As she gave it back to him, he reached again into the bag and drew out a reinforced brown envelope. Before he opened it, he explained that he was always on the look-out for the missing audio cassette recording of the concert at which Isabel and Paul had sung their duet.

'I've not found it yet,' he said, 'but something did turn up today: photographs of them performing together.'

Sophie and I gasped in unison.

'Where were they?' I asked.

'I'd looked in the concert folder and the show file— *Under the Greenwood Tree* by Thomas Hardy—but they'd been filed with *Under Milk Wood* by Dylan Thomas.'

I laughed.

'Not entirely random but a little careless.'

'It gives me hope that the concert tape will turn up somewhere similarly random if I go on looking long enough,' Steven said.

He handed the envelope to Sophie and she took out three large black and white photographs and laid them on the table in front of us. I gasped again when I saw them, but she was silent apart from her breathing which I heard become quick and shallow. In the first of the photos, a full-length portrait, Isabel was standing alone in a spotlight; in the next, which was a head and shoulders shot, Paul was standing opposite her, also in a spotlight. He was not conventionally attractive, but even these old, still photographs captured a look that was unusually striking. The third photo caught him placing a sprig of thyme in her hair, just above her ear, and what was so arresting about it, was the barely-concealed look of desire on his face and the rapture on hers.

Without saying anything, Sophie stood up and went over to her handbag which she'd left on a work surface behind us. She reached inside for her phone and came back to sit at the table. It took her a matter of seconds to find what she was looking for, and when she'd blown up an image so that it filled the screen, she put the phone down, next to the photos, and gazed from one to the other. At last she looked up and pushed the phone towards me.

'That was me,' she explained, 'at a dinner at the Crown Hotel to celebrate my twenty-first birthday.'

I studied the picture and nodded, knowing that the resemblance to Isabel at much the same age was undeniable. The similarity was heightened by their hair: Sophie's was long then, and tied back off her face into a ponytail, the effect remarkably similar to that created by Isabel's elaborate plait.

I picked up the phone and handed it to Steven, and just as he'd done earlier when I'd called him and told him about Sophie, he said 'Wow' very quietly.

'That's me isn't it?' Sophie said, her voice shaking.

'I think so,' I said, and Steven nodded in agreement.

'And that's my father,' she said, picking up one of the photos of Paul and Isabel. 'I knew nothing about him until today—my focus has been on finding Isabel—but it's painful to think of him abandoning her—us.'

I put my arm round her shoulder and she laid her head against me and sighed.

'I'm sorry you've had such a lot to take in today, Sophie,' I said.

'Please don't apologise,' she said, sitting up and squeezing my arm. 'You're both being so supportive and understanding—and without you, I'd know nothing about either of my birth parents, so I'm grateful.'

We ate supper soon after that, Sophie picking at morsels of salad, while Steven and I tucked into the shepherd's pie and a bottle of red wine, and all the while we talked. Sophie recounted her mother's doubts and fears about a possible mix-up at the hospital and Steven and I went over all we knew, trying not to leave out anything, even when we knew it would make difficult listening for Sophie.

'Do you know nothing more about Paul?' she asked.

Steven shook his head.

'The only person we've spoken to about him was Kevin, and, as we said earlier, he wasn't a huge fan...'

'You have more photos of Paul, don't you?' I reminded him.

'I do,' he said, reaching into his bag for another envelope, in which were the three production photos he'd shown Kevin.

Sophie studied them quietly before returning them to Steven.

'He must have been quite young when he died,' she said.

'Forty-seven,' Steven said. 'I found his death certificate.'

'Do you know where he's buried?' she asked.

Steven shook his head.

'He was living near Burford at the time of his death and my uncle's shop is a few miles from there.'

'But there's no record of Isabel's death?' Sophie asked.

'No, there isn't,' he replied. 'I've found hardly anything about her online. Some of her reviews have been uploaded, but I found no interviews or features.'

He paused to take a sip of wine.

'It's frustrating because I've found plenty of material about some of Isabel's contemporaries—Wikipedia pages, discographies, teaching positions—and singers who would be older than she is now often appear in multiple listings.'

I frowned.

'Isabel really did disappear after that night in 1980 when she learnt of Paul's death.'

Steven nodded.

'It seems that way, but…'

'What?' asked Sophie.

Steven shook his head.

'I have a hunch that she's still out there somewhere—in London perhaps.'

'Go on,' I urged.

'It may be fanciful on my part,' he said, 'but Kevin said he's seen an elderly woman, looking very changed and strange, and thought it might be her. A woman who helped me when I was mugged was not unlike the woman he described…'

I thought about the woman I'd seen on New Year's Eve, standing in the frosty graveyard, watching the house. To think she might have been Isabel was surely too far-fetched to entertain and for now, I said nothing.

Sophie had taken off her shoes and was sitting on the bed when I went in to give her a nightdress and towel.

'I've left a new toothbrush in the bathroom for you and you can help yourself to anything else in there you need.'

I sat down next to her and handed her something else: the envelope containing the letter Imogen had written to Isabel. She looked at me questioningly.

'I wasn't sure whether to show you this,' I said.

Sophie turned it over in her hands and looked at me for explanation.

'Imogen wrote this to Isabel the day after she went to the funeral of an old flame of hers, in the summer of 2015. It came back, undelivered. I think you should read it.'

I leaned towards her and kissed her lightly on the cheek. 'I hope you sleep well. I'll see you in the morning.'

Back in my own room and standing at the window overlooking the garden, I wondered if the house felt the presence of the two sisters as keenly as I did at that moment. Imogen's letter had touched and troubled me and I had not intended to share it with anyone, but then, I had not expected to meet Sophie.

Dear Isabel,

After so many years of silence between us, it's hard to know how to start a letter I should have written long before now. All those many years ago, I failed you as a sister. I blamed you for the disappointments of my life and, I'm ashamed to say, I wanted to get back at you. How pathetic and spiteful that sounds, and of course, I cannot justify what I did when I denied you and your child a home. I can only try to explain why I behaved in that cruel and heartless way, and hope that if this letter reaches you, it will help you understand something that at the time must have seemed incomprehensible to you.

I confess it has taken the death of Ralph Liddell—do you even remember him?—to make me realise that resentment has fuelled my life. I was so jealous of you. How I raged silently every time Mother complained: 'Why can't you be more like Isabel?' 'Why can't you be sweet-tempered like your sister?' She didn't seem to consider how self-conscious and unattractive or downright ignored I felt when she favoured you so openly. I tried to hide my dejection, but it would leak out in sarcasm or anger. And when Ralph, too, found you more fascinating and alluring than me, I felt utterly worthless and unlovable. So when you asked for my help, almost twenty years after we last lived together, I was still playing out the bitterness and frustrations I'd felt as a child and a young woman.

Believe me, I wanted to be different, wanted to find a way to reconcile with you. I occasionally thought of turning up, unannounced, and asking if we could start again. I even came to see you in The Magic Flute, *thinking I might surprise you afterwards in your dressing room, but when I saw and heard you in all your grace and beauty I was once more a hurt and lonely child who felt hopelessly inferior to you and I went away as soon as the performance ended.*

I have therefore lived most of my life feeling short-changed, grieving for the contentment and fulfilment I thought might have been mine, if only you had not turned Ralph's head and made him see me as second best. In fact, he found lasting love and happiness with a woman he met almost as soon as he left Sandleheath, a woman with whom he was clearly meant to share his life.

I wonder if you, too, eventually found love and comfort? I remember how, as a teenager, you consumed novels that gave you what I always felt was an idealised view of romantic love, and more than once I scoffed that your heart would be broken by a Mr Casaubon or a Heathcliff—I was sure it would be one of those extremes or the other. Perhaps initially, Paul, your actor friend, reminded you of Monsieur Paul, who, inexplicably, I recall was your favourite. I remember you reading aloud from Villette: *'His mind was indeed my library, and whenever it was opened to me, I entered bliss.' In your cards and letters, you said you loved him, though you also spoke of disappointment and disillusion. I hope that despite the rejection and betrayal that followed, you were able to rebuild your life and that your child has been a source of joy for you.*

I have a goddaughter, Alice Wade, who's a singer and I wish you could meet her. She's doing very well, I believe, always busy. A while back, I saw her in The Magic Flute, *but she was Papagena not Pamina, the role you sang. She is such an engaging performer—a clever actress full of spark and spirit—and she had the audience in fits of laughter when she was disguised as an old crone. She's clearly extremely talented but, away from the stage, she's prey to huge insecurity and her love life has been riddled with mis-steps. She may dismiss me as a desiccated old maid who knows nothing of love, and I admit, I know little of it, but I perhaps understand Alice more than she thinks, and I worry for her. I fear that like me, she will make the mistake of thinking that her worth is defined by being in a relationship. As a child she longed for her father to pay more attention to her—to notice her, like her, love her—and she chased after his love and his validation. Sadly, it seems to me that as an adult she has replicated this behaviour in all her dealings with men, and I see her being over solicitous and over forgiving. (Though, she didn't and hasn't forgiven her father.)*

Sylvia Plath apparently said 'When you give someone your whole heart and he doesn't want it, you cannot take it back. It's gone forever.' I gave my heart away and did not try to reclaim it and I believe I would have had a happier life if I had taken responsibility for my own happiness and not believed it was in the gift of others. I have had a perfectly decent life, work I enjoyed and was good at, a comfortable home, a small group of loyal friends and, until recently, good health, but I allowed myself to wallow in self-pity and to hold fast to something that was an illusion. Perhaps, when we're not good at relationships, it's partly our own fault; our own fear, our own caution, our determination to protect ourselves from further harm.

I will finish now because I'm anxious to get this letter into the next post. I know I cannot expect your forgiveness, but I would like us to put an end to our futile enmity and estrangement. This house is by right your home as much as mine and I open it to you now knowing I did not do so when you needed it most. I greatly regret that.

We are not getting any younger, Isabel; please don't leave it too long before you get in touch.

Yours,
Imogen

When Sophie and I had breakfast the next morning, I marvelled that she could retain such composure when her life was in a state of so much turmoil and change. I sat with my back to the garden facing her and watched as she laid the letter on the table beside her. She looked pale and tired, with spidery fine lines under her eyes, but after a mug of tea and a slice of toast, she was ready to talk.

'I read it again before I came down,' she said. 'There was so much to take in last night.'

I nodded.

'I felt the same when I first found it,' I said. 'I had never known Imogen talk about her life or her feelings.' I paused. 'The letter reveals insights I never thought her capable of. She was very serious-minded and could come over as rather buttoned up.'

'But you and she must have talked about personal matters for her to have those insights, surely?'

'You're right, but I'd forgotten those conversations.'

'She cared about you, though.'

'She did,' I said, 'and I regret how little interest I showed in her. I must have seemed very self-centred, and yet she changed her will to leave me the house a few months after she wrote to Isabel.'

'When the letter was returned, perhaps, and she'd lost hope of contacting Isabel?'

'Possibly,' I agreed.

'Perhaps she was trying to assuage some of her guilt towards Isabel and, by giving the house to you in her stead, she was helping another singer she cared for and was concerned about.'

'Trying to make atonement,' I said, nodding.

'You said last night that Imogen knew your father. Did you ever talk to her about him?'

'We did talk about him once, and she brought it up, not me. We'd gone for a walk to Linda Vista Gardens and were having tea in the café. She asked if I was in touch with my father.'

'And were you? Are you?'

I shook my head.

'Not really.'

I poured myself another mug of tea.

'Imogen said what a shame that was and I remember being irritated and saying he'd left me, which was a pretty rubbish thing to do, and he clearly didn't love me.'

'Just because he left, doesn't mean he didn't love you,' Sophie said quietly.

'I never understood why he did leave. He and Mum didn't argue and there wasn't anyone else at the time, so it didn't make any sense.'

Sophie reached over and put her hand gently on my wrist.

'You were very young when he left and people's motivation can be very complex. Sometimes I think we have to accept how unknowable even our closest loved ones can be at some level.'

I considered that for a moment.

'Imogen said Dad felt he and Mum had married too young, that he felt hemmed in and trapped. Having said that, though, he married again a few years later and has two daughters with his second wife.'

'And I'm guessing you find that hard, too?'

I nodded.

'Perhaps, he was readier by then to make a commitment and perhaps his second wife is a better fit for him. There are so many emotional shifts that can happen that we don't expect, that change the dynamic of our lives and influence our choices.'

'Did you have many relationships before you met Tim?' I asked.

'A few,' she replied. 'Nothing that made me think I could give up the life I had.' She laughed. 'I know many people who're in relationships like to maintain that they were always fully functional alone, and so push the 'be self-sufficient' advice onto single people...'

'They do,' I interrupted. 'It gets boring!'

'The thing is,' she went on, good-humouredly, 'I really did feel I was OK on my own. I didn't feel I was missing out or that I was somehow inadequate, but when I met Tim, something shifted.' She laughed. 'Perhaps I was hijacked by my biological clock.' She fiddled with her wedding ring. 'He's the only man I've met who I would want to have children with.'

I envied her such clarity.

'Is there anyone in your life right now?' she asked.

'Do you really want to talk about me?' I laughed. 'You're here to find out about Isabel.'

'I know, but we talked about me all last night. I want to know about you, too.'

I liked her and felt totally at ease with her and so I told her about my chequered love life.

'I'm troubled by how much I allowed myself to be bewitched by Christian,' I said, when I'd reached the end of the story. 'I feel humiliated, too, and wish I could have treated him with the same indifference I sometimes saw in his eyes.'

I thought how sad that sounded and, momentarily, my eyes brimmed with tears. I recovered myself quickly and tried to make light of it.

'I need to learn how to stop myself attracting bad men,' I laughed.

Sophie shook her head.

'I don't think it's so much about stopping yourself from attracting bad men—you're an attractive woman, you can't help who's going to notice you—but it's learning to see the red flags, and then refusing to allow bad men into your life.'

I blew my nose.

'So what triggers the red flags?' I asked.

'I think it's when you recognise that the relationship is unhealthy.'

'And what's your definition of healthy and unhealthy?' I asked. 'I don't seem to know the difference.'

'The relationships you've described sound all-consuming, so that you think about the person constantly. The relationship becomes a blanket you want to sleep in all day. Does that sound healthy? Is it really love or is it an obsession? Or a way of coping, hiding, and feeling safe in the world?'

I pulled a face.

'I guess that's the only version of love I've known.'

'So it may be powerful and you get your shots of dopamine from it, but you're powerless, too.'

'So what's healthy love like then?' I demanded.

'I think it's rare,' she said quietly. 'It seems to me that healthy love is feeling powerful and independent. It's kind and accepting and it requires a tremendous amount of honesty and a willingness to take responsibility.'

I slumped back against the settle, feeling neither powerful nor independent.

'Love should make you happy and contented,' she said, 'not miserable and anxious like you've been in so many of your relationships. It takes time to know if the love is healthy because it takes time to truly get to know someone.' She paused. 'And realistically, even when you do, there's no certainty. People change. Feelings change.'

'Oh great!'

'You have to be realistic, Alice. At least fall in love with the man in front of you, not with the notion of perfection you impose on him.'

I recognised how often I had done that.

'Do you think Isabel did that with Paul?'

'It sounds like it,' she said sadly. 'The quote she used from *Gone with the Wind* suggests she idealised Paul and only later, when he'd shown himself to be immature and irresponsible, did she realise what she'd done.'

'I think Christian was irresponsible,' I said at last. 'I doubt he ever had any intention of leaving Monica.'

'There's a fecklessness about both of them,' she said.

273

We were silent for a while, drinking our tea, both lost in thought.

'Do you think you and Tim have a healthy love?' I asked at last.

She didn't answer immediately.

'What we have is not necessarily what I thought love was until I met him. We've all been conditioned to go on a narrow search for romantic love in the expectation that it can fulfil us or cure us, but he's taught me that love is broader than that. That love is pouring all you are—the best of you—into everything you do.' She thought for a moment. 'I think Tim makes me a better person.'

'That's powerful,' I said with feeling.

'It is,' she agreed. 'Whereas, the way you talk about love sounds scary to me. You sound as if you lose yourself, so that in the end you have no sense at all of who you are.'

'That's right,' I said. 'Sometimes, when I'm clinging and wheedling, I really don't like or respect myself, but I don't seem to be able to stop.'

'With these men, you've become invisible, lost yourself in them, lost your true voice,' she said. 'And when you lose your voice, you live muted. And that's not living. That's existing.'

I winced and she took my hand, but we both jumped in alarm as there was a heavy clattering against the double doors. I turned round to see a blackbird hurling himself against the glass. After several futile assaults on the doors, he settled down in front of them, pecking at the ground, and occasionally stopping to sing through the window at full voice.

We laughed.

'I know this analogy may be painful for you right now,' Sophie went on, still holding my hand, 'but you need to find your voice and allow yourself to speak up and be heard again.'

Alice

My phone pinged with a text from Steven: *I've been thinking of you, hoping the news is encouraging. Let me know if you fancy/ need a drink and a chat when you get back tonight.*

I was touched that he'd remembered my appointment with Dr Mackenzie and, while Marie negotiated kettle, plates, mugs and milk in her minuscule galley kitchen at the flat she was renting near Euston, I texted back to tell him the time my train was due in to Stoke.

'Here we are,' Marie said, putting two mugs of tea and two slices of chocolate cake onto the small round table.

'That looks delicious,' I said.

'It will be,' she replied. 'The Stage Manager seems determined to fatten us all up, so she's bringing in a regular supply of home-made cakes.'

'How's it going?' I asked.

'Not bad, given how fiendishly difficult the music is,' she said, laughing. 'I sometimes look around and see fear etched on everyone's faces. It's very nice to have an afternoon off—it's been a relentlessly intense rehearsal period so far.'

She leant towards me.

'But look, how did it go with the doc? And what's this mystery you mentioned in your email? I want to hear all about it and we have an hour and a half before your train leaves, so start talking.'

'Well, it seems I have a mildly under-active thyroid, and that can cause the vocal chords to thicken and the timbre of the voice to drop.'

'So you'll take thyroxine to correct it?'

'I will,' I said slowly. 'He says that in time my range should come back, but there's no guarantee that my voice will fully recover and return to how it was before the problems started.'

'How do you feel about that?' she asked with a frown.

'I'm not sure. Positive, I think,' I said hesitatingly. 'Dr Mackenzie suggests I continue to rest my voice for a while longer and give the medication time to kick in and then— well, we'll see.'

'How come this wasn't spotted sooner?' Marie asked. 'You seem to have had masses of tests.'

'It was missed,' I replied. 'Dr Mackenzie queried where the test results were, assuming that I'd had the tests done by one of the other doctors I saw, and it turned out I hadn't.'

'Well, better late than never,' Marie said, cutting off a corner of cake.

My phone pinged again, this time Steven suggesting a bar meal at the Johnny Jim at seven-thirty.

'Sorry,' I said, picking up the phone to reply.

'And what's this about a mystery?' Marie asked, as I put my phone away.

I had told her snippets about Isabel, but now I told her the full story.

'Whew!' she said. 'That's quite a tale.'

I nodded.

'What will happen about the house?' she asked. 'Is it Sophie's decision?'

'She's being wonderful about that,' I replied. 'Says it's our decision and there's no need to rush it.'

'That's very decent,' Marie said.

'It is,' I agreed. 'She's very nice.' I laughed. 'You'd like her—you'd get on well.'

'Oh?'

'Yes, she certainly shares your views on my approach to men. Actually, even Imogen shares your views on that, so you're all singing from the same hymn sheet.'

'Imogen?' she asked, confused.

I told her about the letter and about Sophie's response to it.

'You've never told me much about your father,' Marie said. 'It must have been hard work, constantly trying to get him to notice you, to impress him.'

'I suppose it was,' I agreed. 'I just never felt good enough.'

'Did you think you would feel better about yourself if someone 'important' like Christian liked you?'

'Maybe,' I admitted sheepishly. 'As you have said, wise friend, on more than one occasion, I have tended to go for men like him who're talented and successful ...'

'And get what they want by turning on the charm, but are self-centred and don't take responsibility,' she said, seizing hold of my hand. 'I've been in this business long enough to know what people like Christian are like, to see them scattering the magic fairy dust around them, always playing a part.'

I pulled a face and thought briefly about challenging her, but she sighed loudly and I sensed another sermon coming.

'You know Alice, you're gorgeous and yet you attach your self-worth to how close you are to finding everlasting love, you view every passing white knight as your one-way ticket out of the barren, lonely hellscape of singledom, and you date every suitor you're even mildly attracted to, especially the manipulative or emotionally unavailable ones.'

I shrugged and said nothing. Her description made me feel uncomfortable and embarrassed.

'I'm sorry to go on at you,' she said, 'especially as it sounds as if Sophie's also had a go.' She relaxed her grip on my hand. 'I hope you know it's because I want you to be happy.'

'I do,' I said. 'You miserable old bag.'

'Less of the old.'

She looked at her watch and as we laughed at each other, we stood up and hugged.

'What time will you get home?' she asked.

'The train's due in just before seven and I'll go straight to the pub to have a drink with Steven.'

She raised an eyebrow and smiled.

'That's good,' she said. 'I like the sound of him. Nothing you've told me makes him sound in any way unsuitable or dangerous.'

I pushed her away gently.

'He is living with his mother,' I said reprovingly.

'Don't knock it,' she said. 'His mother could be a very good thing.'

'True,' I said, thinking of mine.

Marie came downstairs with me to the lobby, where we said our goodbyes.

'I know I make out I've led a blameless life and never made any foolish choices,' Marie said, 'but when I was twenty-three, I had a passionate thing with an actor who was in a West End show and who went around scattering mountains of magic fairy dust. I adored him and he broke my heart and I swore I would never get over him.'

I laughed.

'My mother still takes the credit for me getting together with Peter,' she said. 'He was my neighbour when we started going out together and I thought he was nice but dull. So while Mum was constantly saying how lovely he was, I was still adamantly declaring I would never again meet anyone I liked, so she quoted one of her favourite homilies at me: 'When one door of happiness closes, another opens; but often we look so long at the closed door we don't see the one which has been opened for us."

'Good one,' I laughed.

She paused.

'What are you going to do, now you have the diagnosis? Will you stay in Sandleheath or come back to London?'

'I don't know yet,' I said. 'I've enjoyed having a break from the crazy merry-go-round I was living on, but I'm starting to feel bored. I've been asking myself what I'll do with my life and how long can I—should I—wait to see if my voice recovers.'

'I guess you may have to be open to the possibility of doing something else.'

A large glass of white wine and a pot of comforting fish pie were exactly what I needed when I joined Steven at the pub.

'Do you want to tell me about it?' Steven asked, as he watched me enjoying a forkful of the creamy, cheesy topping of mashed potato.

By now, I was in reflective mood and though I repeated much of what I had told Marie a few hours earlier, I felt and sounded more ambivalent about the prognosis than I had then.

'So, what he says could be interpreted as hopeful?' Steven ventured, picking up on my subdued mood.

'Or, it could simply turn out to be a case of deceptive expectation,' I said gloomily. 'I'm struggling with the uncertainty of it all, the sense of still being in limbo.'

He nodded and I knew he understood.

'My experience was different,' he said. 'I knew immediately my career was over and, for a long time after the attack, my focus was simply on recovery, on being able to do the basic things we take for granted. At first it was difficult to talk and people found me hard to understand; my hip was very painful so I could only walk short distances before I felt knackered; I had to drink using a straw and even that was tricky. My jaw was broken in several places, I lost six top teeth so I needed implants, and the damage to my top lip required corrective surgery. All pretty grim, but I think the worst thing was the loss of that satisfying feeling I used to have when I took my bassoon out of its case—that was gone.'

He munched on a chip and washed it down with a swig of beer.

'But I can eat and drink unaided now, so that's a win.'

I laughed.

'That's better,' he said. 'I'm sorry you're feeling down.'

'I just don't know how I'll make a living if I can't go back to singing,' I said. 'The rent I'm charging on my flat in London more than covers the mortgage, but I will need to work. I want to work.'

'I'm in a similar situation,' he said. 'Support from Help Musicians saw me through the first few months and paid for some of my treatment, and my living costs here are minimal and, like you, I have income from my flat in London, but I know this can't be a permanent solution.'

'No?' I asked. 'You don't see yourself staying here?'

'I don't know,' he said, 'but wherever I live, like you, I'll want to work and the job at the archive is short-term.'

'You seem to enjoy it,' I said, 'so perhaps it will give you some clues as to what you might want to do longer-term.'

'It might,' he agreed. 'I've always been interested in history and even at school I enjoyed looking at old records. I'm naturally inquisitive, I suppose, and I seem to be methodical and logical in the way I go about retrieving and arranging materials.' He paused, as if saying these things out loud was helpful. 'We'll see,' he said, smiling as he gazed into his pint.

'I always felt lucky to be doing a job I loved—dressing up and playing about on stage, what's not to like?—and I pitied people who spent their working lives longing for the time when they could retire. Now I envy people who can choose when to give up a job they've loved.'

He looked at me.

'And at the other extreme,' he said, 'there are professional sportsmen and women whose careers are ended prematurely by injury, often when they're still very young. My experience is not unlike theirs.'

'I envy you your stoicism,' I said. 'I wish I had your courage.'

'But you do!' he said, and stopped me when I pulled a face. 'You haven't lost that courage you showed when you went on stage at barely any notice to sing a role you barely remembered and in a production you'd never seen.'

'That was different,' I protested.

'The context's different, I agree, but the spirit and bottle you must have had to do that will be something you can rediscover, in time, I'm sure. You're just battle-weary right now.'

I nodded and smiled and he smiled back at me.

'What do your parents do?' I asked, realising I knew almost nothing about his family. 'Are they musical?'

'My mum's a book illustrator and appreciates music, but no more than that. My dad? I've no idea. He disappeared on the back of a motorbike when Mum was six months pregnant. I'm not sure she knows where he is.'

I gasped.

'So you've never known him?'

'Nope. He was Stage Carpenter at Hope Street Theatre and Mum was a volunteer there. She said he arrived on said motorbike and left the way he came.'

'Does that bother you, not knowing him, I mean?'

'Not really,' he replied. 'I always accepted that was the way it was.' He looked at me. 'It's more complicated for you, isn't it?'

I nodded.

'How old were you when your father left?'

'About nine.'

'And you don't see him now?'

'Not often,' I said.

'You miss him.'

I took a long time to answer.

'I have photos of us as a family, at Christmas or in the garden or on holiday, and I still grieve for our family, for those happy times, and I want it to have worked out for us.'

'But they've both moved on, haven't they?' he asked. 'Made new lives?'

'They have, that's true.'

'Cod psychology advises us to move on,' he said, 'but I know some people find that harder than others.'

I sighed loudly.

'Just saying!'

'I hear you,' I said with a smile, recognising he was trying to help. 'One of the things Dr Mackenzie helped me understand was how much my voice might react to unresolved stuff from the past.'

'That makes sense,' Steven said. 'Soon after the attack, one of the consultants, who worked on my jaw, arranged for me to see a counsellor. It wasn't my thing at all, but I was in no state to argue so I agreed to see her while I was still in hospital. She warned me that I would feel as if there was a gaping hole in my life and talked about facing up to my loss and dealing with it so that it didn't fester and eat me up.'

'Dr Mackenzie said something similar today, that loss that's unmourned can occupy a huge space in a person's psyche.' I paused. 'I'm not sure if he was referring to my voice and my career or my father.'

'Perhaps both,' Steven said.

I sighed.

'Isabel suffered her share of loss, too,' I said.

'She did,' he agreed. 'And what happened to her…?'

He stared into his beer before taking a final swig to finish it.

'You know, perhaps if you talked to your father now, he would help you understand why he did what he did.'

He paused.

'Perhaps that would help.'

Steven

He went down to the canteen later than usual, by which time, it was very busy and he was forced to sit in a part of the room he normally avoided; an area where student chatter competed with the sound of the television that was mounted on the end wall and was kept on all day. A large group of students had pushed together four tables and were conducting an animated debate about a potential rent strike, forcing Steven to take the only free table, which was directly in front of the television.

He tried to ignore the din around him and concentrate on his paper but, occasionally, his attention was drawn to the lunchtime news which was showing on the screen above him. The local news programme followed and he went back to his paper. He looked up to reach for his mug of coffee, when a news item caught his interest.

Police are investigating the circumstances of her death, as she was found by staff when they opened the gardens at first light on Tuesday morning, the woman having apparently been there all night. She had no pulse when emergency crews arrived and paramedics were unable to revive her on the way to hospital. Detective Inspector James Entwistle of the Metropolitan Police said: 'A friend of the dead woman, the Reverend Benjamin Kyle of St Mary's Church in Hanford, reported Elen missing on Monday night. We're making enquiries to trace her next of kin to inform them of her death, but so far we have been unable to identify any.'

Steven had missed the beginning of the story and wondered why an item involving the Met and the Reverend Kyle should make the *Midlands Today* news bulletin. He took a final bite of his sandwich and a gulp of coffee, before hurrying back to the archive. Once there, he fired up his computer and did a search of the BBC News website. The item came up about half way down the list of local headlines and a click on the link gave him the full story. The second half of the paragraph was exactly what he'd heard on the television news, so he focussed on the first part of the story, hoping to find the explanation he wanted.

> *A woman who was found dead two days ago in Russell Square Gardens in London has been identified as Elen Daniel. Little is known about Ms Daniel, but it's understood she came originally from the Potteries and lived in London after having gone there to study music in the 1960s. It's believed that at the time of her death she may have been homeless.*

The office was temporarily deserted and was silent apart from the hum of the computers. Steven reached into his satchel for the notebook in which he'd made notes of the meeting with Kevin. He found the page he wanted and frowned.

GAIL SEBREY
GISELE RABY
GAYLE BIRES

He'd been mistaken and was about to put the book away, when he glanced across to the left hand side of the page which he'd headed *Kevin Stevens, The Nellie Dean of Soho, Dean Street, 1 pm 21st February 2017*. He scanned his notes, but his eyes were drawn back to the name of the pub.

He let out a low whistle, followed by a long sigh of disbelief and sadness.

There it was: an anagram hidden in the name of a song. The signature song of a woman whose life had been brought to life by Isabel Grey on the stage of Hope Street Theatre.

Elen Daniel.

He took out his mobile phone and scrolled through his contacts.

'Hello, Reverend Kyle?' he said. 'You may not remember me, but I called you just as you were leaving for the airport last month. I was enquiring about someone called Isabel Grey.'

'Ah yes, I do remember,' came the reply. 'I'm sorry I didn't have time to ask you more questions about her and why you thought I might know her. Did you find her?'

'No,' Steven said slowly. 'But I think you do know her—or rather you knew her.'

He hesitated, not quite sure what to say.

'I'm afraid it's possible that your friend Elen Daniel was really Isabel Grey and was the woman I've been looking for.'

Isabel

What cruel trick of fate led me to *Jenufa* that night? Watching Jenufa's bereavement, at first quietly accepted, emerge with terrifying force when the dead body of the child was discovered under the ice and she recognised the tiny red cap that she had knitted for him, ignited my own gnawing grief. I wanted to cry out in the darkness of the theatre as she and I shared the same devastating loss. Immediately afterwards, to learn that Paul was dead, proved to be a tipping point that separated me irrevocably from the self I had once been. Though I escaped unharmed from a fire that took hold of my flat that night, it left me homeless and uprooted. Having inspected the damage, the landlord told me to leave. Before I did, I cut off my long hair with a pair of kitchen scissors and scattered the straggly offcuts into the pond beneath the willow tree.

My physical and emotional transformation had begun.

At first I thought of returning to the New Forest, the place where Lucy was born. The morning after I abandoned the performance of *Ariadne* and fled from the theatre, I took an early train from Waterloo to Brockenhurst. As the train left London further and further behind, I toyed with the idea of assuming a new identity and beginning a new life in the Forest. I'd even decided on a name, only to be wrong-footed by the woman whose cottage I rented. I was dazed and tired and relieved to find somewhere that was available for as long as I needed it, so that when the friendly young owner asked for my name, without thinking, I gave it as Isabel Grey, and Isabel Grey I remained throughout my time there.

While I waited for the birth, I got to know the Forest. Its landscape was largely unchanged since the days of William the Conqueror, a living time capsule of a by-gone age. I was gladdened and calmed by the sights all around me of life going on almost as it would have done in medieval times and I took to roaming the narrow lanes and bridle-paths, watching the animals go about their peaceful ways. One day, a chestnut mare and her two spindly colts sauntered across the path right in front of me and I watched as they ambled towards a glade of ancient oak and beech. On the day before Lucy was born, when I felt the first stirrings that warned me her birth might be imminent, I walked too far and it was almost dusk when I realised I should go back. As I turned a bend near the entrance to my cottage, I met a group of young deer in the middle of the road. They stopped, startled and transfixed, their eyes full of a fear I guessed was mirrored in my own.

I became Elen Daniel a few months later in the porch of Holy Trinity Church in Sandleheath when my sister turned her back on me and a kindly curate appeared offering help.

After the fire in my flat in Shepherd's Bush, I had nowhere to go. I thought of Matthew and knew he would help me unquestioningly, but it seemed wrong to prevail on his love when I had shunned him all these years. I felt the tranquillity of the Forest calling me back, but I couldn't summon the energy or the will to make the move. I turned instead to Reverend Kyle, who took me to the nuns at the Stella Maris Convent.

The Sisters of Stella Maris allowed me space and silence, knowing enough about grief to accept that its paths are different for everyone who endures it. Sister Angelica, who I had met at the Good Shepherd in Sandleheath, urged me to be patient. She, too, had known suffering, having lost her parents and sisters in a road accident when she was nineteen years old. The transformation from grief, she said, is a slow, laborious and difficult undertaking.

A less devout soul might have added that not everybody makes it.

Loss had left me hollowed out and desolate. I'd lost everything that mattered to me, and I let the pain of loss seep silently into the very core of my being, encasing myself in a reserve that was hard for others to penetrate. Time lost all definition, and days and weeks and months went awry.

All my life I had been a voracious reader of fiction and I searched my memory for novels that conveyed the aftermath of loss, hoping to recognise myself somewhere and feel less strange and unhinged, but nothing depicted by even the finest writers compared to the excoriating reality of it. I was not exactly insane, like Heathcliff in *Wuthering Heights* grieving for Cathy, but I was not unlike Hamlet after the death of his father, becoming increasingly wayward and eccentric, as if my fundamental self had been rewired. The norms of ordinary behaviour were also lost, so that sometimes I did things that were hard to explain, things I knew were outlandish and bizarre, things I would not have done before. Being unanchored by loss affected my every action, my every thought, even when I was not consciously thinking about it.

Eventually, within the shelter of the convent community, I regained a sense of purpose, living simply among them, dependent upon their charity, but trying to be of service to them, too, by tending to their vegetable gardens and orchards. Sister Angelica became a trusted friend and when she and I worked together in the gardens, I counted myself happy.

If you were to walk past the Convent, tucked away in a quiet corner of west London, you would see an attractive circular drive, flanked on both sides by mature trees, leading to an imposing redbrick house that looked like a comfortable private home. The handsome Victorian villa was able to house up to twenty women, though there were never that many when I lived there, and the numbers declined inexorably, leaving the Convent prey to the overtures of property developers who coveted its large and desirable site. From its location, you would not guess that behind the house were two acres of gardens that retained much of the original Victorian landscaping. Close to the house to one side was a vegetable garden and a potager, while a stone stairwell from a small formal garden led down to split level terraces, large lawns, a pond, and an orchard. The surrounding woodland belonged to a Cambridge college and gave the appearance of being an extension to the garden, giving the property a surprisingly rural feel.

I lived at Stella Maris for thirty six years and for much of that time, I was one of the younger women there and my work in the gardens was greatly appreciated by the older sisters who were no longer able to tend them, and by the few young nuns, whose work among the poor and needy of the area left them little time for gardening. As they grew older and more frail, some of the nuns retired to the Mother House in the midlands; some—including Sister Angelica—died while still in service. She was younger than me, but her health had been compromised by the tuberculosis she suffered in her twenties. Her death was sudden and unexpected, from pneumonia which developed after a stubborn bout of bronchitis. It was yet another loss. Her grace and gentle wisdom had helped to steady and fortify me and with her gone, I once more found myself adrift and increasingly lonely.

In my early years at Stella Maris, I stayed close to the convent, not venturing much into the outside world, but now I resumed the long walks I'd begun during my time in Shepherd's Bush, ramblings on foot and journeys on the underground that took me all over the city. In those later years, I rarely went to concerts but, in the summer, I would chat to crowds queuing for the Proms at the Albert Hall or for the open air theatre in Regent's Park. I enjoyed a sense of friendly communion among them, but when everyone had taken their seats, ready to soak up an evening's entertainment of music or theatre, I was often overwhelmed by a sense of emptiness and came to doubt the wisdom of looking for human contact in this way.

Perhaps that was why I increasingly came to think of trees as friends. From a young age, I'd loved woodlands and forests, and as I grew older I longed to know more about the different species and their origins. I befriended a young forester called Diego who worked in the woodlands that bordered the convent. He helped me sometimes in the gardens at Stella Maris, and from him I learnt about the secret lives of trees. We would walk together through our woodlands and he would point out the different species, explaining that trees are part of an extended family that lives and breathes and communicates like we do. He told me how trees were able to survive the harshest winters and that when they shed their leaves in autumn, they are preparing to shut down until spring. In the New Year, we would walk amongst these beautiful sleeping giants, waiting for them to burst back into life again and become once more like the forests in Shakespeare, full of magic and romance. However lonely I was, within these woods I felt part of a community that was alive with activity and sociability, and at those times, I felt less alone.

Benjamin was Chaplain at the Convent when I first arrived but left sometime later to run his own parish. He was always nearby if I needed him and, on Sundays, I would go to his services. For a while, when his twin daughters were young, I would take them to Sunday School and read from the scriptures to them and the other children.

As the number of sisters dwindled until there were only a handful of us rattling around the large and increasingly shabby house, Benjamin warned me that the Mother House was minded to sell to developers and, though I did not want to believe it or face it, I knew that one day soon I would once more be homeless.

The prospect of leaving the gardens and orchards and woodlands was one I did not feel I would survive and I clung to Stella Maris long after the nuns had gone and the developers were in possession. I need not have lived the way I have. I could have made different choices, less peculiar, more conventional and comfortable, but the seeds of my odd behaviour were sown over three decades earlier when I suffered a derangement of self so profound that what I did afterwards was not always easy to explain.

The builders set about gutting the house and began the painstaking task of turning it into a hotel, but I refused to leave the convent grounds and despite the protests of the developers, I moved into a bothy tucked away near the orchard on the boundary of the garden. It had originally been a journeyman's cottage, a space to stay for someone who travelled around different estates to learn their trade. Later, in the days when the house was a gentleman's residence, the Head Gardener's office was situated downstairs while the upstairs was used as a fruit store for apples, pears and other produce from the garden. Angelica and I had kept the bothy clean and tidy and used it as shelter from the weather and somewhere to have a cup of tea and a break, and in her case, an occasional cigarette. It was weatherproof and dry and had a basic washroom outside. I slept upstairs on a narrow bed Diego helped me salvage from the house and, together, he and I brought over some small pieces of furniture to create a sitting room downstairs. There was still a functioning fireplace and I learnt to use it for cooking as well as for warmth.

The modest lifestyle of the convent had prepared me for these privations. Though Diego and Benjamin never stopped supporting me, they opposed my decision to stay, fearing the hardship would weaken my health. I could have afforded a flat. I had lived frugally for so long that I still had some savings and Benjamin had insisted I claim my state pension, though it took me several years to get round to it. For a while, he would bring me details of houses with bedsits to let, saying that the day would come when the developers would forcibly evict me and I should move out before that happened. I knew, though, that my spirit—and therefore, most likely my health—would be broken by a move into a characterless flat with no outside space I could call my own. I was stubborn and determined to stay put, and though the winter was harsh and felt longer than usual, the knowledge that all the trees around me were surviving the cold and the frosts, the wind and the rain gave me strength, and I imagined myself as one of them, weathering the worst of the elements and looking forward to spring.

As the hotel began to take shape, the developers engaged a landscape designer to advise on the gardens. She was young and inexperienced, and seemed grateful for the information I gave her about the garden's history and its various plantings. I looked forward to her visits as it gave me an opportunity to talk about herbs and trees and plants to someone who had time for me and took an interest. One day she told me that the orchard was to be cleared to make way for a spa in the corner of the garden. The bothy would be pulled down as part of the development and she said that planning consent would almost certainly be secured. She urged me to find somewhere to move to and I know she spoke to Benjamin about it, because he intensified his campaign to persuade me to find what he called a 'proper home'.

I became increasingly anxious and restless. During the day, the site was busy and noisy, with men and machines destroying what had for so long been a peaceful sanctuary. At night and on Sundays, silence was restored but it was short respite in an increasingly fraught situation.

My trips into the centre of London were a form of escape from the din that penetrated all corners of the site. Occasionally, I walked through the gardens at Embankment and Russell Square and, on fine days, I would find a bench from which to sit and watch. I'd rescue unwanted newspapers and pass the time doing crosswords. Sometimes, someone would come and sit next to me and we would chat about all sorts of inconsequential things and it was on one of those occasions, when a woman even older than me was bemoaning the challenges of travelling on the Circle Line, that I saw Matthew for the first time since he had come to my dressing room before the first performance of *Ariadne*.

I remembered that his family business had offices on Euston Road and I guessed he was cutting through the gardens on his way home. He was still tall and upright and his hair was now the colour of light silver, not the nondescript pale brown I remembered. He stopped to make way for a boy on a skateboard and I was struck by how handsome he was and wondered why I had never noticed that when he was a young man.

I feared that age had withered me cruelly and I was self-conscious about my unconventional appearance, so I didn't want him to see me now but I watched him closely out of the corner of my eye, trying not to be distracted by my garrulous companion. When he had disappeared out of sight, I hung my head, thinking how lovely it would be to talk to him, to find out about his life and how he was.

I sighed, sensing that however much I might want that, I would lack the courage to go after him or call on him and let him see what had become of me. It was in this downcast mood that I returned to Stella Maris to find Diego and Benjamin waiting for me at the end of the drive. I knew at once that something was wrong.

'No,' I cried as I got closer and saw their anxious faces. I tried to push past them to make my way towards the side entrance into the garden, but Benjamin seized hold of me as gently as he could. I looked into his kindly face and knew that my time there was over.

'It's all gone, Elen,' he said sadly. 'Diego saw what was happening and made them stop long enough for him to gather up your possessions. We've put everything we could find into black bags in the back of my car.'

I pulled away from him crying out and sobbing, my legs threatening to buckle beneath me. I took Benjamin's hand and pulled him towards the garden and reluctantly, he and Diego came with me, gripping my arms the whole time.

Nothing remained of the bothy and almost all the trees in the orchard had been felled. In the few hours I had been away, my little piece of earth had been laid waste.

Over the following weeks, my desire to see Matthew intensified and though the hardships of my living conditions had weakened me, I felt stronger than I had for many days, my congested lungs seeming to clear. Having first taken a shower in the Old School—a laborious routine I tried to stick to, however unwell I felt—I took a bus into the city to look for him in the park near his home. I walked from the stop near Euston station to the Russell Square gardens, trying to ignore the stares my appearance elicited from curious onlookers. It was a grey, chilly day and, as usual, I was swaddled in layers of shabby clothing which kept me reasonably warm but slowed me down. As I trudged wearily towards the park gates, I realised it was my wheezy chest that was the true culprit and by the time I reached the nearest bench, I was struggling to take anything other than the shallowest of breaths.

It was mid-morning when I arrived and all day long, I waited and watched but, as dusk approached, there had been no sign of Matthew. I was cold now and through the long, uncomfortable vigil I had drunk only a cup of tea brought to me by a concerned passer-by. I'd lost track of time and it was the encroaching darkness that told me it was time to leave. Though the noise of the traffic was incessant, the gardens were quiet now and I appeared to be alone.

Time to go and come back another day.

Or perhaps, I thought, I should walk southwards through the park and on to Matthew's home to call on him there. I ignored a nagging fear that a meeting with him now in my altered state would be more humiliating than heartening and instead, I hoped he would welcome me and be glad that I had come.

Alice, Sophie and Steven

Benjamin Kyle and his wife were waiting for us when we reached the vicarage, a short distance from St Mary's Church in Hanford. Sophie's husband was at a conference in Amsterdam, so Steven had insisted on taking the day off work to come with us and we were both glad of his reassuring, steadying presence.

'Come in. Come in,' said Benjamin, taking us through to a homely sitting room overlooking the small front garden. His wife, Julie, disappeared to make coffee while we settled ourselves apprehensively, Sophie and I sitting side by side on a large sofa, Steven facing Benjamin in one of the matching chairs on either side of the fireplace. An inquisitive Welsh terrier was keen to make friends of us all, and Sophie, in particular, was grateful for his playful affection.

'Here we are,' said Julie, re-joining us with a tray of coffee which she set down on a table in the bay window before handing round the mugs and a plate of biscuits.

'So,' said Benjamin, when Julie had sat down in a chair next to his, 'this is a sad affair. I had no idea Elen was not who she said she was, though I admit, I'm not surprised to discover that she had changed her identity.'

'No?' asked Sophie.

He shook his head.

'It's hard to put into words, but something about how she experienced her loss and her grief gave me the feeling that the person I was seeing was not the person she had been before.'

'How did you first meet her?' I asked.

'I was just starting out in my ministry as Chaplain to the Sisters of the Good Shepherd near Sandleheath and, when I met Elen the first time, I was also working temporarily at Holy Trinity Church, covering for the elderly vicar who'd been unwell for a long while. I'd been visiting a bereaved parishioner and, on my way home, I slipped into the church office via the side entrance to collect some notes I needed for a wedding the next day. As I came round to the front of the church to make my way to my car, which I'd left on Vicarage Road, I heard the cry of a baby through the open door of the porch.' He closed his eyes and shook his head. 'So plaintive it was. I can still hear it now.'

He paused and took a sip of coffee.

'The child was clearly unwell and the woman—the mother—was stricken with worry to the point that she could barely speak. It was obvious she needed help, so I decided to take her to the convent because the nuns there were nursing sisters. After we'd gone a very short distance, the woman started wailing and keening and by the time we got to the convent, the baby had already died.'

We let out a collective gasp of shock, and I squeezed Sophie's hand as I felt her shudder at his words.

He nodded in sympathy.

'What happened to the baby after that?' Steven asked after a long silence.

'We buried her in a corner of the cemetery at Holy Trinity,' he said simply.

'Near the oak tree!' Sophie said.

'That's right. The Sexton was a kind man and I took him into my confidence. We saw to it together. It was much later that Elen told me why she'd been taking shelter in the church but, at the time, I guessed she was local and afraid of a scandal, her being unmarried you see, so we kept the burial between ourselves.'

'Does the baby's grave have a headstone?' I asked.

'It does,' he replied. 'Elen arranged it while she was staying at the convent to recover her strength, but she went back to London before it was put in place.' He paused. 'It was many years before she came back to see it.'

Immediately, I knew when that had been.

'Last New Year's Eve,' I said.

Everyone looked at me questioningly.

'I saw you,' I said to Benjamin. 'I'd intended to go for a walk but, when I opened my front door to set off, it was snowing and I changed my mind, but I saw a woman looking down at the house from behind the wall of the graveyard. Of course, I had no idea who she was, but I thought the man with her might have been wearing a dog collar.'

'Indeed,' he said sadly. 'By that time, I think she feared that if she didn't go to visit the grave soon, it might be too late. She told me that her family had lived in the end house of the terrace, but she didn't know if her sister was still there.'

'She died last March,' I said. 'I'm her goddaughter and she left the house to me.'

'What does the baby's headstone say?' Sophie asked.

'Just her name, Lucy, and her dates, 14 September 1977–14 October 1977, and a single, closed rosebud. Nothing else.'

'When did you meet Elen again?' Steven asked.

'She contacted me a few years later. She was in a terrible state—she'd hacked off her beautiful hair and, until it grew again, there was something quite freakish about her appearance. She'd learnt that the man she loved had died unexpectedly and, the night she heard that news, she lit a candle in her flat in his memory, but fell asleep and a gust of wind through the open window caught the candle and it toppled over. Elen woke in time to save herself and put out the flames, but the room was full of smoke and it was that which did the damage. The owner told her to leave, and though she could have afforded to find somewhere else to rent, she was in no state to do so. She needed looking after, and once again I took her to the nuns I was working with here in west London, the sisters of Stella Maris. She lived happily among them for the next thirty-six years.'

'Thirty-six!' Sophie cried.

Benjamin and Julie nodded.

'It suited her there,' Julie said. 'She liked the nuns and they were kind to her.'

'They accepted her funny little ways,' Benjamin said with a chuckle.

'They did,' Julie agreed. 'And she was useful to them, too, working night and day in the gardens, growing fruit and vegetables. Their way of life didn't change much the whole time she was with them and I think the longer she stayed there, the harder it became for her to adjust to change.'

Benjamin agreed.

'She was very close to a sister called Angelica—I suspect she shared secrets with her that she did with no-one else—and Angelica's death was another grievous blow for someone who was not emotionally robust.'

'What was she like?' Sophie asked.

'She was beautiful,' Julie said quietly. 'Strange and eccentric by the time I got to know her, but beautiful.' She wiped her eyes. 'Our girls loved her.'

'She was a solitary soul,' Benjamin said, 'usually alone, and she nearly always wore black. As she grew older, her long hair grew wilder and she used to wind it into a huge bun at the back of her head.'

Steven smiled and nodded and we knew that it was Elen who had helped him on the night he was attacked in Embankment Gardens.

'She had a very particular gaze,' Benjamin continued. 'Kind and sad but sometimes oddly distracted.'

'But it had a funny strength to it as well,' his wife suggested.

'It did,' Benjamin said, laughing. 'Defiance.'

We all laughed.

'Where was she living at the end?' Sophie asked, leaning down to ruffle the head of the dog who was lying across her feet.

Benjamin and Julie looked at each other and hung their heads.

'I feel so bad about it,' Julie said, getting up to offer round the plate of biscuits again.

'I can take you to see it if you like,' Benjamin said. 'And the convent—or what remains of it now. The nuns sold the house and the grounds to developers and it's being turned into a hotel. Elen was distraught at the prospect of leaving. She simply wouldn't accept it.'

'So stubborn, she could be,' Julie said with feeling, and for the first time, I heard faint traces of an Irish accent.

'The grounds were every bit as much her home as the house was, so when all the nuns had left, she moved into the gardener's bothy at the furthest boundary of the garden and she lived there for about a year.'

Sophie gasped.

'But what was that like?' she asked.

'Basic,' Benjamin said, getting up to take our empty mugs and put them on the tray. 'But it was dry.'

'Cold in winter, though,' Julie said, shaking her head. 'And the outside washroom and toilet froze up many a time.'

'She never complained though,' Benjamin said. 'She was remarkably resourceful. Learnt to cook all sorts of nutritious meals on a fire. Wore layers of clothes to keep warm.'

'That was a sight, to be sure,' Julie added.

'Her vegetable broths were delicious,' Benjamin recalled. 'And if she had any to spare, she'd take a bowl round to someone in the neighbourhood she thought might be in need.'

'I guess, eventually the developers wanted to do something with the bothy?' Steven said.

Benjamin nodded.

'They kept giving her warnings, ultimatums to get out, but she ignored them, until one day, after she'd been out on one of her long walks—she tramped all over London, you know—she came back to find it all gone. It was awful for her. We rescued her possessions—she didn't have much—and we found her a room in the home of one of our parishioners, a lovely woman called Caitlin Dixon.'

'Elen couldn't settle there,' Julie said with a grimace, 'and I don't blame her. Caitlin's a good woman but she has a son in his twenties who's gone way off the rails and, out of the blue, he turned up, saying he was homeless and needed somewhere to stay.' She paused and glanced at her husband. 'It may be un-Christian to say this, but I wouldn't want to stay under the same roof as him.'

'What happened?' Sophie asked in alarm.

'Elen spent as little time there as she could,' Benjamin said. 'She took to wandering the streets for longer than ever, but one day she got back to find him in her room, going through her things. She didn't have much, but what she did have was precious to her and she... Well, Caitlin said she went berserk, that's the only word she said could describe it.'

'She gathered all her stuff together into black bags and left as fast as she could and, for a few days, we didn't know where she was,' Julie said.

'We hunted for her all over the neighbourhood,' Benjamin continued, 'asking everyone we met if they'd seen her, until someone said they'd noticed a makeshift shelter made out of an old tarpaulin and half-concealed by vegetation at the rear of the Old School—a community centre, not far from here. When we went to see for ourselves, Elen wasn't there but her black bags were tucked away under a torn green tent draped between low-hanging branches of a weeping willow tree. The weeds had been cleared and it looked as if she'd set about turning a scrap of land in an abandoned corner into an improvised home and garden.'

'When the Old School *was* a school,' Julie explained, 'right up until the 1960s, the area at the back was a playground and a garden. The old building's been refurbished and modernised and a car park built at the front, but the trust which runs it ran out of money and the land at the back has been left to run wild.'

'So Elen moved in and made it her own and had been living there for the past six weeks.'

We were all stunned into silence and before Benjamin spoke again, the only sound in the room was the gentle snoring of the dog.

'She wouldn't accept any offers of help and said she was staying put.'

'All we could do,' Julie said, 'was make sure she had enough to eat and could stay reasonably warm but…'

Her voice trailed away and Benjamin reached over and took her hand.

'She cooked on a fire she made from sticks and newspapers,' he said. 'We open the church hall on Saturdays to people who're homeless, and we give them a meal, but Elen said that wasn't for her. The manager of the Old School let her shower in their facilities and she was glad of that.'

'She continued to go on her long rambles,' Julie said, 'though she hadn't been well for a while. I think all the shock and upheaval had battered her usual resilience. I felt sure she had a chest infection but she wouldn't go to the doctor. The last time I saw her, on the morning before they found her, she said she felt better.'

'She did,' Benjamin agreed. 'I remember watching her set off. Despite her recent ill health, she was walking very purposefully, and there was something really quite poignant about the sight of her, all wrapped up, but having attempted to look smart.' He paused. 'I saw a glimpse of the beautiful woman she once was. She said she was going into the city, hoping to see an old friend.'

'Do you know who?' I asked.

Julie shook her head.

'We've no idea, have we Benjamin?' she said. 'It's a mystery why she was in that park. We can only assume she became unwell and nobody noticed she was still there when the gardens were locked for the night.'

'There'll be a post-mortem, of course,' Benjamin said softly.

Sophie was holding herself together but was very pale.

'My dear,' Benjamin said gently to her. 'What makes you think you are Elen's daughter, rather than the child we buried?'

Sophie repeated what she'd told me and he listened intently.

'Did your mother's pregnancy go to full term?' he asked unexpectedly.

'It did,' Sophie replied, 'and she was warned to expect a larger than average size baby.'

'And yet you were small?' he said.

Sophie nodded.

He rubbed his chin.

'Lucy was a really bonny baby, despite being almost four weeks premature. Elen said when she first held her she was surprised and relieved that she wasn't small and weakly.'

'Did you find anything amongst Elen's possessions that can help Sophie confirm this?' Steven asked.

Julie nodded.

'We have her hair brush.'

Benjamin stood up.

'Let's go for a walk,' he said, gently nudging the sleeping dog with his toe and offering Sophie his outstretched hand.

They took us first to the site of the former convent, its entrance blocked by steel fencing beyond which contractors were still at work, completing the transformation into an up-market hotel.

'It'll be opening soon,' Julie said.

'It looks nothing like it used to,' Benjamin said sadly. 'The sisters would barely recognise it.'

We stayed for only a few minutes, and walked on to the Church Hall which was nearby. Externally, it still retained the appearance of the grain store Benjamin said it had once been until the church bought and refurbished it. He led us to an office at the back, where Elen's few possessions were laid out on a small table against a wall.

'The clothes had seen better days,' Julie said, 'and we didn't think you'd want to see them, but we kept everything else. There wasn't much. Elen wasn't a hoarder, so what's here must have been important to her.'

'Go ahead,' Benjamin said. 'Have a look.'

There was a battered blue folder, four books tied together with a leather strap and a sealed, clear bag containing a matching hair brush and mirror. Sophie, Steven and I moved along the table and examined the relics of Isabel's life.

Steven opened the folder, while Sophie went first to the brush and mirror, examining them through the clear plastic. They were a striking pair, embellished with blue enamel backings and ornate silver handles.

'There are some initials on the handles,' Sophie said peering at them closely before handing the bag to me. 'Looks like O M.'

'They look expensive,' Steven said, leaning over my shoulder to look.

'They do,' I said, wondering to whom they'd belonged before Isabel.

I handed them back to Sophie and turned to look at the books. On the top was Isabel's copy of *Villette*. It was old and well-used and, throughout it, there were sections underlined, some in pencil, others in ink.

304

I believe in some blending of hope and sunshine sweetening the worst lots. I believe that this life is not all; neither the beginning nor the end. I believe while I tremble; I trust while I weep.

I blinked back tears and showed the page to Sophie.

Underneath *Villette* was a large illustrated book called *Trees of the World* and beneath that was *A Grief Observed* by CS Lewis. Again, Isabel had been through it, underlining sentences, marking some sections with ticks in the margins.

Alone into the Alone was one that caught my eye.

The final volume was not a book but a score of the Brahms Requiem, again well used and with many pencil markings, suggesting that Isabel had performed the work many times.

Steven had emptied the contents of the folder onto the table so that we could all see what was there.

The funeral service for Isabel's father at Holy Trinity Church.

A programme for the event at Hope Street Theatre at which she'd performed with Paul.

Her copy of 'Let no man steal your thyme'.

A cream envelope.

A pile of sketches and drawings, many of them of Isabel herself.

A bundle of hand-written notes from Paul, the text full of flourishes and doodles.

Sophie was flicking through the sketches.

'Paul could certainly draw,' she said.

'He could,' agreed Steven. 'Look at this.'

He held up the manuscript of the song, on the back cover of which Paul had sketched a branch of willow and a spray of flowering thyme.

'That's lovely,' Sophie said, taking it from him.

She put it down and opened a stiff cream envelope from which she took out a handmade card. She gazed at it for a long while before handing it to me.

'The moment Paul stepped back into her life.'

Our final stop was about a mile away at the Old School. It was set slightly apart on the edge of the village, close to what had once been the Hanford Estate. It had been a small Victorian school for the children of the estate and, at first glance, it looked as if it might have been made of gingerbread and that you could snap off pieces of its ornate exterior and eat them. Its octagonal school clock tower had been retained and restored, and there were Gothic features everywhere, at the windows, the carved wooden fascia boards and the blue brick patterns.

'It looks like something out of Hansel and Gretel,' I gasped.

'Hopefully nothing as sinister went on here,' Benjamin said, laughing.

We walked past a handful of parked cars, round to the back of the building, most of which was, as Julie had said, a wilderness of weeds and long grass and unkempt shrubbery. The garden to the right, however, was dominated by a majestic weeping willow tree which created a canopy of cover in one corner, around which was a carpet of flowers and cards and candles.

The others watched as Sophie and I stepped forward to read some of the messages. One read: *Good-bye Elen—a real lady, honest and true, who will be missed and fondly remembered by many.* Another said: *A charming, dignified and highly cultured lady.* Everywhere we looked there were outpourings of sadness and regret at the passing of a woman who had clearly left a mark on the community in which for so long she had lived a highly unconventional life.

With the candles flickering and the leaves and petals of the flowers fluttering gently in the breeze, it was a poignant sight. By now, Sophie was crying openly. She's taller than me but I took her awkwardly in my arms.

'Oh my goodness,' I whispered. 'What a way to live. What a life. What led her to this?'

'I don't know,' she said, clinging to my shoulders and trying to recover herself before she raised her head. 'She endured so much but perhaps some things are impossible to come back from.'

I hugged her close, fearing she was right and that, at the end, Isabel had made herself a cave into which, like Ariadne, she could retreat from the world.

Alice and Steven

There was a delay of several weeks before the funeral and I was overcome by a powerful sense of anticlimax. The mystery around Isabel and the quest to find her had been a welcome distraction and had given me a sense of purpose.

The post-mortem revealed that as a complication of a common strain of flu, Isabel had contracted a bacterial infection that had spread rapidly through her blood, provoking sepsis. The report said that her blood pressure would have dropped to a dangerously low level and, deprived of oxygen, her vital organs would have begun to fail. She might have become confused and disorientated, trying to find her way out of the park as she became increasingly unwell.

'Tim says that sometimes the immune system goes haywire, attacking the patient's own body as well as the invading bugs,' Sophie told me.

On the day she rang to say that the DNA test, using Isabel's hair, had confirmed Isabel was her mother, I laid flowers on the grave of the other baby born in Brockenhurst in September 1977. As I walked to the back of the graveyard towards the oak tree in the corner, I sensed the tranquillity that Sophie had described but felt, too, an air of desolation, my modest bunch of snowdrops being the only flowers there.

'I didn't want her to be forgotten,' I told Steven later.

'Isabel never forgot her,' he reminded me.

How true, I thought.

We were walking through Linda Vista Gardens having had Sunday lunch in a pub near the entrance. It was a cold, bright day and the park was busy with people coming to see the first signs of spring.

'A penny for them,' Steven said when we sat down on a bench near the statue.

'I can't get over the sadness of it. That Isabel lived such a long and lonely life mourning a child who was not hers, not knowing that her true daughter was alive and was looking for her.'

Steven looked at me and nodded.

'How different her life might have been if she'd been given her own baby,' I said, kicking at some dry twigs. 'She might have made different choices, had a different life.'

'She might,' Steven agreed. 'Who knows?'

As we made our way back to the entrance and prepared to go our separate ways home, Steven asked if I'd been to the theatre since I moved back to Sandleheath. I hadn't.

'The Artistic Director is retiring after thirty years in the job and his last production is *The Tempest*. Do you fancy seeing it?' he asked.

'OK,' I said, pleased at the suggestion. 'It will make a change.'

Once home, I felt restless. On the table in the hall was the copy of *Villette* I had bought a few days earlier.

Time to read it, I thought, this book that had so obsessed Isabel. I found it in many ways a difficult novel, perversely strange and suffused with a loneliness and melancholy I found hard to stay with. It took me a while to get into it, but gradually it drew me in. I wondered what threads might be traceable between Lucy's storyline and Isabel's: two Pauls, two loves, two separations. Did Isabel regard the book as a lucky charm and devour its pages hoping the outcome of her own narrative might be found hidden within Lucy's story? I knew that many nineteenth-century novels ended in marriage, but I was shocked at the implication at the end of *Villette* that Lucy and Paul are never reunited, that her happiest years were those when they were apart as she waited in blissful anticipation for his return. Did that gossamer thread Isabel had fantasised as a lifeline between herself and *Villette* survive so that she could continue to believe that, one day, she and her Paul would at last enjoy the plot trajectory of most romantic novels?

Perhaps it did—until the news came that he had died and, with it, the certainty that for her there would be no deliverance.

Steven and I met in the bar before the performance began.

'Do you know the play?' I asked, flicking through the programme and sipping a glass of red wine.

'I did it at school,' he replied. 'How about you?'

I shook my head and reached for one of the cheese-filled oatcakes he'd bought at the bar.

'I saw the opera by Thomas Adès a few years ago,' I said, licking hot melted cheese off my fingers. 'My agent thought that one day I might sing the role of Ariel.'

'And did you?'

'No fear,' I said, shying away from him in mock horror. 'It's possibly the highest role ever written for a soprano. She has to enter singing seventeen, full-voiced top Es and her music continues in a similar range for most of the opera.'

'Wow.'

'On the page, it looks so head-spinningly high you fear that all anyone could produce would be homicidal-sounding shrieks, but the soprano I saw nailed it, no problem. She had the audience watching her with mouths agape one minute and laughing in amazement the next.'

'Respect,' Steven said, with feeling.

'Indeed,' I said, knowing it was a part I would never now tackle.

Our seats were five rows back from the acting area—a shiny, rippling blue floor cloth—in a completely round auditorium which had been transformed into a mysterious sea green cavern full of whispers and strange sounds. Silken drapes and the detritus of a rotted boat were veiled in half-light so it was hard to decide what they were or what they represented. The lights dipped further and the play began with an almighty bang as Prospero stage-managed a fearful storm, before, like a conjuror, he stilled it to reveal the ramshackle home that he and his daughter Miranda had created on their desert island.

I'd been afraid I would struggle to understand the language but the actors made everything they said sound not just melodic but conversational, as if iambic pentameter was the most natural way of speaking in the world, without any of the fussy grandeur I associated with Shakespearean acting. There were other unexpected pleasures to be had, too. The comic scenes involving the shipwrecked drunkards *were* funny and Miranda was no drippy wimp, but a girl fast approaching womanhood who like everyone else on the island, was seeking her own personal liberation.

The greatest delight, however, was Ariel, an irrepressible imp, encased in a close-fitting body suit of green and turquoise, set off by an oversized wig of peroxide quiffs and spikes. It was she who held the audience spell-bound with her daring athleticism, her otherworldly tricks, but most of all, her ethereal singing of some hauntingly evocative music. In everything she did, she exuded an angelic grace and it was her compassionate spirit, her empathy and goodness that was the catalyst for Prospero's change of heart; for his acceptance that 'the rarer action is in virtue than in vengeance.'

We stayed in our seats during the interval, neither of us wanting to break the spell the show had cast by being jostled in a crowded bar. We sat quietly, chatting about the play and listening to the conversations around us, impatient for the second half to begin. When it did, I didn't want it to end. I cried when Prospero finally let Ariel go 'to be as free as the air', and again during the Epilogue when Prospero laid down his magic and asked the audience to set him free.

Afterwards, we had a drink in the theatre bar. While Steven went to the gents, I studied the programme and found an interview with the director in which he was asked why he chose *The Tempest* for his valedictory production.

> *It's one of my favourite plays and I've waited thirty years to direct it. Love and hatred, passion and revenge, humour and sadness—*The Tempest *has them all—but I hope audiences can watch this production and still feel good at the end of it. Of course, loss is a powerful theme in this play, but it also shows us the power of forgiveness to heal when all seems lost, and it makes a strong case for art's ability to set you free by helping you to understand yourself.*

I was deep in thought when the door that led to back stage opened with a flourish and the diminutive girl who had played Ariel bounded towards the bar where a group of actors were waiting for her and pointing to a pint of Guinness.

'Was't well done?' she cried.

'Bravely, my diligence,' said a man I recognised as Prospero.

She seized her drink with relish, before slumping against the bar with a grin of relief. I recognised the adrenaline-fuelled high, the giddying mix of exhilaration and utter fatigue and couldn't help smiling at her. There was much joshing banter among the actors as they assessed their performances, recalling nerve-wracking near-misses and high-spots alike. They'd worked hard and the audience had been responsive and appreciative.

I was surprised and pleased that far from saddening me, I was cheered by their high spirits and I felt something inside me shift.

Alice

A winding path, flanked on both sides by high walls, provided a short-cut from the station to the church. As we reached the end of the lane and turned left, my eye was caught by a cluster of gravestones, worn and covered in lichen, peeping out through bushes and shrubs. Stepping through the lychgate, we saw that a particularly old section of the churchyard that bordered the lane was fenced off and designated as a 'wild area', allowing plants and habitats for birds and insects to flourish, an unexpectedly rustic haven in an otherwise urban setting.

The most distinctive feature of the churchyard was a picturesque archway in the middle, just beyond the main entrance to the church building.

'This looks as if it might once have been part of the structure of the church itself,' Steven said, standing underneath it to examine the stonework, while I looked beyond the arch to where I could see a newly-prepared, open grave.

I turned away and we stood in the patchy sunshine waiting for others to arrive. A squirrel darted in and out of the gravestones and a pair of magpies strutted around, while, out of sight, some pigeons cooed softly. The clouds were parting, allowing the sun to break through and I lifted my face to feel its warmth.

'What a peaceful resting ground,' Steven said, as if he'd read my thoughts.

I nodded.

'It's so beautifully well-cared for,' I said, pleased to imagine Isabel amid such tranquillity.

The heavy oak door of the church was open and I stepped inside to take a look. The church was surprisingly small given the size of the burial ground, and I guessed it could seat only about a hundred people in the pews in the main body of the church, with two rows of additional seating at the back, and choir stalls that would accommodate a few dozen singers. What struck me most powerfully was how bright and airy it was, with many of the church windows filled with glowing colour, and others left plain to allow the daylight to stream through.

I stood in the central aisle and looked towards the far end of the church where Isabel's coffin had been placed beneath a window depicting Jesus as the Good Shepherd. I stepped closer and saw that the coffin was made of willow, its lid covered in willow branches amongst which a spray of wild flowers and sprigs of flowering thyme leaves had been woven. I closed my eyes and breathed in the sweet, herby aroma, when I heard voices outside and recognised the warm timbre of Benjamin's deep baritone.

I walked back up the aisle and stood in the doorway, watching as groups of people gathered along the path, exchanging greetings. I spotted Matthew and Kevin and guessed the others were local people who had known Elen. Benjamin and his wife and daughters had arrived with Sophie and her husband, and were talking quietly with Steven a short distance from the door. Dressed in black and holding the hand of a man a little shorter than her, Sophie had her back to me, and as she shifted her position, I could see that her pregnancy was more visible now and she looked tired.

I stepped forward and touched her gently on the arm. She turned and greeted me with a relieved smile and a long hug.

'You look pale,' I said. 'How are you?'

'I'm OK,' she said quietly. 'It's been a long wait.'

'I know,' I said, squeezing her tight.

'Have you spoken to him?' she whispered in my ear.

I looked at her with surprise and nodded.

'And?'

'I'm not sure. Maybe…'

I heard Steven talking to Tim and relaxed my grip on her so that I, too, could say hello. He was as kindly and friendly as I'd expected and I felt instantly at ease with him.

'A strange day for all of us,' he said, 'but I'm glad you're both here. I know Sophie appreciates it.'

I smiled and nodded and stood aside to allow people to pass us on their way inside.

'I suppose we should go in, too,' I said, glancing towards the lychgate for signs of late-comers.

'You'll sit with us, won't you?' Sophie asked anxiously, taking my hand. As Tim led the way, I heard the sweet voice of a soprano, at first unaccompanied, then joined by a gentle backing of strings and piano. I didn't recognise the singer, or the tune, but guessed it was an American gospel hymn. We took our seats at the front and listened as the recording played out.

> *Softly and tenderly Jesus is calling,*
> *Calling for you and for me;*
> *See, on the portals He's waiting and watching,*
> *Watching for you and for me.*
>
> *Come home, come home,*
> *You who are weary, come home;*
> *Earnestly, tenderly, Jesus is calling,*
> *Calling, O sinner, come home!*
>
> *Why should we tarry when Jesus is pleading,*
> *Pleading for you and for me?*
> *Why should we linger and heed not His mercies,*
> *Mercies for you and for me?*
>
> *Come home, come home,*
> *You who are weary, come home;*
> *Earnestly, tenderly, Jesus is calling,*
> *Calling, O sinner, come home!*

Time is now fleeting, the moments are passing,
Passing from you and from me;
Shadows are gathering, deathbeds are coming,
Coming for you and for me.

Come home, come home,
You who are weary, come home;
Earnestly, tenderly, Jesus is calling,
Calling, O sinner, come home!

Oh, for the wonderful love He has promised,
Promised for you and for me!
Though we have sinned, He has mercy and pardon,
Pardon for you and for me.

Come home, come home,
You who are weary, come home;
Earnestly, tenderly, Jesus is calling,
Calling, O sinner, come home!

Benjamin was standing by the side of the coffin, head bowed and hands crossed in front of him. As the hymn drew to a close, he climbed into the pulpit.

'Welcome to St Mary's,' he said, 'where we have come to lay to rest our dear friend and neighbour, a woman most of us here today knew as Elen Daniel, but a woman who had a whole other life as Isabel Grey.'

A breathless hush descended on the church as the congregation was drawn into his words.

'I'm sure some of you are asking why we played that hymn,' he said, looking round at the faces looking up at him. 'Well, it's simple. Julie and I chose it because it was one of Elen's favourite hymns from one of her favourite films. The hymn recurs as the theme music in *The Trip to Bountiful*, a film Elen loved, in part because of that hymn and the singer who sang it. 'Her voice is so pure and so full of love,' she once told me. 'Whenever I hear it, I'm inspired to be a little bit better, a little more in touch with my heart and my spirit." He paused and looked around. 'And what a spirit Elen was.'

I looked at Sophie and saw her eyes were glistening. She reached into the pocket of her coat for a handkerchief as Benjamin invited the congregation to stand and sing *Lord of All Hopefulness*, a hymn I had always loved, its Irish melody perfectly suited to the words describing the course of a day, from waking to sleeping.

> *Lord of all hopefulness, Lord of all joy,*
> *Whose trust, ever childlike, no cares could destroy,*
> *Be there at our waking, and give us, we pray,*
> *Your bliss in our hearts, Lord,*
> *At the break of the day.*

> *Lord of all eagerness, Lord of all faith,*
> *Whose strong hands were skilled at the plane and the lathe,*
> *Be there at our labours and give us, we pray,*
> *Your strength in our hearts, Lord,*
> *At the noon of the day.*

I heard the church door open and close and turned round hopefully. The pews were full and I saw my father slip into one of the few empty seats. I turned back to the service sheet and sang with as much conviction as I could and, at the same time, tried to steady my nerves for the reading Sophie had asked me to give.

> *Lord of all kindliness, Lord of all grace,*
> *Your hands swift to welcome, Your arms to embrace.*
> *Be there at our homing, and give us, we pray,*
> *Your love in our hearts, Lord,*
> *At the eve of the day.*

Lord of all gentleness, Lord of all calm,
Whose voice is contentment, whose presence is balm,
Be there at our sleeping, and give us, we pray,
Your peace in our hearts, Lord,
At the end of the day.

When the long final chord of the organ had died away, Sophie and I stood up and went to the front of the pews.

'Next, we have two readings,' Benjamin said. 'The first is from Sophie—Isabel's daughter—and the other from Alice, a friend of Isabel's family.'

I heard an intake of breath and saw people craning their heads to see us as we stood side by side, both of us clutching the sheets from which we would read.

'The first reading,' Sophie said, in a voice remarkably clear and steady, 'is a passage from Shakespeare's play, *Cymbeline.*'

I fixed my eyes on the ground, but sensed her gathering herself before she started.

Fear no more the heat o' the sun,
Nor the furious winter's rages;
Thou thy worldly task hast done,
Home art gone, and ta'en thy wages:
Golden lads and girls all must,
As chimney-sweepers, come to dust.

Fear no more the frown o' the great;
Thou art past the tyrant's stroke;
Care no more to clothe and eat;
To thee the reed is as the oak:
The scepter, learning, physic, must
All follow this, and come to dust.

Fear no more the lightning flash,
Nor the all-dreaded thunder stone;
Fear not slander, censure rash;
Thou hast finished joy and moan:
All lovers young, all lovers must
Consign to thee, and come to dust.

No exorciser harm thee!
Nor no witchcraft charm thee!
Ghost unlaid forbear thee!
Nothing ill come near thee!
Quiet consummation have;
And renownèd be thy grave!

Her voice wavered slightly on the last word and her face was flushed as she folded her prompt sheet and waited for me to start.

'The second reading,' I said, 'is a poem called 'Life' by Charlotte Brontë, a writer Isabel loved from a young age.'

I cleared my throat and took a deep breath. I had learnt the poem by heart but was glad of my crib sheet, though I determined to rely on it as little as possible. From the corner of my eye, I saw Steven watching me intently and as I glanced over at him, he smiled.

Life, believe, is not a dream
So dark as sages say;
Oft a little morning rain
Foretells a pleasant day.
Sometimes there are clouds of gloom,
But these are transient all;
If the shower will make the roses bloom,
O why lament its fall?
Rapidly, merrily,
Life's sunny hours flit by,
Gratefully, cheerily

Enjoy them as they fly!
What though Death at times steps in,
And calls our Best away?
What though sorrow seems to win,
O'er hope, a heavy sway?
Yet Hope again elastic springs,
Unconquered, though she fell;
Still buoyant are her golden wings,
Still strong to bear us well.
Manfully, fearlessly,
The day of trial bear,
For gloriously, victoriously,
Can courage quell despair!

When I had finished, Sophie took my hand and led me back into our seats on the front row. As I edged past Steven and before I sat down, I saw my father lift up his hands to mime silent applause. I sat down with relief, glad that my part in the service was over and had gone passably well.

'Thank you Sophie and Alice,' Benjamin was saying from the pulpit. 'Thank you Alice for choosing such an uplifting poem. It strikes me as remarkable that a woman who suffered such hardships and tragedies as Charlotte Brontë did could write a poem so full of optimism. She urges us to believe that life is a wonderful thing and that though there are aspects of it that are unpleasant—like death and sorrow—hope and courage will ultimately defeat them.

'And thank you Sophie for inviting me to give the eulogy. I knew Elen well for thirty-six years but of her life before we met, I knew little, but I've pieced together as much as I can from friends here today who knew her as Isabel, and I will call her Isabel when I talk about her early life and career, and Elen when I describe the woman I knew.'

There was a rustle as the congregation settled itself to listen. He started with an outline of Isabel's early life in Sandleheath, before moving on to talk about her career.

'I have read about this time and am struck by how much joy she brought through her voice and her art. One writer said: 'She was a compelling and elegant stage personality, and while pure lyricism is obviously Miss Grey's strong point, there is more to her than that for she is a singing actress of some depth.' I never heard Elen sing opera, but I did hear her sing hymns—all over the place. You would even hear her singing in the street! She reminded me of Carrie Watts, the indomitable heroine of *The Trip to Bountiful*, who would drive her daughter-in-law mad by singing what she dismissed as old fashioned hymns all day.'

He laughed and the congregation laughed with him.

'But,' he went on more seriously, 'the collapse of her voice in the late 1970s must have been a grievous blow for her. Some of her friends from that time are here today and for them, the story of what happened to Isabel will make painful listening.'

I looked across the aisle and saw Matthew bow his head.

'I met her when she was afflicted by the first of a number of great sadnesses,' Benjamin continued. 'She had had a baby—a little girl she called Lucy—but that baby died, a death for which she felt responsible. I believe the loss of that child was a turning point for her. It marked the time when she started calling herself Elen Daniel and turned her back on the life and the people she had known before.

'Elen was soon to suffer another grievous loss. Even before her baby was born, the man she loved had left her, and a few years later, she learnt that he had died unexpectedly.' He paused. 'His name was Paul and with his death, I think part of her died, too. That was when I met her for the second time and when she came to live among us.'

He seemed to brighten at the memory.

'She was quite a character,' he said, 'and she could be rather obsessive about strange things. For instance, she became an ardent protector of nature and had a vehement dislike of drawing pins in trees. 'What have the trees ever done to deserve this?' she'd cry, snatching down posters appealing for lost kittens.'

There was another murmur of laughter and even Matthew looked up and smiled.

'On her long rambles around London, she liked to chat to the queues outside the Albert Hall during the Proms and tell them about the music they were going to hear.'

I heard Steven gasp and turned to see him nodding enthusiastically as if he knew that.

'On the top of her coffin,' Benjamin was saying, 'there are sprigs of thyme, a herb that derives its name from the Greek word *Thymus*, meaning courage, and Elen was a woman who combined great courage with great gentleness and kindness. A bed of thyme was thought by some to be a home for fairies and, when she was tending the garden at Stella Maris, Elen often set aside a patch for them and sometimes slept there... Though she was always fastidious about her hygiene, a sweet, earthy smell clung to her from all the days and nights she spent sleeping under trees with leaves and vegetation for cover.'

I looked around and saw people shaking their heads in astonishment.

'She was very public-spirited and frequently went about picking up rubbish,' Benjamin continued, 'and she helped to care for the graveyard here and worked especially hard with parts that had become derelict. I'm sure that everyone in the parish who knew her would agree that she never lost the charm and intelligence we know marked her out as a singer. Long before she died, she'd become something of a local institution and when news of her death was announced, the local website was swamped with good wishes, kind thoughts and offers to donate to her funeral or a memorial service. One message said: 'She had dignity. She did things her way but she would go out of her way to help you.'"

Benjamin looked round and sighed.

'Most people would say she made some unconventional life choices but I think we have to put ourselves in her shoes. All deaths have consequences for someone left behind, and baby Lucy's death was a calamity with terrible consequences for Isabel. Some might liken her later life to that of Diogenes the Cynic, the Greek philosopher who shows his contempt for the material world by sleeping in a barrel. She certainly never wavered in the frugal life she had chosen for herself—whether out of madness, grief or to punish herself for some perceived wrong deed.'

Benjamin paused and the silence in the church was palpable.

'But my friends, I have to tell you that a terrible mistake at the hospital where Isabel gave birth meant she took home another woman's child and her own child—Sophie, who read so beautifully earlier—eventually discovered this and a few months ago began searching for her blood mother.'

There was a gasp and an outbreak of whispering as the congregation took in the enormity of what he had said.

'How different Isabel's life might have been if she had known the joy of a child who lived and thrived, we can never know.'

He bowed his head and took a few moments to compose himself.

'Sophie, I'm sorry that you never knew your mother, that you found her too late, but this church is full of people who will be only too happy to talk to you about Isabel and Elen and share their memories with you.'

Sophie nodded and smiled.

'And now,' he said quietly, 'let's take some time to reflect and remember our friend while students from the Royal College of Music, where Isabel studied, will sing for us 'Lay a Garland' by Robert Pearsall. The text is taken from the Beaumont and Fletcher play *The Maid's Tragedy*, and is spoken by a heartbroken woman who has been parted from her betrothed.'

He stepped down from the pulpit and stood near the coffin as two young women and six young men got up from the choir stalls and moved to stand at the front of the pews. One of them quietly hummed a note and after a short pause, they began to sing. Their voices blended exquisitely and they sang with tender expressivity, drawing out the mournful suspensions to almost anguished lengths.

Lay a garland on her hearse
of dismal yew.
Maidens, willow branches wear,
say she died true.
Her love was false, but she was firm
Upon her buried body lie
lightly, thou gentle earth.

Throughout this, Benjamin stood alongside the coffin, as if keeping watch over Isabel, and after the song was over and the group had returned to the choir stalls, he completed the service from the same position with prayers and a blessing. He then asked us to stand. Six black-suited men walked discreetly up the aisle to move the coffin from the church and out into the graveyard. They approached the coffin to the accompaniment of the fifth movement of the Brahms Requiem, and as they lifted the coffin from its catafalque, the soprano soloist soared above the chorus and orchestra, offering comfort and serenity.

And ye now therefore have sorrow: but I will see you again, and your heart shall rejoice, and your joy no man taketh from you. Look upon me; for a little time labour and sorrow were mine, but at last I have found comfort. As one whom his mother comforteth, so will I comfort you.

As the pall-bearers lifted the coffin through the side door and out into the sunshine, we left our pew to follow Benjamin, the rest of the congregation quietly waiting their turn to file outside for the committal.

Afterwards, we walked up the street to the Church Hall, inside which tea and cake and sandwiches awaited. Sophie reached for my hand as we made our way there and I knew she was struggling to hold herself together. I was anxious to support her but glanced over my shoulder to look for my father amongst the dozens of mourners who were following us and was relieved to see him chatting to Isabel's cousin, Les, and his wife Betty. When we entered the hall and saw the tables laden with refreshments, I realised that in the space of three years, Sophie had laid two mothers to rest and endured two such funeral teas. I squeezed her hand and smiled reassuringly as Tim led her to a chair at the side while I hurried away to fetch her a cup of tea.

Steven was chatting to Kevin and Matthew and, having delivered Sophie's tea, I went to join them.

'I often cut through that park on my way to the office,' Matthew was saying, 'and I can't stop wondering if Isabel was ever there when I walked through.'

He shook his head.

'I hate to think I might not have recognised her,' he said sadly.

Kevin nodded.

'I thought I saw her a few times,' he said, 'but something stopped me from approaching her. I regret that now.'

Both men were gazing across at Sophie. She was talking to Benjamin's daughters who'd sat down beside her and were showing her a scrap book or photograph album.

Kevin looked at Matthew.

'She looks so like Isabel, doesn't she?' he said.

'She does. It's uncanny.'

'I know she'd love to meet you both,' I said, and was pleased when they went over and introduced themselves.

'Would you like a cup of tea?'

I heard Steven ask this just as I looked towards the door and saw that my father was waving good-bye and making the sign of a phone.

I turned away, disappointed.

'Not just yet,' I said distractedly.

He was looking at me closely.

'Beautifully read, by the way,' he said.

'What? Oh, the poem, thanks.'

'Are you OK?' he asked.

'Yes, fine,' I said, and then, 'No, I'm not.'

After a moment's hesitation, I rushed towards the door and ran after my father. He was almost out of sight, heading back in the direction of the church, when I called after him.

'Daddy!'

He stopped and turned round and I hurried to catch up with him. The childish diminutive seemed to have surprised him as much as it had me but, as I got closer, he opened his arms and I ran towards him.

'Oh Daddy,' I cried, as he clasped me in the sort of bear hug I remembered from my childhood.

'It's OK,' he said, holding me tight and stroking my hair. 'It's OK.'

'I've missed you so much,' I said. 'Missed having you in my life, missed having a father, but I've been so angry with you and didn't know how to allow you into my life when you'd abandoned me and hurt me so badly.'

The words came out in a rush but all the time, he simply stroked my hair with one hand and wiped my tears with the other.

'I know,' he said at last. 'I know. I'm desperately sorry that I hurt you and your mum so badly. It wasn't her fault or yours that I left, it was mine. I was too young and immature to cope with everything that went with marriage and fatherhood. It wasn't that I didn't love you. I just wasn't ready for any of it, so I walked away. I was selfish and feckless, I admit that, but it cost me. I've never stopped loving you and being proud of you and wanting you to be happy.'

I looked at him in disbelief but could see that he was sincere. We stayed talking for a while longer and after he'd got into his car and driven away, I made my way slowly back to the church hall. I blew my nose and wiped my eyes before I reached the doorway but when I stepped inside, Steven was waiting for me, concern written all over his face. He took me gently by the arm and led me to a table in a quiet corner. He left me there briefly before returning with a cup of tea and a piece of fruit cake.

'Aren't you having anything?' I asked, still sniffing as he sat down next to me.

'I've had something,' he said. 'I'm fine.'

He asked no questions and simply waited for me to recover myself. When I did, I told him what had happened and what had been said.

'I've wasted so much time,' I cried, 'by shutting him out and thinking I could punish him by denying him the chance to be part of my life. It's taken me almost thirty years to realise that I punished myself every bit as much as I punished him.'

'Perhaps it takes that long to understand these things,' Stephen said quietly. 'Don't be too hard on yourself.'

I sniffed and smiled.

'Thanks.'

I looked around at the people who'd stayed behind and was glad that so many had come to pay their respects to a woman who'd spent more than half her life living in the shadows. Sophie and Tim were moving amongst them, listening to their memories, and I remembered something from the service.

'Did you see Isabel outside the Albert Hall?' I asked.

'I did,' Steven said. 'She was chatting to a couple of old fellas about the cricket score; England were playing Australia in the Ashes and were being walloped.' He laughed. 'She sounded as if she knew what she was talking about.'

'And I've been meaning to ask you how you came to think that Elen Daniel might be an anagram?' I asked.

'I knew it wasn't an anagram of Isabel Grey but something about the name bugged me and after we had lunch with Kevin in the Nellie Dean I got to thinking about the song. It was one of Gertie Gitana's signature tunes, and Isabel sang it when she was young and just starting out. I thought perhaps it reminded her of when she was still hopeful and untouched by disappointment.'

'Clever stuff,' I said, nudging him gently.

'I guess she wanted to put distance between herself and everyone who knew her in her prime as Isabel Grey. She dreaded them seeing her humiliation and shame so she changed her name and disappeared.'

I sighed.

'It must be so painful for Sophie to think of her mother ending up the way she did.'

Steven nodded.

'Isabel's story proves that grief's hard and the truth is that nobody else can get you out of it. You're on your own. It's just you.'

His blunt insight surprised and startled me, but before I could respond, Matthew came to say goodbye and Steven and I stood up.

'Thank you for finding her,' he said, taking hold of one of my hands and one of Steven's. As Sophie and Tim joined us, he said: 'I'm so glad to have met her daughter.'

He squeezed Sophie's hand.

'Sophie has shown me the mirror that was found in Isabel's things. I gave it to her—and the matching hair brush. They'd belonged to my mother, Odile.'

'She must have treasured them to have kept them safe all those years,' Sophie said, smiling at him. Turning to me, she added: 'Matthew's invited us to go and see his Gainsborough painting, and I've promised that that will be one of our first outings after the baby comes.'

After Matthew and Kevin had gone, we worked our way round the room saying goodbye to everyone else, lingering a while with Benjamin and Julie, before we headed back to the station together. We planned to take the short cut near the church but, as we came to the lychgate, the graveyard looked so peaceful that I stopped, not yet ready to leave. Sophie read my thoughts and nodded.

We pushed open the gate and made our way up the path, under the arch and through to the side of the graveyard where Isabel had been buried under the shade of an ancient yew tree.

I looked down at the newly turned soil, which was strewn with the willow branches, the wild flowers and the sprigs of thyme. For now a simple wooden cross marked the grave but Sophie had commissioned a marble headstone. I breathed in the pungent aroma of grass and earth and thought of the woman who lay at rest in her coffin made of willow. I felt a powerful bond with her and I knew that her story would haunt me for the rest of my life. But I also knew that I wouldn't let my life become a sad echo of hers.

I opened my eyes and squinted as a shaft of bright sunlight pierced through the branches of the yew tree. Sophie and Tim were talking quietly a little way off, wrapped up in their own world, but Steven was watching me anxiously and I felt myself blush under his searching gaze. I knelt down to gather up some of the loose foliage, out of which I made a nosegay of thyme and willow. I stood up and showed him my handiwork, before offering him a sprig of flowering thyme.

He looked at me quizzically and smiled, and I took his arm and we turned to go.

Also by Carole Strachan

If you've enjoyed reading *A Song of Thyme and Willow,* make sure you get a copy of Carole's debut novel, *The Truth in Masquerade.*

An unusual story of love, loss and the possibility of second chances, *The Truth in Masquerade* follows Anna Maxwell, struggling to understand the abrupt and unexpected ending of her marriage. Haunted by memories of her husband, Edwyn, and of another man who once loved her, she returns to Oxford to sing the role of the Governess in Benjamin Britten's spine-chilling opera, *The Turn of the Screw.*

Caught up in a world of secrets and uncertainties, Anna has to confront the reasons her marriage unravelled, questioning what was true or illusory, and facing the challenge of a demanding dramatic role; a part that has increasingly painful emotional resonances with her own life. Meanwhile, Edwyn, too, is haunted, by ghosts from his past, and a mystery of identity is revealed that Anna must resolve for both of them, if either is to move on with life.